Alice Emma Sauerwein Lord

The Days of Lamb and Coleridge

A Historical Romance

Alice Emma Sauerwein Lord

The Days of Lamb and Coleridge
A Historical Romance

ISBN/EAN: 9783743367487

Manufactured in Europe, USA, Canada, Australia, Japa

Cover: Foto ©Andreas Hilbeck / pixelio.de

Manufactured and distributed by brebook publishing software (www.brebook.com)

Alice Emma Sauerwein Lord

The Days of Lamb and Coleridge

Dedicated

TO THE MEMORY OF

MY FATHER,

WHOSE WIDE CULTURE AND SCHOLARLY TASTES

INTRODUCED ME TO THESE,

HIS FRIENDS.

PREFACE.

In this Historical Romance, built upon the Lives of Lamb and Coleridge and their intimates, I am indebted for facts to careful study of the books mentioned below, and, perhaps, to some others read during the many years of preparation given to the subject.

I have carefully acknowledged anything taken *verbatim* from another writer; and all letters of my characters, copied from their "Lives" or "Histories" are acknowledged by reference to my authorities. I have used such letters as often as possible to complete the mental photographs of my heroes. But all conversations, arguments, and table-talk not so marked, are, of course, my own, and are made as characteristic of the speakers as long familiarity with their writings and lives has enabled me to paint them.

If in collaborating facts, events, and history, I have erred, or have been misled, as is very possible in gleaning history from so many sources, I trust to the leniency of a Public who can appreciate the difficulty of painting portraits from so many sketches—making, as it were, composite photographs of these well-known men.

The Author.

SOME BOOKS ABOUT LAMB AND COLERIDGE
AND THEIR TIMES

AINGER (ALFRED) Letters of Charles Lamb.

ASHTON (JOHN) Dawn of the 19th Century in England.

BRANDL (ALOIS) and EASTLAKE (LADY) Coleridge and the English Romantic School.

CAINE (HALL) Life of Coleridge.

COLERIDGE (S. T.) Biographia Literaria.

COTTLE (J.) Coleridge and Southey.

GILLMAN (JAMES) Life of Coleridge.

HAZLITT (WM.) Spirit of the Age.

HAZLITT (W. CAREW) Mary and Charles Lamb.

HOWITT (WM. and MARY) Homes and Haunts of the British Poets.

HUME (DAVID) History of England.

KNIGHT (WM.) William Wordsworth.

LAMB (C.) Essays of Elia.

LEE (EDMUND) Dorothy Wordsworth.

MARTIN (B. E.) In the Footprints of Charles Lamb.*

MESEN (R. T.) Personal Traits of British Authors.

ROSSETTI (L. M.) Mrs. Shelley.

RUSSELL (LORD JOHN) Thomas Moore's Diary.

SALA (GEORGE AUGUSTUS) Living London.

SANDFORD (MRS. H.) Thomas Poole and his Friends.

TALFOURD (T. N.) Essays and Letters of Charles Lamb.

TALFOURD (T. N.) Memorials of Charles Lamb.

* Appeared after the present volume was written, but before it was published.

CONTENTS.

THE DAYS OF LAMB AND COLERIDGE.

CHAPTER I.

A GRAY DAWN.

> Our birth is but a sleep and a forgetting:
> The Soul that rises with us, our life's Star,
> Hath had elsewhere its setting,
> And cometh from afar:
> Not in entire forgetfulness,
> And not in utter nakedness,
> But trailing clouds of glory do we come
> From God, who is our home:
> Heaven lies about us in our infancy!
> Shades of the prison-house begin to close
> Upon the growing Boy,
> But he beholds the light, and whence it flows,—
> He sees it in his joy;
> The Youth, who daily farther from the east
> Must travel, still is Nature's Priest,
> And by the vision splendid
> Is on his way attended;
> At length the Man perceives it die away,
> And fade into the light of common day.
>
> WORDSWORTH.

THE London of 1780 was not the present thronged, gigantic city whose streets seem wellnigh limitless, and which has incorporated all the suburban towns of the last century. It was not blazing with gas and electric lights, and pulsating with the tramways connecting the farthest limit with the throbbing heart of thè great metropolis, so much of whose busy thought and life now vibrate through its telegraph and telephone nerves. Still, it was a mighty city for those days. Fashion thronged through Bloomsbury and Piccadilly; and misery abode in Whitechapel, just as to-day. Holborn and the Strand teemed with people hastening to the Exchange and the Bank, as now. The stately dome of new St. Paul's rose majestically above the surging streams of life coursing through these marts, and sent its vibrant tones across to the Mansion House. Westminster Abbey looked down upon St. Margaret's and St. Martin's in the Fields, and near it stood the old Parliament buildings. But the superb gothic Westminster Palace, with its many towers and myriad windows, has risen since those days, as have the National Gallery, the Nelson Monument, and the lions of Trafalgar Square, and the palatial hotels flanking the square.

Quaint inns like the old "Staple Inn," and the "White Horse Cellar," and the "Three Feathers" were the centers of life, and, during the day, the busy coaches for the suburbs and provinces in the North, South, East, and West of England, bustled into the courtyards under the great gateway with outriders and merry horns, deposited their tired occupants and luggage, changed horses, and dashed off again with a fresh supply of passengers and mail-bags.

Beyond the old Staple Inn of Holborn and past Newgate Prison there still stands, behind an iron paling, a quaint gray-stone building with gothic windows and a great doorway. By this main entrance one passes through a churchyard, with low slabs and a few box- graves, into the court. Had you—in the year mentioned above—walked under the arched gateway, and across the cloisters into the quadrangle, you would have seen about you the dingy walls of the Christ's Hospital, or "Blue-coat School." Amid the furious din of "several hundred wrestling, shrieking, racing boys, kicking their footballs along the cloisters, and playing leap-frog on the flags," far off in a sunny corner crouched a couple of little fellows of eight and eleven years. The poor little lads are young enough to need home shelter, and tender enough for a mother's watchful care, but their black pates are pressed together over a book, and they have forgotten home, mother, and the uproar around them, so absorbed are they in their treasure.

Suddenly a football sends their book sprawling upon the flags. The younger boy springs like a cat upon the foremost of a group, who are jeering at the result of the well-directed aim.

"Go it! Cholley!" "Hit 'im again!" and similar cries greet the well-aimed clawings of the little black-headed imp, who has landed on the shoulders of the aggressor. In a moment the two are rolling over and over, entangled in the long skirts of their blue coats. Meanwhile, the older of the two friends has collected the scattered leaves of the beloved book, and is looking with sorrowful gray eyes upon the scuffle.

"Why don't you pitch in, Esteecee? you're always afraid of your skin!" "Mollycod!" called out several interested by-standers.

But a great bell interrupts further demonstration, and the din ends in a mad rush for the entrance to the dining-hall. The old pump nearly has its handle wrung off, as dozens of boys cluster round the trough to administer hasty dabs at grimy faces. The long blue skirts are hauled out of belts, where they were tucked back to give free play to the yellow-leather-covered legs. Confusion and bustle subside into stately order, as, two and two, the boys file into the long hall chanting the grace to the rather shaky twang and blare of violin and cornet. The young voices rise in melodious cadence and the harmonies fill the fine old dining-hall of the Blue-coat School—one of the handsomest antiquities of London.

Our little friends linger in the rear, Cholley mopping his curly poll with his sleeve, and giggling.

"I say Es, did'nt I l-l-lamb Jem like a h-h-hero? I just thought I was one of those fellows at Th-Th-Thermopylæ."

. "But O, Cholley, what will Boyer say to that torn Plutarch?" said Esteecee, trembling.

"N-never mind, I'll say I did it, he's always so hard on you; and he don't lick fellows that o-o-own up half as bad as when he d-discovers," said the philosophical little Charley.

The twang of violin and pipe, of clarionet and flute, interrupting, they joined in the decorous grace, chanted before meat. What a burst of harmony rose from those hundreds of young throats and echoed along the oaken beams of the roof, and vibrated from the great gothic windows! Truly, so rich a chant might have served for richer fare than the pease soup, brown loaf, and bitter beer in the homely wooden piggins! Perhaps the long red sunbeams streaming through the stained-glass windows gave a *couleur de rose* to the meager dole ; but methinks the Monday's tasteless milk-porridge, and the Wednesday's bowls of millet and treacle, and the Thursday's boiled beef were scarcely flavored and seasoned by golden rays. And very, very often there were not even sunbeams in smoky, drizzly London. But empty stomachs, after hard study and harder play, found even these "unsavory messes" acceptable because necessary, and few were the crumbs and remnants for those on table duty to clear away. In a twinkling the orderly sets of boys on table duty had tucked up skirts, whisked leavings into baskets, piled platters and "piggins" in, polished the oaken tables until they shone like mirrors, and, filing into the scullery, had deposited, washed up, and set away the dishes.

Lessons again after dinner. And woe to him who brought imperfect recitations to the head-master, Boyer ! He was of a furious temper, and used his cane without stint upon the idle or the listless.

"What, sirrah ! are ye dreaming again ? " he would shout to poor little Esteecee, who tremblingly stumbled over the Latin verbs and Greek roots he knew so well an hour before.

"Stand forward, sirrah!" And upon the cowering form the rod or strap would fall with whistling thuds until the burly Irishman espied some fresh victim tittering over a book. He seemed to gloat over the slips and mistakes of the nervous, shambling boy, who shrank from his terrible eye. And after each thrashing the poor, discouraged lad would fix his gaze upon his books, and try to gather his scattered wits for a fresh tussle with the slippery Latin conjugations.

"Eh, Cholley," Esteecee said to his sympathizing little chum, at the next intermission, "if he would but wait until I can get it out. I know those stanzas as I do my own name: listen." And he repeated page after page of his Horace to his wondering friend, without a pause, save for the sobs that shook his delicate frame.

"He chases it out of me with his wild eyes, glaring like a Satan's demon."

A heavy step, not heard before amid the babel of the boys' voices and games, caused the terrified children to turn, just in time to catch the uplifted strap right upon their faces.

"And ye two devils criticise the master, do ye? 'A Satan's demon,' because I dare chastize the idle and laggard!" But they had fled ere again the cruel thong could leave its marks upon the blanched faces.

The next day being the usual weekly holiday, the Blue-coat boys were turned out as usual, to pass the time as they might, through the long hours of a gray, drizzling, winter's day. They shivered along the streets, drenched and miserable. Some were fortunate enough to have friends or relatives in London ; and let us hope the poor fellows found cordial welcomes on those frequent holidays and half-holidays, after the bare halls and dreary cloisters of the Blue-coat School.

Blue-coat boys might be seen all over London and its suburbs on these half-holidays. The bare heads (for no covering is worn on the head) and the blue gown mark the Blue-coat boys to this day, and being set apart by their dress, the boys have a pride in maintaining the dignity of their position. They are not charity boys, but " protégés of the nation," and have always held aloof in pride from other asylums and hospitals, considering the power and dignity of their establishment. The system of governing by "sizars" and Grecians; the promotion for merit, and the gradual development into Grecians with full-fledged honors, give a collegiate air to the institution, and 'tis but a step to the great Universities for a Grecian of Christ's Hospital.

One sees them strolling along the Thames and lounging about the bridges, or sauntering on Cheapside and Paternoster Row with their noses pressed against the show-windows, especially those of book-stores. They peer into the pastry shops, and after a careful study of the riches in the window, the more fortunate ones spend a penny or halfpenny in a judicious bun or a dyspeptic muffin for dinner. They throng the Tower, passing the guards fearlessly on their oft-repeated visits to the crown jewels, or shuddering over the fatal Traitor's Gate, or the stairway where the young Princes were buried, or admiring the fine old armor and the splendid arrangement of weapons with flower and vine designs. Many happy days are passed amid these splendors. One often wonders what those homeless wanderers would do on the many rainy half-holidays, without the Tower or the British Museum.

On this rainy Saturday, "Cholley" had permission from home to bring his home-sick friend to the paternal roof. How briskly they trotted through Fetter Lane to the Strand, and through the old arch into the Inner Temple! There, at the end of the long, dingy brick building, with its rows of windows staring into the Temple Garden, was Crown Office Row, and there was Sister Mary waiting to welcome her boy. How warm and cosy the papered walls, the high-backed chairs and great cushioned settle looked to the boys, after the bare walls, wooden benches, and stone floors, of Christ's Hospital! What a world of comfort and cheer in the great kitchen fire, throwing its glare on chairs and table, and redolent with the appetizing fragrance of roast beef, suet pudding, or hot muffins!

"Eh, Cholley," said his friend, "how nice to have a mother and sister waiting for you and expecting you! Your sister is always so glad to see you."

"So would yours be if they were here, in London, Estee; a f-f-fellow's mother kind of b-belongs to him, you know."

"No, Cholley, my mother had too many to look after at home to need me. I was one too many, always; and I was forever being sent out of the way," and the large gray eyes had a wistful look that made Charley's heart ache, young as he was. He opened the great mahogany book-case and found their favorite "Spectator," and the two were soon curled up in a corner over its pages. After a while they got out the volume of Shakespeare, of which they never tired.

Esteecee's cheeks would flush as he read "Julius Cæsar," and Charley's black eyes flashed in responsive enthusiasm.

"How horrible for his own friend to have stabbed him! To die with his friend's treachery before him was worse than the pain of the blow," exclaimed Esteecee with flashing eyes.

"B-b-but we could never have had the Oration without that," said Charley, doubtfully.

"There were enough to kill Cæsar without Brutus's stab."

"Yes, that was the most b-brutal blow of all," said Charley.

"Oh, you midgets, to spend your holiday curled up over books! Don't you have enough of them at school?" asked Sister Mary, patting her little brother's curly locks, tenderly. "Such learned young gentlemen as these Blue-coat boys with their Latin and mathematics! Why, Charley is growing now beyond his sister's reach."

"N-no; only trying to catch up, sister; you started on f-f-far ahead; I'll have to climb on Latin and Greek to get even."

"And the poor little colts have been urged too hard," said Mary, noticing the long red welts across the boy's faces.

"We were talking of Boyer, and he heard me call him, 'devil'," said Estee. "We generally know in the morning what sort of a day we'll have by old Boyer's wig. When he comes in with that wig cocked over his left ear, by jingo! I try to find some old cloth or newspapers to put layers in my breeches and shirt; he thrashes the very Grecians on those days."

"And a f-fellow hit back, and gave him an awful black eye, last Candlemas. And d-didn't we smile!" piped in Charley.

"Old Boyer couldn't hit straight for a fortnight, and the boys slipped between the licks," said Estee, laughing.

Charley's holidays were occasions for killing the fatted calf, and the steaming roast mutton and suet pudding received full justice from the hungry boys, and seemed a sumptuous repast after the meager dole at Christ's Hospital.

Charley's big brother, John, was rather a quietus to the boys' chatter when he dined at home. He was big, and "such a swell," as Charley admiringly termed him. Somehow the room always seemed smaller and more crowded when brother John came in. His gorgeous waistcoats and neckcloths, and the shining brass buttons on his coat rather overwhelmed the boys and oppressed them with a sense of his magnificence. John represented the elegance of the family.

Mary was soft-eyed and very sweet-looking, but the plain mob-caps and folded lawn neckerchiefs gave her a very demure air for a young woman of nineteen years.

She was very silent, save when she and Charley were together, when she was gay and genial, and chatted as fast as her pet brother.

Esteecee hovered admiringly around her, and his tongue became eloquent over some late country ramble or a new book. His holidays spent with his friend were the happiest days of his boyhood.

CHAPTER II.

UPS AND DOWNS.

Verse, a breeze 'mid blossoms straying,
Where Hope clung feeding, like a Bee,
Both were mine !   Life went a maying
With Nature, Hope, and Poesy
                When I was young !
When I was young ?—Ah, woful when !
Ah ! for the change 'twixt now and then !
This breathing house not built with hands
O'er aery cliffs and glittering sands.
How lightly then it flashed along
Like those trim skiffs, unknown of yore,
On winding lakes and rivers wide,
That ask no aid of sail or oar,
That fear no spite of wind or tide !
Naught cared this body for wind or weather,
When Youth and I lived in't together.

COLERIDGE.

ONE half-holiday, some weeks later, Estee burst into
the house in high spirits. He hunted up his friend,
Miss Mary, exclaiming breathlessly : " Oh, what do
you think has happened ! I was walking along the
Strand imagining I was Leander swimming the Helles-
pont. I had my eyes shut and was striking out with
my arms, when I struck an old gentleman's back, and
got my arm twisted in his coat-tails. He grabbed me,
and shook me while I was trying to explain to him, and
he wanted to call a watchman. I begged him to listen,

and see that I was no thief, and after a long talk he laughed at the idea of my swimming on a London street, and asked me all about Hero and Leander, and ended by taking me to King's Library, on Cheapside, and buying me a membership ticket. Oh, think of it! *think of it!* I can always have some place to go on those awful holidays, and I can read and read all day long." The boy's face glowed with the illumination of happiness until he seemed another being. Mary rejoiced in the child's pleasure, and Charley capered about in glee.

" I sha'n't mind now saving half my breakfast loaf for dinner, for I can enjoy it over—oh, everything, in that library. Addison and Pope and Chaucer and Spenser and Goldsmith are there. And you can come with me, Cholley, and I can lend you the books, too."

The friends went to their dreary dormitory that night, full of a new hope, with long vistas of delight stretching out before them ; so little does it take to lift a child's heart from the slough of despond to the heavenly hills of enthusiasm and hope.

Life's burdens are heavy enough upon old shoulders ; 'tis pitiful to see them weighing upon the young, when so little can scatter them. I wonder if that kind old man ever remembered afterwards, or knew, the stores of happiness he had provided for the lonely Blue-coat boy, wandering penniless and friendless in the great, busy London ? He was only a charity boy, a Blue-coat lad with shambling gait and blowsey head ; but that fledgling grew to be a *rara avis* that shall sing through the centuries, when you and I lie forgotten.

That library was indeed a blessing to the two boys.

Estee flew from Boyer's blows and tyrannical tasks to hours of quiet and peace. He read everything within reach ; poetry, history, metaphysics, classics, all were welcome to fill the void of loneliness and longing in the imaginative youth's heart. The works of Voltaire and Hume had recently been added, with other new writers, and our greedy Estee devoured everything, ignorant of any danger. His mind expanded to the new theories, and he felt like a young bird trying its own pinions for the first time, amid the wild flights of older birds who had flown far from the safe home nest of orthodoxy. Before long he found much to lure him into strange, new paths. The old beliefs and faith of his father, and the safe dogmas of the Church as inculcated daily in the school routine, grew too narrow for the tempted fledgling. So months and years went by.

Charley was less tempted by these dry metaphysicians. He was too young to venture into the unknown regions. Besides his beloved Shakespeare, he read diligently the earlier English dramatists and the minor Elizabethan poets, and upon such models his taste was formed. They were the dear friends of his boyhood in these King's Library days ; and they ever remained the richest treasures of his life.

Charley would coax Esteecee into the Tower, after they had been reading of the Lollards or of Henry VIII. and his wives ; of the sorrows of Anne Boleyn, Lady Jane Grey, or of Cromwell and his times. They would hunt up the historic rooms, and picture the celebrated prisoners who had chafed and pined there, or find the spot where they had forfeited their lives. They would imagine themselves confined prisoners in those gloomy cells, and follow the sufferings of the heroes, and imagine they, too, were prisoners of state, until, in trembling and terror, they would rush past the keepers and beyond the gates, only breathing freely when, safe outside, they could look across to the walls and towers from the opposite hill.

Upon these holidays Charley shared with Esteecee the home spoils of cold mutton or veal-pie which old Aunt Hetty had smuggled into the school for her boy.

Poor Aunt Hetty used to come hobbling into the play-yard at noon, peering amongst the noisy horde for her little curly-pate.

" Hello, auntie ! " shouted several large boys, " let's see what's in that basket," and they would flock around her, and lift the cover of the bowl containing the coveted morsels, whilst she would mumble and snarl and strike out with her cane, giving many a sharp rap upon inquiring knuckles.

The ungrateful Charley would sneak shamefacedly up, and hustling the old dame into some quiet corner, hastily gobble all he could cram into his mouth, stuff the rest into his coat-pocket, or tuck it under his gown for future use, striking out at inquisitive groups of boys who tried to follow and tease.

" Why don't you come just before recess, auntie ? I would meet you behind that gate; the boys jeer so at thy cane and call me ' mollycoddle.' " So youth criticises age and appropriates kindness as its just due, little thinking how empty the stomach would be, after porridge and blue skim-milk, if poor old auntie did not hobble up with extras from the home-table.

Charley was fond enough of the edibles, but liked not the ridicule and importunities of his comrades. The broken hot loaf and bowl of pudding would be but a crumb if shared with all that noisy crowd. They often snatched the greater portion from him; but Charley was as wiry as he was diminutive, and could defend his rights against a reasonable number of assailants by darting between their legs, or twining himself around their shoulders, and many such cat-like maneuvers.

Poor fastidious Esteecee would have grown even more starved and lean over the boiled beef and bitter beer and millet, if Charley had not always shared his home spoils with his friend. Aunt Hetty came almost daily, and the boys knew where and when to watch for the little hobbling dame with her basket. They often changed the rendezvous, as the other boys discovered the clandestine meetings and demanded their share of the feast. Many bloody noses and bruised heads were the results of these surreptitious feasts, while Aunt Hetty learned to snub her tormentors, and Charlie learned to improvise corners and hiding-places for his goodies as a dog learns to hide a bone.

" Poor Estee was always building imaginary castles of gingerbread and plum-cake, and eating out rooms and corridors, during these long, hungry, Christ's Hospital days." *

The long holidays came year after year, and Esteecee went home to Ottery St. Mary to visit his family. But the kind father was dead, and the elder brother, who had the living and the little parish school, had a family of his own, and dreaded the irregular habits and independent ideas of the London school-boy. Esteecee would go off into the woods and forget to come home at meal-time, or would return dripping from a swim-

---

* " Life of Coleridge."—HALL CAINE,

ming expedition, where he had worn his clothes into the water, from very indolence. He was a visionary dreamer beyond the ordinary rules of well-organized families, and his relatives did not know what to do with him. The tired mother had nursed and reared eleven children; and the queer pranks of this alien, who had left her for the city school, wearied her. He compared his chilly welcome with the love and tenderness Charley found in his home, and the oppression would tighten round the young heart, and the yearning, "Why, why?" kept eating into his very soul.

He would throw himself down on the soft grass and watch the drifting clouds speed over the blue dome above him; he would peer into the mirror of the quiet little brook that meandered through the meadows, but nowhere could he read an answer.

"Why was life so hard for him?"

Other boys had kind fathers and loving mothers who lavished tenderness upon them; what had he done to miss all this from his life? He saw other lads driving in gay coaches with happy faces and fine clothes; he had no coach; no fine dinner was awaiting him—only a scolding for not knowing the time, and this would remind him that he was late again, and he would run home breathlessly.

After a few weeks of rambling through these pleasant fields, he must go back to those stone walls and bare floors, and mingle again with that wild herd. Would it always be so? What could come next? Perhaps he might win further honors—even be a Grecian; perhaps he might be sent to Oxford or Cambridge, and then what?

Well! that was something to work for, something to

dream over, and perhaps comfort and home and happiness might be his some day. As he cogitated thus, in his rambles, a warm ray of hope would come back to his tired young heart. And Charley would be glad to see him! Charley had written him a long letter from a famous old mansion in Hertfordshire, where he and Mary were staying with their grandmother, who was housekeeper in this stately old place. What a nice way Charley had of describing those wide halls, the great stairways, and the fine old galleries filled with such wonderful paintings, and the tapestried walls, the statuary and marble balconies! Esteecee had seen something like this at Dudley House, and at Holland House, when he peeped through the gateway with the crowd, watching the gayly-dressed ladies and gentlemen passing from their carriages and sedan chairs into the brilliantly-lighted halls. He might get into one of these splendid homes himself some day. Was not Addison, like himself, the son of a poor clergyman in a country parish? He had gone to the Charterhouse, no better than Christ's, and then to Oxford, and had worked hard and studied well, and had written poems and essays and dramas, which had opened the doors of these very houses to him. He wrote some of his poems in a garret in the Haymarket. "I know the very house," said Esteecee to himself, "and he afterwards lived in that very Holland House in Kensington that I have seen blazing with light and flowers. "Shakespeare, himself, was but a poor country boy: why cannot I rise? Even old Boyer grunts a compliment over my essays, and sometimes says my Latin verses will pass. If work can raise a fellow from this infernal poverty and dinginess, why need I question fate? I'll be my own fate."

So reasoned the youth of fourteen; he felt the divine inspiration within, and listening to the call, believed he could do anything. So, often, reasons youth, but genius must poise the wings and balance the body for the flight to fame and success. Many just as ambitious as Esteecee have fallen, broken-winged, by the way.

Esteecee returned more hopefully than usual to Christ's Hospital, and Charley rejoiced at the change. The boys had much to relate of their holidays, and Estee was full of his new-born hope. Charley listened with great admiration to his voluble friend's plans and hopes. They studied hard, and for a time Estee struggled against the rheumatism that seemed to chain his limbs to the ground. He studied well, and read everything within reach.

Boyer still thrashed him whenever he found an opportunity. He often said he gave him an extra blow " because he was such an ugly, shambling blockheaded fellow "—a fine reason for a master's castigations !

The cold rooms gave poor Estee rheumatics, and on the half-holidays, when he was forced to roam about, the frosty streets gave him chilblains. He felt less and less able to begin the literary career that was to open the doors of paradise to him. He was much in the sick ward, and was put on nauseous gruels, and not allowed his beloved books, because hospital nurses of that day, certainly, did not cure patients by humoring their idiosyncrasies. A special liking was a bad symptom, and must be suppressed. So the days went wearily by.

Charley was moping for want of his friend, and ever waiting for chances to share his best morsel with him. As often as possible Estee accompanied Charley home on the holidays, and there found rest and comfort.

CHAPTER III.

> To me the Eternal Wisdom hath dispensed
> A different fortune and more different mind—
> Me from the spot where first I sprang to light
> Too soon transplanted, ere my soul had fixed
> Its first domestic loves ; and hence through life
> Chasing chance-started friendships a brief while.
> Some have preserved me from Life's pelting ills ;
> But, like a tree with leaves of feeble stem,
> If the clouds lasted, and a sudden breeze
> Ruffled the boughs, they on my head at once
> Dropped the collected shower.
>
> COLERIDGE.

IN Estee's wanderings, on the "halfs," he had found a kind cobbler and his wife, who sheltered him at their fire, laughed at his droll stories, and looked upon him as quite a philosopher. The warmth and cosy comfort of the narrow home seemed very desirable, after the chill atmosphere of Christ's Hospital and the drizzly streets, and he was so hopeless of earning fame or even a pittance by the uncertain pathway of literature, that he decided to renounce future ambition for present comfort, and learn cobbling. There seemed even a touch of elegance in the warm little kitchen behind the shop, where the good wife kept the bit of raisin-bread and pot of soup hot for the lean Blue-coat boy who honored the small establishment with his friendship.

Estee and the cobbler had long talks about the possibilities of life, and the probabilities of success.

" 'Tis feow that rise into affluence and fame, me lad ; the rawd is sleow, and 'tis only them as hes genus that hits it," said the shoemaker. " Didn't Holiver Goldsmith live in this very street right 'ere in Brick Court ? 'Asn't me fayther hoften tawled me of the great scholard that writ and writ, and yet ne'er could lay by enough to keep the wolf from the dawer. A rael gentleman he was, sent pomes and hessays by the scores to the magazines, an writ books 'nough to make his fortune, yet pore he were until his last days. My fayther remembered his berryin' like it was yestere'en. 'E moved haway to Hedgeware Rawd ; but they laid him in the Temple grounds anigh the church, with great ceremoniousness. And I've heard that the chaps in Parliment hev put up a muniment to him in the Habbey, like he were a great person."

" Oh," said Estee, thoughtfully, " I've seen both his grave at the Temple, and the slab at Westminster, and I've read his books dozens of times at King's Library. His ' Animated Nature ' is delightful ; and ' The Deserted Village ' is one of the most exquisite poems in the English language."

" Eh ! well ; you air a scholard tew ; yet 'e lived and died a pore man, after all his books was writ and published. I've heerd fayther say so, yit they honored 'is name, and put 'im in the Habbey after he were dead."

Estee grew very sober at this bit of history with its implied pessimism. It was another fling at his air-castles, and he felt his hopes sink ; for work as he might, he could never excel Goldsmith or even Burns, and their lives were failures if their works were not. He sighed a deep, heartfelt sigh which was almost a sob, and after a long silence : " Sandy," said he, " would you take me as an apprentice and teach me to make shoes ?   I must earn my living ; I have no one to help me, and if I learn a trade, I can help myself ; and the sooner I begin, the better."

" I'll tak ye, lad, ye're an honest chap, and not above 'umble friends, wi' all yer larnin'.   I could teach ye," he added, doubtfully, " but it wad tak time."

"Would you see old Boyer, the master, for me ; he might listen to you better than to me," said Estee, with a formidable vision of purple wrath and torrents of abuse, rising before him.

" I wull, lad."

" He's very violent, I've told you about him, before," faltered Estee.

"I knows it, lad ; but he cawnt do more nor shake 'is stick at me ; for I've a pair of fists of me owen."

Estee lay back and laughed and shouted over a vision of the bristling Boyer and the valiant cobbler in a pitched battle, until the good wife came into the shop to hear of the plan.

She shook her head rather ominously at the prospect of her " gude mon " coming into those awful clutches ; but her affection for their young protégé overcame her wifely fears, and she concluded : " Sandy allus could stand up pretty well to a tussle."

Charley was distressed at the result of his friend's meditations and discouragements.

"Oh, Estee! if you give up all your plans and ambitions it is for l-life. You are throwing away all ch-chances that might c-come," he stammered.   " You are l-l-losing the honor of being a G-G-Grecian and g-g-going to college, and being among your b-betters. I b-b-believe you only want to be a sh–shoemaker to get shoes big enough for your ch-chilblains. It is g-g-going to the f-f-foot of everything," he said, with a laugh.

But Estee held to his purpose, and in a few days the two conscious boys saw a stranger enter the school-room and ask for Boyer, and they recognized the cobbler.

Boyer took him to his own sanctum and soon a roar of voices was heard. The schoolboys were all agape with excitement, and our friends trembled guiltily when the cobbler rushed wildly past with Boyer, as red as a hunter's coat, staggering after him. The violence of his kicks, which missed the fleeing cobbler each time, spun the irate teacher nearly off his balance.

"Come forward, sirrah," he said, glaring at poor Estee. "You want to be a shoemaker, sirrah, I hear."

"I did, sir," faltered poor Estee.

"A noble aim, and worthy of so excellent a pupil! And why do you aspire to such a height, sirrah?" hissed the master.

"Oh, sir, I see no hope of ever earning a home by writing or literary work of any sort. I see how Burns and Goldsmith——"

"I'll Burns and Goldsmith ye," he panted as he laid on the strap with unmerciful blows. He called the sizars and ordered the trembling lad into the dungeon with the usual bread and water diet.

For any lad of sixteen to be shut in this horrid vault was awful; but for a lad of Estee's nervous temperament it was brutal. Charley begged his own preceptor, Field, a gentle, lenient man, to interfere, but to no purpose. To the dungeon Estee went, and in the chill loneliness and darkness of the stone cell, the last spark of hope died out of that young heart. He doubted God's care; he rebelled against Him for placing his helplessness in such straits.

"What have I done to be marked out for naught but sorrow and pain!" he exclaimed. "Had I wronged any one, or murdered a fellow-creature, or stolen food, some days when I was hungry, I might have been left to such a fate. But I have studied my best; I have harmed no one, yet here I lie, in a dungeon, crawled over by these cursed vermin; and gnawed at by rats if I forget myself in sleep. Where in this world or the next is an atom of pity or help?" and the bare, mouldy walls echoed—"Where?"

There was great pity and sympathy in one heart, although the ability to help scarcely equaled the will.

Charley, taking a hasty flight home for a supply of books and eatables, on the first half-holiday after Estee's imprisonment, bribed the old porter, who was also jailer, to let him visit his friend.

Estee's heart melted when he saw Charley's faithful face, and warmly welcomed the books. His mood softened. "Perhaps God did not forget me, since he sent you to me in this gruesome hole," he said. The very act of yielding his rebellion brought new peace, and the lads wept together in the dismal cell.

"Cholley, dost think God sent thee to me, lad? He seems to have forgotten me and given me over to the Devil."

"Be comforted, Estee. If I had not had God's help I could never have reached you. Think of all the rules and restrictions. It was like P-P-Peter passing the sleeping guard for me to come through all and find you. This is a j-jolly time to think out a p-plan of work for the f-future, you know. You can just fill the d-d-dark old room with plans and visions, until it sh-shines."

After the episode of the shoemaking scheme, culminating in the dungeon, the lads studied harder than ever. Estee became a fine classical scholar, and won honors and prizes, and finally became a Grecian, and ranked high among that envied band of Blue-coat magnates. His universal reading had made him famous, and his companions were proud of his wonderful eloquence. Gradually he gained great supremacy amongst them, and became their oracle. His study of metaphysics and philosophy from the promiscuous assortment of literature at King's Library had greatly unsettled his faith in the simple doctrines of the English Church, and had filled his mind with a chaos of new beliefs and philosophies that rendered him a most interesting, if not dangerous, companion.

In the mean time, Charley had patiently plodded on under Field, a more lenient master than Boyer, and was a good scholar, though not so brilliant as his friend Estee. He was satisfied to drift along in the old channels, and preferred the lighter fields of literature to his friend's restless searchings after truth and groping into mystery. Charles liked to dip into the older English dramatists and novelists, such as Beaumont, Massinger and Richardson, and he gleaned all the poetic fields within reach. He was a good scholar, and when promoted to Boyer's charge, that choleric individual had grown too rheumatic to wield the rod with the frequency of old. Charles being a winning and apologetic fellow escaped tolerably well.

Esteecee or Coleridge, as he was now called (the Esteecee being merely a nickname from his initials, S. T. C.) had on his Saturdays met a pleasant family, the friends of a schoolmate. The Misses Evans were learning millinery with a milliner on Great Russell Street, and whenever Coleridge could escape the vigilance of sizars, and upon his holidays, the big Blue-coat lad with the waving black locks would escort the girls home. Mrs. Evans found the young scholar useful and agreeable, and often invited him to the friendly tea-table; his ceaseless ripple of wit and humor being a most pleasant addition to their quiet circle.

Charles and Coleridge would scour the fields and gardens within a dozen miles of Christ's Hospital, for the violets and daisies to be laid at Miss Mary's feet.

"Ah, Estee, you no longer c-c-care to browse in our poor pasture, since Miss Mary has filled all your d-d-dreams," sighed Charles. "Pray God the p-passion may be evan-nescent," he said, with his sunny smile. "You've grown so masterful since you have become a Grecian and a l-l-lover, that your poor L-L-Lamb may bleat in vain for his old chum."

"Nay, Charley, 'not that I love Cæsar less, but Rome more,' you surely do not grudge me this warm ingle-nook after these long years of cold and starvation; I feel that the sun is but beginning to shine, and I am basking in its warmth and light; 'tis like sparkling new wine."

"Hello! he grows poetic! Perchance thou'lt tipple

just a bit too long and find thyself in the ' slough of despond ' ; the lassie may bid thee get along."

"No, she is wondrous kind, and my soul seems aflame with hope and love," said Coleridge with a glorious light in his eyes.

" But, Estee, you are but eighteen, and since the shoemaker's b-b-bench has been denied you, and college st-stretches out its promises to you, what p-p-purpose can you have in this love-making ? " stammered Charley.

" Purpose ! " echoed Coleridge ; " ah, you practical grandfather, that is all in the future. It is enough to love and be beloved. This is happiness enough for me. And after ten long years of friendless Blue-coat days, you need not fear for your place, old fellow. You will always have your corner in my heart."

And so the dreamer dreamed on, weaving his fancies into poetic work. He wrote sonnets to his beloved, and sent her poems upon the sweetness and beauty of life, with the flowers filched from suburban gardens.

She found her young Adonis very amusing ; but I fear the roses and pinks were sweeter to the young milliner than the rhythmic flowers ; for song is nothing to deaf ears, and to the unpoetic heart poetry is often nonsense, though love sometimes stirs depths that can receive the pent-up torrents of another's enthusiasm.

CHAPTER IV.

FIERCE DOUBTS, AND A VITAL ANSWER.

" Sad lot, to have no hope !   Though lowly kneeling
He fain would frame a prayer within his breast ;
Would fain entreat for some sweet breath of healing,
That his sick body might have ease and rest. . . . .
That hope which was his inward bliss and boast,
Which waned and died, yet ever near him stood,
Though changed in nature, wander where he would—
For love's despair is but hope's pining ghost ! . . .
. . . . . Yet this one hope should give
Such strength that he would bless his pains and live.

COLERIDGE.

ON the half-holidays, Coleridge had a new enthusiasm opening to him ; and to him, as to all dreamers, a new enthusiasm was a source of rapture and energy. His brother Luke had come to London, and was a practicing physician in the London Hospital and allowed his eager young brother to assist him. Coleridge could hold bandages and minister in many ways to the sick, and a desire to study medicine sprang up in his heart.   He devoured the books upon the subject in King's Library, and, as usual, mastered much of it in an incredibly short time.

Luke's tiny home and his young wife were an additional factor in Coleridge's life, which seemed gradually broadening in interests and hopes.   And with the relief from the loneliness and bareness of Christ's Hospital came a more peaceful spirit. But again hope was dashed to the ground, and sorrow fell upon his heart.

Luke became ill, and, in spite of the faithful nursing of his young brother, whenever he could escape from school duties, died, leaving his young wife and lovely boy to struggle with want and with the hard world. Poor Esteecee! the blow fell hard upon him. He was becoming hopeful of a future of congenial work, and had made considerable proficiency in his medical studies; but Boyer meant him for a different career.

He was expected to study for the Church. Blue-coat boys are provided with trades or professions according to merits, and Grecians have college fellowships open to them. Coleridge's aptitude for study, his classical attainments, and exceeding volubility and fluency in argument, decided Boyer and the directors on sending him to Cambridge to study for the Church.

" But I have no taste for the life," pleaded Coleridge.

" No *taste!* What has that to do with it? Pray what has that mule-pate a taste for, save kicking in the harness?" roared Boyer.

" I feel entirely unfit for the life and its duties, sir," said Coleridge.

" And ye would rather moon and dream on the housetop, and scribble verses to the stars and garters!" bellowed Boyer; " or maybe ye are still longing to make shoes ?" he sneered.

" But I do not believe the doctrines taught by the Church of England," stammered Estee, looking the criminal he felt.

"Hoots! thunder!" roared the irate Boyer, whose wig fairly rose from his head. "What do you know of this or that doctrine, that you dare deny what your betters hold sacred?" he hissed.

He knew nothing of the ten years of omnivorous reading that Coleridge had lived upon. Voltaire, Kant, Hume, Gibbon, Swedenborg, were unknown at Christ's Hospital, and the master little dreamed of the many hours spent at King's Library, when young Coleridge had been endeavoring to assimilate this mental pabulum until his digestion was upset.

"I am an Atheist, sir," boldly asserted the refractory youth, "and I will meet you upon any point you name, and give you my reason."

"An *Atheist!* an Infidel!" shrieked Boyer, administering such a thrashing that the timid fellow turned, and bit and fought, until the panting master, now purple with rage, called the sizars and again condemned the unlucky youth to the dungeon. He sent also a liberal supply of theological literature, and ordered him to prepare for an examination upon the " Evidences of Christianity " and other standard text-books of the Church.

Coleridge had so carefully read all he could find upon the other side, and had so long been weighing the Socinian beliefs, and Kant's denials, that this sudden and severe method of argument was not likely to convert our refractory student. He had imbibed too many Socratic and Idealist theories to descend at bidding to the level high-road of Evangelical doctrines. His wayward fancy had fed upon too many Atheistic treatises, and had reveled too freely in Voltaire's airy flights, to come quietly back into harness. His mind was like " sweet bells jangled and out of tune," and a flogging and cramming of cut-and-dried theology could not bring back the key-note of faith, especially while his heart was lacerated with loss and disappointment.

His friend Charles Lamb had read much of his metaphysics with him, without, however, developing the same religious skepticism, for sorrow and disappointment had not embittered his nature. Charles warned Coleridge again and again that there was nothing comforting, nothing helpful, in these wild speculations and denials.

" How much better, Esteecee, is it t-to lift the heart, thankfully and p-prayerfully to the one only God, than t-to lose yourself and your hold on faith in these wild th-theories," he would stammer, as his friend argued for this or that atheistic theory.

" What difference does it make to you whether we are but i-ideas, and only im-im-imagine we feel and suffer, or whether e-e-everything is real, and the mind but a part of the machinery. Either theory of the Idealists, or the R-Realists, is but empty q-q-quibbling. We do feel and suffer whether in real materialism, or in our minds ; a-a-and what we want is the *c-cure.*

" In sickness we need m-medicine to relieve obstructions and help nature, and in mental d-distress we need the medicine of God's help—our only h-h-healing. Whether we project this from our ideas of God, or accept it from his S-Spirit, the healing and the help c-come, if we ask it ; and we are c-comforted. So what matters it about these theories ? "

" But I cannot shut my eyes, Charley. They have been opened to see whole worlds of reasoning and seeming truth beyond those set dogmas prescribed for us by

men who believe in other seeming truth.   I am not prepared to affirm or deny what you say of God's help.   I
have tried all my life to find mercy and help from
God, and I must say the comfort and help, if any, have
been infinitesimal, while the staggering blows have been
only too visible and evident.   Nevertheless, I grant a
possible purpose in trials, and a possible help from a
Higher Power; but I want to weigh the matter and sift
the evidences."

" And who are y-you, to weigh and j-judge ? " asked
this wise young philosopher, made wise by his love and
fears for his friend.

" The ostrich hides its head and feels safe because
it cannot see the danger," said Coleridge ; "but I am
not satisfied to swallow theology whole, or to hide my
head under dogmatic sand-piles;" he added, smiling at
the mixed metaphor.   " The very Fathers differ among
themselves and quarrel about vital points ; and each
denounces the other as worse than an Atheist.   Look
at the quarrels between Origen and the Bishops of the
early Church, between Pelagius and St. Augustine, between the Protestant and the Romish churches, between
Calvinists and Churchmen, and then say that they
have found *The Truth*.   Now, what *is* Truth ? "

" Is it for you, a y-youth of eighteen, t-to question the
convictions of the learned F-Fathers, and sift the t-truth
between them and the railing Atheists ?   Will you in-
vent s-s-something to suit yourself, the ' Coleridgean
doctrine,' f-founded upon K-Kant's Idealism, and general upsetting of all the other philosophies, on Hume's
Atheism, which cannot p-prove God in the universe or
in man ; on Sp-Spinoza's Pantheism, or God in everything ; on Voltaire's mocking Deism ? "   Charles was

so utterly in earnest, that he stuttered out these questions before Coleridge could interrupt, and then added, breathlessly :

" Boil 'em d-down, simmer them well over the f-fire of vain-g-glory; sk-skim them with the l-ladle of opinion ; d-d-dish them in manly independence ; and you have the new religion, flavored with a strong essence of Q-Quakerism.   No, no, old boy, I don't p-pretend to share your l-learning; but I don't w-w-want it.   I have a s-simple old b-book that has served Christians for living and d-dying, 1700 years, and it is g-good enough for me, without cracking my skull with hair-splitting ' isms ' and ' ologies.'

" That is just where all start from, for or against; and the Bible is only a human vessel for—Divine truth —if you will," said Coleridge, amazed at Charles's volubility.

" As far as I can see, *everything* must have a human vehicle, except, perhaps, light and air.   Thought and ideas *must* be put into words for expression, and hence the theories and philosophies you would exterminate. Why should they not have the same chance as your Bible ? "

" You know why, Estee.   You know the B-Bible is inspired.   You know it c-carries a power and c-comfort that are utterly wanting in all the philosophies of the world.   It is the s-simplest religion and the c-clearest because it is *God's word.*"

" I don't *know* that, Charley, and I will not swallow it whole until I find that out, or else find Truth somewhere."   Coleridge had chafed so long against the trials and denials of his life, that he could not feel the help and comfort that happier people find in relying upon God's care.   Yet he was not wholly an unbeliever, nor was he at all a willing one.

Charles's reasoning was pretty good for a lad of sixteen, who had dipped into many of his friend's metaphysical researches and shared his difficulties.   Only a spirit of faith can so answer the world's troublous questionings.

All this conversation between Coleridge and Lamb had occurred months before the scene with Boyer. Boyer's attack upon his infidelity came whilst he was still wandering and groping amid these mazes ; and the wholesome dose of doctrine thrust upon him whilst in the cell helped more than he realized.   Later, he could thank the stern mentor for his summary harshness. The dear old father's early teaching in the country parish came to him strong and clear during the weary imprisonment, and with the remembrance of it were mingled longings for the peaceful charms of Nature.

Coleridge passed the test examination creditably, and gave such clear answers and objections to his inquisitor's questions, that they thought it wiser not to push the matter too far.   It is probable that finding they had a powerful and well stored mind to deal with, they wished no open rupture or scandal, for example's sake.

The long holidays soon came, and Coleridge turned hungrily to his old home with its peaceful woods, and the smiling Otter.   George Coleridge, who occupied the father's parish and pulpit, had many long discussions with the obdurate young pedant, to the sore ruffling of his temper.   He began to feel that the younger brother was too deep for him, so regarded him as a willful renegade.

Poor Estee sighed and yearned for tenderness and comprehension from his mother.   But her interest was in the fortunate son who trod in his father's steps ; and her sympathies were for his young brood.   The weary, heart-sore wanderer was looked upon as a sort of prodigal who carried home much mud and filth of the struggling world ; and who must be black at heart to have so wandered.

Esteecee returned to Christ's Hospital, winning for his last term prizes and distinction in both Greek and Latin.

As a Grecian, his stomach was somewhat better filled than in the early days of blue milk and millet ; the small stipend attached to the position enabled him to add sugar and coffee and potatoes to the rigorous fare of those days.

His friend Charles Lamb at the close of the term had gained the position of deputy Grecian, and some honors, but he was now a clerk in the South Sea House, where his elder brother had long been employed.

Scarcely had Coleridge returned to the gloomy cloisters before Charles Lamb appeared, to engage his friend to dine with him on the next half-holiday.

"We have moved from the Inner Temple to more c-commodious quarters at 72 Queen Street.   Come and d-dedicate our household gods; Mary is p-pining to see you," he stammered, with the same old, comical hitch in his speaking.

"Odds bobs ! parson Charley, is this you in clerical black and a hat, with no more coat-tails fluttering round your attenuated shanks ? " laughed Estee.

" Estee, my boy, I have l-left your bookworms behind, and am p-p-promoted to the second floor of yon p-pillared palace, at £50 per annum. I s-slip in l-like the noonday shadow of the venerable John and reflect s-some of his refulgent glory," he said, looking at the black gaiters buttoned to the knees. " I have not yet achieved those neck-ties, Estee, that were our boyhood's envy."

On holidays, when Coleridge was not carrying bouquets to his sweetheart, he would walk up the Strand to Cheapside, and on to the South Sea House and wait for Charles, and the two would stroll back, chattering like magpies, and enjoying the bustle of the passing vehicles. My Lady Holland's carriage would dash by, spattering mud upon the young cockneys; and they would have glimpses of Edmund Burke on his way to or from Parliament, and Pitt, the popular premier, whose speeches were known even to Blue-coat lads, would roll by in his coach. But they strolled merrily on, caring more for the hot dinner awaiting them, and for Mary's joyful greeting, than for these statesmen and grandees. Mary was thin and pale in these days, sewing day and night to increase the scanty income. The father was no longer clerk with a snug little salary; but was tottering to feeble old age, and Charles's small salary and Mary's earnings seemed scarcely enough for the family needs. Their uncomplaining adaptation to the narrow limits of their poverty, and the exquisite neatness of the small house made it very cosy and homelike to the homeless stranger, and he greatly prized these evenings over Shakespeare or Massinger, which were Charles's delight. Charles had become a great lover of the drama, and often spent his evenings at Drury Lane or Covent Garden. He was so captivated with Mrs. Siddons' acting, that he wrote several sonnets to her, which were afterwards published.

Coleridge slipped off with him one evening, but as theater-going is entirely prohibited at Christ's Hospital, he was obliged to lay aside the marked Blue-coat dress, and wear coat and breeches and hat belonging to the venerable John, unknown to that worthy. The two youths were so alarmed at their temerity, that the stolen pleasure scarcely compensated for the awful fears of detection. They did not repeat the experiment, so Coleridge had to enjoy the theater by proxy.

Mary sometimes accompanied Charles, and enjoyed the Kembles and Mrs. Siddons quite as intensely as did her brother. "The Rivals" and "School for Scandal," now in the first flush of their fame, were heartily enjoyed by both.

Another great pleasure of their lives was the Sunday walk to Hampstead Heath, or through the green lanes of Islington, then a village several miles from London.

With dinner-basket, ale-bottles, and a merry flow of wit and humor, the frolic seemed a charming treat, after the smoke and dullness of London. Often Coleridge and his sweetheart would join them, and sometimes Leigh Hunt, a witty, clever, ease-loving schoolfellow, was of the party, and then the fun would wax high. Seated in some shady nook, beside a babbling brook, with the towers and spires of the city jeweling the horizon, they would discuss poetry, politics, everything, in fact, over the sandwiches and cold mutton, and Coleridge's eloquence was not more charming than the stammered puns and witticisms of Charles, and the grave, sweet, interludes of Mary. The whispering trees and murmuring stream, and the distant hum of the city bells, were a dreamy and lovely accompaniment. In the spring, the friends watched the trees budding into fairy gauzes, and blossoming into pink and snowy bouquets ; in summer they enjoyed the calm, deep skies, and shady denseness of the oaks and plane-trees ; and in autumn the golden skies, ripened fields, and russet-trees, with the occasional crimson vine. Their Sundays were flower-crowned, and were marked days in their calendar.

But after many years of these delightful holiday rambles and sweet, dreamy confidences, a parting came. Coleridge was sent to Jesus College, Cambridge, and the brother and sister had their rambles alone. Their parents needed constant care, as the feeble health of each slowly failed, and the poor old father developed a childish petulance and helplessness ; then Charles's evenings were often claimed for cribbage by the querulous old man. His holidays from his desk were less free than formerly. Mary, too, was daily and nightly in attendance upon the ailing mother, often stitching wearily during the intervals of nursing—not the sewing of the nineteenth century, with the fairy machines to rattle off long seams and turn work into play ; but slow, tedious work in the lightest corner of the gloomy room, or often by sputtering, flickering candle-light.

CHAPTER V.

CONTRASTING DESTINIES.

And to be placed as they with gradual fame,
Among the archives of mankind, thy work
Makes audible a linked lay of Truth—
Of Truth profound, a sweet, continuous lay
Not learnt, but native—her own natural notes!
Ah! as I listened with a heart forlorn,
The pulses of my being beat anew,
And e'en as life returns upon the drowned,
Life's joy rekindling roused a throng of pains.

COLERIDGE.

THUS patiently the brother and sister plodded on, taking life as it came. Life to them meant ceaseless toil and unchanging drudgery for the bare necessities. A few books in the great mahogany book-case were the only luxury; the plain, hair-cloth sofa, and straight-back, high, old mahogany chairs, and center-table were good and substantial, but suggested no thought of beauty or even comfort.

But the Lambs were content; they knew little else. Their aspirations were simple, and had not been poisoned by contact with the great world of fashion around them. What cared they for the balls and routs of nobility, or for the great dinners of the rich! Those jewels and flowers and courtesies of gay beaux and belles belonged to another world than theirs, and were as far off as heaven. They had glimpses into it in the passing coaches and at the theater. But having no contact with such gayeties, there was for them no temptation to envy or aspire. The simple content of those whose eyes are not opened to the gayeties and pleasures of life, with all their attendant struggles and heart-aches, is happier than the emulations and ambitions of those who live on the edge of the world's favors.

Even to those who reach the summit, there is so much of care and toilsome detail, and of corroding anxiety, that their hearts are strangers to the content of the unstriving poor. As we rise in affluence and position, we see greater heights beyond which must be reached. Therefore, said Wolsey, who had gained the summit : " Cromwell, I charge thee, fling away ambition : by that sin fell the angels."

How fared it with Coleridge in these days ? He found a new source of delight in the long shaded avenues of stately elms and limes of Cambridge. The winding river, reflecting the towers and spires, gave fine opportunities for bathing and boating or the easier drifting. The beautiful, historic buildings, with their battlemented tops and oriel and Tudor windows; with their spires and towers, their stately archways, quadrangles, and smooth-shaven lawns, filled his poetic heart with rapture. The great libraries, with more volumes than even his greedy appetite could devour in a lifetime, gave him a happy sense of repletion. He donned the cap and gown and felt at home within these stately halls filled with scholars like himself. Groups and cliques could pass from college to college and discuss the topics dear to students' hearts. Political feeling waxed high. France's days of riot and shrieks of liberty were commencing, and the ferment was stirring the Whig circles of England, and giving Toryism anxious occupation.

Opinions grew hot among the fiery young souls gathered in the colleges, and the ferment of liberty was rising in the form of independence, in the scorn of tyranny, and in a spirit of opposition to all control.

"What if barbarities do result, and murders stalk abroad ; was ever revolution accomplished without?" asked Coleridge, now a rabid revolutionist. "Of course blood flows and prisons teem ; is Liberty not worth the cost?"

The staid old English towers frowned down upon such heresy. The solemn professors frowned even more blackly upon the suspicion of disloyalty among college men, and the firebrand was quenched by stricter rules, and more watchful vigilance over college hours and work. The French populace had risen, and were sweeping down king, nobles, and laws in a wholesale devastation. Hideous mobs pillaged and murdered in the name of Liberty. Blood flowed like water down the streets of Paris, and, like a red rag to a bull, red caps and rosettes excited fresh horrors. Setting up their goddess of Reason in the Notre Dame, they massacred bishops and priests, for Liberty.

And our mad young Englishmen felt the passion for license in their souls, and shouted for Liberty too, and wildest of them was our dreamer Coleridge, who ever welcomed a new sensation or enthusiasm as the voice of God. There was no Boyer now to hold him in check; the revolutionary yeast must rise until it soured. So he worked on in secret meetings and debates, a recognized leader, with his golden eloquence and his boyish enthusiasm.

Upon his arrival at Cambridge, a fine gentleman had called, offering to furnish his room, as though sent by the authorities, and telling him of the necessity for establishing himself properly among his associates.

He took orders for refurnishing, sending a couch and table, chairs, an escritoire for books and papers, and dishes, etc., to entertain a few friends properly. Coleridge, a stranger to college ways, and provided with the modest stipend belonging to a Grecian with class honors coming up from Christ's Hospital, gave the orders for the needed articles. Greatly did he enjoy his cosy room with oriel window looking upon the campus, with roses climbing up the gray walls and wreathing about his window, shaking their rich fragrance into his room. Greatly did he enjoy the soft bed and luxurious couch ; and his table was often graced by the brighter spirits of the college.

His old friend, Middleton, of Christ's Hospital, had preceded him to Cambridge, and was ready to welcome him. Many happy evenings were spent around the cosy table whose simple viands testified a ready welcome. Coleridge strove for honors during this first year, and gained the gold medal for the Greek Ode. His room became the favorite meeting place for enthusiasts like himself. Robespierre was discussed and admired, and the dreamers were ready to emulate the struggle for liberty. Religion was freely discussed, and Coleridge again had wide scope for his theories and wild fancies. From Voltaire to Priestley ; from Berkeley to Hume ; from Pitt to Robespierre—all the questions these names suggest were hotly discussed and freely handled by the young fools who "rushed in where angels fear to tread." Coleridge drifted past the shoals of infidelity, that had threatened to wreck his soul's life, to Unitarianism. But within the sacred precincts of an English college, founded upon the Church of England, this was as heretical as dangerous, and the brilliant youth was in greater danger of expulsion than he knew.

Of his intimates, one friend was called before the college authorities to answer charges of schism and Unitarianism. The questioning was very close and searching, the replies were bold and clear, and the argument grew hot and eager. In the midst of a telling reply from his friend, Coleridge involuntarily clapped his hands. A proctor immediately charged the man next to Coleridge with the breach of decorum, and he was called to stand before that august assembly of prelates and professors. "Would that I could," he replied, holding up the stump of a right arm; and thus the danger drifted by, but it was all really through the proctor's friendliness to the real offender. When Coleridge afterwards confessed to the proctor that he was the transgressor, the latter replied, "I knew it, and it would have cost you your place in college. You are on dangerous ground, morally and politically, and you will be expelled if you do not change your course."

But youth is fearless of results and courts danger as evidence of bravery, and the warning was unheeded.

Charles Lamb was overjoyed at his friend's hopeful and happy letters, and he and Mary pored over the charming accounts of the fine old buildings, with their beautiful avenues of English oaks and limes, and the trim college bowling-greens. If Charles sometimes sighed

over the stern fate that kept him from following his
friend to the University, and enjoying the opportunities for which he was almost as well fitted, he kept
his discontent to himself, save for an occasional longing to run off and investigate these classic scenes. He
was needed at home to care for his failing father, and
to throw his earnings into the family purse to keep
starvation from the door. He was too much a philosopher to waste time in complaints; but in the silent
nights how often he lay and thought of those delightful possibilities forever closed to him! His sweet nature
learned patient acquiescence in the colorless lot laid
out for him, but his imagination pictured those splendid
halls and venerable walls, those charming groups of
congenial souls, the teeming life, the wholesome friction of spirit on spirit that kindles such fires of enthusiasm.

The absence of this opportunity for noble thinking and
hopeful doing is harder to bear at life's threshold than
poverty or toil. The spirit has not learned the hopelessness of mental and spiritual struggle, and the new
soul-wings feel ready to soar, if space and chance are
given. To yield all that ambition and hope promise
to the drudgery for daily bread is a bitter blow.
Charles knew but one path lay before him, and so he
patiently plodded on at the South Sea House for a
year or so, until his father's old patron, Samuel Salt,
procured a better position for him in the India House.

"I have changed my location," he wrote to Coleridge; "I, also, am in classic halls with Doric columns
and stately façade. I take my daily seat at my ac-
countant's desk in a lofty chamber, with statues and
pictures of moguls and begums around me, almost

fancying myself Prime Minister to India. Around me are fine specimens of Eastern elegance, carved Bombay chairs and settees, delicately wrought elephant tusks and ivory idols, quaint Hindoo gods, etc. I have but to imagine myself the happy possessor, as I gaze upon them from my daily tasks, and what could be better? You know the sense of happiness and possession lies in the *idea*, according to your German theories; and since I daily have these treasures about me, I formulate the idea that they are tributes to my greatness; *ergo*, I become their owner, and a personage of consequence; *ergo*, all the Indies with their stores of wealth do honor me. Below, are vast museums of these curiosities. I keep them under lock and key, lest some less fortunate beings should be tempted to dispute my possession."

So, with quaintest vein of humor, Charles Lamb transformed his daily routine to a pretended diversion, and, year by year, great folios of figures accumulated to witness the patient daily drudgery.

Coleridge, at the University, was becoming daily more of an enthusiast for liberty. Robespierre's all-conquering power inspired wonder and enthusiasm. Liberty, as shrieked by the revolutionists; liberty, as profaned by the Jacobins; liberty, as proclaimed from the council halls to sanction the massacre of king and conservative Girondists; liberty, as prostituted by Robespierre for his own wild ambitions, seemed a glorious watchword to the infatuated young fools who wanted vent for their own awakening aspirations. "Here is the path to glory, through the freeing of the people from kings and aristocrats!" Such were the sentiments smouldering throughout the colleges and among

the young madcaps of England, and causing frequent
riots and disturbances. The arrest of Horne Tooke
and Thelwall and other revolutionary enthusiasts somewhat quenched the rising flames ; but for years there
was an occasional flickering of liberty fires.

The brand left a mark upon that college set and their
friends, which in after years greatly marred their fortunes
and destinies.

CHAPTER VI.

DE SCYLLA EN CHARYBDIS.

Repine not, O my son, that Heaven hath chastened thee.
                     Behold this vine,
I found it as a wild tree, whose wanton strength
Hast swoln into irregular twigs, ...
And spent itself in leaves and little rings,
So, in the flourish of its outwardness,
Wasting the sap and strength
That should have given forth fruit.
But when I pruned the tree,
Then it grew temperate, in its vain expense
Of useless leaves, and knotted, as thou seest,
Into these full, clear clusters, to repay
The hand that wisely wounded it.
          Repine not, O my son!
In wisdom and in mercy Heaven inflicts,
Like a wise leech, its painful remedies.

SOUTHEY.

MEANTIME, less heroic matters were occupying Coleridge's attention. The visitor who had generously suggested little improvements in his student's quarters was dunning him unmercifully. Coleridge found to his surprise and sorrow that those same chairs and tables were not part of the college outfit. His family resented any demands for " extravagant luxuries." " Have I not helped send you to the University, at the cost of considerable pinching, and must I be rewarded by bills for debaucheries and luxuries, whilst I and my family are living on almost nothing, but at least keeping clear of debt ?" wrote his brother.

On festive occasions, a certain grimy money-lender would walk in unannounced, and make himself appallingly at home upon those same chairs. If Coleridge had a few friends to dine or sup with him, a hook nose and piercing eyes were sure to appear at the door. It was Coleridge's ever-present skeleton at the feast, and he would hastily call his tormentor aside to beg a few more days of grace. Our dreamer had willingly given a note of hand to free himself from this apparition; but when the day of settlement came, with no funds to meet the note, the "skeleton" seized upon the furniture, and confiscated all movables. The man's disappearance, though the furniture went with him, was a relief. But the present value of the goods was far below their original cost six months ago; and again the hook nose and eagle eyes became ubiquitous, until the disgust and shame of it, and the hopelessness of ever getting rid of him, sent Coleridge a fugitive to London. He took the coach to town one black night; and when he reached the city with no money and few friends, he knew not where to go. The old horror was slowly creeping upon him. Whilst sitting disconsolately upon the door-step of a deserted house, a miserable beggar, more hungry and wretched than himself, asked and received his last penny.

"He is more hungry and helpless than I," Coleridge muttered ; but when he sat supperless upon the lonely steps all night, and roamed breakfastless and faint around the street in the drizzling dawn, he thought perhaps he was the more miserable, not being accustomed to the gnawings of hunger in these days.

"Where shall I go; what can I do?" kept churning
and turning over in his mind. All the philosophies of
all the sages could not coin him a penny for a bun.
His friend the shoemaker had left London, and he was
unwilling to apply for help to his already overburdened
school-fellow, Charles Lamb. He felt the old Blue-
coat-days' horror fastening tighter around his heart as
he wandered aimlessly on, when suddenly he espied
the sign of a recruiting officer : " Men wanted, to enlist
on the 15th, in Elliot's Light Dragoons."*

As he had always had a deep antipathy to soldiers
and their cut-throat trade, and was a coward about
horses, the call was not an attractive one. He read
and re-read the sign, and in his wretched depression
said: " Well, if there is a devil, he is holding out an
enchanting bait! It seems a call to the most distasteful life that my unfortunate feet could enter; so it must
be my fate." Doggedly he told the old sergeant he
wished to enlist. The sergeant looked, first carelessly,
then attentively, at the hollow-eyed young man. He had
seen something of life, and, noting the weariness and
despair in the young fellow's face, suspected he wished
only to escape some difficulty or hide some disgrace.
The sergeant asked him where he had slept, and
finding his fears correct, made Coleridge rest on his
bed and share his breakfast. He tried to dissuade
him from enlisting. " Take this crown, young man, and
go to the theater, and come back to-morrow, and see
if you are not in a different way of thinking," he
urged.

Coleridge gratefully accepted the man's sympathy
and much-needed help, spending the crown for food
and a decent lodging for the next night. The following

---

* " Homes and Haunts of British Poets."—HOWITT.

day he again presented himself before his new-found friend, and insisted upon enlisting under the name of Silas Cumberbatch, or "Cumberback," as he was soon called, from his awkward riding.

"I could not disgrace the family name by being a common working private," he murmured. "Poor brother James was an officer when he died last winter, and Frank is now a lieutenant in India. It would not do to disgrace him by giving him a brother who may be appointed officer's servant," he said, scornfully. "Not that I owe the captain, the clergyman, or the lieutenant much family fealty," he muttered, bitterly, "but that Cambridge shark will better lose my scent under my new name."

The company marched to Reading, and poor Coleridge, or "Cumberback," found the life a sorry exchange for the comforts of the past year at Cambridge.

A stumbling horse, which delighted in tossing up its hind legs in good, rousing kicks, and landing the awkward rider in the mud, was not calculated to improve his taste for riding. He never could stick on that horse, but wobbled around in most disjointed fashion, to the constant amusement of his companions. He was continually under punishment for rusty accoutrements and ungroomed horse; for in his fits of abstraction he would forget to rub the animal down. His rheumatic pains made stooping and grooming and all menial duties most painful, and the exposed life added to his physical miseries. "*De Scylla en Charybdis,*" he often murmured after some ignominious tilt into mud or dust, or after a reprimand for untidiness.

But in camp or hospital, the clumsy dragoon was a universal favorite. His endless stories charmed his companions. His reading and writing were marvels of wisdom to them, and he was always ready to write their home letters, or recite poems and scenes from his old favorites. They recognized his superiority, and were eager to serve him in return. In this way, with ready hands to groom his horse and clean his gun, he slipped along, much comforted by his great popularity.

He nursed a companion through small-pox, when no one else would approach the shed to which the contagion was banished. His life was novel and full of hardships, yet the affection of his rough associates made it bearable.

He was appointed orderly to Captain Ogle, where the duties were less irksome; for his Christ's Hospital days had taught him lessons in setting and clearing the table which were useful at the mess-room. In a fit of despondency he scribbled upon the stable-door the words: "*Eheu quam infortunii miserrimum est fuisse felicem !*"

Captain Ogle was astonished to see the correct Latin, and suspected the author, having noticed his shambling orderly's excellent grammar and refined speech, so different from the unlettered ignorance of most English privates. Calling him, he requested him in Latin to saddle his horse and attend him upon some mission, and the immediate reply proved Coleridge to be the writer of the lines.

" How came you in such a position, Cumberback? I see you have led a different life. Your awkwardness in your duties, and your education, prove you belong to a different sphere ; have you been unfortunate ? " asked the captain, looking keenly at the abashed Coleridge.

"Naw, sur," he stammered, in broad north-country dialect ; "oive picked up a little larning at me fayther's country-school; but there was a big lot of us, and the eldest was sent into the world."

Captain Ogle looked searchingly at him, and remembered to have heard, heretofore, a speech entirely free from dialect, but said nothing more.

After the mention of the fact of the orderly's Latin attainments, and his endless classic and historic tales, which were widely discussed among the men, Coleridge found himself uncomfortably conspicuous among the officers. The fear of detection was realized at Hounslow, when an old college friend, Allen by name, recognized him as he rode behind his officer.

"Why, Coleridge! where have you been hiding these six months? Why did you leave Cambridge so suddenly? Your friends and family have been searching everywhere for you," he added, running breathlessly after the trotting dragoon.

"You are meestaken, sur," shouted Coleridge, " I never seen your loike befar."

"No! you need not pretend I'm mistaken ; I'd know those gray eyes in Egypt, and that black poll," called his friend.

Captain Ogle turned inquiringly, and Coleridge blushed painfully, looking every inch a detected culprit.

"He's meestaken the pursun, sur," said Coleridge, digging his spurs into his steed's side and galloping away.

Coleridge's six months of military drill and reprimand had somewhat straightened the stooping shoulders and bent knees, and improved his awkward gait, and the plain, wholesome fare and out-door exercise had strengthened the delicate frame; but the poet, metaphysician, and logician of the University was not yet transformed into the typical dragoon.

His friend persisted in hunting him up at head-quarters, and Coleridge's persuasions could not induce Allen to conceal his whereabouts.

"You are throwing away your life, with your talents and attainments. An officer's servant !—a stable groom !" said Allen, indignantly, whilst Coleridge's astonished companions gaped curiously.

"Aw said ee were a scholard," said one ; " ee telled us aboot Cromwell and Charles, who had ees 'ed cut off, and about Robeyspear, who sarved the Frenchey Louis a loike treek."

"Be quiet, will you !" thundered Coleridge, cursing .the foolish tongue that had led to this scrape. " 'Tis an ill turn my wits have done me," sighed the discouraged dragoon. "They never gave me a pennyworth of bread, and now they rise like Nemesis to force me out of an honest living."

" Come back to Cambridge, Coleridge ; if those small debts drove you away, we will pay them and set you up again. It is wicked to waste such attainments here," urged Allen.

Some weeks later his brother appeared and angrily demanded his return.

"What, sir ! have we all helped you enter the University, for you to disgrace the family thus—a dragoon ! to hide the results of your debauches ? "

"I tell you I have not been leading a wild life," angrily answered the poor fellow. " How can a man live anywhere on the interest of nothing. 'Twould take a new arithmetic to demonstrate that ; bread, meat, clothing, and bed on £10 a year ! Much room this leaves for debauchery and extravagance! I tell you I could not squeeze shillings from my book covers or my finger ends, and your liberality of £10 a year was simple starvation after I lost my tutorship. Those debts were for mere furniture and necessaries. Where did you suppose those would spring from, I not having a fairy godmother or 'wonderful lamp'?"

" Well, well! " said his brother, " come back to Ottery and help me with the school until the next term, and then go back to Cambridge and fit yourself for a place in the world."

Reluctantly Coleridge applied for and gained his discharge from service, and went down to his birthplace and toiled faithfully among the boys. But his dreaminess gave them many opportunities for shirking lessons and sliding over difficulties. How hard boys will work to shirk an appointed lesson or duty! Why does the young idea always aim astray? Coleridge, being young and fresh from school himself, was too lenient with their slippery ways, and George Coleridge saw with indignation that their progress in Latin and Greek was but slow and uncertain.

This, and the air of disapproval hovering round Coleridge like á gloomy cloud, made him restless to get back to Cambridge.

To his latest days he never forgave his mother and brother their distrust and coldness. It rose before him like a wall of discouragement. One sometimes wonders if the early deaths of the more fortunate sons, following so closely one after another, were not the Nemesis avenging his unsheltered, sordid youth on those who should have offered helping hands, yet left him lonely and uncared for.

CHAPTER VII.

THE DREAMS OF YOUTH.

Wisdom doth live, with children round her knees;
  Books, leisure, perfect freedom, and the talk
  Man holds with week-day man, in the hourly walk
Of the mind's business; these are the degrees
  By which true sway doth mount; this is the stalk
True power doth grow on; and her rights are these.
WORDSWORTH.

COLERIDGE took up his broken course at Cambridge, and wrote to his friend Lamb, whom he had neglected during his days of masquerading as dragoon.

"Don't mention this subject to me again, my friend. I never want you to imagine I enjoyed the delights of being groom and stable-boy and servant. I am now again among my friends the books, free from settled debts, and shall strive to gain a College position. To the Church I cannot turn; I have no stomach for its bands and ligatures of doctrine, and cut-and-dried and digested pabulum for diseased digestion. Let those whose consciences are clear of doubt, or dried to prescribed form, take the fat livings from her hands; I will not perjure my truth. Moreover, I could not gain admittance even if I would." *

Later, Charles and Mary Lamb received a letter more like his cheery self:

* " Life of Coleridge."—BLONDL.

" I've just come across a volume of poems by a
young fellow named Wordsworth ; he was a graduate of
Oxford the year I entered Cambridge, and he is now
in London, a Westmoreland fellow with the sweetness
of the hills clinging around him.   Do read his poems ;
they breathe true heavenly music.   Of course, the
' Monthly Review ' minced it ; all modern poetry must
pass the fires of criticism, and the fiends who light
these fires eternally borrow their sulphur from a hot
place that never is suffered to cool.   These poems
are exquisite pictures of the scenes he loves.·   They are
mirrors reflecting Nature's sweetest smile ; the fools cannot see it through their own smoked glass.   Read them,
my gentle Lamb, and bleat thy opinion to me.   If you
could find this bard of Nature in your great London,
where they say he and his sister are living, you and
your dearest Mary might find most congenial spirits." *

But Lamb and Mary had their heads too full of work
and heavy household cares to take Coleridge's hint,
and Wordsworth and his sister, after trying to stifle their
yearnings for the hills and woods, left London and
settled in Somersetshire, living upon a small legacy
left the poet by an admirer named Calvert.

This godsend of £900 kept the wolf from the door,
and enabled the poet to follow his bent in spite of literary critics and want of success.

Coleridge, hearing of his friend Allan Cunningham's
success at Oxford, determined to visit him and compare
Oxford with Cambridge.   He set out on a pedestrian
tour along the beautiful, shady, English roads, and
reached Oxford in a couple of days.   If Cambridge
was picturesque, what raptures did the glorious towers

* " Life of Coleridge."—BLONDL.

and spires and domes of Oxford awake in him! He rambled through the beautiful stone archways to the college greens. He strolled along the shaded avenues of Magdalen College, called Addison's Walk. Through the long vistas of noble limes, interlaced overhead, he saw the turrets and spires gleaming, and dreamed of the poet Addison. He recalled the beautiful rhapsodies and elegant metaphors of the classic " Cato," and found at every turn inspiration for a poet's dreams. On, through the " Tom quad " of Christ's College, where the gothic windows and spires of the beautiful Cathedral charm with their beauty and with their historic associations. Visions of Wolsey's magnificence arose, as he contemplated the splendid buildings of his munificent gift.

On he passed through the Roman arches and pillars of Queen's College, in severe classic contrast with the gothic pinnacles of All Souls' and the oriel windows of St. John's, with the crimson and gold roses climbing to its battlement roof, and enwreathing the rugged brown walls. He walked through the beautiful gardens to the shaded river-walk back of the colleges, where spires and towers peep from the embowering green. He reached Magdalen with its ivy-crowned towers, duplicated in the river, where the Isis and Cherwell are spanned by the bridges, which seem warders of the ancient moats around the beautiful, hoary, old piles that have outlived so many generations of men. Truly it is a place for visions and dreams, and our dreamer wandered in silent uninterrupted ecstasy through the shaded avenues, and over the emerald lawns, before he broke the spell, and hunted up his friend Allan Cunningham.

Intimate with Cunningham was a most radical fellow who had been expelled from Westminster for daring to write an article against school tyranny. He had been refused admittance to Christ's the orthodox head of the colleges, for his radicalism and his unsettled views and independence. Baliol had ungraciously admitted him. It only tolerated the young scapegrace, who was an avowed free-thinker in theology and politics, and who dared, as undergraduate, to throw off the conventional college wig. Between this young man, who was always scribbling poetry,—this Robert Southey,—and Coleridge, a warm intimacy sprang up. There was a great congeniality between them. They were both strong advocates of the French Revolution, which was so dearly buying "liberty, equality, and fraternity." They inveighed against the tyranny of college authority in requiring such deference to Church and State. They rebelled together against the autocracy of the Church, and the enforced attendance upon the services, which they called but remnants of Popery and the Scarlet Woman.

From their contagious sympathy in moral, mental, and religious liberty, college life seemed to both more and more distasteful ; Coleridge found the splendid old palaces of Oxford but the hoary shells of most rotten kernels.

He wrote to Southey, after departing for a pedestrian tour of Wales : " Verily, Southey, I like not Oxford nor the inhabitants of it. I would say thou art a nightingale among owls. Thy nest is in the blighted cornfields where the poppy nods its red-cowled head."

They had rhapsodized together over Coleridge's

favorite, Bowles, and his later admiration, Wordsworth. Together, they read their poets, strolling along the classic avenues, and discussed them at night, sometimes interpolating with their own fancies, as poets will. Each had read snatches of his own poems and thoughts to the appreciative ear of the other. Both felt the upspringing of the poet's flame within, and each required a kindred spirit's sympathy and encouragement. Our young poets had feasted upon Shakespeare, Gray, Addison, Pope, Thomson, and Bowles, and were eagerly discussing the later poets, Cowper and Goldsmith, whose works were slowly creeping into notice.

What sweet depths of kinship lie in this meeting of soul with soul on the plane above the every-day world ! They felt the fire kindling in their own souls, and each found inspiration in the other.

Allan Cunningham and Southey had been studying Rousseau's theories, and were growing enthusiastic over a plan of socialism which they afterwards called Pantisocracy, when Coleridge joined them in the scheme. The dreamers found it a very Utopia. Pantisocracy was to be a government of entire equality, where all the members of the community should divide the manual labor, the expenses, and the results.

These dreamers talked about the scheme, day by day and into the night, until " big Tom's " curfew drove them reluctantly apart. The friends parted at the expiration of Coleridge's visit with vows of eternal friendship, each feeling stronger for the other's sympathy.

Coleridge had heard of Wordsworth's rambles through the North of Wales, and he, too, wished to drink from the fountain-head of beauty. He and some friends started for a pedestrian tour amid the picturesque glens and brawling ghylls of Wales.

Southey lingered on until the close of the term ; but his growing impatience of church and college restraints drove him at last to forego his examination.

He determined to leave Oxford and go to his aunt's, in Bath. After his father's failure in business she had taken him to raise and educate, and had great aspirations for the brilliant youth. She was bitterly disappointed at his refractory spirit, which was cutting him off from the career she had planned for him.

The Pantisocratic scheme seemed to others too absurd for more than a passing sneer. But it was a growing plan among the young men with whom it originated. They commenced to give their socialistic theories a practical turn, agreeing to collect funds, charter a sailing vessel for America, and procure a small tract of arable land, lying along the Susquehanna River, where they might become farmers. They were to marry, and their wives would attend to the dairy and the domestic economy of the new settlement. This plan of carrying practical wives with them was well arranged, and seemed available. Southey was already madly in love with a Miss Fricker, a sister of the wife of Lovell, a young Quaker poet living at Bristol, who for many years had been a friend and admirer of Southey, and was as eager as he for the new scheme. The young women were as enthusiastic as the men.

Lovell's father was a wealthy Quaker who would not listen to the plan, but Lovell was about the only member of the Brotherhood with the shadow of money, and even his was mainly shadow. But the young dreamers were hopeful and trusted that fortune might at last smile upon so rational and modest a scheme. George Burnet, another of Southey's Oxford friends, joined them at Bristol, and Charles Lloyd, a Christ's Hospital graduate and friend of Lamb and Coleridge, was also of the party. Their numbers were rapidly increasing, and upon Coleridge's return from Wales, he hastened to Bristol, to join his friends.

Cambridge had become too distasteful with its strictly marked theological lines. He was in constant danger of incurring reprimand and expulsion for his " obstinate, heterodox views."

" I never could control my erring member ! " he wrote to Charles Lamb. " I like not the pompous masters and the begowned and bewigged dons, who always look askance at me. I feel a continual desire to quiz them upon their own tenets, and in fact I believe the ' Logos ' would stir up more mud than their waters of rhetoric and reason could clear. During the examination, when Dr. Camedon was holding forth upon the Trinity and denouncing the Arians, I asked what authority they found for believing the early Fathers taught the Divinity of Christ."

" ' What ! ' thundered the Doctor, ' you presume to introduce heresies here ! '

" ' Nay, sir, but Tertullian and Origen seemed but the originators of the belief in the economy ; and Chrysostom apologizes for the apostles not teaching it, because of the early Christians being unprepared.'

" ' Do you dare, sir, quote the Fathers for your heresies ? ' he asked.

" I trembled lest I should be called before that august body of college magnates to answer for the awful crime of Socinianism, and yet I should have liked to hear their answer.   The miracles, the resurrection even, could they not be simple manifestations of God's power, like the plagues of Egypt, and the raising of the widow's son ?   I *should* like a clear, unbiassed opinion and fair argument, Charles Lamb ; but in this Churchly establishment, at the first question, they cry, Infidel, meddler with sacred things ! and 'tis just so at Oxford ; yes, 'tis worse there, for a set of high Anglicans are carrying forms and ceremonies and externals to the verge of Papacy.

" If they are so sure of their ground, why not answer fair questions ?

" I shall not return from these free fells and glades to Cambridge.   I have done with the old order of things into which I cannot fit myself.   I shall follow Southey, Lloyd, and Allan Cunningham to Bristol, there to hatch the golden egg we have been sitting upon— the Pantisocracy.

" How I wish you and Mary would join us in our flight to the New World !   Think of starting upon new life, new hopes, new work, new religion, with utter freedom, in that land of the free !   We have studied all the history, philosophy, religion, science, and political economy bearing upon a socialistic government, and have a most admirable system.   'Tis a colony where *all* shall have equal rights of labor, profit, principle and government.   It will be a refuge for the oppressed of all nations and sects.   We will show the beauty of having all things in common, which the apostles practiced and dropped, after a short time."

Coleridge settled in Bristol with Southey and Lovell, and deep were the schemes these plotters laid.

Southey's Aunt Tyler, finding him determined,

raised such a scene as that youth was not likely to forget, and turned him out forever from the house where he had always been treated as a son.

Thus Coleridge and Southey were thrown upon their own resources, which were most meager. Southey's "Joan of Arc" and a few other poems had been published before he left Oxford, and brought him a small sum. They found a few pupils to coach for college. Aunt Tyler's servant "Shad" had also grown enthusiastic over the new plan, and was likewise turned adrift for meddling with such heathenish ideas.

Coleridge, on seeing the lugubrious youth come like a whipped dog, exclaimed: " Shad goes with us; he is my brother." *

Our impecunious socialists also wrote poems and magazine articles, which a Bristol publisher, Joseph Cottle, himself something of a poet, published, giving them a slender pittance.

Coleridge had long ago awakened from his early passion for the young milliner. College life and soldiering had driven love from the field, and an unexpected meeting with Miss Evans in a Welsh inn had been anything but a pleasure, since the vows had waned to silence and indifference.

Being thrown constantly with Southey's *fiancée* and her family, he immediately proceeded to fall in love with her sister. Sarah Fricker seemed just the wife for him. Southey looked somewhat suspiciously upon a flame so hastily kindled, and Lovell doubted its expediency, seeing Coleridge's very slim prospects of making a living. But Coleridge, believing in Pantisocracy, —where all should fare alike,—was much enchanted

* "Life of Coleridge."—HALL CAINE.

with Miss Sarah, and believed himself greatly in love. Those great, earnest eyes, and the illuminating poet's glance, fascinated men and women, and Sarah's heart soon yielded.

Our dreamer was on the heights now; Pantisocracy, Southey, America, and Miss Fricker were rounding into blessed realities, and again Fortuné seemed beckoning to him.

He wrote poems and essays, and folios of impassioned eloquence; but Bristol, the most unpoetic spot in England, was rather a limited sphere for so many young poets. So Coleridge decided to try his fortunes for the winter in London.

CHAPTER VIII.

A SPRING SONG.

But Love is indestructible,
Its holy flame forever burneth ;
From Heaven it came, to Heaven returneth.
Too oft on earth a troubled guest,
At times deceived, at times oppressed,
It here is tried and purified,
And hath in Heaven its perfect rest.
It soweth here with toil and care ;
But the harvest time of Love is there.

SOUTHEY.

DURING this summer, whilst Coleridge was dreaming of Pantisocracy and making love, Charles Lamb had had a sleeping and an awakening.

During his holiday he visited the fine old house in Hertfordshire where his grandmother was housekeeper. In these stately halls and galleries, with their lines of ancestral portraits looking smilingly or scornfully down at the bright-eyed youth, he loved to dream his dreams. The family being absent in London for the season, he could wander at will through the great library, and browse upon the rich pastures displayed there. He often fancied himself the young heir, and sauntered amid the statuary and pictures as one "to the manner born."

Good Mrs. Field knew well that her sedate young grandson might bask in these rich apartments all day without the slightest danger to the worshipful contents. Here Charles reveled in the beauty of the mellow Titians and the serene Raphaels, in the rich tints of the Gainsboroughs and the quaint satire of the Hogarths. They so haunted his imagination that his first possessions in after-life were copies of some of these pictures.

In his fortnight's visit the young clerk, with Blue-coat garb laid aside forever, and a neat suit of black small clothes, gladdened old Grannie's heart.

"Eh ! Charles, but ye are a man now."

" B-b-but not a big one, Grannie, nor ever shall be, I m-m-much fear."

"But a most bonnie, comely lad, wi' winsome eyes, and the air of a born gentleman," said Grannie.

"And so I am, grandam. The son of John L. Lamb of Inner Temple can hold up his h-head with the b-best, so please you," he said, with a good hug and kiss, to the fond old lady, who gave him the freedom of the house, inwardly wishing my lady could see the dainty, handsome youth who whistled cheerily around the dull old halls. Who knows but he might find a home here as secretary to my lord, and then—— But

> " The dreams of age and the dreams of youth
>   Seem wasted thought in this world's hard truth,
>   And there's nothing sure but Heaven."

In his long strolls around the fine old manor, beyond its great brick walls, covered from ground to turret with the rare, rich English ivy, he met a timid, blue-eyed girl of sixteen or seventeen. He was only in the springtime of life, and amid the buds and blossoms of the sweetest land upon God's earth, the two young turtle-doves must fall to billing and cooing.

His daily strolls turned to the tiny stone cottage with the diamond-paned casements, and the roses clambering to the thatched roof.

From the roses the pretty human bud peeped out, and, espying her lover in the distance, flitted down the shady path to the shadow of the giant oaks, where were the mossiest rocks and the largest primroses; and where the tiny beck purled and rippled a soft accompaniment to the pretty babble of their innocent young hearts.

"Oh, Alice! that we might wander thus forever! How sweet these woodlands are! how sweeter still are thy sunny tresses and c-c-clear blue eyes! Thine eyes are just the c-c-color of this stream where it reflects the sky!"

"I think your eyes are like my gentle doe's eyes, which I have always loved for her tender looks," she said.

And so they chattered on, in the glad, bright to-day, not heeding the to-morrow that would find them far apart. It was hard for Charles to tear himself from this short dream of bliss, and wake to the realizing of what he had done.

How could he, with but £70 a year, and a sick mother and almost imbecile father to support, dare to think or speak of love? Was he blind, was he a fool or a villain to win that dear, innocent heart for mere pleasure? It was with a bitter struggle that he left her without a promise of returning, without a hope of even hearing from him. Should he further rob that trusting heart, since he had but now awakened to the theft?

Alice wondered that he spoke so bitterly of the parting, with no word of future meetings or letters. She wondered if he forgot all that in the grief of saying farewell.

Alas! he remembered only too well, if too late; and his silence about the future was more generous than idle promises. The poor child pined and grieved through the sweet summer. By the winter, she had taught herself that he was but a faithless city man who was only amusing himself with her; and gradually her proud young spirit asserted itself, and she learned to despise the young lover who had stolen her heart for mere pastime. Charles at his desk in the dingy rooms of London fared so badly that his loving sister, seeing a great change in him, tried to win back the old cheerfulness, to lure him to see Mrs. Siddons and Sheridan and the Kembles, whose wondrous representations had always delighted him beyond all else. But he was too listless to enjoy the cold comfort of the theater. Even Hyde Park and Piccadilly, with their gay throngs, ceased to interest him. His work at the dreary desk was but a loathsome task that seemed to press the life out of him, with its deadly round of sameness. All was wrong, all was upset and awry, and his very pleasures turned to loathing. The ceaseless cry in his heart was: "Why, why, did I spoil her dear life and mine? Why was I such a blind, blind fool? If she would wait for me these dozen years it would be the same! Oh God! the bitterness of being poor! Others, with no better chances than I, can stretch out their arms to take thy sweetest blessings, and I, because I have so little now, must forego all the best dreams of life!"

The daily, nightly, hourly strain was tasking his sensitive spirit beyond its powers. An attack of fever and delirium left his mind in such a state of turmoil, that they feared he would take his life. Mary, who watched unceasingly at his bedside, now knew the secret of the change of those three months. But as his mind grew no clearer, it became necessary to place him in an hospital, where he could have constant watching and wise medical treatment. She and John found a retreat at Hoxton, and taking him in a cab, they drove to the Insane Asylum, Charles gazing with a stony stare that saw but the desolate delusions of his own brain.

Six weeks of careful treatment and wholesome country air gradually cured the mental disorder and soothed the wounded heart. He returned home in December, 1795, quite restored, and wrote at once to his friend Coleridge at Bristol :

"My life has been somewhat diversified of late. The six weeks that finished last year and begun this, your humble servant spent very agreeably in a mad-house at Hoxton. I am got somewhat rational, now, and don't bite any one, but mad I was. Can your fantastic imagination picture the phantasmagoria of facts, fancies, angels and devils that held possession of my senses,—yes, possession to the exclusion of all else. I felt like the ghost of some one else haunting the shadow of myself—a wild, half-sad, half-merry existence, with fancy and lies running riot, mixing up the real and the imaginary in a wholly bewildering manner. And all because of a clear, fair face, and some foolish, happy days that are gone forever—yes, *forever!* Well! what next ?—Yours,

"Carolus."*

* "Letters of Charles Lamb."—Alfred Ainger.

CHAPTER IX.

DROPPED STITCHES.

It is not now as it hath been of yore ;—
  Turn wheresoe'er I may,
  By night or day,
The things which I have seen I now can see no more !
. . . But yet I know, where'er I go,
That there hath passed away a glory from the earth.

WORDSWORTH.

SOON after Lamb's return to London, Coleridge also came to town for the winter to further his fortunes and Pantisocracy. They resumed their old intimacy, and many were the cosy evenings spent over pipes and egg-hot in a little tavern in Newgate Street, which they had known, in Blue-coat days, as the " Salutation and Cat." It was a quaint little den in a narrow court, entered through an archway on Newgate Street, with narrow stone hallway and slits of windows with diamond panes, and a cheerful back parlor with open fire-place, where the chops could be grilled before their eyes, and their noses regaled with the savory odor. Perhaps Goldsmith and Dr. Johnson had enjoyed this very same little den ; it was within easy reach of the dwellings of both.

Here our friends made the dingy room blue with tobacco smoke as they discussed metaphysics, sociology, and poetry. They never reached the end of their many theories and hobbies, and the talk and jokes rippled on like a merry mountain stream.   Here, too, many congenial spirits were attracted by the brilliant though stammering talk of the young clerk of India House, whose witticisms and logic mingled with the poetry of his more brilliant companion, who was trimming his wings for flight.

This cultured scholar and metaphysician, who was more than a match for Cambridge professors, yet as dreamy as a wild-wood bird warbling its carols, would talk the night away.   Lamb had greatly recovered health and spirits since his friend's return to London, and, with his kindly satire and inimitable puns, was as irrepressible as newly-opened champagne.

At Little Queen Street, Mary was still nursing the sick mother day and night, and helping to eke out Charles's small salary by sewing, until the patient head seemed reeling with its pain and weariness.   It was her delight to have Charles repeat their fun and wisdom, and she joyfully welcomed her old favorite, Coleridge, on his Sunday visits.

Mary and Charles were keenly interested in the Pantisocratic scheme, and were never weary of hearing Coleridge expatiate upon it.   George Dyer, author of " Complaints of the Poor " and other works, was struck with the plan.   He often joined them at the " Salutation and Cat " and discussed it.   Dr. Priestley, the eminent metaphysician and theologian, also thought well of it and promised aid.   A friend of Coleridge, who had been in America, described graphically the wonders and advantages of that splendid republic, picturing the beauties of the Susquehanna and its surroundings. They calculated that a few thousand pounds would buy the hundred acres and the needed outfit, and a dozen men could easily clear and cultivate that in six months. They would have an experienced builder among them, who could run up their buildings between times, and somebody who could tell them just where to locate, and with that soil and sunshine their crops would easily support the community, and their wives could spin the flax and weave their linen. They could write for the magazines and papers of the adjoining cities of New York, Philadelphia, and Baltimore, which were flourishing towns.

Winter, he was obliged to confess, was rather different from an English winter. Snow lay on the ground during several months, and the rivers sometimes became frozen over solid, as in Holland ; and in the spring the ice-cakes often floated together and formed great walls and dams, which sometimes caused floods. But winter, with an abundance of fuel from the great forests everywhere, was a fine time for study and writing and building fences, etc., for the coming season. He was not sure about the maples in this locality ; but in some places one had only to tap the maple trees in winter, and out poured gallons of delicious syrup for making sugar. It was a wonderful country ! In the summer, everywhere along the roadsides, cherry trees bore fruit, and every country path and lane was bordered with raspberry and blackberry bushes laden with most delicious fruit, ready for any passer to enjoy and carry home. It was certainly a land " flowing with milk and honey," and its riches of nature were free to all. He had not found coined gold easy to pick up, but any quantity of the ore could be dug from the ground in certain regions, and silver too. This was faithfully reported to Southey and the rest of the

Brotherhood, and Pantisocracy grew apace. They had found the right spot for such a community in a land that offered them fruit at every turn, without even the need of culture.

But, as the winter advanced, and Coleridge grew more absorbed in his London friends and pursuits, his correspondence with his Bristol friends languished. After awhile, he forgot to write to Southey, and even to his sweetheart, who became alarmed at her absent lover's waning passion.

Towards spring Southey took the Bristol coach for London, a long journey in those days. He hunted up the truant swain, and reproached him for his neglect, but finding him writing constantly for the " Morning Chronicle," furthering their cause, and faithful in heart to Miss Fricker, he devoted his stay in London to making the acquaintance of Charles Lamb and Coleridge's other intimates. Coleridge returned with Southey to Bristol, where the love-making progressed so rapidly, that nothing would do but immediate marriage. He felt the ground beneath his feet firm enough for it, because having in Bristol and the vicinity lectured upon the French Revolution, and upon the Civil War and Charles I. ; also upon " Revealed Religion," and the necessity of having reason and faith go hand in hand, his wonderful eloquence had made him very popular.

Southey and Lovell disapproved of a speedy marriage, knowing that Coleridge was earning but a bare subsistence. But Joseph Cottle, the poetic publisher of Bristol, had great faith in the young poet's rising star, and offered him thirty guineas, in advance, for a volume of poems, and upon this slight basis of ready money Coleridge insisted upon the wedding.

CHAPTER X.

LOVE IN A COTTAGE.

> Low was our pretty Cot, our tallest rose
> Peep'd at the chamber window.   We could hear
> At silent noon and eve, and early morn,
> The sea's faint murmur.   In the open air
> Our myrtles blossom'd ; and across the porch
> Thick jasmines twined : the little landscape round
> Was green and woody, and refresh'd the eye.
> It was a spot which you might aptly call
> The Valley of Seclusion.
>
> COLERIDGE.

ON a golden day of October, 1795, when the heather along the hillsides was lying rosy and purple, and the gorse and broom had attained their full plumage along the woodsides, and the ferns were heavy with their russet seed-scales, the wedding chimes pealed from the ivy-crowned spire of St. Mary's Church, Redcliffe. The small wedding party included, besides the principals, Southey and his *fiancée*, Edith Fricker, acting as bridesmaid and groomsman, and a goodly number of our Pantisocratic friends and Bristol acquaintances.   The bride was in simple dove-colored silk, with the huge sleeves and short waist of the times, and Coleridge in new brown small-clothes, with long coat and high rolling collar and wide neckerchief, and both felt supremely happy.

At Clevedon, near Bristol, they had found a tiny, one-story rose-embowered cottage, with diamond-paned windows and thatched roof.

Here they came after the wedding, and the bride looked with courageous heart upon the bare walls and rather meager furniture, feeling it was indeed love in a cottage, a very tiny one, yet quite large enough for two people who were going to turn farmer and dairy-maid in America. What if the whitewashed walls were bare, her poet's voice would fill the place with music and pictures! What if the tiny kitchen was the only other room, did not the roses peep into the windows and encircle the door like a bridal wreath—these glorious cloth-of-gold roses that pressed their soft cheeks against the ragged stone wall!

The Severn rippled along within sight of the front door, promising fishing and boating for their idle hours, and the oaks and vines almost hid the tiny house, like a nest, with one great old yew stretching long, shadowy arms as if to protect the little bower. So poetry, sweetness, and love folded their wings and brooded in this charming nest. A speedy letter reached Mr. Cottle, praying him to send by return coach: " A candle-box, two glasses for wash-handstand, one dust-pan, one small tin tea-kettle, one pair of candlesticks, a Bible, a keg of porter." * In due time these and other forgotten necessaries arrived, and the little wife was singing like a bird, finding the simple housekeeping more like play than work—save when the chimney smoked and the roof leaked.

Different offers of employment came to Coleridge in the months following. He tried a tutorship at Bristol, but the exceeding stupidity of his pupils drove him to abandon that effort. A Unitarian pulpit was offered him, and he preached for some little time for the

* " Homes and Haunts of British Poets."—WM. HOWITT.

delighted people ; but journalism seemed better suited to his tastes.   He wrote for the "Morning Chronicle" and "The Critical Review."

The question of daily bread was finally solved by starting the project of a weekly journal.   He canvassed the country and the midland counties, finding much to discourage and little to encourage.   But he started "The Watchman," a miscellany of thirty-two pages, containing : 1st, History of the domestic and foreign policy of earlier days.   2nd, Speeches in both Houses of Parliament.   3rd, Original essays and poems.   4th, *Résumé* of interesting and important events.

The new editor found great discouragement, in the stolidity of farmers and the stupidity of manufacturers, who did not appreciate the new project to the extent of 4d. per week.   He was the ablest canvasser who ever spent breath in talking up a paper.   He smoked with farmers until his head reeled ; he argued with "Brummagem" tradesmen until his temper failed ; but with all his eloquence he gained few subscriptions. Many were swayed by his eloquence and promised subscriptions, but failed to pay when the magazine was sent.   He worked early and late, writing most of the articles himself.   Ten numbers only of "The Watchman" were issued, before, between poor sub-scriptions, heavy expenses, paper tax, and cost of printing, the funds were exhausted, and Coleridge, to his bitter disappointment, was forced to abandon the enterprise.   To add to the cloud of darkness that was lowering over him, the Pantisocracy scheme seemed dying out.   For some months Southey had been growing cooler over it, while Lovell and Burnet were also losing interest.   Southey found that newspaper work in England paid better than farming in America. He had a tempting offer from his Uncle Hill to go with him, as secretary, to Spain. The chances for writing from these new vistas of experience and scenery were not to be lost; so he was hastily married to Edith Fricker, and leaving his disconsolate bride at the church door to the care of her brother-in-law, Lovell, he sailed with his uncle. The raising of the necessary £2,000 now seemed an utter impossibility to the impecunious enthusiasts; so, with the opening of new interests to some, the dream slowly faded out, and the dreamers were forced to turn their waking thoughts to the bread-winning struggle which leaves little time for visions.

When Coleridge returned from his canvassing campaign, he found a sobered and depressed little wife awaiting him. He looked anxiously at the clouded brow and veiled eyes.

" Why, my love, where is the sunshine I left in the little nest ? " he asked, taking her in his arms.

" Sunshine, indeed ! " wailed Sarah. " It has rained until the chickens have all been washed into the Severn; and the chimney has smoked until I am like a side of beef——and oh, Esteecee, it was bitterly lonely in all those weeks, with no one to speak to me, or even to bring me a letter. The very postman thinks this place too far to come to."

" And I," said Coleridge, rather grimly—"do you think I have been reveling in fun and fancy? Imagine me haranguing ' Brummagem ' tradesmen by the hour for a few fourpenny subscriptions. Let us change places ; you canvass, and I'll sit by the fire and smoke with the chimney."

"Oh, my love," said Sarah, "I did not mean to greet thee with complaints; but in truth it has been solitary, and then—then—Esteecee," and she hid her face upon his bosom, " I am afraid, I see months before me when I dare not be alone; I must be near women-kind," she said, with quick blushes scorching her face.

And Coleridge guessed the secret of the new loneliness, and agreed that before another winter they must be nearer friends.   He, too, in his writing, felt the need of reaching libraries and publishers.

So the tiny nest was forsaken, with its roses, its jasmines, and its leafy bowers, and they moved to Bristol for the winter.

Mr. Poole, of Nether Stowey, a wealthy manufacturer and a warm friend of Coleridge, persuaded the young couple to take a small cottage near him.

As the rent was but £7 a year, and the cottage a pretty tidy place, they concluded to move there.

"We are settled again," Coleridge wrote to Lamb, "in another little nest with its roses and gardens.   You should see my hands from tilling that garden.   No farmer's lout e'er toiled with more honest sweat than I, in furrowing, sowing, planting that sacred soil. Come to us, friend, and see the bantling and the nest. We long to see thy sunny smile amid our Quantock hills. Sarah sends thee greeting and bids thee come." *

At the little cottage was another inmate.   Charles Lloyd, the son of a banker of Birmingham, having become charmed with Coleridge and his poetry and Pantisocracy, his father persuaded Coleridge to take the young man as a boarder, that he might have the advantage of the poet's conversation, and the benefit of his poetic

* " Life of Coleridge."—HALL CAINE.

tastes and proclivities. As Lloyd was willing to pay well, Sarah rather reluctantly consented to receiving him into the sanctity of her home.

Soon after they were settled, whilst Coleridge was absent from home on a visit, a little son was born. In a tumult of delight, the young poet hastened home to greet his child, commemorating the event by several pretty sonnets.

CHAPTER XI.

A TRAGEDY.

In fancy (well I know)—
From business wandering far and local cares,
Thou creepest round a dear-loved sister's bed,
With noiseless step, and watchest the faint look,
Soothing each pang with fond solicitude
And tenderest tones, medicinal of love.

Coleridge.

But, poor Lamb! a tragedy was to prevent the coveted visit—a shadow, that would forever darken his patient life.

Ever since his return from the asylum, Mary had done her best to brighten him and help him forget his past. She was his constant companion, when she could escape from the fretful mother's sick-room. She plodded on with the sewing, and vainly tried to finish the gowns promised her customers.

But nights of unrest and nursing, after days of sewing and ceaseless headaches, caused such depression, that even the beloved brother could no longer win a smile. Poverty had overtaxed the strength she so needed for nursing the sick mother and attending to the querulous father. Charles saw with alarm the hopeless cloud of melancholy settling upon her cheerful spirit, and several attacks of nervous excitement warned him of the terrible strain.

"She shall have rest and medicine," said Charles;

"her dear life shall not be wrecked by this cursed poverty."

He called to see a skillful apothecary, but he was out, and so the matter rested over night.

The next day, upon his return from India House, he heard shrieks issuing from the upper room, and flying upstairs past the screaming, terrified little maid, he found poor Mary, with eyes gleaming in unconscious mania, rushing at her helpless mother with the carving-knife.

Her father, in trying to wrest the knife from her, was cut, and before Charles could reach her, the knife was plunged into their mother's heart, and the mad woman was flourishing it wildly for fresh victims. She did not know Charles, and they struggled for the knife. He gained it, and she hurled forks and knives at every one in sight, believing she was defending her life from attack. Finally, Charles and some men who had heard the noise, and had come to his aid, over-powered her and bound her arms.

She knew nothing of the poor bleeding body which they carried to the bed, but was taken, raving and singing, to the insane asylum, where a few months before Charles had recovered from his first and last spell of madness.

The shock to poor old Aunt Hetty kept her ill for weeks, and nearly destroyed her kind old wits. Neighbors poured in, and curiosity peered upon the tragedy until Charles claimed protection from the police, and quietly buried the murdered mother, carry-ing the helpless father and aunt to another home in a different part of the city—to Pentonville. Here they lived for a couple of years.

After the awful event, the papers of the day were most considerate and reticent, not making capital out of each harassing detail, as is too much the custom in these later times. The London "Times" merely gave the sad, unvarnished facts of the tragedy.

Names were suppressed, and there was no gloating over scenes and details.

No : the curtain fell upon the personality of this horror. The young clerk's grief was too sacred to be paraded before the public as a bit of entertaining news. The London "Times" only spoke of "the sad death of an elderly woman, by the frenzied hand of an insane daughter, in the neighborhood of Holborn. . . . . The coroner's jury, after sifting all the evidence, found the verdict—*Lunacy.*"

Even after this generous reticence of the press, Lamb's sensitive spirit shrank from the publicity inevitably connected with such an affair. He felt the awful loneliness of soul that such an experience gives.

Charles visited Mary as often as allowed, and gradually saw the wild light softening in the dark eyes, and the sweet, natural tenderness returning. The recovery was slow, but with it came for a time entire oblivion of the awful deed of madness.

After a few months, when reason and calmness had returned, Charles pleaded to have Mary released from surveillance in the asylum, promising to be surety for her during the remainder of their lives. Their brother John, who had assumed neither responsibility nor expense, protested against her release—fearing, perhaps, that some of the care or odium might fall on him. But Charles urged and entreated, promising to take the entire charge upon himself as soon as his father's death would leave him free to care for Mary. He finally gained the magistrate's consent by signing a pledge to watch over his sister while he lived—a terrible responsibility for a man of twenty-one years! No hope of wife or child, no hope of wealth or fame— even in the far future! He was entangled in the meshes of a horrible tragedy, that was like the iron hand of Fate; and he was forever bound to a sister whose future was as uncertain as the wind.

Here were calamities to either craze or sober a man. Poor Charles! whose heart had preyed upon his reason when he had to crush out his love-dream, now arose in new strength. He threw himself upon his knees and prayed long and earnestly for guidance and strength in these terrible days. If his spirit quailed before such an abyss of misery, his very agony of grief led him to the only source of comfort and help.

He remembered the words, "Underneath are the everlasting arms," and he cried out in helpless agony : "Though He slay me, yet will I trust in Him."

And the strength came from that Infinite Mind that alone brings strength out of weakness.

Fancy this genial young fellow of twenty-one years hastening from his desk day by day to the distant rooms, and to the poor, invalid father, who demanded constant amusement with cribbage and cards! Patiently, tenderly, the man who seemed the tool of fate gave his evenings to the imbecile father, who only complained if the tired clerk wanted a little rest before the evening games. "If you cannot play when you come home, why need you come home at all?" he whined. The argument being unanswerable, Charles put aside book or paper with a most reluctant sigh. The elegant John had, long before the tragedy, fled into comfortable bachelor quarters, and now kept aloof more than ever; never offering aid in supporting either father or sister.

Lamb's heart turned for comfort to his friend Coleridge, and his letters at this time were mirrors of the pathos of his lot and the patience of his soul.

Coleridge was sitting before his hearthstone, where the blazing logs cast long rays of light and flickering shadows upon the floor, with the cooing baby on his knee, when Lamb's letter was brought by the carrier.

"My God! Sarah, Sarah, come read this letter," he said, "I think my eyes are playing me false."

With frightened, tearful eyes she read aloud:

"Sept., 1796.

"My dearest Friend,—White, or some of my friends, or the public papers, by this time may have informed you of the terrible calamities that have fallen on our family. . . . My poor, dear, dearest sister, in a fit of insanity, has been the death of her own mother. I was at hand only time enough to snatch the knife out of her grasp. She is at present in a madhouse, from whence I fear she must be moved to an hospital. God has preserved to me my senses. I eat and drink and sleep, and have my judgment, I believe, very sound. My poor father was slightly wounded, and I am left to take care of him and my aunt. . . . Write as religious a letter as possible, but no mention of what is gone and done with. With me, 'the former things are passed away,' and I have something more to do than to feel. God Almighty have us well in His keeping. . . . Mention nothing of poetry; I have destroyed every vestige of past vanities of that kind. . . .

"I charge you don't think of coming to see me. Write. I will not see you if you come. God Almighty love you and all of us.

"C. LAMB." *

Together they wept over the dreadful blow to their friend, and over his sad, brave letter. Coleridge paced the floor and wept, and for hours could not calm himself to write a reply to such sorrow. Finally, feeling he must not delay sending what comfort he could, he wrote :

"DEAREST BROTHER,—

"Your letter struck me with a mighty horror. It rushed upon me and stupefied my feelings. You bid me write a religious letter. I am not a man who would attempt to insult the greatness of your agony by any other consolation. Heaven knows that in the easiest fortune there is much dissatisfaction and weariness of spirit, much that asks for patience and resignation; but in scenes like these, that shake the dwelling and make the heart tremble, there is no middle way between despair and the yielding of the whole spirit to the guidance of faith. And surely it is a matter of joy that your faith in Jesus has been preserved. The Comforter that should relieve you is not far from you. But as you are a Christian, in the name of the Saviour who was filled with bitterness, and made drunken with wormwood, I conjure you to have recourse to frequent prayer to His God and your God—the God of mercies and Father of all comfort. Your poor father is, I hope, almost senseless to the calamity; the unconscious in-

---

* "Letters of Charles Lamb."—AINGER.

strument of Divine Providence knows it not; and your mother is in heaven. It is sweet to be roused from a frightful dream by the song of birds and the bright rays of morning. Ah! how infinitely more sweet to be awakened from the blackness and amazement of sudden horror by the glories of God manifest amid the hallelujahs of angels ! . . . .

" As to yourself, I approve of your abandoning what you justly call 'vanities.' I look upon you as a man called by sorrow and anguish, and a strange desolation of hopes, into quietness, and a soul set apart and made peculiar to God. We cannot arrive at any portion of heavenly bliss, without, in some measure, imitating Christ. And they arrive at the largest inheritance who imitate the most difficult parts of His character, and bowed down, and crushed under foot, cry in fullness of faith : ' Father, Thy will be done.' I wish above measure to have you, for a little while, here. No visitors shall blow on the nakedness of your feelings. You shall be quiet, that your spirit may be healed. I see no possible objection, unless your father's helplessness prevent you, and unless you are necessary to him. If this be not the case, I charge you write me that you will come. I charge you, dearest friend, not to dare encourage gloom or despair. You are a temporary sharer in human miseries, that you may be an eternal partaker of the Divine nature. Come to me.   S. T. C." *

This letter, coming into Charles Lamb's desolation, brought the consolation of friendship. Written by one Unitarian to another, it was yet full of practical

---

* " Life of Coleridge."—HALL CAINE.

Christianity, upon the plane where all who love and serve Jesus Christ can meet.

Charles immediately replied :

"Oct. 3, 1796.

"My dearest Friend,—Your letter was an inestimable treasure to me. It will be a comfort to you, I know, to know that our prospects are somewhat brighter. My poor dear, dearest sister, the unhappy and unconscious instrument of the Almighty's judgments on our house, is restored to her senses—to a dreadful sense and recollection of what has passed—awful to her mind. . . . but tempered with religious resignation and the reasonings of a sound judgment, which in this early stage knows how to distinguish between a deed committed in a transient fit of frenzy, and the terrible guilt of a mother's murder. I have seen her. I found her, this morning, calm and serene—far, very far from an indecent, forgetful serenity. She has a most affectionate and tender concern for what has happened. Indeed, from the beginning—frightful and hopeless as her disorder seemed—I had confidence enough in her strength of mind and religious principle to look forward to a time when *even she* might recover tranquillity. God be praised, Coleridge! wonderful as it is to tell, I have never once been otherwise than collected and calm ; even on the dreadful day, and in the midst of the terrible scene, I preserved a tranquillity which bystanders may have construed into indifference—a tranquillity not of despair. Is it folly or sin in me to say that it was a religious principle that *most* supported me ? . . . . I closed not my eyes in sleep that night ; but lay without terrors and without despair. I have lost no sleep since. I had been long used not to rest in things of sense—had endeavored after a comprehension of mind, unsatisfied with the 'ignorant present time,' and *this* kept me up. I had the whole weight of the family thrown on me; for my brother, little disposed (I speak not without tenderness for him) at any time to take care of old age and infirmities, had now with his bad leg, ['twas broken from a fall] an exemption from such duties, and I was now left alone. . . .

"Our friends have been very good. Sam Le Grice, who was then in town, was with me the first three or four days, and was as a brother to me; gave up every hour of his time to the very hurting of his health and spirits in constant attendance and humoring my poor father; talked with him, read to him, played at cribbage with him (for so short is the old man's recollection, that he was playing at cards as though nothing had happened, while the coroner's inquest was sitting over the way). Samuel wept tenderly when he went away; for his mother wrote him a severe letter on his loitering so long in town, and he was forced to go. . . .

"A gentleman, brother to my godmother (from whom we never had right or reason to expect any such assistance), sent my father £20; and to crown all these —God's blessings to our family—an old lady, a cousin of my father and aunt's, a gentlewoman of fortune, is to take my aunt, and make her comfortable for the short remainder of her days. My aunt . . . . has generously given up the interest of her little money (which was formerly paid my father for her board) wholly and solely to my sister's· use. Reckoning this, we have, Daddy and I, for our two selves, and an old maid-servant to look after him when I am out. . . . £180 a year, out of which we can spare £50 or £60 at least for

Mary, while she stays at Islington, where she must and shall stay during her father's life, for his and her comfort. I know John will make speeches about it; but she shall not go into an hospital. . . . Poor thing, they say she was but the other morning saying she knew she must go to Bethlem for life; that one of her brothers would have it so; but the other would wish it not, but be obliged to go with the stream; that she had often as she passed Bethlem thought it likely, 'here it may be my fate to end my days;' conscious of a certain flightiness in her poor head, oftentimes. . . .

"If my father, an old servant-maid, and I can't live. . . . on £130 or £120 a year, we ought to burn by slow fires.

"The lady at this madhouse assures me that I may dismiss immediately both doctor and apothecary, retaining. . . . a composing draught. Of all the people I ever saw in the world, my poor sister was most and thoroughly devoid of the least tincture of selfishness.

" Yours,

" C. LAMB." *

Thus the patient soul tells his own story of this sad time. Brave, cheerful, and trusting as he was, that wonderful uplifting of spirit under such trials was indeed God's very mercy.

Coleridge wrote often, describing wife, child, and home, and often invited Lamb to visit him. But one can see it was no time for taking even a much-needed holiday.

Coleridge, with his poetic temperament, was always

* Letters of Charles Lamb."—AINGER.

subject to great fluctuations of spirits, and was ever hovering between the depths of despair and the heights of ecstasy. With more of seeming happiness in his lot than Lamb, he was less cheerful; he was cursed with the restless longings of poet and thinker, and harassed for means to supply his family's needs. In writing to Lamb, he poured out much of his discouragement and restlessness.

After receiving several depressing letters, Lamb wrote:

"DEAR COLERIDGE,—I feel myself much better for that spirit of confidence and friendship which dictated your last letter. May your soul find peace at last in your cottage-life! I only wish you were but settled. I read your letters with my sister, and they gave us both abundance of delight. Especially they please us when you talk in a religious strain; not but we are occasionally offended with a certain freedom of expression, a certain air of mysticism, more consonant with the conceits of pagan philosophy than with the humility of genuine piety. . . . In your last letter you say: ' It is by the press that God hath given spirits, both evil and good (I suppose you mean *simply* bad men and good men), a portion, as it were, of His Omnipresence.' Now, high as the human intellect, comparatively, will soar; and wide as its influence, malign or salutary, can extend, is there not, Coleridge, a distance between the Divine Mind and it which makes such language blasphemy? . . . . God, in the New Testament (our best guide), is represented to us in the kind, condescending, amiable, familiar light of a *parent;* and in my poor mind, 'tis best for us to consider Him as our *Heavenly*

Father, and our *best Friend*, without indulging too bold conceptions of His nature.

"C. LAMB." *

* "Letters of Charles Lamb."—AINGER.

CHAPTER XII.

NEW SCENES AND FRIENDS.

And now, beloved Stowey! I behold
Thy church tower, and, methinks, the four huge elms,
Clustering, which mark the mansion of my friend;
And close behind them, hidden from my view,
Is my own lowly cottage, where my babe
And my babe's mother dwell in peace! With light
And quickened footsteps thitherward I tend,
Remembering thee, O green and silent dell!
And grateful, that by Nature's quietness
And solitary musings, all my heart
Is softened, and made worthy to indulge
Love, and the thoughts that yearn for humankind.

COLERIDGE.

WHILE Lamb was patiently plodding on day by day at India House, and spending his evenings playing cribbage with his helpless father at Pentonville, Coleridge's life was widening into new interests and pleasures.

Coleridge had sheltered himself in the little dell among the woods where Stowey lies, like a well-filled partridge's nest, at the foot of Quantock hills. The hills rise in rose and purple splendor above the great elms and the dark yews of the vale, and brood protectingly over the little hamlet with its gray-stone cottages facing the tiny, purling stream. Quite near Coleridge's little cottage was the large, old-fashioned, stone mansion of his friend Thomas Poole. The pleasant gardens, filled with old-fashioned larkspurs, pinks, and nasturtium, lit the front with friendly cheerfulness, while, behind, the stable-yard sloped to the fine green meadows. Soon after he had settled here, Wordsworth came to visit him, and being also charmed with the beauty of the heather-covered Quantock hills, decided to settle at Alfoxden—which was a bower of beauty—upon the slope and near his new friend Coleridge. Amid these hills and vales the brother poets strolled from morning until night.

The bond of genius is often stronger than the ties of blood. And as the electric spark of genius finds its poles in hearts and leaps out in sudden flashes of joy at the touch of a comprehending spirit, they looked into each other's souls and knew they were akin.

Wordsworth's early poems had met with so little recognition, that Coleridge's delight in them touched his heart. The "Monthly Review" of 1793 had sneered at "the eternal changes rung upon upland, lowland, budding forests, and snowy clouds."

"Are we forever to be inundated with floods of maudlin trash called poetry of Nature?" the sneering critics had asked.

But the young Wordsworth had gone on writing his lays in his own style. He had been chary of printing, and would have been crippled in means had not his friend Calvert left him a legacy of £900, upon which he and his sister Dorothy contrived to live.

Coleridge's little volume, published by Joseph Cottle, had attracted some attention, and rather more favorable criticism than Wordsworth's.

Again and again have the critics threshed down the grain striving to ripen, and needing but the sun of human favor, only to turn at last with the popular voice and help gather in the harvest. Milton, Burns, Goldsmith, Wordsworth, Coleridge, Keats, Lanier, suffered poverty and scorn. Their poems, that did not win their bread, have since become household words. After their death they are. gods, and their monuments are placed in the world's fane, Westminster Abbey, whilst a tithe of the sum so expended and the fame so granted would have warmed their cold firesides, and filled their tables with bread and their hearts with thankfulness and hope.

Are we so blind that we cannot see genius until a half-century has gathered evidence that this man is a poet? Or is it because men fear to trust their own ideas of the true and beautiful, that they must first criticise and anatomize before they dare admit talent? Is it not so with the other arts of painting and music? Beethoven's name was almost forgotten during his later years, and Mozart but gained success by dying ere his manhood ripened. Why did Millet and Delacroix and the other artists of that school struggle through their lives with poverty to rise, too late, to pinnacles of fame?

Is any fate so sad as fame, love, appreciation, which have come too late? Too late! when the ears that longed for praise, even for toleration, are cold in death; when sympathy and admiration only awake to strew flowers on a tomb! Talent struggles out because you fear to stretch your hands in welcome; yet you help and encourage the very bubbles that float on the surface of stagnant pools—the novels of flimsy sentiment and false life. Let me plead with critics for a little more patience and hopefulness towards beginners, and with readers for a little more confidence. The help thus given would be worth an occasional mistake. Make way for all that is brave and pure and true in art and life, in heart and soul; and thus help " Ring out the false, ring in the true." So shall God's Truth come uppermost in the long roll of the centuries that shall carry down the false and elevate the true.

Back to our poets, whose fortunes have elicited this monologue, and tempted this lifting of the veil.

Coleridge and Wordsworth grew into such close sympathy whilst browsing in each other's fields that each needed the other's encouragement to spur him on. Wordsworth delighted in the brilliant flow of humor, as well as the deep thought and erudition of Coleridge. Like Coleridge and Southey, Wordsworth had sought truth in philosophy and metaphysics, being wearied of the narrow limits of the Church, which seemed to place form above principle. After shaking off college fetters, he had wandered amid the wild glens of Wales with his sister. They had later sought the beauties of the Continent, and were caught while in France in the meshes of the " Reign of Terror." He, too, had imbibed the spirit of " Liberty " from those whose later acts so belied her name.

But the thieving, selfish spirit of faction riding down faction, and their horrid thirst for blood, disgusted him; and, like Beethoven and others, who had adored the bravery of the young Napoleon, he learned to loathe the tyrant who seized a throne under cover of the name of Protector and Consul.

In Bristol, Coleridge and Wordsworth, Southey and

Poole, had debated such questions.   And now upon the breezy Quantock hills, and along the shady sequestered vales, they continued their long arguments, quoted their poetry, and discussed the sphere and scope of the muse.

Wordsworth's home at Alfoxden was one of the loveliest nooks in England, surrounded by noble trees, with the blue hills rising, range on range, around, and the green meadows winding down to the blue waters of Bristol Channel, scarcely a mile away.   The loftiest hollies of England fringe these Quantock hills, amid their environment of splendid oaks.   It was a most appropriate setting for the poetic jewels of thought and inspiration.

Wordsworth and Coleridge roamed the hills and haunted the dells and woodlands along the trickling streams, until the simple rustics grew afraid of the solemn townsmen who went peering into rocks and streams, arguing, talking, quoting, declaiming.   To the astonished innocents who followed them at a safe distance, and shook their heads at the droning monologues of the tall man with the green glasses, they seemed bewitched.   The observers "knowed no good would come of they 'uns as allus had their 'eds in clouds." "They made signs with they arms, and talked treason," said others.   And at the village pot-house, the rustics whispered over the strange wanderings of the mysterious roamers who seemed "allus a-lookin' and a-lookin' for sommat."

"Depend upon it they're spies of they French cutthroats.   I heerd them talking of Bonypart and Robyspear," said Hodge.

A county magnate, hearing the talk of the rustics and his lackeys, actually notified some London officials of the dangerous characters loitering in the neighborhood. A spy was sent to watch the suspected men, who were entirely unconscious of criticism or danger, and dogged them until, finally, Coleridge, noticing a suspicious looking person following their daily rambles, agreed with Wordsworth to lead the man a dance.

To the top of Eagle's Crag and down the roughest glens they clambered, the weary spy clumsily following. Back and forth wandered the poets, declaiming in mock heroics, and surreptitiously watching their man until he gave up the chase and reported that "those fellows were only innocents talking poetry. Their 'Spy Nosey,' which Hodge heard so much about, was only one of the book people they was discussin'."

The baronet was still unconvinced, but after some further watching, the innkeeper also testified that "they fellows was naught but poets a-writing up the Quantock hills." *

How Wordsworth and Coleridge roared with delight over the joke, when they finally discovered that they were "suspects;" and with what fiery and frantic declamations they astonished any natives they chanced to meet on hill or glen !

After that episode they delighted in appearing as eccentric as possible. Small wonder that the lank, dark man with green glasses, and the wild-eyed, shambling fellow beside him, with shaggy black mane and endless torrent of words, were an incomprehensible pair. It was rather hard on pretty bright Dorothy and the more demure Sarah to be considered the improper allies of these dangerous creatures. They did not enjoy the joke quite as much as their lords.

* "Biographia Literaria."

Of Wordsworth, Coleridge wrote to Lamb : " The giant Wordsworth—God love him ! When I speak in the terms of admiration due to his intellect, I fear lest these terms should keep out of sight the amiableness of his manners. He has written near 1,200 lines of blank verse, superior, I hesitate not to aver, to anything in our language which any way resembles it. As to Dorothy, she is a woman indeed in mind and heart. Her person, is such, that if you expected to see an ordinary woman you would think her pretty." * " She has brilliant, dark eyes flashing with quick intelligence and sudden tenderness ; glossy, dark, waving hair, and an everchanging color flitting on her nut-brown face," he wrote later.

Cottle, Poole, and the Wedgwoods often joined the poets at home and in their expeditions. Dorothy was continually with them, but Coleridge's wife was often kept at home by her child and home duties. She used to look wistfully after the merry party as they started for a day's frolic, with lunch baskets and ale bottles. She bravely fought down the envious demon that came whispering : " Why cannot you share your husband's pleasures and holidays as well as Dorothy ? " But as their expeditions sometimes lasted several days, and became more frequent, the imp's suggestions gathered weight and persistence.

" Not again to-day ? " she said, after Coleridge had been spending a week with the Wordsworths. " Not to-day, Esteecee ; you have scarcely been with your wife this fortnight." And the tears, so often repressed, rolled down the flushed face that looked so pleadingly into his.

Coleridge frowned. " Would you keep me tied here

* " Life of Coleridge."—HALL CAINE.

when Wordsworth and I are planning such beautiful verses? You know I must have inspiration, and I am working for you and the little birdie, my love."

" But it is every day and always, whilst I must sit at home and mend the socks and tend the fire," she sobbed.

" My dearest, come with us; we men who live by our wits must keep up the fuel for our fires, and fires must burn or there will be nothing to put in the pot. Come with us, and you and Dorothy can bring your sewing for a quiet chat whilst we are climbing."

" Little Hartley is not well enough for me to leave, you know, Esteecee; and Dorothy has pleasanter company than mine in those rambles," she said, with a suspicious ring in her voice, and a flush over neck and brow. There! the secret was out! Coleridge looked angrily at the clouded brow, and within him also rose a demon in resentment. But he checked it, and taking his wife into his arms, settled into the warm chimney corner for a long cosy chat such as they both loved. Sunshine soon returned, and they were gabbling merrily, when Lloyd came in from his little study, beyond, and joined them. Sarah sighed as she sank into the cushioned chair by Esteecee, and took up her sewing. It seemed hard that in these days of ceaseless rambles, visitors, and intimates, they could rarely have an evening to themselves as in the little nest at Clevedon. Lloyd was always here, and Mr. Poole, or Mr. Cottle, or the Wedgwoods, or Southey, who had now returned from Spain, and was settled at Bristol. So poor Sarah again saw Coleridge prepare for his day's wanderings. She hid her face in little Hartley's soft curls, and ere long the baby caresses had soothed away the disappointed tears that came so readily in these days.

Far up the purple slope, above the hollies and the oaks of the glens, the poets again met to continue their discussion upon the requisite qualities of true poetry.

"Poetry must, of course, have imagination," said Wordsworth; "fine fancies emanate from such scenes as these. But more necessary still is the soul's utterance, suggested by the glories of God's beautiful creation, and whispered into the listening ear."

"Whispered by what? I do not quite understand your drift," said Coleridge.

"I only use the word 'whispered' for want of a better term for the still, small voice within. In all beautiful scenes; in the heart of Nature, amid her mighty forests or her tiny trickling streams, there is a voice, whether without or within, I know not. Listen for it in all sweet solitudes, and the attentive soul will always hear God's message of love and wisdom."

"But this is very Quakerism, the key-note of George Fox's teachings," said Coleridge.

"Call it Quakerism or inspiration, or the Divine Spirit, I know not, nor do I care, since I can hear and follow that inner voice," said Wordsworth, pacing rapidly along.

"I entirely agree with you as to the imagination and the inspiration, which are the true soul of poetry. But to my mind they are the workings of the poet's own thought and fancy, from within, not from without," answered Coleridge. "I build my poems from my own fancies, the response of my brain to the external world."

"Perhaps we mean the same thing," said Wordsworth, with one of his grave smiles. "I write from the inner consciousness of God's meaning in His creations, and you from their suggestions to your brain. I believe in following Nature closely, and in depicting rustic scenes and the simplicity of rustic life, as far as possible using their own language and expressions."

"But *you* interpret their passions and feelings from your own experience and imagination," argued Coleridge.

"Yes; as I read them through their acts and lives. Their loves and hates and sufferings must have their own proper setting and language, which my inner voice must discover."

"Well," said Coleridge, laughing, "we may differ slightly as to our method of writing; but we certainly have the same faith in Nature and her inspirations."

About this time, Wordsworth wrote the poems giving the key-note of his poetic faith :

> " The eye it cannot choose but see ;
>   We cannot bid the ear be still ;
>   Our bodies feel, where'er they be,
>   Against or with our will.
>
> " Nor less I deem that there are Powers
>   Which of themselves our minds impress ;
>   That we can feed this mind of ours,
>   In a wise passiveness.
>
> " Think you, 'mid all this mighty sum
>   Of things forever speaking,
>   That nothing of itself will come,
>   But we must still be seeking !"

And in another poem, he says :

> " Come forth into the light of things,
>   Let Nature be your teacher.

> She has a world of ready wealth
>   Our minds and hearts to bless—
> Spontaneous wisdom breathed by health,
>   Truth breathed by cheerfulness. . . .
> Enough of Science and of Art;
>   Close up those barren leaves !
> Come forth, and bring with you a heart
>   That watches and receives."

It was during these days of constant intercourse and inspiring rambles that Wordsworth wrote the " Lyrical Ballads," and Coleridge wrote his " Religious Musings " and his most beautiful poem, " The Ancient Mariner." The weird fancy of the mysterious wedding guest took hold of his imagination until he has given us a real ghost. But the exquisite expressions and thoughts here seem as familiar as David's Psalms, and almost as dear.

> " An orphan's curse would drag to hell
>   A spirit from on high,
> But oh ! more horrible than that
>   Is the curse in a dead man's eye,"—

is a picture to remember for life, and the lovely benediction is a watchword to our hearts:

> " He prayeth best who loveth best
>   All things, both great and small;
> For the dear God, who loveth us,
>   He made and loveth all."

CHAPTER XIII.

The world is too much with us; late and soon,
Getting and spending, we lay waste our powers.
Little we see in Nature that is ours,
We have given our hearts away—a sordid boon.
The sea that bares its bosom to the moon,
The winds that will be howling at all hours,
And are upgathered now, like sleeping flowers. . . .
For this, for everything, we are out of tune. . . .

WORDSWORTH.

This City now doth, like a garment, wear
The beauty of the morning; silent, bare,
Ships, towers, domes, theaters, and temples lie
Open unto the fields, and to the sky . . . .
Ne'er saw I, never felt, a calm so deep!
The river glideth at his own sweet will.

WORDSWORTH.

WHILST the new friends were gaining help and inspiration from one another, the old friend was still plodding at India House, spending his leisure time with his poor father, and in constant visits to the sister who was also patiently enduring her incarceration in the asylum.

Lamb's letters to Coleridge through all this dreary time breathe almost a spirit of exultation, in the beautiful patience and resignation they show. To a sensitive soul relying on God's grace, such states of mind often accompany a great sorrow. The sense of the

Divine presence and help, as Lamb said, "gives a feeling of brotherhood to the man of sorrows." He could hear without envy of the new friendship, and Coleridge's letters came like a sweet breath of the free country to the smoky, dusty London.

He rejoiced in his friend's poetry, wept over the "Ancient Mariner," and treasured the "Religious Musings" next to his Bible. He was the admirer, critic, and "public opinion" of everything Coleridge wrote; and many suggestions of his improved and polished those poems before they were crystallized into print for the world.

Coleridge, in publishing his new poems, kindly offered to include those of Lamb and Lloyd. He wrote to Lamb: "Give me, my friend, those poems you saved from your holocaust and what you have since written, and let them have a being and a place among my brain children. They are at least first cousins, and it would prevent loneliness to send them into the world together."

Lamb was pleased at the tribute to his unpretending work. The sonnets and poems were added to Coleridge's with a dedication to his dearly-loved sister, as she must henceforth share in any good thing that should befall him. The dedication reads: "The few following poems, creations of the Fancy and Feeling, in life's most vacant hours, produced for the most part by love in idleness, are with a brother's tenderness inscribed to Mary Anne Lamb, the Author's best friend and sister." *

He wrote to Coleridge: "With this pomp and paraphernalia of parting, I take my leave of a passion

* "Letters of Charles Lamb."—AINGER.

which has reigned so long within me. Thus with its trappings of laureateship I fling it off, pleased and satisfied with myself that the weakness troubles me no longer. . . . I am wedded, Coleridge, to the fortunes of my sister and my poor old father. Oh, my friend, I think sometimes, could I recall the days of the past, which among them would I choose ? Not the 'pleasant days of hope,' not those ' wanderings with a fair-haired maid,' which I have so often and so feelingly regretted, but the days, Coleridge, of a *mother's fondness* for her *schoolboy*. What would I not give to call her back to earth for *one day*—on my knees to ask her pardon for all of those little asperities of temper which, from time to time, have given her gentle spirit pain. And the day, I trust, will come. There will be time enough 'for kind offices of love,' if ' Heaven's eternal years ' be ours. . . .

" Ah, my friend, cultivate the filial feelings ! And let no man think himself released from the kind charities of relationship; these shall give him peace at last. These are the best foundation of every species of benevolence. . . . Send me an account of your health; indeed I am solicitous about you.

" God love you and yours,

" C. LAMB." *

"Sacrifice your little ' Epitaph on an Infant,' or sell it to a country statuary. Commence in this manner: 'Death's prime poet-laureate,' and let your verses be adopted in every village round instead of those hitherto famous ones :

" ' Affliction sore long time I bore ;
Physicians were in vain '. . . .

" With regard to my lines, ' Laugh all that weep,' I

* " Letters of Charles Lamb."—TALFOURD.

would willingly sacrifice them; but my portion of the volume is so ridiculously little, that, in honest truth, I can't spare 'em. . . . Ah, Coleridge, think when we writ them,—'twas two Christmases ago, and in that nice little smoky room at the Salutation, which is even now continually presenting itself to my recollection, with all its associated train of pipes, tobacco, egg-hot, welsh-rabbits, metaphysics, and poetry!   Are we *never* to meet again? How differently I am circumstanced now! I have never met with any one, never shall meet with any one, who could or can compensate me for the loss of your society. . . . I lack friends, I lack books to supply their absence; but these complaints ill become me. My sister is quite well now, but must not, I fear, come to live with us yet a good while. . . . One man has pressed it on to me that she should be in perpetual confinement. What has she done to deserve this?

" I am *starving* at the India House, near seven o'clock, without my dinner, and so it has been, and will be all the week.   I get home at night o'erwearied, quite faint, and then to cards with my father, who will not let me enjoy a meal in peace; but must conform to my situation, and I hope I am, for the most part, not unthankful."

" I got home at last, and after repeated games at cribbage, have got my father's leave to write awhile; with difficulty got it, for when I espostulated about playing any more, he very aptly replied : ' If you won't play with me you might as well not come home at all.' The argument was unanswerable, so I set to work again. . . .

" . . . . When I read the ' Religious Musings,' I think how poor, how unelevated, unoriginal my blank verse is. . . . and I ask what business they have with yours; but friendship covereth a multitude of defects."

" I have been reading ' The Task,' with fresh delight. I am glad you love Cowper. I could forgive a man for not enjoying Milton, but I would not call that man my friend who should be offended with the 'divine chit-chat of Cowper.'

" I have almost lost thy letters, Coleridge; I have given them to a friend out of the house to keep safe from my brother John's sight, in case he comes to hold inquisition over our papers; for much as he dwelt upon your conversation whilst you were among us, he has not ceased to depreciate you, and cry you down. You were the cause of my madness, you and your damned, foolish sensibility, and melancholy, and lamented we had ever met; e'en like that father who, when his son went astray upon the Mount of Parnassus, is said to have cursed ' wit, poetry, and Pope.' " *

Again he writes: "Ah, Coleridge! I would rather hear you sing ' Did a very little Baby,' by your family fireside, than hear you repeat one of Bowles's sweetest sonnets in your sweet manner, whilst we two were indulging sympathy by the fireside of the ' Salutation '. . . . Not a soul loves Bowles here; scarce one has heard of Burns; few but laugh at me for reading my Testament. They talk a language I know not. I conceal sentiments that would be a puzzle to them. I can only converse with you by letter and with the dead by their books. My sister is indeed all I can wish, in a companion. But our spirits are alike poorly; our reading and knowledge from the

* " Letters of Charles Lamb."—TALFOURD.

self-same source, our communication with the scenes of the world alike narrow. . . . Love to Mrs. Coleridge and little Hartley, and remembrance to Lloyd, if he is still with you."

At another time he wrote: "Coleridge, where am I to look for friends? I know not one Christian, not one but undervalues Christianity. What am I to do? Wesley (have you read his life? was *he* not an elevated character?)—Wesley has said: 'Religion is not a solitary thing.' Alas! it necessarily is so with me, or next to solitary. 'Tis true you write to me; but correspondence by letter and personal intimacy are so widely different! Do write to me and do some good to my mind, already too much warped and relaxed by the world. Good-night. God have us all in His holy keeping.—C. L." *

Coleridge had written to Lamb of his discussions of Hartley and Berkeley with his new friends, and Lamb replied:

"Are you yet a Berkeleyan? Make me one. I rejoice in being speculatively a Necessarian. Would to God I were habitually a practical one! Are you finishing your 'Evidences of Natural and Revealed Religion?' Or are you doing anything towards it? Make to yourself other ten talents. . . . Woe is me that I am constrained to dwell with Mesheck, and to have my habitation among the tents of Kedar. I know I am no better than my neighbors; but I have a taste for Religion, an occasional earnest aspiration after perfection, which they have not. I gain nothing in being with such as myself; we encourage one another in mediocrity. I am always longing to be with men more

* "Letters of Charles Lamb."—AINGER.

excellent than myself. . . . I have been reading Priestley on 'Philosophic Necessity,' in the thought that I enjoy a kind of communion (a kind of friendship even) with the great and good. Books are to me instead of friends; I wish they did not resemble the latter in scarceness." *

One can fancy the cravings of the young scholar amid the commonplace herd of fellow-clerks, who knew and cared for little besides ledgers and task work, and the easiest way to shirk all other responsibilities. I hope my readers will pardon me for introducing so many of Lamb's letters; but how better could I give a true insight into heart and character and surroundings, than by this outpouring of his spirit to his bosom friend? Happy is the man who has one true heart into which he can unreservedly pour his pent-up cares and thoughts! It is a wondrous safeguard against the bitterness, perhaps the unbelief, that follow silent, secret grief.

As Coleridge read his friend's tender and touching letters to his wife, she, too, learned to love the gentle clerk who was chained to his desk and his family troubles. She constantly added postscripts to Coleridge's replies, and her invitations to his for the long-desired visit. In September, 1797, Lamb made one more effort for a holiday, and gained it.

* "Letters of Charles Lamb."—AINGER.

CHAPTER XIV.

FRIENDS IN COUNCIL.

Well hast thou said and holily dispraised
These shapings of the unregenerate mind—
Bubbles that glitter as they rise and break
On vain philosophy's aye-babbling spring.
For never guiltless may I speak of Him—
The Incomprehensible! save when with awe
I praise Him, and with faith that inly feels,
Who with His saving mercies healed me,
A sinful and most miserable man ;
'Wildered and dark, and gave me to possess
Peace, and this cot, and thee, heart-honored maid.

COLERIDGE.

ONE day in September, a slight, thin-legged little
man in black small-clothes and leggings, with huge
green overcoat nearly to his heels, mounted the Bristol
coach at the "White Swan Inn." He took an outside
seat near the driver, and from the innumerable questions and stammering jokes and puns, as the coach
spun down the Strand and rattled through the streets
to the broad highway, one could recognize Charles
Lamb. Away they sped over the shady roads, rattling
through the towns of Berkshire and over the meadows
of Wiltshire to Bath, leaving the well-stuffed mail-bags
at the inns by the roadside, amid the din of clattering
hoof and the strident horns, and the joking and swear-
ing and drinking of guards, lackeys, drivers, and the

ever-thirsty passengers, who must stretch their legs, and have a pot of beer or ale at each stop. Dinners at the quaint stone inns with their huge fire-places and savory roasts on the spit; and a night's lodging at another town seven hours further on, where the lights of the inn stream out over the reeking horses and bustling servitors.

The meadows swell to hillocks as they spin through Gloucester the next day; and beyond lie the long blue lines of the Quantock hills in the far distance, and then comes Bridgewater, where Coleridge meets him with that greeting so sweet to loving hearts after long parting. How pleasant for each to look into the other's eyes and read the tenderness that men's tongues are too stiff to utter to another man!

As they walked to Stowey, along the pleasant country road, Lamb looked with delight at the scenes so new to his cockney eyes. " Ah, Esteecee, how quaint are these st-st-st-stone cottages lying along the way, with their b-b-brown wigs shading their eyes! How b-beautiful th-those ranges of hills with this sunset t-turning them to mountains of limpid g-g-gold."

And the friends basked in the golden light and quiet beauty as they walked arm-in-arm along the shady lanes between the hawthorn hedges. Where the cottages clustered along a shady road, with a tiny stream flowing along the center, Coleridge pointed beyond to one peeping from its overshadowing trees, as from it toddled a wee chubby baby to welcome " daddy " home. Sarah came out with warmest greetings to the long-expected friend.

When Mr. Poole came, during the evening, Lamb was in his richest vein of fun and humor; and with

Lloyd the friends found topics to interest them until midnight.

For days and weeks Joseph Cottle and Poole came almost daily to enjoy the bright-eyed cockney who was so keenly alive to the charms of their pretty country.

"Nay, t-talk not of your hills and dales," Lamb would say, with his inimitable stutter; "g-give me this for a holiday, b-but for a c-constancy the streets of London, with their smoking lamps, the shops, the t-tempting bookstalls, and b-bustling coaches are best of all for me.   M-m-man made the town; but G-G-God found it g-g-good."

The serious, sedate Wordsworth was longer in becoming acquainted with the voluble stammerer.   He looked askance at the ceaseless flow of puns and witticisms; and Lamb, feeling the magnetic current checked, said, after their first evening together: "C-C-Coleridge, your g-g-giant is on too high a pedestal for such p-pygmies as I.   He does not know my g-g-genus. He thinks my W-Words-worth n-n-nothing."   But in the recitations and poets' talk of later days the "giant" found a reverent listener, and they became warm friends ere the visit drew to a close.

Dorothy Wordsworth, who had often heard from Sarah Coleridge the story of Lamb's devotion to his sister, took him into her heart at once; and many long talks they had of Mary's condition and Charles's hopes and plans for the future.

"She is so serene and calm," he said, "you would w-wonder at the strong spirit that without the least f-forgetfulness has so accepted the m-m-miserable accident, as being an unconscious instrument in God's hands. She has had but one r-r-return of the terrible mania since that d-day, and then she lived over in frightful v-v-v-vivid-ness those awful scenes," he said, shuddering and covering his face with his hands. "She is now in p-pleasant quarters with a family who k-keep careful watch over her symptoms; and she is very s-sunny and happy keeping her little establishment in order. Sh-she is her own cook, and every Sunday she has a fine pudding for me after our walks in the fields."

"How lonely you must be without her at home," sighed the sympathetic Dorothy; "you two seem as congenial as brother and I."

"Your unanimity of thought and p-purpose constantly r-r-remind me of my home life with Mary," said Charles, with one of his beaming smiles. "God grant I may have the comfort of her d-d-dear presence soon; but I feel it would as yet be bad for my f-father; he needs m-much attention, and his irritability might unnerve her, and her p-presence might arouse d-d-dead memories with him."

As they rambled amid woodlands and hills these talks drew the friends in closer sympathy, and all Coleridge's friends learned to love Charles Lamb as he deserved.

They must show him the beauties of the Quantock hills, and Wordsworth was the pilot. Coleridge, having sprained his ankle the day after Lamb's arrival, was unable to accompany them in the first rambles.

During their absence Coleridge wrote a poem to his friend Lamb, called "My Lime Tree Bower," in which he bemoans his imprisonment and absence from their tramps.

> "My gentle-hearted Charles! for thou hast pined
> And hungered after nature many a year

> In the great city pent, winning thy way
> With sad, yet patient zeal, through evil and pain
> And strange calamity! Ah! slowly sink
> Behind the western ridge, thou glorious sun!
> Shine in the slant beams of the sinking orb,
> Ye purple heath flowers! richlier burn, ye clouds!
> And kindle, thou blue ocean!   So my friend,
> Struck with deep joy, may stand, as I have stood,
> Silent with swimming sense. . . . gazing till all doth seem
> Less gross than bodily; and of such hues
> As veil the Almighty Spirit, when yet He makes
> Spirits perceive His presence."

Southey, too, came from Bristol to renew his friendship with Lamb, but Lamb noticed a slight restraint between Coleridge and his old friend. They seemed less intimate and less congenial than of old. Southey's year in Spain had made a break in old ties, and the friends were growing apart in thought and spirit. Southey now disapproved of vain theorizing, and the mischief from setting up opinions against the established order of things. He was also disgusted with French politics and with Bonaparte, whose ambition had overbalanced his patriotism. He was becoming a stanch Churchman, and a royalist, since freedom seemed but an excuse for violence and crime. Coleridge, on the other hand, was still studying philosophy and metaphysics, while settling into Unitarianism, the Divine Spirit within having conquered many of the old doubts and atheistic unbeliefs.

He and Lamb had long discussions about the Arians and Socinians, about Necessity and Free-will, as in their earlier days. They fully agreed that Unitarianism is not a belief, 'tis a *way* of thinking. "I believe in nature, and in human nature as parts of God's creation. Righteousness, not dogma, is true religion, and Jesus' life is our example, and His death the crowning act of that life," said Coleridge. " I have come to this resting-place after my wanderings among the Sophists."

" You have c-come, dear Esteecee, to where I have always stood, although I c-c-could not formulate the b-belief so well as you. Christianity is Divine power in our l-lives and souls, and over all is G-God, and the inspired t-teacher, Jesus Christ," said Lamb reverently.

" But you both want to go a step further to find the real truth of the Bible," said Southey. " I wandered through the mazes of doubt and questioning as you did, Coleridge ; I sought to reason out a God ; but I have found it vain, hopeless, to step from the finite to the Infinite. The only step or bridge is faith—the voice within—proclaiming a Creator. And the same inner voice whispers faith in His revealed Word—the Bible ; and the Bible says : 'God so loved the world that He gave His only begotten Son, that whosoever believeth in Him should not perish.' If I believe part of that Word, I must believe all. I find that ' Christ died for the ungodly,' and ' Being justified by His blood, we shall be saved from wrath, through Him.' "

" You scorned this once," said Coleridge.

" Yes, Esteecee, I set my obstinate will against Church and State, and vainly tried to find a better religion than the doctrines and the interpretations of Mother Church ; but I have humbly acknowledged my errors, and, like the prodigal, I have gladly returned to my father's house. The Schools are utterly impractical and a useless maze of reasoning in a circle that is but knocking the head against a stone to gain a cracked skull."

"Ah, Southey! that is the secret of your sudden return to wisdom and the Church; 'tis worldly wisdom, I fear; you have thrown away all your Ideals, for what? To gain favor and place?" asked Coleridge.

"No; I have curbed a turbulent spirit, and harnessed it for life's duties," replied Southey, with a hot flush called up by Coleridge's insinuations. "I have mouths to feed, Samuel Coleridge; I dare not waste my time in vain speculation, or in pursuing an *ignis fatuus* into every ditch that lies before me; and the satisfaction of the good old beliefs makes the surrender a delight."

"You are a brave, honest man, Southey, and I beg to shake hands with you," said Wordsworth.

"And I also," added Lamb.

"And I," said Coleridge; whereupon the friends grasped hands like the knights of old when starting on some sacred quest.

"He who first does his duty as a man will find his faith rising, like the guiding star over Bethlehem, to lead him to the truth in God and Christ," said Wordsworth.

"Does he not evolve his faith from his needs?" asked Coleridge.

"Nay, the spirit from within speaks; God's Spirit guides each listening soul to His truth, and we listen best when sorrow or fear turns our gaze from outside to within," anwered Wordsworth.

"Ah, f-friends, if I could but have this blessed intercourse in my stupid London life, where no one thinks or c-cares for aught but the petty cares or empty fashion of the day!" sighed Charles Lamb. "A l-little friendly human conversation is better than f-folios of wisdom," he stammered, looking lovingly at Coleridge. "I shall soon go b-back to my desk among the Ishmaelites; God g-grant you may drift d-d-down our way, some of you poets. We need ideality, in London, to l-leaven the old city."

"Who could write a sonnet in that smoke-blackened spot ?—my wits grow beggared there," said Wordsworth.

"Nay, there is much to f-feed a p-poet's thought," said Lamb, always quick to defend his beloved London. "Did not Addison and Pope and M-Milton live in London. We have an excellent p-poetaster there now, Samuel Rogers, who wrote th-those beautiful descriptions of Continental Scenes and the 'Pleasures of Memory.'"

"Bah ! delicate cameos for my lady's boudoir !" cried Wordsworth.

"No; finely polished g-gems, but the real t-thing," stammered Lamb; "and there is a new star rising, an Edinburgh scholar who is becoming vastly p-popular in London, one Campbell, who writes for some of the R-R-Reviews."

"I have not heard of him," said Wordsworth; "but city poems seem to me too much like highly-wrought jeweler's work: they pale before God's sun and His great hills and shining lakes."

"City life may cramp a writer's fancy; but I think a poet's mind and heart are so filled with the scenes of his dreams—his visions—that he might write well even in a dungeon," continued Southey.

"Such poems would surely take a melancholy tone ; they would lack the freedom and freshness of nature," said Wordsworth.

"B-b-birds sing well in cages, and m-m-many a prisoned spirit beguiles its m-melancholy with lightest fancies, to forget its en-environments," answered Lamb.

The point was carried ; for who wrote happier fancies than this same prisoner of fate, whose life, ambitions, and hopes were fettered by chains of adamant ?

" Here we are, a party of friends much given to scribbling," laughed Southey. " We are all beginners together ; who knows but some of us shall write our names beside those very bards you mentioned ? "

" Methinks our pens must be tipped with gold to win a smile from Dame Fortune," sighed Coleridge. " Not one of us could earn the money by our poems to pay our funeral expenses."

" Whoever deserves Dame Fortune's f-favor shall conquer the f-fickle coquette at last. Your ' Ancient Mariner ' has b-beauties that will live th-through the centuries. I am p-prophet enough to read that in your f-future, Esteecee."

" I wish the heartless hussy would pay in advance," said Coleridge, " 'tis most discouraging to wait upon her pleasure."

" And yet, 'tis what we all must do," said Wordsworth gravely. The friends started for a long ramble among the Quantock hills to shake off the cobwebs they had conjured up.

A few days later, the Stowey party started for a picnic at Alfoxden. Joseph Cottle brought a wagon from Bristol to carry some of the party over ; others preferred to walk. They prepared a great picnic-basket, with lettuces, bread, cheese, and a bottle of prime cognac ; and many jokes were cracked about the expected feast. Coleridge's gray eyes were blazing with fun and frolic, and Lamb was a very imp of mischief. Dorothy Wordsworth had been visiting the Coleridges, and was brilliant and saucy, as usual.

The women chatted gayly and were happy, and the projected picnic dinner, to be spread under a shady oak, was a fruitful topic. They found a mossy couch in a sheltered nook where cresses grew in the brook, and, after depositing the precious basket, the men proceeded to unhitch the horse, and wait comfortably for those who were walking.

But the question arose: How should they get the horse's collar off? Each philosopher in turn tried to pull off that collar. The horse's head had certainly swelled since it was adjusted, for no head could get through that narrow opening. Wordsworth pulled and tugged, but the head was wider than the collar. Coleridge, who had groomed and saddled many a horse whilst in his country's service, said : "Let me try." But "the stubborn collar had shrunk, that was obvious; and the beast was hydrocephalous." Several rustics were attracted by the struggles, and a small group was forming around the patient beast, who must have longed to speak.

"Hi!" one wise native finally said, "hi! muster, lemme turn it roond and it wull coom roight."

With a good laugh over their helplessness, agreeing not to divulge their joke upon themselves, they turned their attention to the lunch basket, but behold! some of their audience had stolen their cold beef and cheese, and nothing remained but the loaf and lettuces!

"At least we shall have something to drown our sorrow in," said Coleridge, diving after the brandy bottle.

Alas! it slipped through his hands and, falling upon a stone, baptized mother earth with the precious contents.

"Alas! alas!" said Coleridge, looking at their rueful faces, "what a waste!"

"It shall be our li-li-libation to propitiate the m-muses," laughed Lamb.

" See how a planet shines when the moon is eclipsed," said Dorothy, holding up a bottle of ale she had provided for Sarah and herself. " You men would not have looked at this in the presence of the cognac, but now it seems a treasure."

So the feast of bread and lettuces, with foaming ale, and sparkling water from the brook, was as merry as a Lord Mayor's dinner. Joseph Cottle* often told the story of this day as did the others ; for it seemed too good to keep to themselves.

Thus, with pleasant rambles and picnics, with friendly chat and pipes, the days sped by, and Lamb was forced to say farewell. He sighed to leave the pleasant home and the " young philosopher, Hartley." The little one had been an endless delight to the young fellow who, as yet, had seen nothing of babyhood.

Before leaving, he said, with his stuttering earnestness : " Coleridge, sh—shake off your melancholy spells, they are but constitutional. With a wise, tender w-wife and sweet toddling baby, what more could a mortal ask of the g-gods ? If the purse be slender your wants are few; do not l-l-let this d-discontent ruin your happiness and your wife's." And the friends wrung hands and parted ; Lamb to go back to the smoky little room at Pentonville and the dreary desk at India House. He comforted himself with long walks along his beloved streets, browsing upon the musty treasures on the book-stalls, and carrying home some of the coveted volumes, as yellow and spotted as his favorite cheeses.

---

* " Life of Coleridge and Southey."—COTTLE.

CHAPTER XV.

> For, not a hidden path that to the shades
> Of the beloved Parnassian forest leads
> Lurked undiscovered by him ; not a rill
> There issues from the fount of Hippocrene,
> But he had traced it upward to its source. . . .
> Piercing the long-neglected holy cave,
> The haunt obscure of old philosophy. . . .
> O studious poet, eloquent for truth !
> Philosopher, contemning wealth and death !
>
> COLERIDGE.

DESPITE all Coleridge's articles for the London papers and reviews, and the poems he was continually writing and sending to any paper that would accept them, he was scarcely able to provide the necessaries of life for his little family. He was invited by a congregation at Shrewsbury to preach for them. His ability and deep scholarship were well known, and such requests were not infrequent. William Hazlitt, rising at daylight and walking ten miles to hear him, thus describes the young enthusiast of twenty-five, who, "in his ordinary blue coat and breeches, with no ceremony of vestments," stood up to preach :

" Mr. Coleridge gave out the text : ' He departed again into a mountain, *Himself alone.*' As he gave out this text his voice rose like a stream of rich distilled perfumes ; and when he came to the last two words, which he pronounced loud, deep, and distinct, it seemed to me, who was then young, as if the sounds had echoed from the bottom of the human heart, and as if that prayer might have floated in solemn silence through the universe. The idea of St. John came into my mind, of one crying in the wilderness, who had his loins girt about, and whose food was locusts and wild honey.

" The preacher then launched into his subject, like an eagle dallying with the wind. The sermon was upon peace and war—upon Church and State—not their alliance, but their separation—on the spirit of the world and of Christianity, not the same, but as opposed to one another. He spoke of those who had inscribed the Cross of Christ on banners dripping with human gore. He made a poetical and pastoral excursion ; and to show the fatal effects of wars, drew a striking contrast between the simple shepherd-boy driving his team afield, or sitting under the hawthorn, piping to his flock, ' as though he should never be old,' and the same poor country lad crimped, kidnapped, brought into town, made drunk at an ale-house, turned into a wretched drummer-boy, with his hair sticking on end with powder and pomatum, a long cue at his back, and tricked out in the loathsome finery of the profession of blood.

" Such were the notes our much-loved poet sung, and for myself I could not have been more delighted if I had heard the music of the spheres. Poetry and Philosophy had met together ; Truth and Genius had embraced under the eye and with the sanction of Religion. This was beyond my hopes." *

* " Spirit of the Age."—WM. HAZLITT.

He was indeed a poet-preacher, and was much inclined to accept the Unitarian pulpit as his mission.

Coleridge was restless, dissatisfied, and often deeply melancholy. Sarah saw this with grieving bitterness of spirit; and she could not always hide her disappointment. The shadow of lost illusions is often harder to bear than graver trials. So the dissatisfied wife fretted the moody husband, and the few tears or reproaches that *would* run over from the surcharged heart angered the sensitive Coleridge, already discouraged by his literary failures. The meager purse made all harder to bear, and there soon came another little mouth to feed. Coleridge often fled from the gloom at home to Wordsworth's quiet dwelling. The poet, and Dorothy with her bright sallies and warm friendship, soothed the ruffled philosopher, who needed constant sunshine to keep his plumage smooth. This intimacy was not at all pleasing to Sarah, who felt bewildered. She, the wife, could not give her poet the counsel and sympathy he needed; and she, left alone during their long absences of days and weeks, was pining for appreciation and sympathy, herself. Wordsworth's year at Alfoxden was drawing to a close, and the owners refused a longer lease to a tenant who was so suspected and feared in the neighborhood. There must be something wrong where there was so much talk, and they could not afford to bring odium upon the place. So, in disgust, Wordsworth was obliged to give up the beautiful little home among the Quantock hills, and he and Dorothy decided to take a trip to Germany.

Thomas and Josiah Wedgwood, the great potters, hearing of this, and knowing Coleridge's thirst for German poetry and philosophy, now made him a generous offer. Seeing that he was in danger of sacrificing his noble gifts, they offered him a pension of £150 yearly, and offered to pay his expenses to Germany for the opportunity of studying the subjects lying so near his heart.

Coleridge gratefully accepted their kind gift, and decided to profit by the promised trip. He settled the pension upon Sarah, and felt she could be comfortable during his absence. Poor Sarah was slowly learning the sad lesson of withdrawing her heart from her husband's companionship.

Sarah's grief was almost inconsolable when she found that her innocent rival in her husband's affection was to be of the party. Her sister, Edith Southey, and also Southey himself, reproached Coleridge for his wandering instincts.

But he would not heed. The schools of Germany were beckoning, and he resolved to take the good the gods had provided for him.

Before Coleridge sailed for Germany, he and Lamb had the only misunderstanding of their lives. "Coleridge had, in a spirit of mischief, written a satire upon the poets of the new volume of Lyrics and Sonnets —Coleridge, Lloyd, and Lamb." * Lamb, greatly piqued, replied most bitterly, and for once in his patient life wrote the sharp things that came uppermost.

Lamb had himself written jestingly of the absurdity of three young men composing sonnets and verses to their grandmothers. As he was ever quick to catch at an absurdity, such " venerable love-making " struck his

* " Life of Coleridge."—HALL CAINE.

sense of the ludicrous. But Coleridge's ridicule stung like a whip, and from this interchange of sarcasms sprang the only coolness of their friendship.

Coleridge left England without a farewell. Before he left he sent a half satiric message to Lamb : " Tell Lamb to apply to me for knowledge ; I am going to the fountain-head."

Coleridge and the Wordsworths sailed for Hamburg, and had a rough voyage. His letters home (afterwards published in his " Biographia Literaria,") were a charming mixture of wit and observation, from a poet's standpoint. He described his fellow-passengers with vivid power : *

The " frog-colored appearance " of those who remained on deck amid the miseries of the " exportations from the cabin " was most graphically described. " I was well enough to join the able-bodied passengers, one of whom observed, not inaptly, that Momus might have discovered an easier way to see a man's inside than by placing a window in his breast. He needed only to have taken a salt-water trip in a packet-boat." He says : " Your companions are of greater importance to you than in a stage-coach, from the uncertainty of how long you may be obliged to house with them."

He had studied the different passengers, and was interested especially in two Danish brothers who talked English with marvelous fluency and ludicrous incorrectness. " The Danes christened me ' Doctor Teology,' and dressed as I was, all in black, with black worsted stockings, I might have passed for a Methodist missionary." His dialogue with the Danes is a

* Satyrane's Letters : " Biographia Literaria."

rich picture of pedagogue and pride, with most absurd misapplication of terms.   .

His description of a comical matrimonial squabble between another couple, and several other character sketches, prove that he would have been an admirable humorist, had he not been a poet and a philosopher. In Germany he found Blankaness "a most interesting village, scattered amid straggling trees over three hills, in three divisions. . . Each of these three hills stares upon the river with faces of bare sand, with which the boats with their bare poles, standing in files along the banks, made a sort of fantastic harmony. Between each façade lies a green and woody dell, each deeper than the other. It is a village with a labyrinth of paths, or rather a *neighborhood* of houses." *

Writing of his experiences and impressions of the Continent, he said: "Pipes and boots are the first universal characteristic. The character of gentleman is frequent in England, rare in France, and found, when it *is* found, in age, or the latest period of manhood; while in Germany, the character is almost unknown. But the proper antipode of a *gentleman* is to be sought for among the Anglo-American democrats.

"I walked on, feeling like a liberated bird that had been hatched in an aviary, who now, after his first soar of freedom, poises himself in the upper air. Very naturally I began to wonder at all things—Dutch women, with large umbrella-hats, shooting out half a yard before them, with a prodigal plumpness of petticoat behind—the women of Hamburg with caps plaited on the caul, with silver or gold or both, bordered around with stiffened lace which stood out before their eyes,

* Satyrane's Letters: " Biographia Literaria."

so that their eyes sparkled through it—the Hanoverian women with the fore part of the head bare, then a stiff lace, standing up like a wall, perpendicular, on the cap, and behind *tailed* with an enormous quantity of ribbon which lies or tosses on the back. . . . The ladies all in English dresses, all rouged, and all with bad teeth, which you notice from their contrast to the *almost-animal*, too glossy, mother-of-pearl whiteness of the laughing, loud-talking country women and servant girls, who, with their clean white stockings, and with slippers without heel-quarters, tripped along the dirty streets, as if they were secured by a charm from the dirt." *

" The street narrows ; to my English nose sufficiently offensive, and explaining, at first sight, the universal use of boots, without any appropriate path for the foot-passengers. . . . The gable ends of the houses all towards the street, some in the ordinary triangular form and *entire*, as the botanists say ; but the greater number notched and scalloped with more than Chinese grotesqueness. Above all I was struck with the profusion of windows, so large and so many that the houses look all glass. Mr. Pitt's window tax, with its pretty little *additionals* sprouting out from it like young toadlets on the back of a Surinam toad, would certainly improve the appearance of the Hamburg houses. The water intersects the city everywhere—it might have been a rival of Venice. . . . . . *

" I passed through streets and streets, as happy as a child : amused by the signboards of the shops, on which all articles sold within are painted, and that, too, very exactly, though in grotesque confusion (a useful sub-

* Satyrane's Letters : " Biographia Litteraria."

stitute for language in this great mart of nations) amused with the incessant tinkling of the shop and house door bells, the bell hanging over each door and struck with a small iron rod at every entrance and exit;—and finally amused by looking in at the windows as I passed along; the ladies and gentlemen drinking coffee or playing cards, the gentlemen all smoking. The long pipe of one gentleman rested on the table, its bowl half a yard from his mouth, fuming like a censer by the fish-pool,—the other man who was dealing the cards, and of course had both hands employed, held his pipe in his teeth, which, hanging down between his knees, smoked beside his ankles. Hogarth himself never drew a more ludicrous distortion both of attitude and physiognomy. Nor was there wanting beside it one of those beautiful female faces which the same Hogarth (in whom the satirist never extinguished that love of beauty which belonged to him as a poet) so often and so gladly introduces, as the central figure in a crowd of human deformities; which figure (such is true genius) neither acts nor is meant to act as a contrast; but diffuses through all, and over each of the group, a spirit of reconciliation and human kindness, which blends its tenderness with our laughter, and thus prevents the instinctive merriment at the whims of nature in the foibles or humors of our fellow-men from degenerating into the heart-poison of contempt or hatred." *

Thus in his letters Coleridge poured out the voluble eloquence that made his conversation so charming. His keen observation of everything new, strange, or beautiful constantly suggested interesting trains of

* "Biographia Literaria."

thought ; such as the views of Hogarth and art in this last letter.

He further wrote : * " Our *hotel* has one great advantage for a stranger, by being near the market-place, and the next neighbor of the huge church of St. Nicholas, a church with shops and houses built up against it, out of which *wens* and *warts* its high massy steeple rises, *necklaced* near the top with a round of large gilt balls. A better pole-star could scarcely be desired. Long shall I retain the impression made on my mind by the awful echo, so loud and long and tremulous, of the deep-toned clock within this church, which awoke me at two in the morning from a distressful dream occasioned, I believe, by the feather-bed which is here used instead of bed-clothes. I will rather carry my blanket about with me, like a wild Indian, than submit to this abominable custom."

Meeting in Germany many French refugees and emigrants who had fled from the French Revolution, he had become so disgusted with their " profligacy, treachery, and hardheartedness," and their "corrupt principles which so many have carried into the families of their protectors," that his change of feeling became complete. He wrote : * " My heart dilated with honest pride as I recalled to mind the stern yet amiable characters of the English patriots who sought refuge on the Continent at the Restoration ! O, let not our civil war under the first Charles be paralleled with the French Revolution ! In the former, the chalice overflowed from excess of principle ; in the latter, from the fermentation of the *dregs !* The former was a civil war between

---

* Satyrane's Letters : " Biographia Literaria."

the virtues and virtuous prejudices of the two parties ; the latter, between the vices."

At Hamburg, Coleridge met the poet Klopstock, and discussed poetry and the drama with him, comparing Kotzebue, Molière, and Shakespeare, and upholding English poetry and Milton. He says : * " Klopstock appeared to know very little of Milton, or indeed of our poets in general. . . . He told us his first ode was fifty years older than his last. I looked at him with much emotion—I considered him the venerable father of German poetry ; as a good man, as a Christian ; seventy-four years old ; with legs enormously swollen ; yet active, lively, cheerful, kind, and communicative. Klopstock wore a toupée periwig, powdered and frizzled. By the by, old men ought never to wear powder—the contrast between a large, snow-white wig and the color of an old man's skin is disgusting, and wrinkles in such a neighborhood appear only channels for dirt. It is an honor to poets and great men that you think of them as parts of nature, and anything of trick and fashion wounds you in them as much as when you see venerable yews clipped into miserable peacocks. The author of ' The Messiah ' should have worn his own gray hair—his powder and periwig were, to the eye, what *Mr.* Virgil would be to the ear. Klopstock was nearly thirty years composing ' The Messiah,' but of these thirty years not more than two were employed in the composition. He only composed in favorable moments. He called Rousseau's ' Ode to Fortune ' a moral dissertation in stanzas. . . I spoke of Dryden's St. Cecilia ; but he did not seem familiar with our writers. . . . He had not heard of Cowper. . . . He said Lessing was the first of

* Satyrane's Letters: "Biographia Literaria."

their dramatic writers. . . . He spoke favorably of Goethe, but said his ' Sorrows of Werter ' was his best work, better than any of his dramas. Schiller's ' Robbers ' he found so extravagant that he could not read it. . . . He said Schiller could not live. . . . Bürger he said, was a true poet and would live ; that Schiller, on the contrary, must soon be forgotten ; that he gave himself up to the imitation of Shakespeare, who often was extravagant, but that Schiller was ten thousand times more so. . . . He asked whether it was not allowed that Pope had written rhymed poetry with more skill than any of our writers. I said I preferred Dryden, because his couplets had greater variety in their movement. . . . He found the works of Kant utterly incomprehensible—that he had often been pestered by the Kanteans ; but was rarely in the practice of arguing with them. His custom was to produce the book, open it and point to a passage, and beg they would explain it. This they ordinarily attempted to do by substituting their own ideas. . . . Until the appearance of Kant about fifteen years ago, Germany had not been pestered by any sect of philosophers whatsoever."

After these long talks with Klopstock, Coleridge went to Ratzeburg with a letter of introduction from Klopstock to the Antmann of Ratzeburg, who introduced him to the pastor with whom he boarded during his stay there. He says : "On the road to Ratzeburg the inns and farm-houses at which we stopped . . . were all alike, except in size : one great room like a barn, with a hayloft over it, the straw and hay dangling in tufts through the boards which formed the ceiling of the room and the floor of the loft. From this room, which is paved like a street, sometimes two smaller rooms are enclosed at one end.   These are commonly floored. In the large room the cattle, pigs, poultry, men, women and children live in amicable community ; yet there was an appearance of cleanliness and rustic comfort. . . . The stalls were on each side, eight feet in depth. The faces of the cows, etc., were turned toward the room." *

After lingering awhile at Ratzeburg and visiting other interesting points, the Wordsworths traveled further, whilst Coleridge settled at Göttingen to study philosophy and metaphysics and natural history at headquarters. After five months of eager study and novel German experience in the quaint University town, Coleridge undertook a pedestrian tour through the Hartz Mountains with a party of college friends. He was his old buoyant self again, drifting along in the sunshine from one splendid pine-clad height to another; reveling in the glorious scenery and quaint old buildings of the ancient German towns.

His poet's eye sought the picturesque in the old five-storied roofs, with the stork's nest on the apex, and the long-legged birds soaring aloft, or feeding their young from the rim of their nests.

* " Biographia Literaria."

CHAPTER XVI.

> Ye ice falls! ye that from the mountain's brow
> Adown enormous ravines slope amain—
> Torrents, methinks, that heard a mighty voice
> And stopped at once, amid their maddest plunge!
> Motionless torrents! silent cataracts!
> Who made you glorious as the gates of heaven,
> Beneath the keen full moon?   Who bade the sun
> Clothe you with rainbows?   Who, with living flowers
> Of loveliest blue, spread garlands at your feet?
> God! let the torrents, like a shout of nations,
> Answer! And let the ice-plains echo, God!
>
> COLERIDGE.

IN all these months Coleridge had not sent one line to his life-long friend Lamb. To Coleridge's last message to him, "Tell Lamb to apply to me for knowledge," Lamb, piqued at the insinuations, had replied with his usual ready wit, sending Coleridge the following:

"DEAR COLERIDGE,—The 'frog' has not yet jumped into the last ditch, but he is contemplating such a leap. Will you gratify his last request and present these Theses to the University for solution, dilution, and circumlocution, with proper doses prescribed;

"I. Whether God loves a lying angel better than a true man?

"II. Whether the archangel Ariel *could* knowingly affirm an untruth, and whether if he *could* he *would?*

"III. Whether honesty be an angelic virtue, or not rather belonging to that class of qualities which the schoolmen term ' virtues *minus splendidæ et hominis et terræ nimis participes?* '

"IV. Whether the seraphim archangels do not manifest their goodness by way of vision and theory ; and whether *practice* be not a sub-celestial and merely human virtue?

"V. Whether the higher order of *seraphim illuminati* ever *sneer*.

"VI. Whether pure intelligences can *love*, or whether they can love anything but pure intellect?

"VII. Whether the beatific vision be anything more or less than a perpetual representation to each individual angel of his own present attainments and future capabilities, something in the manner of metal looking-glasses ?

"VIII. Whether an 'immortal and amenable soul' may not come to be *damned at last*, and the *man never suspect* it beforehand ? "*

Coleridge laughed on receiving this message with a sting in its tail, and showed it to some of his colleagues with whom he was forming intimacies.   But he deigned no reply.   With his studies and his tobacco fumes, his new scenes and new friends, he was drifting away from the old alliance of a lifetime.   Even wife and children seemed far-away visions amid the new experiences.

The young English poet was a lion and a hero, and his learned and brilliant conversation attracted notice

* " Letters of Charles Lamb."—AINGER.

and admiration wherever he went. The pines and great mountains towering to heaven inspired him with awe; the spirit of poesy had hold of him. He and his companions would climb to some mountain eyrie perched upon a crag amid the clouds, and in a stable, or upon the kitchen floor, Coleridge would sleep, and forget life and its tangles and uncertainties. The German frau or maid found his gentle manners and broken speech irresistible, and the freshest *pumpernickel* and richest *schwadermachen* were placed before him. He blinked at the strength of the *schweitzer-Käse* and the fumes of the *sauer-kraut*, and ate them with what relish he could, the long mountain tramps and the bracing, pine-scented air giving him the best relish for any meal—a good appetite. He climbed the Brocken's crests, and the witching fragrance of the pines cast its spell upon him. His poetic senses were inspired by the wild beauty, and the Specter of the Brocken took him by the hand and led him to the pinnacle where all the world lay beneath, softened by cloud shadows; and dreaming of home amid these noble scenes, he wrote:

> " I moved on
> In low and languid mood; for I had found
> That outward forms, the loftiest, still receive
> Their finer influence from the Life within:
> Fair ciphers else; fair, but of import vague. . . . .
> My native land!
> Filled with the thought of thee this heart was proud,
> Yea, mine eye swam with tears; that all the view
> From sovereign Brocken, woods and woody hills,
> Floated away, like a departing dream,
> Feeble and dim. . . . . .
> Who can feel
> That God is everywhere! the God who framed
> Mankind to be one mighty family,
> Himself our Father, and the world our home."

He tramped through the dense wildernesses of the Black Forest, amid those mighty pines that ever sigh and sigh for the dead centuries. He followed the winding roads cut by men up giddy heights and down the great gorges where leap in endless frolic the swift mountain torrents, and the plunging Rhine, freed from Lake Constance and the Rhine Falls, to sail majestically past the Lorelei and its thousand sister mountains, past castled crags and towered cities and smiling vineyards, to the low sands of Holland, with its vigilant windmills and myriad canals, down to the sea.

Coleridge did not follow it in all its windings to the North Sea. But to him, as to all thoughtful travelers before and since, the storied Rhine, that has been the main artery of the German Fatherland for centuries, was full of charm and mystery. And in those days, when France and Austria and Prussia and Belgium were wrangling over its borders and constantly changing the ownership of its boundaries, it was of vital interest to the young enthusiast. For the river plunges through the Via Mala, and glides through smiling Lake Constance, and rushes past the castles and fortresses of Alsace-Lorraine, as happily when the French hold Coblentz, as when the Fatherland grasps all. Men and nations change; but the Rhine goes on forever.

CHAPTER XVII.

> Alas! they had been friends in youth,
> But whispering tongues can poison truth,
> And constancy lives in realms above;
> And life is thorny, and youth is vain,
> And to be wroth with one we love
> Doth work like madness in the brain.
>
> COLERIDGE—*Christabel.*

COLERIDGE's charming letters greatly comforted his wife in the far-away English village; but she had many anxious hours thinking of her wandering poet. She kept up a brisk correspondence with Lamb, after his visit to them, and Lamb's pleasantries and bright jokes coming like sunbeams into her lonely home, with Coleridge's brilliant letters from Germany, swept away the melancholy that her loneliness engendered.

Lamb often wrote to Southey, in Coleridge's absence, taking this mutual friend to fill the woful gap in his life which Coleridge's estrangement caused. He took Southey roundly to task for writing a criticism of "The Ancient Mariner" in the "Critical Review." * "I am sorry you are so sparing of your praises to the 'Ancient Mariner.' So far from calling it, as you do, with some wit, but more severity, a Dutch attempt, I call it a right English attempt, and a successful one, to dethrone German sublimity. You have selected

* "Letters of Charles Lamb."— TALFOURD.

a passage fertile in unmeaning miracles, but have passed fifty passages as miraculous as the miracle they depict. I never so deeply felt the pathetic as in that part :

> "'A spring of love gushed from my heart,
>   And I blessed them unaware.'

" It stung me into high pleasure through suffering; and this :

> "'So lonely 'twas, that God Himself
>   Scarce seemed there to be.'

" But you allow some elaborate beauties ; you should have extracted them."

It was brave of Lamb, and so like his true heart, to vindicate his estranged and absent friend. He always was thus loyal, and this fealty made him so beloved by all his friends. Southey richly deserved the reproach ; he was an old friend, and a brother-in-law, and took the relative's privilege of unsparing criticism. And 'tis just here that Southey's traits grow unlovely. He criticised without tenderness, and he always placed candor above generosity. The hardness of intolerance and bigotry was growing around the once open, impulsive nature. It was the root of bitterness which spread as life's trials increased. Southey was over conscientious about fulfilling certain duties. He hampered himself with Lovell's widow, and others who were not properly cared for by their natural protectors, but his generosity was ever tinged by a certain bitterness towards those who shirked duty.

It was at this time that Charles Lamb's father died, and was buried beside his wife in St. Andrew's Church, Holborn, a place which has since been swept away by the march of improvements. It was a pretty little church where the New River purled along by the graveyard, and not far distant from Lamb's old quarters, Christ's Hospital, and his old home in the Temple.

At last Mary could return home! She had waited very patiently for the coveted release from her lonely isolation, and her return to her beloved brother, whose frequent visits, during the Sundays spent with her at Islington, only made her long more keenly to be with him, as of old. And now that their father was laid in the grave, Charles was alone, save the old servant, Hetty.

It was two years since the brother and sister had lived together, but the long gap of suffering and distress was bridged over, and the cosy tea-table, the book and sewing during the evenings, gave Lamb the most exquisite pleasure.

" 'Tis worth the p-pain of separation, Mary, to have thee in the old ingle nook l-like the genius of h-h-home," he stammered, looking with his sweet smile into Mary's placid face. " I fear this s-s-smoking has grown upon me in the lonely evenings, and in the e-e-effort to keep awake for poor Daddy's interminable c-c-c-cards."

" I will help you do without this poisoned pleasure, dear. Read Coleridge's poems to me, and then you will not care to smoke to-night."

Charles laughed at her promptness in assuming the generalship, and doing battle against his enemy—tobacco.

"Well, it is like having one's wife and f-f-family back," he sighed, in the comfort of the cosy fireside.

After a few days of the pleasant home-life, Mary saw that another habit had taken hold of her beloved brother; he was too fond of his "night-cap," as he called his glass of whisky and hot water.

"We must banish another enemy, eh! Charles?" she asked, placing her hands tenderly upon his shoulders. "Shall we not let the old tankard of ale come back, instead of the hot whisky?"

"Ah, B-B-Bridget, but you are hard on a s-s-sinner; I have given you my s-s-sword, and will you take my staff too? But you are right, those confounded p-p-pipes and cups are my worst enemies, and we w-w-will defeat them—some day," he added, looking anxiously at the corner cupboard—" but to-night——"

"No, Charles, to-night is better than to-morrow, and I have sent Hetty for fresh ale."

"W-w-well, tyrants must have their way," he stammered, ruefully.

"Have you had no letter from Coleridge, brother?"

"Now, Mary, you want to drive me straight to the arms of my enemy for c-c-comfort! He has not written to me for a y-year, and they say he will soon be h-home."

"This estrangement must have been doubly bitter to you in this year of loneliness, dear, and I am glad he is coming home; he cannot see you without going back to the old pleasant relations with his chum."

"I hope so, Mary, I h-h-hope so," said Charles earnestly. "I think the death of dear little B-Berkeley will soften his heart to old friends who love him and his little ones."

After a few months of serene domestic happiness, Charles noticed the fatal symptoms returning. A certain nervous irritability was hovering around his placid sister, and a sudden stupor showed him that Mary was threatened with one of her spells of insanity. He seized the boiling tea-kettle and held it close to her spotless cap to arouse her. The poor girl realized what was threatening her, and quietly submitted to the strait-jacket. With bitter tears the unhappy brother and sister walked to Hoxton, and there poor Mary remained for six weeks, wildly singing, reciting, or imagining herself now a leader in the French Revolution, and now a court dame.

Meantime Charles returned home more desolate than ever, after the winter's pleasant companionship with one who understood and sympathized with every phase of his high spirits or his dullness, and only required of him what he was ready to give.

"Few wives could do this," thought Charles. "Wives are always peering into their husband's affairs, and expecting a man's moods to suit their own."

He sighed deeply, and closing the now deserted room, sought the "Salutation and Cat," where he and Coleridge had spent so many happy evenings a few years before. He smoked and drank among the convivial spirits gathered there, and went stupidly home, forgetting to take off his gaiters and shoes on going to bed.

When he awoke late the next morning, with a headache, and the evidences of last night's potations, he was disgusted with himself and all the world.

"This won't do," he grumbled; "I wonder if old Mac won't give me a week's leave to run up and see Lloyd."

In a few days, he was on the coach for Cambridge, where Lloyd had settled after his marriage.

Lamb, always fond of classic scenes and time-honored buildings, gazed with delight upon the exquisite old towers and pinnacles of the colleges, and feasted his soul upon the hoary, ivy-covered walls and arches and oriels. " The lime avenues of Oxford are finer, and the forest of sp-spires and t-t-towers there outvie the beauties of C-C-Cambridge," he said, whilst studying the place ; "but either is g-good enough for an Englishman's p-paradise."

Here Lloyd introduced him to Manning, a professor of mathematics at Trinity, and the two at once became warm friends, finding innumerable points of sympathy. Manning was as great a wag as Lamb, with an inimitable faculty of facial expression, and whilst Lloyd would, as Lamb expressed it, " run the gamut through all the keys of idiotism, until he felt like one possessed, Manning could out-gamut Lloyd, in all the keys, from the smile to the glimmer of half sense and quarter sense, and on to the grin and hanging lip of imbecility." *

After Lamb's return to London he wrote : " I do long to see your honest Manning face again." Manning promised to visit him, and Lamb eagerly looked forward to his congenial companionship.

* " Letters of Charles Lamb."—TALFOURD.

CHAPTER XVIII.

"HEADS OR TAILS?"

O meek retiring spirit !   We will climb,
Cheering and cheered, this lovely hill sublime;
And from the stirring world uplifted high
(Whose noises faintly wafted in the wind
To quiet musings shall attune the mind) . . . .
We'll smile at wealth and learn to smile at fame,
Our hopes, our knowledge, and our joys the same."
COLERIDGE.

MEANTIME Coleridge had reached England in July
and hastened to Stowey, where Sarah was once more
happy in having her husband with her.   How foreign
he seemed with his German pipe, and the broad laugh,
instead of the gentle smile of old !   It was so sweet to
have him again after all those weary months, that she
started in terror when he spoke of London and work,
and the lines gathered around the tired mouth at the
thought that his return was but temporary.   She tried
all the little wifely tricks and endearments that bind
a man's heart to home.   Little Hartley was an endless
delight to him, and was so proud of "the great papa."
Coleridge felt a new tenderness for the mother who
was shorn of her little nursling, the baby Berkeley.
But he must find immediate work, and the wanderer
felt the restless cravings for change creeping upon him.
His wife's sadness, when he showed signs of restless-

ness, oppressed the sensitive man, and in September he again left home to join the Wordsworths in a trip to Westmoreland, where Wordsworth was thinking of settling. They visited the beautiful Lake Windermere that winds down the long valley at the foot of Orrest Head, and the long line of beautifully wooded low mountains that form the lake's environment. They came to quaint Ambleside, with its low stone cottages in their pretty flower gardens, with the nasturtiums trailing like red and yellow flames over the old stone walls. They stopped at one of the quaint stone inns, and visited the old mills at the foot of the cascades that plunge into the wooded valley from the mountain top. They followed the fine old coaching road, on past Rydal Mount, where Rydal Water reflects the beautiful villas, and Leigh Hall, with Nab-Scar rising like a sentinel guarding the jewels, on to Grasmere. There, between Nab-Scar and Scawfell, nestle the pretty stone cottages with climbing roses peeking into the diamond-paned windows and fringing the roofs. The arched stone bridge over the rippling Rothay lay close to the little stone church with its tiny graveyard back, bordered by the murmuring stream, that forever and forever sings its requiem over the quiet dead in this peaceful spot. Wordsworth found a tiny cottage at Grasmere, where he and his sister settled, and Coleridge went to London. He found work at the office of " The Morning Post," and for months his articles were the most popular matter in that paper. He took lodgings upon Buckingham Street, just off the Strand. The street is a short one, running but from the Strand to the Thames, and from his garret windows he could see the sails passing up and down the river;

and here the air seemed purer and lighter than in the more densely packed streets.

Lamb, hearing where his old friend was staying, pocketed his pride, and hastened to welcome Coleridge back to England. When he was announced, Coleridge hesitated a moment, remembering those Theses; but the moment he saw the well-known little figure in the black small-clothes and gaiters, with the angelic smile on lips and eyes, he held out his arms, and the old friends were reunited after the only estrangement in nearly twenty years of friendship. They talked the night away. Lamb told Coleridge of Mary's return home, and of her illness a few months before, and of her many inquiries about him. Lamb feasted his eyes upon his bronzed friend, and exclaimed, " What a Th-Theseus you are ! " and the two laughed over the sly allusion to their wrangle.

" I do believe you would pun on my grave," laughed Coleridge.

" No; I draw the line at that, C-C-Coleridge, 'tis too grave a subject," said Lamb, with a twinkle in the merry brown eyes.

" Oh, you wagging wag ! what have you written since I climbed the Alps ? " asked Coleridge.

" I'll read you ' Rosamond Grey ' when you c-c-come to-morrow. Southey likes it well, " he added. " Your old friend Lloyd is married, and I have just returned from a delightful visit to him at Cambridge, and met there a fine f-fellow named Manning. He will visit me s-soon, and I want you to know him. And you, what have you to show for all these months, besides your b-bronzed skin ? "

" I have written some descriptive poems, and absorbed many new ideas ; and shall settle down at once to translate Schiller's 'Wallenstein,'" said Coleridge.

And this erratic genius actually did make a splendid free translation of that work in six weeks, adding a couplet which so pleased Schiller that he translated it into German, and published it in his next edition.

His political articles in the "Morning Post" attracted much notice. His admiration for Bonaparte and the French Revolution had materially changed since the "little Corsican" had shown the cloven foot of ambition. Napoleon, having returned from Egypt, after his reverses on the Nile, had proclaimed himself First Consul, and written a most plausible letter to George III. of England, expatiating upon the glories and advantages of peace, and recommending a pacific mutual understanding between the two countries. But Pitt and his party were utterly opposed to allowing England to sleep while the treacherous Napoleon should gain time to recruit his shaken armies.

And now Coleridge, suffering from the reaction of feeling after his wild and misplaced enthusiasm for Napoleon, shifted around as strongly to the other side. His horror at the French atrocities had sent him to the opposite extreme of upholding the powers that be, rather than encourage the license committed in the name of Liberty. And now, when the usurper urged peace, Coleridge, having learned to doubt his integrity, joined the formerly despised Tories in advocating war and the punishment of the tyrant. His articles in the "Morning Post" upholding Pitt's course did much to continue the war. He was thus in the anomalous position of a man battling vigorously for the very party he had always denounced, and denouncing the leniency he had formerly upheld. He and Lamb had many hot discussions upon this change of party ; Lamb entirely agreeing with the disgusted Fox, who refused to take part in these gratuitous war troubles.

Again was Coleridge carried away by his overwhelming ideality. The leader of the people had betrayed his cause, therefore he must be annihilated, and no treaties must be entered into with a perjured usurper ! One sees here the same high ideal of truth and right ; and in upholding this, the shifting of one's platform in politics is as nothing. He wrote in his usual desultory way, sending out innumerable articles when the spirit was upon him, and sinking into his ease-loving lethargy when his enthusiasm waned. He became assistant editor upon the " Morning Post," Lamb and Southey also contributing to his department. His success was such, that in March, 1800, Stuart of the " Post " and " Courier " offered Coleridge a half interest, with £2,000 a year, if he would become sub-editor. This was the chance of his life, the pivotal point ! Regular occupation and plentiful means would have saved the man ; and it need not have killed the poet, as he feared. He needed the money sadly ; he needed the check to his restless spirit, as a wayward horse needs bit and bridle. What did he choose ?

To him it meant a life of toil in paths he especially disliked, and the restriction of personal and mental liberty. A poet feels that he can write only when the voice within claims to be heard. Coleridge felt that he was listening to his conscience when he declined. He knew he was yielding up a competence and regular work for the sake of those poetic dreams which haunted his spirit. He little knew the result of his choice. "If men could but see the turning-point in their lives, how much better and easier life would be! Such an era comes to each one of us. We may make our decision conscientiously, selfishly, or stupidly. But the choice is given us if we but realize it; and our own decisions make or mar our lives," said Wordsworth upon hearing of his friend's choice.

The die was cast, Coleridge's heart was set upon an untrammeled life amid the charms of nature, with freedom to interpret her voice. He wrote to his old friend Thomas Poole:

"If I had the least love of money I could make sure of £2,000 a year; but I would not so give up the country and the lazy reading of old folios for 2,000 times £2,000. In short, beyond £350 a year, I consider money as a real evil." *

His poor wife, living on the Wedgwood pension of £150 a year, might have said: "If money be an evil, the want of it is by far a worse evil."

Our hero did not, however, consult his wife about a paltry £2,000 a year. Of course she would say: "Stick to your work and accept the position—and the money." Of course she could not see the importance of a poet's being free from the requirements of routine work, and from printers clamoring at stated times for so many columns of brain-product.

Lamb saw his friend's tendency to drift with each tide, and felt that he needed a rudder and sail. He urged Coleridge, with all the eloquence of his earnest, loving heart, to accept the position. He knew, from his twenty-five years of experience, that work might cripple,

* "Thomas Poole and his Friends."—SANDFORD.

but need not kill poetic fancies and inspirations. He knew that Coleridge was too erratic to trust to steady purpose in working, with no especial impetus. He felt that success as a writer would make a man of him ; but that harsh criticism would shrink his powers, as a touch does a sensitive plant.

But Coleridge was determined to remain unfettered. He felt great thoughts and beautiful poems burning for utterance, and he loved to dream of the past, the present, and the future. He had tried to edit and write for a magazine ; "The Watchman" had been a nightmare ; but then he was hampered by having no money to meet the expenses. Journalism meant unremitting toil with no release from bit and bridle. So, he let his golden chance go by.

The air was softening, and even in smoky London the summer sun sent golden rays through the trees in Hyde Park, and dotted with daisies the grass in St. Paul's Churchyard and around the Abbey. Coleridge, feeling his soul answering to the voices of nature calling from the hills and lakes, fled to Westmoreland, where Wordsworth was living a poet's idyl at Grasmere.

Looking about for a rest for himself and his family near his friend, he found Greta Hall, upon the hill above Keswick. From the house, one could look down upon Keswick, and across pretty meadows where the Greta ripples by under its arched bridges, to Derwentwater. Behind Greta Hall stretched out a long line of lofty peaks, with Skiddaw, towering to the clouds. It was a picturesque spot, rustic, yet homelike enough to touch a poet's fancy. The house stood, broad and inviting, with its central hall and wide doorway. One half was occupied by the owner, Mr. Jackson, who had a fine library and afterwards became a warm friend of the Coleridges. The poets could easily walk the ten or twelve miles separating Greta Hall from Grasmere; even though the road lay over the Dunmail Raise, a constant succession of heather-covered mountains and yew-clad vales. Thirlmere Lake, and the "Mighty Helvellyn," lying just beyond Grasmere, added to the charm of the walk. At twenty-seven, Coleridge was an inveterate walker and he climbed those mountains in all weathers, regardless of the pitiless storms that often burst upon their crowns. The many wettings of those wild rambles increased the rheumatism and gout that became the torment of his life.

He had always suffered with rheumatism since the days at Christ's Hospital, and the careless baths in New River and the Otter. The chilly Lake country, with its shut-in vales and mountain mists, was the worst location he could have chosen for a home. But he considered being near Wordsworth a sufficient off-set. Thomas Poole, their kind neighbor at Stowey, protested against the Coleridges leaving. And it was equally hard for Coleridge to part from so dear a friend; but he had learned to look upon Wordsworth as necessary to his poetic development, and clung to him as the ivy to its fostering oak. So, gathering up their household gods, and bidding farewell to Stowey and their Bristol friends, they took the stage-wagon to the North, and settled in their third and last home, Keswick.

Sarah hailed this new residence gladly, as promising a more settled life for her husband. She had long ago relinquished her feeling of resentment against Dorothy Wordsworth for filling a place she knew she could not reach in her husband's intellectual life; and she now felt that Wordsworth was the real attraction. She saw Coleridge's reverent admiration for his serious friend, and knowing him to be a good man, she rejoiced in the intimacy which she believed of so great a benefit to her husband. She found some new friends in their new home, especially Miss James, the vicar's daughter, who lived in an adjoining cottage.

In the years following, the Coleridges had their little circle in the Lake country, where their children grew up.

Coleridge himself found few friends among the plain people of the Lakes ; Wordsworth and Nature were enough for him, and he filled his heart with both. During his many long absences it was often a dreary life for the young wife, but she was learning not even to look a complaint.

Does any man know how hard it is for an earnest, warm-hearted woman to learn to suppress the many anxieties and discontents born of her love? An in-different woman can accept indifference, but the very semblance of it stings a loving wife. The continual hypocrisy of hiding all traces of the struggle to keep a waning love might well kill hers soon ; but love dies hard in some natures. Her poet was often moody and silent, but she must not wonder at it. When cheerful, he often became wildly hilarious, and she must be ready to respond in a moment, lest she should check the mirth, and bring scowls or depression. She was trying hard to learn all the moods and tenses of a poet's soul ; but it is a most irregular verb to conjugate, and does not always agree with its subject. She must not expect him to respond to her little griefs or pleasures. No man likes to see a woman depressed or uneasy. So she made the new home bright and cheerful, and

Coleridge awoke to a new happiness amid the lakes and mountains, with the warm fireside and pleasant rooms, with his great easy-chair drawn before the hearth, and a fine old organ making an artistic background. He placed an Æolian harp in an upper window, and the winds from Skiddaw sang weird chaunts through the poet's home, and inspired him to dreams as melodious as their chords. Surely, now, his restless spirit might learn the charms of repose and peace !

CHAPTER XIX.

There's Allan C——, the large-hearted Scot, and Procter, candid and affectionate as his own poetry. . . . And Coleridge himself, the same to me still as in those old evenings when we used to sit and speculate at our old 'Salutation' tavern, upon Pantisocracy, and golden days to come on earth. And Wordsworth. . . . (H. C. R.), unwearied in the offices of a friend; and Clarkson, almost above the narrowness of that relation,—and the gall-less and single-minded Dyer, and. . . . the veteran Colonel B., with his lusty heart, still sending cartels of defiance to old Time.

CHARLES LAMB.

CHARLES LAMB wrote often to his friends, glad to have back the old friendship, without which his soul had limped, crippled, through the weariness of the clerk's desk and his home troubles. He wrote gay letters, sad letters, witty letters, critical letters, the overflow of a deep, true nature. He criticised Coleridge's writings, and sweetened the criticisms with judicious praise. He wrote: "For God's sake, don't make me ridiculous any more, by terming me 'gentle-hearted' in print; or do it in better verse. It did well enough five years ago, when I came to see you and was moral coxcomb enough to feed upon such epithets; but besides that, the meaning of 'gentle' is equivocal at best, and almost always means poor-spirited. The very quality of gentleness is abhorrent to such vile trumpetings. . . . I hope my virtues have done *snaking.*" " Please to blot out 'gentle-hearted' and substitute drunken dog, ragged head, seld-shaven, odd-eyed, stuttering, or any other epithet which truly and properly belongs to the gentleman in question." *

Of the death of the faithful old servant, which so shocked Mary that she had another spell, and was obliged to go to the asylum again, he wrote :

" I shall be quite alone, with nothing but a cat to remind me that the house has been full of living beings like myself. . . . My heart is quite sunk, and I don't know where to look for relief. Mary will get better again ; but her constantly being liable to such relapses is dreadful. We are in a manner *marked*. Excuse my troubling you, but I have no one else to speak to." *

He felt keenly the notice caused by their affliction, and longed to return to London from their house at Pentonville. He wrote to Manning : " We are in a manner marked people, and can be nowhere private except in the midst of London." †

At this time Coleridge paid him a visit of three weeks, and after this pleasant break in his loneliness, he wrote to Manning : " March 17, 1800. I am living in a continuous feast. Coleridge has been with me for nigh three weeks, and the more I see of him in the quotidian undress and relaxation of mind, the more cause I see to love him and believe him a *very good man*, and all these foolish impressions to the contrary fly off like morning slumbers. He is uncommonly kind and friendly to me. He ferrets me day and

* " Letters of Charles Lamb."—TALFOURD.
† " Letters of Charles Lamb."—AINGER.

night to do *something*. He tends me amidst all his own worrying and heart-oppressing occupations, as a gardener tends his young tulip. Marry, come up! what a pretty similitude and how like your humble servant! He has dragged me to the brink of engaging to a newspaper, and has suggested to me the forgery of a supposed MS. of Burton (the anatomist of melancholy). . . . If I can pick up a few guineas in that way, I feel they will be most refreshing, bread being so dear!" *

Lamb sent on a number of Coleridge's promiscuous chattels, after that most careless individual had gone home without them, and wrote: " Besides the papers and books I sent a case of razors and a shaving-box and strop. This it has cost me a severe struggle to part with. . . . 'Bonaparte's Letters,' 'Arthur Young's Treatise on Corn,' and one or two more light-armed infantry, I have torn up for waste paper."

Manning also visited Lamb in his lonely days, during Mary's absence. They smoked and chatted, and dined, and I should say *wined*, together, save that Lamb could only afford whisky and the cheaper liquors, in which they indulged rather freely. Manning met Lamb's old friend, George Dyer, the absent-minded scholar, whose quaint sayings and queerer doings caused them much merriment. After his return Lamb wrote: " And now, when shall I catch a glimpse of your honest face again?—your pure, dogmatical, skeptical face by *punch* light? Oh! one glimpse of the human face and shake of the human hand is better than whole reams of this cold, thin correspondence. . . . George Dyer, that good-natured

* " Letters of Charles Lamb."—AINGER.

heathen, is more than nine months gone with his twin volumes of ode, pastoral, sonnet, elegy, Spenserian, Horatian, Akensidish, and Masonic verses (Clio prosper the birth !).   It will be twelve shillings out of somebody's pocket. . . . Well, God put it in the hearts of the English gentry to subscribe by shoals, for He never put a kinder heart into flesh of man than George Dyer's. . . . Dyer says : " Charles Lloyd, Charles Lamb, and Wm. Wordsworth in later days have struck the true chord, of poesy. . . . O George, George ! with a head uniformly wrong and a heart uniformly right, that I had power and might equal to my wishes ! " *

He told Manning of Dyer's weakness for buying every book he heard praised, or even spoken of, although so poor he could ill afford the luxury. " Would I could lock him up from all access of new ideas ! . . . The oftener I see him, the more deeply I admire him. He is goodness itself.   If I could outlive the period of his death, I would write a novel on purpose to make George the hero ; I could hit him off to a hair." *

Poor George Dyer was so forgetful that he would wear his summer clothes in winter, or put salt into his tea, and snuff into his soup, and commit all the absurdities of the absent-minded and near-sighted. At one time Lamb heard he was dying, and upon visiting him, found he had been living solely upon water-gruel for weeks, and being in the last stages of weakness, had sent farewells to his nephews and friends. Lamb insisted upon taking the starving philosopher home with him, and having prompted the physician, had a heavy prescription of beefsteak ordered, which he had previously bought and prepared. The dying philosopher

* " Letters of Charles Lamb."—AINGER.

was so stuffed in a week, that he went home plump and blooming.

About this time, Amos Cottle, the brother of Lamb's and Coleridge's friend, Joseph Cottle, died, and Charles Lamb and George Dyer paid a visit of condolence, which Lamb described to Coleridge in his matchless way : "Cottle was in black, and his younger brother was also in black, and everything wore an aspect suitable to the respect due to the freshly dead. For some time after our entrance nobody spoke till George modestly put in a question ' whether " Alfred " was likely to sell.' This was Lethe to Cottle, and his poor face wet with tears, and his kind eyes brightened up in a moment. Now I felt it my cue to speak. I had to thank him for a present of a magnificent copy, and had promised to send him my remarks. I ventured to suggest that I perceived a considerable improvement in his first book, since the state in which he first read it to me.

" Joseph, who had sat till now with his knees cowering in by the fire-place, wheeled about with great difficulty of body, shifted the same round to where I was sitting, and first stationing one thigh over the other, which is his habit in sedentary mood, and placidly fixing his benevolent face right against mine, waited my observations. At that moment it came strongly into my mind that I had got ' Uncle Toby ' before me ; he looked so kind and so good. I *could* not say an unkind thing of ' Alfred.' So I set my memory to work to recollect the name of Alfred's Queen, and with some adroitness recalled the well-known sound to Cottle's ears of Alswitha. At that moment I could perceive that Cottle had forgot his brother was so lately become a blessed spirit. In the language of mathematicians, the author was as 9; the brother, as 1.   I felt my cue, and in pity beslobbered 'Alfred' with most unqualified praise, only qualifying my praise by the occasional politic interposition of an exception taken against trivial faults, slips, and human imperfections, which, by removing the appearance of insincerity, did but in truth heighten the relish.   Perhaps I might have spared that refinement, for Joseph was in a mood to hope and believe *all things.* What I said was beautifully supported by. ... George on my right, who has an utter incapacity for comprehending that there *can be* anything bad in poetry.   All poems are *good* poems to George, all men are *fine geniuses.* .... The author repeatedly declared that he loved nothing better than *candid* criticism.   Was I a candid greyhound now, for all this, or did I do right ?   I believe I did.   The effect was luscious to my conscience.   For all the rest of the evening Amos was no more heard of, till George revived the subject by inquiring whether some account should not be drawn up by the friends of the deceased, to be inserted in 'Phillips' Monthly Obituary,' adding that Amos was estimable both for his head and his heart, and *would have made a fine poet if he had lived !* . . .

" In reality, Cottle imitates Southey, as Rowe did Shakespeare, with his 'Good-morrow to ye, good Master Lieutenant.'   Instead of a man, a woman, a daughter, he constantly writes, 'one a man, one a woman, and one his daughter'. . . . Instead of the king, the hero, he constantly writes: ' he the king, he the hero ;' two flowers of rhetoric borrowed of ' Joan.'   But Mr. Cottle soars a higher pitch ! !   When *he is* original, it is in a most original way, indeed.   His terrific scenes are indescribable.   Serpents, asps, spiders, ghosts, headless bodies, staircases made of nothing, with adders' tongues for bannisters! What a brain he must have! he puts as many plums in his pudding as my grandmother used to do. . . . And then emerging from hell's horrors into light, and treading on pure flats of this earth—for twenty-three books together." *

And so Lamb ambled on, with his keen sense of the ridiculous and his kindly human fun. He never thrust a sword or even a needle into a tender spot, yet he always relished absurdities, even though he saw them with the eye of love. The good qualities he detected in his friends always made their foibles touching or lovable. Such is the alchemy of a loving heart and nature: it turns all baser metals into its own affinity—pure gold.

Poor Lamb had a lonely time while Mary was at the asylum. He wandered to his friends' houses for company—to Godwin's, and to Dyer's untidy Noah's ark; to the theaters; and took his daily walk down the Strand, watching the busy crowds with unvarying interest. He wrote Manning of an amusing experience at a sort of menagerie, whose placard promised sight of a rattlesnake ten feet in length: I went to see it last night by candle-light. We were ushered into a room very little larger than ours at Pentonville. A man and woman and four boys live in this room, joint tenants with nine snakes, most of them such as no remedy has been discovered for their bites. We walked into the middle which is formed by a half-moon of wired boxes —all mansions of snakes; whip snakes, thunder snakes, pig-nose snakes, American vipers, and *this monster*. He lies curled up in folds. Immediately a stranger

* " Letters of Charles Lamb."—AINGER.

entered (for he is used to the family and sees them play at cards !) he set up a rattle like a watchman's in London, or near as loud, and reared up a head from the midst of those folds, like a toad, and shook his head. I had the foolish curiosity to strike the wires with my fingers, and the devil flew at me with his toad mouth wide open ; the inside of his mouth is quite white. . . . It frightened me so much that I did not recover my voice for a minute's space. . . . I wish you could have seen it. He absolutely swelled with passion to the bigness of a large thigh. I could not retreat without infringing upon another box ; and just behind, a little devil not an inch from my back had got his nose out with some difficulty and pain quite through the bars. . . . But this *monster*, like Aaron's serpent, swallowed up the impression of the rest. He opened his cursed mouth, when he made at me, as wide as his head was broad. I hallooed out quite loud, and felt pains all over my body from fright." *

Charles Lamb had a great scare, and considered it tempting Providence to visit such an inferno, and pave the way for a certain distemper that follows lax habits, in which he too frequently indulged during Mary's many absences. His health, never very robust, began to suffer more and more from constant tobacco, late hours, and evening potations to drive away the blue-devils of his lonely bachelor life.

Mary returned, and the little home grew cheery again. Manning kept urging a visit to Cambridge, and Coleridge and Wordsworth begged him to visit the Lake country. He even thought of a visit to Coleridge before Christmas, and wrote to Manning : " Perhaps I

* " Letters of Charles Lamb."—AINGER.

shall be able to take Cambridge in my way going or coming. I will not describe to you the expectations which such a one as I, pent all my life in a dirty city, have formed of a tour of the lakes: Coniston, Grasmere, Ambleside, Wordsworth, Coleridge.

" I hope you will send hills, woods, lakes, mountains, to the devil. I will not eat snipes with thee, Thomas Manning. My taskmasters have denied me a holiday season, so I shall transfer my expectations back to my mistress. . . .

" I confess I am not romance-bit about *Nature*. The earth and sea and sky (when all is said), is but as a house to dwell in. . . . Streets, markets, theaters, churches, Covent Gardens, shops sparkling with pretty faces of industrious milliners, neat sempstresses, ladies cheapening, gentlemen behind counters lying, authors in the street with spectacles, George Dyers (you may know them by their gait), lamps lit at night, pastry-cooks, and silversmiths' shops, beautiful Quakers of Pentonville, noise of coaches, drowsy cry of mechanics; watchmen at night, with bucks reeling home drunk; if you happen to wake at midnight, cries of 'fire,' and ' stop thief ;' Inns of Court, with their learned air, and halls and butteries, just like Cambridge colleges ; old book-stalls, 'Jeremy Taylor,' 'Burton on Melancholy,' and ' Religio Medicis,' on every stall ! These are thy pleasures, O London ! with thy many sins. . . . For these may Keswick and her giant herd go hang ! " *

By such monodies the quaint cockney tried to comfort himself for his disappointments about projected trips which were doomed to remain but day-dreams.

---

* " Letters of Charles Lamb."—Ainger.

To Wordsworth he wrote : " With you and your sister, I could gang anywhere, but I am afraid whether I shall ever be able to afford so desperate a journey. Separate from the pleasure of your company, I don't care much if I never see a mountain in my life.   I have passed all my days in London, until I have formed as many and intense local attachments as any of you mountaineers can have done with dead Nature.   The lighted shops of the Strand and Fleet Street " (lighted with smoking oil lamps in those days !) ; " all the bustle **and wickedness** around Covent Garden ; the sun shining upon houses and pavements ; the old book-stalls and fruit-shops, coffee-houses, steams of soups from kitchens ; the pantomimes,—London itself a pantomime and masquerade—all these things work themselves into my mind and amuse me without a power of satiating me.   The wonder of these sights impels me into night walks about her crowded streets ; and I often shed tears in the motley Strand, from the fulness of joy at so much life.   My attachments are all local, purely local.   I have no passion (and have had none since I was in love, and then it was the spurious engendering of poetry and books) for groves and valleys. The rooms where I was born, the furniture which has been before my eyes all my life, a book-case which has followed me about like a faithful dog (only exceeding him in knowledge) where I have moved, old chairs, old tables, streets, squares where I have sunned myself, my old school—these are my mistresses.   Have I not enough without your mountains ? " *

What a mirror of his quaint fancies and likings this quiet London scholar held up to his friend, the poet

* " Letters of Charles Lamb."—AINGER.

of Nature! How Wordsworth must have sniffed and
snorted amid his admiring circle when he reccived this
confession! That Lamb meant every word is proved
by his later writings. He has crystallized just these
impressions and *penchants* into the charming descriptions of his essays. Like Dr. Johnson, he adored every
nook and corner of smoky, crowded, fascinating London,
and he has immortalized her Inns of Court, her chimney-
sweeps, her streets, parks, shops, and mysterious old
by-ways better than Hogarth or Wilkie, or any other
brush or pen artist has done.

Lamb thought he had no love of " dead nature,"
until his eyes were opened; but after seeing God's
gigantic creations, his soul was touched, and his heart
responded to nature's charms as to all else worthy and
beautiful. He was beginning to scribble his fancies
for newspapers and magazines, and slowly the satire
and humor of the unpretending clerk of India House
won admirers.

CHAPTER XX.

"HE WAS A MAN, TAKE HIM FOR ALL IN ALL, I SHALL
NOT LOOK UPON HIS LIKE AGAIN."

> Dear Charles! Whilst yet thou wert a babe, I ween
> That pity and simplicity stood by
> And promised for thee that thou shouldst renounce
> The world's low cares and lying vanities.
>
> COLERIDGE.

> Antiquity! Thou wondrous charm, what are thou ? that being
> nothing art everything! When thou *wert*, thou wert not Anti-
> quity! then thou wert nothing, but hadst a remoter antiquity, as
> thou call'st it, to look back to with blind veneration.
>
> CHARLES LAMB.

POOR Mary Lamb's attacks were so frequent as to
attract considerable notice in their neighborhood,
and they were often requested to find other quarters. The Gutches, who had invited them to lodge with
them, found the notoriety unpleasant, and the stream
of visitors who now found their way to Charles Lamb's
humble dwelling made a home of their own a necessity.
So, on Lady's Day, 1801, they moved to rooms in the
Inner Temple, near their old home in the Crown Office
Row. Lamb always hovered delightedly round the
stately gardens and halls of the Temple. He loved
the plain brick rows and quadrangles, whose many
staring windows looked upon these gardens and halls.
They spoke to him of the scholarly side of life;

and he reverenced the old benchers that haunted their gloomy avenues, and liked to meet the scholars and students and lawyers who frequented these precincts of Court. He adored the old law libraries and gothic dining-halls, with their polished oaken tables and benches, shining as mirrors and black almost as ebony. He reveled in the stately solemnity of the old Temple Church, with its dome and circled pillars, where lie the remains of barristers, Crusaders and Knights Templars, with records on their brass effigies reaching back to the middle ages. His antiquarian soul loved to reach back from the present to the dim past, and in these precincts was an unbroken line stretching back to where the real and the ideal or legendary meet, in the receding vistas of time. He loved the quiet, secluded gardens whose trees and flowers and velvet turf are such a contrast to the grim, dark surroundings ; and like many others, in this dear old spot, he liked to stop at Goldsmith's tomb, just outside the church, and ponder upon the gentle poet who now had the honors and the rewards denied his busy yet pleasure-loving life of poverty and anxiety. The doves and pigeons flocking around the gardens of the Inner and Middle Temple knew Charles Lamb, and hovered round him for the crumbs he often gave them from his pockets, as he strolled down the walks to the Thames. He loved those flower-bordered walks, and the sight of the spires rising over the river, where the sails, passing and repassing, and the turrets and towers of the great Tower of London in the blue distance, made beautiful pictures for his eye and fancy.

Here, in the Lambs' rooms in the Temple, many friends gathered of evenings to chat and smoke and play whist, for Charles was becoming a great favorite with a certain set of writers and thinkers. He who gave such reverence to genius and such kindly admiration to all that was worthy, gained the esteem and friendship of men who were earnestly working and becoming known in the literature and politics of the day.

George Dyer, the author of " History of Cambridge University; " he " with heart of gold," Wm. Godwin, the Necessarian, who wrote the " Political Justice " and " Caleb Williams," and who had but lately married and lost the brilliant and unfortunate Mary Wollstonecraft, were frequent guests; Rickman, who afterwards became clerk of the House of Commons, whom Lamb so sincerely admired, calling him the " finished man," whose memory was as "the brazen serpent to the Israelites—I shall look up to it to keep me honest and upright; " * Thomas Manning, the mathematician and fellow of Cambridge; William Hazlitt, the painter, turned critic and essayist;—all were his intimate and loving friends. They consulted him about their writings, their dramas and poems; all realized his exquisite taste, and no friend published essay, play, or poem without begging his criticism. Sometimes these gratuitous tasks wearied the clerk who had pored over books and figures all day, and needed his evenings for rest. But he was always ready to lend his aid; to criticise, to encourage —to ridicule, perhaps; but with so tender a thrust, that his severe censure never gave a pang. He used the surgeon's knife with the anæsthetic of humor and gentle satire. The lonely clerk was slowly drawing about him a circle of admirers and life-long friends, which greatly

* " Letters of Charles Lamb."—AINGER.

compensated for the sordid poverty and meager comforts of his life.

Charles Lloyd had settled near Grasmere, on the Rothay, not far from Wordsworth; and these Lake Poets made Lamb's home their headquarters when in town, sometimes staying with him and sometimes at an adjacent inn, where they could have frequent intercourse.

They all loved the quiet, gentle sister whose whole soul was wrapped up in her brother. Mary welcomed them all with unfeigned pleasure. She had always loved Samuel Coleridge as a younger brother, and she watched the vicissitudes of his life with tender interest. She reverenced the serious Wordsworth, and there was a warm bond between her and Dorothy. Their brothers were their idols, and they never wearied discussing them as other women compare lovers or husbands. She was more shy of the brilliant Manning; but in the long years of his close intimacy with Charles she learned to love and trust him; and William Hazlitt became as a brother to both. His sharp scalpel spared this gentle pair, in the days when he probed all his contemporaries to the very quick. Hazlitt found the weak spot in every man; and the higher and more pretentious they were, the more ruthlessly did he lay bare their petty foibles or deeper vices. But in Charles and Mary Lamb he saw only purity and kindliness.

The friends would gather round the whist-table, and cards and talk would alternate in most free and easy fashion; and Mary would bring in a dish of smoking baked potatoes and a cold joint and pot of ale; or sometimes it was but bread and cheese, with a bowl of steaming punch that Charles would brew with great *éclat.* Lamb's nervous temperament felt the strain of the daily desk work and nightly card parties, and he determined to make one more effort to break away from London, and visit Coleridge at Keswick. He was successful in gaining his *congé* from the India House, and without even waiting to notify Coleridge, he and Mary took the coach for Penrith, and after a couple of days along the beautiful English highways, they reached Penrith on the third day, and found a stage just leaving for Keswick. As they rode through the glens and over the wild passes at sunset, and saw the long lines of peaks and domes, gorgeous in purple and gold, with the lakes lying like jewels below, the city pair were filled with awe. Skiddaw and its giant brothers, as Coleridge called them, loomed golden in the distance, and, as they approached, towered high above the purple chasms, their bald crowns peering among the fleecy, golden clouds.

" I had no idea of the grandeur of mountains," Charles said, in an awe-struck voice. The sparkle in Mary's eyes told of her delight.

Along the breezy heights, bathed in the purple and rosy haze, they climbed ; up and up, with woods to right and left, and Bassenthwaite and Derwentwater lying in the purple vales, like flashing gems, until they reached the pass and descended into the pretty vale where Keswick nestled at the mountain's foot.

" There is the Greta," said Lamb, as the coach drew up at the old inn. " We can just follow it to the bridge, and there yonder on that hill is G-Greta Hall ; I know it by Coleridge's w-word pictures." They hastened on, in the gathering gloom of the long twilight, and burst in upon the delighted Coleridge sitting before his cheerful, crackling fire.

Sarah gave them as hearty a greeting, and the birdlings were peeped at in their nest.

"I'm converted; turned from a c-c-city drone to one of those d-d-despised tourists, and all because of your sunsets and m-m-mountains. I was happy to sit by my L-L-London fireside, and l-l-listen to the eternal roll of the c-c-city noises, and now, like P-P-Pandora's spirits, I can never again be entirely content, c-c-crowded into the smoky levels of d-d-dirty old London. I have seen Hel-Helvellyn and your grand old Skiddaw, and my s-soul has leaped out to meet them—and it w-won't return. It has e-e-eaten the forbidden fruit," he sighed. "But why this organ? It is big enough f-for a minster," he asked, looking at the large organ at one end of the room.

"Oh, it is harmless," laughed Coleridge; "it belongs to the house and helps furnish up, and it never speaks unless Lloyd comes in, and then it plays the very devil."

Mary insisted upon helping Sarah in the kitchen, knowing well what sudden visitors entailed upon a quiet household, and the women grew confidential and cosy over their little duties.

Meanwhile Lamb looked earnestly at Coleridge, and noticed the haggard pallor which had followed his many attacks of rheumatism. He saw that his friend was changed; he was less open, and less merry-hearted than when he was in London.

Little Hartley was a fine, manly fellow of five years, quite independent, and something of a philosopher, for he must always have the reason for everything. Lamb's stutter puzzled him immensely. "Is that why he is named Mr. Lamb ? " he asked, with some indistinct notion of the bleat of a young sheep, and the eternal fitness of things. Derwent was a tiny roly-poly that bobbed around in his yellow gown and Lamb insisted upon calling him " Stumpy Canary," also because of the " eternal fitness."

Lamb and Coleridge took up their old discussions, and dropped into the old, friendly intercourse, and Mary and Sarah were equally congenial.

They were always ready for the beautiful mountain rambles. They spent long days climbing the exquisite shady roads to the lakes. They visited Thirlmere and Loughrigg Tarn with their bracken and heather beds, and gazed upon the emerald sweeps of mountain and valley. They opened their picnic baskets at the mossy old stone at Thirlmere, under the shadow of the mighty Helvellyn, where their table was the great mossy stone, decorated with sprigs of fern and ivy, and their seats the soft purple heather, covering all the mountain sides. Fresh cresses with the dews of the rill upon them were a dainty salad, and poetic thoughts and fancies were sauce and spice fit for the gods. Southey and Lloyd had joined them upon this picnic, and Joseph Cottle had come up from Bristol for a short visit; so their party was complete, excepting that Wordsworth and Dorothy were off on a pedestrian tour, their last ramble before his expected marriage.

During the day Lamb turned to Coleridge and said : " I must have that exquisite 'Christabel' f-finished, Coleridge ; we can never leave that gentle creature under the s-spell of that mysterious visitor. We see the effort of Christabel to free herself from the l-l-loathsome influence, and her father's anger at his beloved

child's seeming c-c-caprice. You leave us shuddering
at such an influence over the young girl and her noble
father, b-b-but how does it end ? Does the s-s-serpent-
eyed charmer capture the father ? "

" I have the plot completed in my brain," said Coleridge. " You don't expect me to give it away to you
rival poets ? " he asked, rather suspiciously. " Some day
you or Southey will be putting your own ending to my
story."

" Then why not f-f-finish it yourself, Esteecee, and
p-p-prevent the possibility of such d-desecration ? It is
so full of wild charm that even the Scotch critics could
not pluck a f-f-feather from its b-beauty. For God's
sake, f-f-finish it."

Coleridge looked uneasy, and tried to change the subject, but Lloyd and Southey added their entreaties.

" I have often begged him to complete that gem,"
said Southey.

Coleridge flushed angrily, saying : " Come, brother
poets, don't be so ready to pick my bones. Were I to
finish ' Christabel ' without the inspiration, it would be
a failure. I will not finish it hastily ; nor will I give a
hint of its unraveling," he added, impatiently, glancing
at his wife, who had turned quickly to Lamb when he
broached the subject.

She opened her mouth to speak, but seeing his frown,
stopped and bit her lip, and the talk drifted to other
subjects.

Later, Sarah said to Lamb : " I have often begged
him to finish that poem ; he begins so much work and
dreams over it, and seems so reluctant to finish up, that
I am continually begging him to work ; " and she sighed
deeply. " He is growing so moody and fitful in these

days, Charles; there seems some spell upon him since that German tour. I sometimes think the spell of the Lady Geraldine is more real than mere poetic fancy."

"I notice the change that has t-troubled you, Sarah; but with his t-t-temperament you must not urge him too st-strongly, or c-complain of his habits. A p-poet is a sensitive creature, enduring his own fancies and discouragements, and also f-f-feeling the reflex of others' anxiety or c-c-criticism—even when n-n-not expressed."

"But where must a wife's duty cease?" she asked, anxiously. "If a wife sees her husband drifting, drifting to certain ruin of mind and body, can she *bear* it and be still, and not even *try* to keep him safe?"

"If trying and urging accomplished anything it w-w-would be d-different; but did you ever know a man l-l-listen to a woman's warnings and—f-f-follow them?"

Sarah's quick tears were her answer, and Mary coming up, the subject was dropped, and the two women strolled off and were soon immersed in the friendly chat that women love.

The friends carved their initials on a rock projecting over the lake, and Wordsworth and Dorothy afterwards added theirs, and the memorial stands to this day as a token of the intimacy of the Lake Poets.

Day after day, during this visit, the friends walked to the different lakes. One day was spent in enjoying Derwentwater amidst its encircling mountains, and the beautiful Lodore Falls. The varied peaks and crests and domes of the mountains charmed Mary and Charles. The blue peaks in the distance, and lilac shoulders of the nearer heights, with Lodore plunging down their rocky crags and tossing over its pebbly and moss-bordered bed, until it dashes, foaming, into the lake, were a new experience of the wonders and beauty of nature.

Charles confessed to being a complete convert to their mysterious charm. "They seem like a giant host awaiting battle, but some have grown bald in the waiting, and some are hoary with the scraggy growth of centuries. This beautiful fall is always in its fresh, babbling youth—a perennial spring," * he afterwards wrote, in referring to this visit.

They wandered amid the grave old yews of Borrowdale, with Eagle's Crag and Falcon's Nest hovering above the peaceful vale, and after a few more delightful days and rambles, the Lambs bade farewell, and took the coach to Grasmere and Rydal Water for a peep at Wordsworth's home.

They were invited by the Clarksons, warm friends of the Wordsworths and Coleridges, living at Rydal Mount, to visit them. The Clarksons showed them the tiny stone house at Grasmere that Wordsworth had taken for his new home; they strolled amid the little stone cottages and along the babbling Rothay to the little church upon its banks. The Clarksons accompanied them down the beautiful road, shaded by the great elms, that leads to Ambleside. Together they hunted up the pretty falls that dash down the three ravines, and turn the wheel of the picturesque old mill. The drowsy, quaint old towns of Ambleside and Bowness and Windermere had more charms for Mary than for her brother. The old gray stone cottages, the ivy growing over all the stone walls and fences, and the roses and nasturtiums creeping over walls and into windows, were a new delight to the city

* "Letters of Charles Lamb."—AINGER.

woman, who knew but the flowers in Covent Garden market. The wealth of nasturtiums and pinks and pansies and roses, making these old houses like bowers, was most fascinating to her.

They climbed Orrest Head, winding up the paths amid the scrub oaks and heather, and gazed rapturously upon the long, irregular Windermere, with its many islands and peninsulas and its lovely villages, with a castle here and there peeping from the thick foliage.

"Ah! what a p-picture!" exclaimed Charles, as they looked from the lake to the long chains of mountains stretching into the blue distance, with the Langdale Pikes visible here as everywhere in the Lake District. With enthusiasm, Charles said, "What a creature of t-turns and t-twists among these mountains is Lake W-Windermere! It is like a huge c-c-centipede, crawling through the v-v-valley!"

The Lambs started to explore the Wordsworth surroundings for their friends' sake; but Lamb became as "romance-bit" as even Wordsworth could have wished, and he acknowledged upon his return to London that the streets seemed narrow and dark after "the humps and dips of the pretty old straggling streets in the Westmoreland and Cumberland towns. . . . But the glory is here still, the life, the wine of existence," he added. "I can stand on tip-toe and see all the sails on the Thames. I can turn the corner and see the busy stream of life and vehicles on the Strand; the lights, the shops, the beautiful old chimes of St. Paul's, and life seems here full of beauty and interest." *

And thus the double-dyed cockney settled back to

* "Letters of Charles Lamb."—AINGER.

his haunts. But Mary sighed for the sweet woods and mountains, and found her windows very narrow and dark.

The visits of Rickman, and of George Dyer, with his queer stories, were not such a delight to her as to Charles.

"*HE WAS A MAN, TAKE HIM ALL IN ALL.*" 179

CHAPTER XXI.

LIFE'S SHOALS AND QUICKSANDS.

I saw her upon nearer view,
A spirit, yet a woman too!
Her household motions light and free,
And steps of virgin liberty;
A countenance in which did meet,
Sweet records, promises as sweet;
A creature not too bright or good
For human nature's daily food. . . .
A perfect woman, nobly planned,
To warn, to comfort, and command;
And yet a spirit still, and bright,
With something of angelic light.

WORDSWORTH.

DOROTHY WORDSWORTH had written several times to Mary, regretting their absence from home during their friends' visit to the Lake Country, and she had poured out her grief at the thought of her beloved brother's approaching marriage. With a woman's strong sense of possession, she resented sharing her beloved with another, and wrote pathetic letters to Mary of this danger that threatened their peace. "If I were *sure* my brother's happiness would be increased, I might not so dread a stranger coming under our roof. We have for years been such constant companions, I know not how to bear the constant presence of another." And the other devoted sister could well sympathize, reflecting that were such a thing to happen to her, she would be undone. Mary poured out her tender condolences and counseled her friend not to wean her brother's heart by opposition and complaint. " After the first few weeks you will fall into your own old ways. You and William are so entirely congenial, he will not easily turn from the old to the new, if you will be patient, dear Dorothy. The habits of a lifetime are stronger than new ties, and will hold after the honeymoon is over."*

How pleasant for the young bride who was to leave home, friends, and family ties, for the man she loved ! In her secluded home at picturesque Penrith, she was building fairy castles ; dreaming of being all in all to the " noblest poet in England." She would nestle to him while he wrote his beautiful poems; she would have his fireside cheery and bright, and his home, though modest, should be a fitting poet's trysting place, and she would be his ministering angel.

The sister was scarcely thought of, and the future was for herself and her poet, as all true-hearted brides dream of the life ahead.

Sometimes the rocks and quicksands lie further off, and smooth sailing belongs to the first happy months.

But Mary Hutchinson had a lesson of abnegation and self-effacement to learn from the beginning. The highest duty would not lie in the line of the highest pleasure, but directly across it. She could not be first in the heart that had leaned so long upon his sister. Her place was—what she could patiently, gently, but, oh ! so wearily, win ! She might have thought, she should have known, of his dependence upon Dorothy,

*" Mary Lamb."—ROSSETTI.

and so have shaped her dreams and hopes upon a truer basis. She did not understand ; and when after the wedding she reached her tiny home at Grasmere, where the sister had everything ready to welcome the bride, with constrained kindness, the shock of cruel disappointments descended upon her, almost on the evening of her wedding-day. It seemed Dorothy's fate to come as an interloper between the men she most cared for and their wives. Her friendship for Coleridge, who so needed help and comfort, was viewed coldly by his wife. Why did not the wife, then, better understand the poet-soul beside her? And now her own, her very own William, whose every thought was open to her, was nearer to some one else, some one he scarcely knew. She was a brave woman, and a true one ; she had had time to consider this marriage, and she had taught herself to resign some of her old rights. But between these two women war was threatening, and such a cruel war as might overthrow the happiness of their whole empire. They both saw and knew it, and, like brave women, they compromised.

"You must compromise, Dorothy," wrote Mary Lamb. "You must yield self for William's sake. It is not easy, but it is noble, because it conquers your bitterest enemy. Self has such just rights. It is so plausible, so powerful, so sensitive, that it is the hardest enemy in the world to overcome, especially as it always holds our inclinations and specious arguments of duty and right on its own side. But you can conquer for your brother's sake."

Through the winter, the little home was snug and pleasant enough, and the wife would take her sewing and knitting and sit close to her husband's side while he wrote, or frequently she wrote as he dictated, and he found her a most willing listener, who reverenced his beautiful thoughts, and poured her adulation upon his already self-satisfied soul. He thawed in the sun of admiration and love, as most men do; but his women spoiled him, by making him an oracle. His friends, Coleridge and Lamb, looked up to him with the same reverence—Coleridge as to a beloved master, and Lamb as to a superior being who must be honored and court-ed. Wordsworth was fond of Lamb, but looked some-what questioningly upon the constant by-play of wit, and the irrepressible interlarding of puns, in his con-versation. Wordsworth's serious face seldom relaxed at Lamb's levity, and Charles always felt somewhat apologetic for ruffling the surface of the long discus-sions upon learned subjects and poetry, by skimming his pebbles of fun into the midst. They were second nature, and Lamb could no more help punning, and seeing the absurdity which ever underlies the pathetic, than he could help breathing. In later years, when Tom Hood and Lamb became intimates, they often compared notes upon this habit of "squinting at life." Both had had deep sorrows that brought grief and tears very near their hearts; yet each turned the sting aside by the glittering shield of humor.

CHAPTER XXII.

WEIGHED IN THE BALANCE.

Oh ! many are the poets that are sown
By nature ; men endowed with highest gifts,
The vision and the faculty divine,
Yet wanting the accomplishment of verse. . .
           These favored beings,
All but a scattering few, live out their time,
Husbanding that which they possess within,
And go to the grave unthought of.   Strongest minds
Are often those of whom the noisy world
Hears least ; else, surely this man had not left
His graces unrevealed and unproclaimed.
                WORDSWORTH.—*Excursion.*

WHILST Lamb and Wordsworth were cherishing Coleridge more deeply, his old friend Southey was growing away from him.   Southey had long ago thrown aside the youthful vagaries and socialistic dreams that had unsettled him, and had become a sober family man of stanch Church proclivities and untiring energy.   He plodded steadily, writing books, poems, essays, anything that would win fame and money.   He had assumed the care of Lovell's widow (his wife's sister), in addition to his own growing family, and steady work was needed to keep the pot boiling.

He had talked and written with disapproval of Coleridge's wandering proclivities ; and from the standpoint of brother-in-law, did not approve the vagaries which left his home and wife too often lonely and sad.   And

Coleridge resented the good advice and criticisms of his old friend.

How different they all were, this party of friends and poets !

Wordsworth ! sober, serious, introspective, and rather self-centered, yet worshiping nature, and poetry as nature's interpreter, and steadily holding his exalted views until the world came round to his way of thinking. Coleridge ! varying as a weather-cock, warm-hearted but over sensitive, and inclined to indulge his proclivities by right of genius, yet wanting the ballast of steady purpose. He clung to Wordsworth as to a sheltering rock. Lamb ! loving, trusting, generous, self-denying, living a daily tragedy, yet wearing the mask of comedy ; true as steel to friends, to conscience, and duty, yet allowing too great liberty to the few indulgences he permitted himself, and parading his faults with penitent humility. And Southey ! upright, conscientious, censorious, and strait-laced, to atone to the world and himself for the latitude of his boyish dreams and aspirations.

Do the environments make the man, or would each have been modified and different with the other's surroundings ? They were all talented and thoughtful, with the fear of God in their hearts. Would Charles Lamb have sobered into a Wordsworth with the strain of care and servile toil removed ? Would he have had a taste for the oddities and pleasantries of the " seamy side " of life, as he describes them in his charming " Essays of Elia " ? Would Southey have remained a visionary and socialist had he been blest with means to gratify his early tastes ? And Coleridge, the most brilliant and scholarly of all, if he had accepted the editorship of the " Post " and " Courier," with an ample fortune, and the regular requirements of the office, would his nobler possibilities have developed as they ought to have done? And would the fatal habit, now already, when he was but thirty years of age, beginning to close around him, like the arms of the devil-fish upon its prey, have left him a free man ? Who knows ?

It is but the story of every life and every day; this might-have-been romance is but weaving circumstances around possibilities, and guiding the thread to a desired pattern.

The undesired patterns of real life have more of romance than the wildest story-teller dreams of telling, only they are lived out so slowly that we lose the thread, and miss seeing the pattern. A part is faded ere all be completed.

Wordsworth, brave in his love of right, and trusting to his inner voice, kept steadily on writing in his own style and waiting for the eleven stubborn men of the critical juries to come to his way of thinking.

The " Edinburgh Review," started in 1802 by Sydney Smith, Francis Jeffrey, and Henry Brougham, sneered at the love of nature, and the rhapsodies of its inter-preters. The editors, men of active life and practical temperament, could not at all comprehend the introspec-tion of a poetic mind like Wordsworth's. They pro-nounced his poems "trash," "balderdash ; " because they lived in an atmosphere of the practical, that excluded the very idea of inspiration from woods and glens, from the air we breathe, and the sun above us. A keen, critical humorist like Sydney Smith, probing the great questions of the day and of life ; a lawyer like Jeffrey, who must see a wherefore for every why, and a motive for each result, could not comprehend the Quakerism of Wordsworth's poetic inspirations. And to Brougham, who must ever be setting the world to rights, the life of Wordsworth's " rustics " was stagnation worse than death.

Coleridge was but a dreamer, and his fancies were meaningless dreams to these practical Scotchmen. Wherefore the " Edinburgh Review " always held these romance poets in contempt, and denied them any place among poets. And now when a new edition of " Lyrical Ballads " and the " Excursion " appeared, they were sneered at as " child's play " and absurd nonsense. Wordsworth was hurt at their blindness and ruthless bitterness ; but he knew he was right and kept on in his own way.

Coleridge, who had won some praise and applause, was cut to the quick by the sneers of the " Edinburgh Review " and the " Monthly Magazine," and was utterly discouraged.

Long years afterwards, when the " London Magazine " and " Blackwood's " had awakened to the fact that the Lake dreamers were poets who should speak truths to the world, the " Edinburgh Review " maintained a discreet silence, but Charles Lamb and others long remembered its early persecutions.

After Lamb's return from the Lake Country, his friends gathered about him so constantly that he appointed Wednesday evenings for them to meet at his house for their cards and talk. Around the old mahogany table were grouped Wm. Hazlitt, the essayist and critic ; Wm. Godwin, the novelist and philosopher, who usually fell asleep after he had partaken heartily of the hospitable cheer and the steaming punch; George

Dyer, Rickman, the Burneys, father and son, and a constantly increasing circle who spread the fame of the " Round Table," as they called it, far and near.

The late hours, and smoking, and, alas ! drinking at these pleasant gatherings were telling upon Lamb, and therefore upon Mary. Her " spells " were more frequent, and Lamb, after a night's carousing, was nervous and racked with regret and self-abasement. He watched Mary so anxiously, that his terror and uneasiness fretted her, and both grew sleepless and wretched. He determined to give up smoking, and dallying with the thought, and dreading to break with his old mistress, he wrote to Coleridge : *

" What do you think of smoking? I want your sober, average, *noon* opinion of it. Morning is a girl, and can't smoke. She is no evidence, one way or the other. And Night is so indecently *bought* over that he can't be a very upright judge. Ugh ! the truth is that one pipe is wholesome, two pipes toothsome, three pipes noisome, four pipes fulsome, five pipes loathsome, and that's the sum on it.

" But that is deciding rather upon rhyme than reason. When shall we two smoke again ? Last night I had been in a sad quandary of spirits, in what they call the evening ; but a pipe and some generous port, and ' King Lear ' (being alone) had their effect as solacers : I went to bed—pot valiant." *

He wrote Coleridge also that his " poem, ' Man of Destiny,' being a ' *Salutation* ' poem, had the mark of the beast (tobacco) upon it."

For some time he gave up tobacco entirely, and **was**

* " Letters of Charles Lamb."—AINGER.

better for the abstinence ; but after Mary left for the asylum again, he comforted himself with his old enemy, and for years it was war to the knife between him and his tempter, sometimes the one conquering, and sometimes the other.

CHAPTER XXIII.

Too soon transplanted, ere my soul had fixed
Its first domestic loves ; and hence through life
Chasing chance-started friendships.   A brief while
Some have preserved me from life's pelting ills. . . .
                And some, most false,
False and fair-foliaged as the manchineel,
Have tempted me to slumber in their shade
E'en 'mid the storm : then breathing subtlest damps,
Mixed their own venom with the rain from heaven,
That I woke poisoned.

                        COLERIDGE.

WILLIAM WORDSWORTH had not been married a year when the old spirit of roaming rose strong in the hearts of the brother and sister. The young wife saw the restlessness and heard William and Dorothy discussing their old tramps, and longing for another. So she knew her test was coming. She was not able to stand the fatigues and excitement of long walks, and being a brave woman, she looked the thing straight in the face. She knew that the pair were accustomed to these trips, and she also knew she must yield to her husband's wishes in the matter.

She had gradually assumed more of a wife's position in their home, and she was determined that her poet's happiness should be her first duty and pleasure. So she smilingly bade them " God speed," and kept her tears for her own room.

An old book says : " He that conquereth his spirit is greater than he that taketh a city," and she conquered, after a grievous struggle.

Coleridge had also grown restless again, and was sick and miserable, and he determined to accompany the Wordsworths.

Sarah had grown accustomed to her husband's frequent absences, and had ceased to struggle for her old hold upon his heart. She saw him drifting, drifting from home, paying long visits to this friend and that, and only coming again fitfully, until her home-life was but a troubled dream. The sweet companionship of early days had subsided into mere surface-life. Her husband's deeper thoughts and feelings were reserved for congenial friends. He was a loving husband and father, yet all his sympathies lay beyond home. She, whose whole life and heart were bound up in him, grew morose from the strain of trying to hold his heart, and to condone his growing restlessness. Sarah had always envied Dorothy Wordsworth her sympathy and comradeship with the husband she never could wholly win. All Coleridge's pleasantest excursions were shared by these friends. So, with sighs and many tears, she saw him depart with the Wordsworths for a long summer's expedition. She wondered how Mary Wordsworth liked her new rôle of widowhood, and if these long absences caused her tears and anxiety ; and not being a brave woman, she wasted her emotions upon the inevitable. And therein lay the difference between the influences of the two homes.

The poets visited Edinburgh, and looked with delight

upon the stately Greek columns and porticoes of that classic city. Coleridge was not at all enthusiastic about fine architecture, and, whilst discussing some cherished idea, often passed a noble cathedral, merely seeing a great church. But even he was interested in the old Canongate, with its narrow streets, crooked old houses, blind lanes, and antediluvian signs swinging from still more antediluvian buildings. John Knox's house, with its queer clerestory and quaint old windows, appealed to him as the shell that had enclosed so rich a kernel; but Wordsworth and Dorothy gloated over the city's quaint picturesqueness, and enjoyed to the full beautiful Holyrood, with its smooth, round pinnacles, and the great, rugged Castle towering aloft over the city. Where Wordsworth and Dorothy saw grandeur or beauty, Coleridge saw the march of centuries, and the panorama of changing dynasties; and his eloquence expanded into wonderful beauty and charm.

The poets hunted up Burns's grave, visited his old home and youthful scenes in Ayrshire, and found the long, low cottage of his birth, near Ayr, and the " Brig o' Doon," where " Tam O' Shanter " took his wild ride, pursued by the witches on " Hallowe'en." They reached old Stirling Castle, with its glorious panorama of the half of Scotland, and started to walk through the Trosachs' hermit shades and fairy passes, amid the purple, heather-clad mountains, around Loch Katrine. Ben Ann and Ben Venue were almost as fine as their own Skiddaw and Helvellyn; and the new novelist, whose tales and poems were becoming the world's talk, had chosen this beautiful Loch Katrine for his scenes. The " Waverley Novels " were peopling these woods and lakes with romance, and the poets had many discussions about the books whose author was yet unknown. But a miserable Scotch mist followed them from Edinburgh, and the chilling drizzle penetrated their clothing. Coleridge's rheumatism made walking painful, and the cold, gray atmosphere penetrated beyond the skin and bones to his very spirit. He was moody and melancholy, and neither Wordsworth nor Dorothy could rouse him to the cheerfulness usual when with them. At last he left them, and went by coach back to Keswick, where he was ill for several months, suffering terribly from neuralgia, rheumatism, and the many forms of torture belonging to his temperament, and aggravated by this exposure and foul weather. Tenderly did Sarah nurse him through these weary months. He could not use his stiffened and swollen hands to write, and the weeks dragged wearily by.

Some friend recommended the " Kendal black drop," whose principal ingredient was opium, that soothed his pain like magic. Again and again, when suffering, he at once found relief from this wonderful medicine, until he kept it with him continually. He did not realize the insidious poison in the seemingly harmless narcotic. It was sweet to find rest and wild, beautiful dreams, after paroxysms of pain. His fears and discouragements were soothed away by lovely visions ; and he little realized the foul tempter hid in this angel's disguise. He little dreamed of the iron fetters it was riveting around soul and body. He welcomed the poetic fancies it called up ; but the fiend had tied his hands ere he could weave those visions into form.

Sarah's alarm was becoming unbearable as she saw the fine powers so held in abeyance. Her sister, Edith Southey, had lost her only child early in the summer, and had fled to Sarah for comfort. She was there during Coleridge's illness, and helped to nurse and cheer him. Southey decided to leave Bristol and share Greta Hall with the Coleridges. He saw that Coleridge was too ill to do the writing necessary to maintain his family, and Sarah gladly welcomed their board to help pay her bills. Later they moved their household effects to the unoccupied rooms and shared the rent, and thus, for years, the two families lived together at Greta Hall, which Southey never again left. Southey saw, with stern disapproval, the danger of Coleridge's tampering with the fatal drug. He begged Coleridge to give it up ; but constant rheumatism and neuralgia were a good excuse, and opium, once established as a habit, is a monster only shaken off with untold sufferings of mind and body. Alcohol is a monster that admits no escape from slavery but by incessant struggle ; but opium makes freedom almost impossible.

After some time Coleridge improved in health and was able to resume his journalism ; but the new enemy forbade the steady work of early days, and the lassitude fretted him. He went to see the Wedgwoods and Joseph Cottle at Stowey, and then paid a prolonged visit to his friends, the Lambs.

They fell at once into the old congeniality, and Coleridge's brilliant conversation charmed the literary men who were now Lamb's frequent visitors. Coleridge was a star of the first magnitude among the brilliant galaxy around the table on Wednesday evenings. Philosophy, poetry, religion, ethics, politics, were equally fascinating when handled by Coleridge. He and Lamb were both writing for the papers and some of the magazines. Journalism, now considered an honor, as paving the way to favor and position, in the eighteenth century and even early in our nineteenth century, was a mere trade. Contributors to the reviews and dailies were not favored at social entertainments. Francis Jeffrey and Brougham being writers and journalists, and having their own social positions, did much to overthrow this absurd English prejudice. One would scarcely expect brains to be above par in those days, when a Beau Brummel ruled the fashions and dictated style to court and nobility. He was at the height of his glory and of his intimacy with the Prince of Wales, and was the glass of fashion and the mold of form as he strutted superciliously along Piccadilly in his blue coat, buff waistcoat, and Hessian boots, all fitting the dapper figure like wax. Had he worn scarlet or emerald tights, the dandies of the day would have followed his lead as they did the tip of his hat, cocked to the right, and the height of his bands and neckerchiefs, which must reach the ears.

Most of the Lambs' circle were writers—essayists, journalists, critics, novelists, philosophers—and their fellowship was close and intimate, with their witty host ever stirring their mirth, and guiding the topics away from dangerous ground. It was a trying time politically. The cajoleries of the tyrant Bonaparte blinded many to his real intentions; and discussions about settling his ambitious designs or accepting his overtures caused exciting differences, not only in Parliament, but in every class of society. Lamb's friends were principally Whigs; but when Fox and Grenville so bitterly opposed war, Coleridge and Wordsworth and many of the stanchest Whigs upheld Pitt's policy, and, as the world knows, he staked his reputation upon the necessity of subduing and subjugating the "little Corsican."

This and the "Reform Bill" and the "Poor Laws," in which Rickman and Thomas Poole were so interested, became such exciting subjects that Lamb made a rule of excluding politics from his "Round Table," and it required all his tact and *bonhomie* to keep those pleasant evenings free from the all-absorbing topics, especially after the punch-bowl loosened tongues and heated imaginations.

Alas for the mischief of those frequent convivial evenings with good-fellowship, tobacco, and whisky! It was a day of gambling and drinking. No gathering was complete without cards for money, and no hospitality was considered passable without liquors to excess. So universal was the custom, that "card-money" was always placed upon the snuffers-tray by the guests, until the constant abuse of the custom caused its downfall.

Thackeray has pictured the card-parties and social features of those days among the court circle. The coteries of Holland House and Gore House, it is true, rose to a more intellectual plane than the universal card routs. Charles Lamb's coterie stood between the gambling parties and the *salons*, combining cards and conversation, with a decided predominance of the latter.

If opium was wrecking Coleridge's great powers, tobacco and a too free use of liquor were making Lamb nervous and irritable, and each was inwardly ashamed of his thralldom. Lamb complained freely and frequently of his tyrants. He ridiculed them and himself with his own matchless humor, and said more severe things of his own weakness than any one else had the heart to say of the gentle wag.

But Coleridge was too proud to speak of his conscious deterioration. He could never bear a hint of it, resenting a suspicion of it, especially from his wife or Southey.

Only to Mary Lamb would he speak of his growing infirmity. Her own trouble gave her the right to comfort a fellow-sufferer, and she pitied without criticising. Her Madonna-face, full of pity and sympathy, soothed where another would but wound.

CHAPTER XXIV.

> A grief without a pang, void, dark, and drear,
> A stifled, drowsy, unimpassioned grief,
> Which finds no natural outlet, no relief
> In word, or sigh, or tear."
>
> COLERIDGE.—*Ode to Dejection.*

DESPITE the efforts of Pitt and the War Party, the successes of the English arms, and the Whig element, backed by popular acclamation, decided upon the peace of Amiens in 1802. Great was the rejoicing throughout England at the close of a war which had so impoverished the masses. Taxation for the war had become a constantly increasing burden, and bread and wheat were at fabulous prices. Lloyd's and White's coffee-houses were besieged by rejoicing crowds for the latest bulletins; and parades and processions with banners and placards by day, and lanterns and torches by night, made London festal. The gorgeous illumination, when all London blazed with tallow dips in its windows, and lamps and lanterns of prodigious size and smoking capacity, showed the best intention of throwing all the light upon the subject which could be got out of the means then known.

The Holland House coterie were radiant with their party's success, and powdered dames and stately lords, with powdered hair and queues, mingled with the rabble in witnessing the illuminations and rejoicings. The wax tapers of Piccadilly and Mayfair scarcely outshone the tallow dips; and the enthusiasm of party conquest was equal to the rejoicing over the promised return to cheap bread and lower taxation.

In the Lamb coterie, opinions were greatly divided as to the expediency of this peace: whether it would be outweighed by allowing the aggressive First Consul time to strengthen his outposts unmolested. It required all of Lamb's tact and geniality to keep the hot discussions from becoming personal wrangles.

The suffering and poverty that Coleridge saw around him in the thronged Whitechapel districts, where the poor huddle together like herds of starving beasts, ready to prey upon anything and everything in reach, shocked and depressed him. He talked of it and grieved over it, until Thomas Poole, himself almost a fanatic upon the subject of the Poor Laws, rebuked him.

"Why should you rave so over the poverty of the masses? What have you to do with regulating the expenditures of the rich or the penury of the poor and idle?"

Coleridge's great eyes blazed with passion and pain as he turned to Poole with:

"What have I to do with it? What are my voice and talents given me for if not to serve the needy? Do I not know the tortures of working, yes, slaving for the wretched uncertainty of daily bread? Do not I see my own family needing life's necessaries, whilst these London aristocrats' 'Tear Drips' and their '*Soupirs*' pour into their abundance three times the sum we poor men get for work? Do I not know the bitterness of serving—waiting a chance for an honest article to receive a grudging pittance, whilst these pampered money-bags pocket their hundreds of pounds for some simpering or wailing trash they call 'poetry'? I tell you there is no place for the poor. Look at the hundreds of human animals crowded into Hounsditch in filth and want, until they become murderers, adulterers, and mere beasts, whilst the noble Lords owning the tenements squeeze rent out of their very blood. What does the Government do for them? Are there provisions made for supplying them with work or decent quarters? A paternal Government that exacts corn taxes, meat taxes, and taxes on whatever is produced and consumed crushes instead of upholding its children. Who can see these things and not fight them with tongue and pen?" he asked, pacing up and down the room.

"But you need not assume the responsibility," said Poole. "You have your own needs, your own sickness and suffering to bear; why add the burdens of mankind? It is morbid!"

"Nay, Thomas Poole, you who are working unweariedly for these very poor need not teach me to say, 'Am I my brother's keeper?' You have time and money to give, and you do it nobly; I have but the luxury of praying for them, and writing up their wrongs. If those articles harm me with the powers that be, I have at least done my part with the only means given me."

Poor Coleridge was daily learning the cruel lesson of poverty. He added all these other cares to his own struggle, and grew too discouraged to do even his own part. Discouragement and opium were chaining him, and his muse fled from his captivity.

He returned home, but not for a long stay. Sarah's mournful and reproachful looks and Southey's coldness stung him, and his rheumatic pains drove him to the only sure relief. A prostrating spell of illness made him a helpless victim to his tempter, and when he had sufficiently recovered he fled to Wordsworth's sympathizing household for comfort. Whilst there, Wordsworth insisted upon his accepting one hundred pounds for a visit to the tropics, to try if a warmer climate would not cure his rheumatic troubles, and so help him overcome his opium fiend.

Wordsworth insisted that the money was principally due Coleridge from his part of the "Lyrical Ballads," in which the "Ancient Mariner" and some of his other poems had been included. Joseph Cottle and Thomas Poole had added to the sum, hoping that the change might benefit the man who seemed so rapidly becoming a wreck.

Coleridge afterwards wrote of this period : " My convalescence was of no long continuance, but what then ? the remedy was at hand, and infallible. Alas ! it is with a bitter smile, a laugh of gall and bitterness, that I recall this period of unsuspected delusion, and how I first became aware of the maelstrom, the fatal whirlpool to which I was drawing, just when the current was already beyond my strength to stem." *

His friend, Sir John Stoddart, who was Queen's Advocate at Malta, invited him there. Southey and Sarah and every one believed the climate would help to cure him ; so, after dallying at Thomas Poole's and delaying until April, he sailed. The voyage helped him, and the new scenes brightened his spirits. His

* " Biographia Literaria."

eloquence and culture attracted the notice of the Governor, Sir Alexander Ball, who invited him to be his private secretary. He gladly accepted the position, and for a time all went well; but the intense heat and glare of sun and sand oppressed him. He sent home some money, and having left the Wedgwood annuity to his wife and family, and feeling that they were beyond want with that and the Southeys' help, he wrote cheerfully of his convalescence and position.

He was relieved of the dressing and ceremony that always belong to a public office, especially in the colonies, where the Government dignity is maintained by the magnificence of its officers. His quaint, plain dress, that of an English rustic, with no attempt at fashion, and his simple manners, made him quite a marked man in the little community.

But he was not in harmony with his surroundings; he intensely disliked the noisy Malta.

He was made magistrate, and tried to accommodate himself to the dignified position. But it was terribly irksome, and his heart was too tender to punish offenders. He was no aristocrat, and he was too honest to assume the dress or bearing belonging to his office. His eccentricities were tolerated, and his talents were admired; but he never could be popular; and between his distaste for work, and his old enemy, opium, which again came creeping in, his duties became insupportable. He resigned the secretaryship with its magisterial duties. He accepted a Government commission to Sicily, which he fulfilled satisfactorily, and then went on to Rome. His lethargy and inability to stick to regular occupation drove him forth again, a rudderless ship, drifting, drifting, drifting here and there, indulging his fatal opium habit, and sometimes writing and taking notes for the future poems and books that would never be written.

Again Providence had crossed his untoward fate, and given him a second chance in life. The position and favor that were given him in Malta might have built up character and fortune; but the same nerveless hand that relaxed its hold when the editorship was offered him also dropped this rudder now.

He feasted upon the wondrous ruins, and lived on the memories of the Past that hover around Rome, in the columns, arches, and other grand verifications of history written over its antiquities. He basked in the grandeur of the Coliseum, and shuddered over the persecutions of the early Christians, as he penetrated the Catacombs in those classic scenes, familiar from his studies and wide reading. His wonder and admiration were awakened by the superb churches of that city of temples. He dreamed his dreams of great achievement and noble poems that should atone for these months of *dolce far niente*. His brilliant conversation and information made him a favorite with the poets and artists who haunt Italy.

He met Allston, the American painter and writer, who painted his portrait, and always remembered the dreamy-eyed poet who talked like a god. He also became intimate with Humboldt, whose friendship was of service later. But he could not work, and shame at his idleness, and humiliation at his incapacity, made him shun those to whom he owed duties.

Sarah waited and grieved, month after month, looking for tidings or letters, fearing he was dead. Then hearing from the Stoddarts that he had left Malta, and had not given her or his friends a clue to his whereabouts, she lost faith, at last, and felt that her husband was unworthy of her love. She learned little by little to steel her heart against him. She grew worn and stricken, but held the truant's name above reproach, determined to hope to the last.

Month after month passed with no line or message ! His friends first wondered, then feared. Even his beloved Wordsworth had had no message from him for over a year, nor had Charles Lamb.

They wrote to Malta, and some of their letters followed him and deepened the sting of his accusing conscience. He turned from their loving steadfastness to nurse his own bitter humiliation, that he, Coleridge, the poet, philosopher, preacher—ay, the Christian, was drifting, a rudderless wreck, at the mercy of a deadly foe. The bitterest thought was that his worst enemy was *himself.*

He drove out with insane fury the thoughts of wife, children, home. He dared not go back to them a mere shattered wreck, with little purpose and no courage. He spared not himself ; but they should not share his degradation, nor should they know it. Southey, the worker, who excused neither himself nor others, should he scorn him for this cursed want of purpose ? Wordsworth, the simple, noble interpreter of nature, his dear and trusting friend, should he see all that was lovable in him quenched and dead ? And Lamb—dear, tender Charles Lamb, who was calling for him as for a lost brother, should they all know of his life's failure, and *pity* him ? And Coleridge wept the bitterest tears that a man can shed—tears for his lost manhood, his wasted opportunities. He fled farther and farther from their letters, and at last dared not open those that reached him.   He could not bear these reminders of lost home and friends.

Yet, in this time of his worst misery, Coleridge's life was not given up to shame or debauchery.   The wreck was of spirit and energies.   He controlled and prevented bodily degradation ; but he could not master the paralysis of will and energy caused by opium, and he despised himself for being the slave of the destroyer.

Poor, foolish dreamer, by his silence he caused more pain than if he had confessed the worst.   His wife could have borne his death or anything better than heartless desertion.   She grieved and wearied until at last Charles Lamb heard of his being in Sicily, and sent Sarah word of his safety, which was little better than the other news they feared.   Then, whilst he was drifting around, he was lost to them again.   This time the poor wife grieved no more.   She was neither wife nor widow, and she learned to brace nerves and heart against the throes of lost hope.   She had her children to teach and to live for.   She had a pittance to live upon in the Wedgwood pension, and she could sew for Edith Southey, and help her with her family cares, in return for any assistance from them.

Southey gave help and comfort most generously to her, as to Mary Lovell, and shouldered every burden that came in his way.   But, for the wandering husband and father, he had small pity, and no sympathy.

CHAPTER XXV.

> Possessions vanish and opinions change,
> And passions hold a fluctuating seat ;
> But by the storms of circumstance unshaken,
> And subject neither to eclipse nor wane,
> Duty exists—immutably survives
> For our support, the measures and the forms
> Which an abstract intelligence supplies,
> Whose kingdom is where time and space are not.
>
> WORDSWORTH.—*Excursion.*

WHILE Coleridge was wandering around the Continent, England was moving her men on the chess-board, and stupendous changes were going on.

The Peace Party was overwhelmed when Napoleon proclaimed himself Emperor, and proceeded to become conqueror of the world. Pitt was recalled, and war again raged and filled all minds. Bonaparte's messages to George the Third about crossing the Channel and taking possession of England had awakened a fury of patriotism in the English mind. England's great victories of the Nile and Trafalgar were hailed with wildest enthusiasm. The death of Nelson seemed a terrible price to pay for victory ; for where should another Nelson be found? Great victories in battle always mean sorrow to many stricken hearts ; but here was grief to a nation. Amid the flags and banners of rejoicing were hung the tokens of mourning.

Hilarity and enthusiasm at the " Round Table " were tempered with serious regrets.

" I s-saw Lord N-Nelson on Piccadilly just before he s-sailed, and a finer, nobler looking little w-w-warrior I never beheld. There was a de-de-determination in every step. He could fight for the r-r-right with the arm that was l-l-left," said Lamb.

" The funeral will cost the country a pretty penny," added the impecunious Godwin.

" More taxes and high-pressure," said William Hazlitt, with his customary sneer. " These funeral pageants are a frightful addition to the cost of a victory. I wonder how the 'little Hero' feels at such signal defeats; he is not accustomed to being on the losing side," he added.

" Egad ! we must look out for his revenge," said Rickman ; " a defeat turns Bony into the very devil."

The funeral pageant was perhaps the greatest the world has ever known. William Godwin summoned courage to invite the Lambs and a few other friends to witness it from his front windows.

Now, Godwin's second wife was known to be an Amazon, and upon his first call on Godwin, after the marriage, Charles Lamb had fled precipitately from her sarcasms.

" She's an old c-c-cat, with c-c-claws," he had said upon his return, and he never would divulge the particular form of unpleasantness that had routed him.

On this occasion the dame chose to be gracious ; and between her own children (for she had been a widow with two children) and Mary Wollstonecraft's two little girls and the guests there was quite a merry party to witness the splendid display of marines, cavalry, artillery, nobility, and civic societies, with banners and all their paraphernalia, and the wondrous funeral car, with its columns and plumes and beautiful horses. The procession lasted nearly all day. Mrs. Godwin served a fine luncheon to her guests, and was so gracious that Mary Lamb wondered why Charles had been so afraid of her. They became very friendly, and Mary sometimes visited the Godwins afterwards.

She had felt great sympathy for the lonely "professor," as Lamb always called his serious friend with the great head and shaggy mane, after his interesting wife, Mary Wollstonecraft, had died, leaving him with the new-born babe and her little Fanny Imlay. He and his wife had kept separate homes, that he might not be disturbed by her little Fanny. And when he had moved his possessions to the desolate home where nurses had charge of the motherless babies, Mary had pitied him doubly for these increased cares, and had often gone with Charles to visit the little ones and their father. Fanny Imlay was now a pretty, timid child of twelve, and Mary Godwin a most winning little fairy of eight. Mary loved children, and was glad to renew her acquaintance with these motherless bairns who had found so warm a corner in her heart during their babyhood. She was pleased to see that the reputed tartar seemed so kind to the children ; and as they were not overmuch afraid of her, she must be a reasonably good step-mother, in spite of the many reports of her temper and eccentricities.

Scarcely a month after the death of Nelson, the dandies and fashionables who frequented Piccadilly gathered in throngs at Lloyd's coffee-house, this time to read of defeat upon the great placards.

Napoleon, already in possession of Vienna, had defeated the allies at Austerlitz, and was enjoying the triumphant revenge for Trafalgar that Rickman had predicted. All along the Strand and Holborn the coffee-houses were besieged with excited crowds, and at night one could see groups of men striking their flints and lighting their tinder to read the placards, when the smoking lamps that were meant to light them had blown out in the wind and sleet.

Pitt's rage and disappointment were so intense that he went to bed ill, and in a couple of weeks came whispers that the minister was dying, and then came the shock of his death. There was another great funeral, with military and civic honors, and the great Tory leader was buried in Westminster Abbey, near his illustrious father.

They were stirring times, and the Opposition coterie at Holland House discussed the changes with grave decorum. Pitt, their great opponent, was dead, and Napoleon had gained another victory, followed by treaties for peace! It was an anxious time. Grave debates excluded all lighter interests at the dinners and *salons* of Holland House. Lord John Russell and Lord Lansdowne, Lord Grenville and the whole party of " All the Talents," insisted upon Fox giving up his cherished retirement in the country and returning to the ministry. Lord Grenville and Lord Grey refused to serve without the man who had for so long headed the Liberal party. Poor old George the Third, utterly discouraged by Pitt's death, and the war defeats, and troubles with the last ministry, was obliged to throw down the gantlet at last, and imply a desire for his old enemy's return to the ministry. Fox was called to

London to meet the leaders of his party, and was persuaded, sorely against his will, to serve as Secretary of Foreign Affairs. His literary taste and love of quiet were far dearer to him than ambition.

"Your country needs you in her crisis," wrote Lord Holland, his nephew. "I must repeat to you and for you Lord Nelson's great and last appeal : 'England expects every man to do his duty.' Is it not your duty to serve your party and your country?" His devoted wife added her entreaties, and Charles James Fox again accepted public office after an absence from the ministry of nearly twenty-three years. True, he had served in Parliament several times since, and had warmly upheld all reform and liberal movements, and his wonderful eloquence was always a powerful lever to raise the interests of his party. The abolition of the slave trade, so long battled for by Wilberforce and Thomas Clarkson, Wordsworth and Coleridge's friend, was powerfully aided by Fox, and he continually fought for it during his periods of service in Parliament. But his impatience at the Tory party's restraints and opposition to all Liberal measures, and the King's open enmity, had long made the scholarly retirement of St. Anne's Hill far sweeter than the turmoils of public life. He adored his wife and was only happy in her society, and when his country called him from that calm happiness to the bustle and excitement of London, he almost wept at the sacrifice. Even the charms of Holland House, his dearly loved early home, could not compensate him.

For years Holland House had been the great rallying point of the Liberals. In its stately halls, not only aristocratic politicians assembled to talk over the great questions of the times, but the *literati* of the day met and discussed the latest books and the progress of thought. For centuries Holland House had been a marked spot in the literary world. In Queen Anne's time, Addison had made it the favorite rendezvous of scholars and authors. Pope, Gray, Swift, and all the luminaries of that day shone at its dinners. There the unfortunate Charles the First and his adherents had found ready welcome, and in addition to the place's historic claims, Henry Vassail Fox and his brilliant wife now delighted in making it the pleasantest and most popular house in London. He was a man of scholarly tastes, a statesman of some note, and his writings upon Spanish literature gave him a place among the *literati* of the day. The wits and beauties of the times also assembled at the *salons* of Lady Holland, although the eccentricities of her temper and the sharpness of her satire often caused her fair rivals hours of rage or disquiet. Still, invitations to Holland House were always accepted. Who could refuse the coveted chance to mingle among the most brilliant spirits of London—yes, of the world, for here assembled, also, the famous men of other countries : Lavater, Prince Talleyrand, Prince Metternich, Humboldt, and innumerable distinguished foreigners ; and there were met Rogers and Tom Moore, Lord Byron and Campbell ; and Reynolds, Gainsborough, and all the greatest painters and sculptors also graced those gay scenes.

The house itself was beautiful, with its superb library, and the pictures and elegant ornaments and articles of *vertu* which adorned the drawing-room. The brilliant "gilt room," with its mirrors and myriads of soft waxen tapers, set off well the beauty and vivacity of the guests. Amid statuary and rich tapestries, and grouped tropical plants from the conservatories, the soft flow of conversation and ripples of laughter along the halls and galleries, the silken clinging draperies of the day, and dazzling pearly shoulders and high powdered coiffures (slowly relinquishing their hold since the tax upon hair-powder), made Holland House the pinnacle of London society. And amid these charming scenes, in the stormy days of George the Third and the Regency, one could always find groups and couples discussing the public questions—the Reform Bill, the "Catholic Emancipation" question, and the "Poor Law" bill, and all the interests of the Whig party. The future Prince Regent was a frequent *habitué*, and he and "All the Talents" were too strong an alliance for the poor old King to cope with. He had leaned upon Pitt for so many years, and relied so upon his wisdom and influence whenever his pitiful spells of madness incapacitated him, that he now turned to the compassion of his opposers as he felt his mental forces yielding again to care and disappointment. There the many brilliant speeches of Pitt and Burke and Fox, in Parliament, were discussed, and here Jeffrey and Henry Noon Talfourd were welcomed as wits and writers, when elsewhere aristocrats and fashionables had not learned to recognize talent in literary paths.

Tom Moore, however, a young poetaster of Irish extraction, and young Campbell, the brilliant Scotchman, who was coming into notice by reason of several excellent poems, were invited to the Holland House *salons*, whilst our English poets were withering under the sneers and sarcasms of the "Edinburgh Review," which found some merit in Tom Moore's pretty little songs, in the rising young poet of Edinburgh, and in young Byron. There was a great gulf in those days, as to-day, between the rich and aristocratic and the poor, and only those crossed the chasm who were willing to be patronized. Tom Moore made it the ambition of his life to toady to the lords and ladies of the Holland House coterie, and to be invited to their dinners.

Later, it became his business to follow them around, and sing his ditties to entertain their guests. One has but to read his journal and memoirs to see how all-important were their functions and their smiles. And when Lady Holland occasionally turned her sarcasms upon the obliging poetaster, he was miserable until he had made his peace with her ladyship.

Such aims had no place among our sturdy, independent children of nature. They scorned the pretensions of the rich, and sneered at the pomp and paraphernalia of wealth. Not one of them aspired to having more than a mere competency. If they sought friends, it was for friendship's sake, and because of congeniality in mind and taste. And so the gulf remained.

Some came from the other side across to the whist and tobacco and whisky of Lamb's Wednesday evenings; but our friends remained on the hither side, and were damned as unfashionable by London society.

They could not be tempted across; it would be flinging off the prejudices and principles of a life-time. Both Lamb and Coleridge spoke scornfully of the pomp and glitter of their rivals, whilst their rivals (if such they may be termed) ignored them.

"Ay! there's the rub!" What insult stings so keenly as living forgotten and unnoticed? Pride ever clothes itself with a sneer to cover the nakedness of oblivion ; and the little parties around the whist table, with its cold beef and hot punch, rivaled the wit and wines and dinners of " that Lady Holland mob," as Lamb irreverently termed his—betters. But the little gnat-stings do not harm the great folks upon their heights—and they may ease the gnat of a little superfluous venom.

CHAPTER XXVI.

My soul is sad that I have roamed through life,
Still most a stranger, most with naked heart,
At mine own home and birthplace."
                                        COLERIDGE.

DURING these stirring times of victories, defeats,
and deaths, Coleridge was lingering on in Rome amid
its kaleidoscope of scenes and impressions. The news
of Trafalgar and Austerlitz and of Pitt's death reached
him there when he was charming Allston and Humboldt,
Thorwaldsen, Angelica Kauffmann, and other new
friends with his eloquence. But Humboldt had already
warned him that Napoleon had not forgotten those
letters of his in the "Morning Post" advocating war
upon the "Tyrant of Europe." Hearing that the Consul
never forgot or forgave an enemy, Humboldt had warned
him to leave ere Bonaparte should reach Italy. But
Coleridge had not heeded the warning, believing himself
too insignificant an opponent to be worth the great
Napoleon's notice. It seemed impossible that the busy
First Consul should have seen or remembered the attacks
of an English journalist. But he had miscalculated the
power of the Argus-eyed conqueror to whom in his days
of triumph all things were possible. Soon after this, *
in June, 1806, a Benedictine monk came to his chamber

* " Biographia Literaria."

with a message from no less a person than Pope Pius the Seventh. The Pope, learning of orders from Napoleon for the arrest of Coleridge, procured him a passport from Rome as a Benedictine monk; and upon receiving this direct message Coleridge left Rome in monastic dress, with his visitor, who had provided a carriage and the disguise. Scarcely had he left his apartment when several *gens-d'armes* appeared at the door to arrest him. They were greatly mystified at his escape, as the order had been received but a few hours before.

It was a kind and noble act of the head of a Church that Coleridge had always despised. Coleridge, with all his changes of belief and searchings after truth, had felt but one way towards it. He was utterly intolerant of its trammels and paraphernalia, and never hesitated to express his contempt. Yet the head of this Church had graciously rescued the heretic from his vindictive enemy, and sent him into safety, for the sake of his poems and genius.

The two monks reached Leghorn safely. Coleridge bade a grateful adieu to his protector, and laid aside his sheep's clothing for the disguise of a countryman with vegetables, and in this masquerade costume boarded an American ship bound for England.*

His usual eloquence won the captain's promise of protection, and again the wanderer was cared for by strangers, and kindly guided along his way. He saw and acknowledged the loving Father's care over his erring child, and he humbly and penitently confessed how little he deserved it. He prayed for guidance and mercy, for help to overcome his tempter, and the power

* "Life of Coleridge."—BRANDL.

to begin a new life. They had a terribly rough passage, and poor Coleridge was so ill that he hoped death would release him from the enemy that slept by his side and warmed itself in his bosom. But he lived during fifty-five days of tossing and danger.

Napoleon, hearing that his prey had escaped, sent a French man-of-war after the little American packet with its contraband passenger. The captain insisted upon poor Coleridge throwing all his papers into the sea, so that, if the vessel were captured, nothing of a suspicious character should be found to implicate him or his vessel.

With a heavy heart Coleridge threw his letters and his notes of travel and incidents for future work into the jaws of the all-devouring monster, that hourly threatened to swallow them and their plunging ship.

So, shorn of all evidence of his two years' work, and without the foundation for future poems, Coleridge landed in England, August, 1806, friendless, poor, and despondent, feeling that he had been saved from a French prison ; from shipwreck at sea ; from illness almost unto death—for what ?

He hunted up Lamb, who welcomed him joyfully, and made much of him.

Mary received him as a loving sister receives a sick brother, and comforted him and coddled him with the gruels and teas that such souls love to administer. The poor homeless fellow felt that life still held some comforts. Charles wrote that Coleridge had come home as brilliant and lovable as ever—" an archangel slightly damaged." *

He was homeless—worse than homeless ; because,

* " Letters of Charles Lamb."—AINGER.

having a home and family, he had deserted them.   He felt unfit to claim the deserted fireside and the dishonored wife.   But his heart yearned for them; the patient, wronged woman was still dear to him; the little daughter was growing beyond his memories of the tiny baby, and the little sons were strangers to their father.   He went first to Wordsworth, and found floods of sympathy and tenderness.   They had not suffered by his neglect and absence, and it is easy to forgive where there is no personal wrong.

Wordsworth read him "The Prelude," which he had dedicated to the absent Coleridge.   The noble poem stirred him to the depths of his soul.   He wept over his own aimless and misspent years.   He wept in sympathy with the noble thoughts and earnest purpose of his friend.   And those tears of remorse and repentance healed the wounded heart, and stirred the benumbed will into action.

He was inspired again by the wine of his friend's faith in him, and sympathy that was not pity; and he wrote to Wordsworth:

> "O Great Bard,
> Ere yet that last strain, dying, awed the air,
> With steadfast eye I viewed thee in the choir
> Of ever enduring men. . . .
> Ah! as I listened with a heart forlorn,
> The pulses of my being beat anew."

And Wordsworth wrote of Coleridge, referring to this sad time of his return:

> " Ah! piteous sight it was to see this man
> When he came back to us a withered flower,
> Or like a sinful creature
> Would he sit, and without strength or power
> Look at the common grass from hour to hour."

He longed for a sight of his children. They were as dear to him as other little ones to happier fathers' hearts. Yet he dreaded to face his wife, and see her reproaches for those months, yes, years, of silence.

"I love them, yet I must leave them all; my pretty, pretty birdling, with her sweet baby ways, has forgotten her father, and I will not shame her and my bonny boys with the daily sight of my wrecked life. If I ever gain the mastery over my devil, I can go to them with thankfulness and joy."

But as he said it with tears, he heaved such a sigh that Wordsworth was touched to his heart's core, and Mary and Dorothy sobbed outright.

Here, and here only, Coleridge felt he was understood; and under Wordsworth's roof at Allan Bank he felt at home.

The two poets worked the pretty garden, and dug and planted and were happy. Allan Bank was a bower of roses and sweet, old-fashioned flowers, and Mary Wordsworth was a sweet, loving, trusting woman who clung tenderly to her husband, but never let the twining tendrils hamper the spreading boughs, as do so many loving but selfish wives. As tender wife and mother, she claimed gladly her share of her poet's time and attention, and gave him such restful repose that he often marveled at her influence and the secret of her strength.

"So might poor Sarah have been if I had been as patient and tender as Wordsworth," thought Coleridge. "She loved me as truly and watched me as faithfully, but my unfortunate habits made her wretched."

Again the demon tempted him to forget all, in the

wild, blissful fool-dreams where tropical jungles with gay birds singing on every bough changed to vast halls and pillared palaces whose exquisite orchestras lulled his senses, and slaves and houris bowed in homage before him. He was the ruler and god in this fantastic dreamland, and the shame of his wasted life and enchained powers was utterly forgotten. What wonder that the golden enthrallment bound him fast, when it offered not only delights beyond conception, but Lethe for all earthly cares and disappointments.

Soon after Coleridge went to visit Thomas Poole at Stowey, and there met De Quincy, who had long admired Coleridge's poems and sought this opportunity to pay grateful homage to the poet. Coleridge's heart was touched; he accepted the homage. It lifted him to his proper place, and he conversed with De Quincy "like one inspired." De Quincy listened and wondered, and seeing his new friend's hopelessness and sadness behind the gayety, wondered the more. He spoke of taking laudanum for face-ache, and this roused Coleridge to a sense of his new friend's danger. He besought him in terror to let the poison alone. He confessed his own misery.

"Shun opium as you would the devil," he said, laying his hand on his young friend's shoulder. "It is the devil's own emissary, and you are *helpless* before it. Let it alone, I implore you."

De Quincy wondered at his earnestness, not knowing the secret of his life. In after years when he, himself, was in the toils of the beast, he remembered Coleridge's warnings.

De Quincy, finding his idol so depressed, and believing that debt and want were the sole cause, gave Joseph

Cottle £300 for Coleridge, stipulating entire secrecy as to the donor.

Although his prayers for deliverance from his tempter seemed unanswered, still, in his worst days of need, help came from some unexpected source to lift his soul from its depths of despair. How often kind friends had been led to help this song-bird with the broken wing !

The Wedgwoods had assisted him for years; Joseph Cottle and Thomas Poole were ever ready to relieve him in a day of need; and Wordsworth and Lamb were always as brothers, glad to share their small earnings with him. Southey had always taken up the burden of family cares when Coleridge was unable to carry it alone; and now a stranger had sent him a gift which would pay the debts that oppressed him, and enable him to go less like a beggar to his neglected wife.

Sarah's letters assured him of a welcome to Greta Hall, and at last he turned his steps homeward.

The joy of seeing them was great, but it was so mingled with pain that it was but a trying ordeal to all. Should the fatted calf be killed for the wanderer who had sent no messages during his long absence, and who lingered to receive the home greetings last of all ? Sarah felt the hurt more than the joy of his return, and he seemed little better than when he left. He was terribly restless and depressed and quite unable to work, and the reproach of Southey's energy and cheerful labor haunted him. He saw condemnation in their glances; he felt the contrast between him and his brother-in-law; and despair at his lost powers drove him forth to see what he could find to do in London, to earn a living and brace his will to overcome his cravings for opium.

He applied to Stewart for a position upon the "Post" and "Courier," whose editorship he had declined a few years before. Stewart found him somewhat unreliable about regular work, and he was treated as men on the down-hill of life usually are. What he wrote was accepted or rejected at will, and delayed to suit the convenience of editors and printers, and changed and dissected to fit their purposes. This discouraged and enraged him, yet what could he do? He must take what he could get. They gave him an attic-room near the great noisy printing-press, and here Coleridge wrote faithfully five or six hours daily—or nightly—as best suited his shattered powers. It was maddening and utterly discouraging to find that much of his most careful work was cast ruthlessly aside, because the papers were so filled with war and parliamentary matter that they could not place it.

Thomas Poole was also in London working with Thomas Clarkson and Wilberforce for the abolition of slavery. They lectured, wrote, and labored faithfully for this cause of humanity. Pitt had promised help ; but the war and the country's greater needs had kept crowding the Abolition bill out. Yet now that Pitt was dead, Charles Fox and his party also promised to attend to the bill. Again foreign interests crowded this important home reform out, and the House of Lords was slow to see the necessity and advantage, and even the possibility, of producing sugar, coffee, and tobacco without slave labor. They challenged the advocates of the bill to give up those luxuries if their consciences would not permit them to enjoy the fruits of slave labor. Poole, Clarkson, and many of the Society of Friends actually gave up sugar, snuff, tobacco, and all the products of slave labor, in token of their earnestness. Poor Poole yielded his snuff and pipe most reluctantly ; for they were deeply-rooted habits of his quiet bachelor life.

Lamb and Coleridge, both warm advocates of the bill, looked with admiration and wonder at their friends, whose strength of mind and purpose enabled them to make such sacrifices for their cause.

Lamb's Wednesday evenings were as full of excitement and discussion as Holland House. Rickman was terribly in earnest in his efforts to advance the bill in the House of Commons, where he was clerk. He brought the latest news of its progress, and of the parliamentary interests, and of the " Poor Laws Reform," which was equally dear to our friends. As the " Round Table " was undivided upon these interests, the arguments were principally upon one side of the question ; but great enthusiasm and eagerness were expressed in unmeasured terms, and Coleridge went to his attic-room and wrote page after page of burning eloquence in favor of these bills. It was exasperating to have his work line the paper basket when his cause needed all the championship it could get.

CHAPTER XXVII.

> The mighty chiefs sleep side by side.
> Drop upon Fox's grave the tear,
> 'Twill trickle to his rival's bier.
> O'er Pitt's the mournful requiem sound,
> And Fox's shall the notes rebound.
> The solemn echo seems to cry—
> " Here let their discord with them die.
> Speak not for those a separate doom
> Whom Fate made brothers in the tomb;
> But search the land of living men,
> Where wilt thou find their like again ? "
>
> WALTER SCOTT.

ANOTHER bomb fell in the rival camps. Charles James Fox had been taken ill in the midst of earnest work to gain an advantageous peace with the French Consul. The coalition parliament of " All the Talents " was paralyzed on receiving tidings of his death. He who from boyhood had been a power to move and carry on the reforms of the Liberals died but five months after his rival, Pitt.

Lord Grey and Lord Grenville, who but a few months before had refused to serve in the ministry without the co-operation of the great Whig leader, were now forced to bear the brunt alone. Holland House and the " Round Table " of Mitre Court were alike stricken, and but one topic filled men's minds—the death of one who for more than thirty years had been their oracle. Yet this man was but fifty-eight years of age.

His country gave him a fine public funeral, and he was laid in Westminster Abbey, close beside his life-long rival. They, whose lives were spent in antagonism, in their country's service, shared the same bed in the halls of the leveler, Death.

His successor, Lord Howick, introduced the bill that continued to be a bone of contention for many years—the "Catholic Emancipation Bill." The Liberals fought hard to remove the disabilities of the Roman Catholics, and enable them to hold public office. The King and his party so objected, that Lord Grenville and his ministry resigned after first passing the "Bill for the Abolition of the Slave Trade."

Our friends threw in all their efforts to carry this bill. Lord Grenville and his party, seeing their days were numbered, forced it to an issue, and Thomas Poole * and Clarkson sat up all night to await the result. Poole celebrated the victory by taking a vigorous pinch of snuff and smoking a "pipe of peace."

Thomas Clarkson and our friends, the poets, met at Charles Lamb's, and spent an evening in wild enthusiasm at the success of their long-contested cause.

Rickman, Francis Jeffrey, Talfourd, Wm. Hazlitt, Thomas Poole, Mr. Godwin, Captain Burney, Coleridge, and Wordsworth from his quiet hermitage among the Lakes, all met in Mitre Court upon that eventful Wednesday, and drank to the success of freedom, and the prosperity of England and her colonies.

During this winter Coleridge was invited to deliver a course of lectures before the Royal Society. He

* "Life of Thomas Poole and his Friends."

hesitated, knowing his weakness, and the small reliance to be placed upon himself for regular work. Sir Humphry Davy insisted, and Lamb begged his friend to undertake the task—so light a one to a man whose universal reading made him so familiar with all literary subjects. He consented, and Lamb took him home, to watch over and guide him during the time of the lectures and remind him of the hours and subjects. Mary watched him like a mother, providing the regular meals and strengthening food, so necessary to restore shattered nerves to healthy action.

These lectures upon " The Fine Arts " were a great success. Albemarle Street was thronged with the carriages of the *élite* of London. As Coleridge stood before them, with the light of genius illumining the great gray eyes, with its stamp upon the broad brow, and his wonderful eloquence pouring almost faster than the deep, rich tones could utter it, his audience were carried away. He became the fashion ; his lectures were discussed in every drawing-room, and his poems were read and quoted. The poet who had been so long secluded amid his lakes and mountains, and who had come to his garret-room in London to earn a scanty living with his pen, became the oracle of the fashionable world. They would have fêted and flattered him if he had responded to their call.

But the fluttering of the butterflies was not to his taste, and moreover the strain upon him, of the regular hours and abstinence from his poison, was greater than any one but his friend Lamb knew.

He and Mary attended the lectures, and saw, with pardonable pride, Lord and Lady Holland and their friends, and the young Byron and others of the best known people of London, listening with rapt attention to Coleridge's utterances. They were pleased with the congratulations and demonstrations of delight that greeted him after the lectures. It was well worth their anxious watching and careful guarding of the sick soul from its tyrant. But the old enemy was clamoring for admittance, and Lamb and Mary watched and entertained him by day and often far into the night, fearing he might open the door to his tempter. They gave him their tenderest care to the very last of the lectures, and felt fully repaid. What he could yet do if he could free himself from opium was proved to Coleridge. And the £150 which he received greatly encouraged him. But the strain reacted upon poor Mary Lamb. She fell into a stupor from which Charles could only rouse her by sudden and almost violent maneuvers. The brother and sister knew what would follow the preliminary attack—that in a few hours she would be unconscious of her friends and surroundings and live in some wild dream of court life or historic scenes. So Mary put on the strait-jacket, which was always kept in readiness, and with sorrowful tears they walked along the New River, and past the pretty town of Islington, to the asylum, where she remained for six weeks.

Charles returned to his home, where Coleridge had already yielded to his tempter, and was lying in the wild-eyed stupor of his opium dreams. For weeks Charles watched his friend, who was paying for the long strain of the previous weeks in misery and sleepless wretchedness.

Faithfully Lamb went to his daily tasks at India House, from wakeful, trying nights with Coleridge, until his own nerves could no longer bear the strain. Reluctantly he let Coleridge return to the miserable garret over the printing-presses of the "Courier" office, and ran off to Cambridge for a short rest in the companionship of his dear friend Thomas Manning.

CHAPTER XXVIII.

The Poets—who, on earth have made us heirs
Of truth and pure delight, by heavenly lays !
Oh ! might my name be numbered among theirs,
Then gladly would I end my mortal days.
WORDSWORTH.

TOWARDS spring, Sir Humphry Davy insisted upon Coleridge delivering a second course of lectures. The last course had been a great success, and the Royal Society wanted to engage the popular lecturer again.

Coleridge, as before, shrank from the ordeal, fearing to trust himself. But again his friends insisted and persuaded, reminding him of his brilliant success. He reluctantly yielded to their entreaties.

The hour for the first lecture came. Coleridge was not there. The hall was crowded, but the tardy lecturer did not appear. A messenger was hastily sent to his room, and found him in a stupor, with staring eyes, baked lips, and incoherent speech.

Sir Humphry announced that the lecture would be postponed on account of " sudden illness " of the lecturer. The disappointed audience was sympathetic, and hoped he would be well enough for the next week's lecture.

The unmelodious buzzing and cawing of a collection of human beings took a minor tone, and there were everywhere expressions of the greatest interest in the unfortunate sufferer, whom they supposed to be simply attacked by an acute illness.

Lamb hastened to his friend's room and was shocked and indignant.

" How d-d-dare you throw away your last chance th- th-thus? You know this is the f-f-foundation for a new life f-f-for you! " he exclaimed, despairingly. " Oh, Esteecee! oh, my friend! " he pleaded, " d-d-do make another effort! You d-d-did so well last winter. Do f-f-fight against your w-w-weakness."

" I cannot, I cannot," sobbed Coleridge. " I could even now charm a roomful of people, yet I *cannot* break my fetters! "

" You c-can, and you sh-sh-shall! " exclaimed Lamb, and he fell upon his knees, Coleridge following his example. The two friends wrestled in prayer, until a great calm fell upon Coleridge, and he felt he was strengthened against his weakness.

The prayerful spirit lasted, and he earnestly prepared his lectures, and when the day came he poured out his wondrous eloquence as before. He pictured Shakespeare and his times, and quoted from him, commenting and expounding, until his spellbound audience almost feared to breathe for fear of losing a word. He really looked ill and pale, and his mouth was parched, yet this scarcely interfered with the man's eloquence.

Samuel Rogers invited Coleridge and Lamb to a poets' dinner, as Wordsworth was visiting him at the time. Tom Moore and Lord Byron were also at the dinner. Rogers and Wordsworth had been friends for some time, and the rich poet was fond of gathering his brother poets around him, although his sharp tongue would sometimes make keen thrusts at his friends' peculiarities.

Coleridge was glad to measure swords with the author of "Pleasures of Memory." In parrying some of Rogers' thrusts, he was more like his old self than he had seemed for years. But Lamb was rather overwhelmed by the gilt and glitter of his surroundings. He said to Rickman, afterwards :

" The silver plate and l-l-lights d-d-dazzled me. I f-f-felt as though I had stumbled into the B-B-Bank of England. And the s-s-servants, those stately gentlemen in gold lace and calves, that were f-f-forever changing the plates and handing d-d-dishes,—I w-wanted to apologize for the endless trouble I was g-giving. Their great b-b-bulk and s-s-solemn silence g-gave me a Liliputian feeling ; they s-seemed so vastly aldermanic. Rogers is used to this sort of thing ; and T-Tom Moore and B-B-Byron and the rest of that s-s-set take it very philosophically. B-b-but it sp-sp-spoiled my appetite."

At this dinner the poets freely discussed some young writers who were finding favor with the London world. Thomas Campbell, the young Scotchman who had carried off all the University honors at Glasgow, had written " The Soldier's Dream " and " Hohenlinden ; " and lately his " Pleasures of Hope " had attracted much notice.

Rogers, with his usual acerbity, said, in discussing him : " He is a fine stripling and has a touch of true poetic afflatus ; but he carries his head in the clouds. His ' Rainbow ' is a fine piece of poetic diction ; but the jangle of ' Lord Ullin's Daughter ' might have come from a school-boy."

" I cannot understand his popularity, nor why that yarn-spinner, Walter Scott, wins such applause for his pretty fancies," said Wordsworth. . . . "' Blackwood's ' and the ' Edinburgh Review ' laud these young coxcombs to the heavens, while they treat my sonnets and descriptions of my native woodlands with scorn ! I have made no reply to their abuse ; but when I see the blunders of those who profess to be critics of English poetry, I confess I hold the critics of to-day as the veriest penny-a-liners, who truckle to aristocrats and bow to the passing fashion," added Wordsworth, hotly.

Lamb and Coleridge looked with some alarm at Rogers during this tirade against his friends Jeffrey and Henry Brougham of the " Edinburgh Review."

But Rogers let the thrust pass, only saying :

" There is a blindness that pays better than using a microscope upon the wrong object. They soon found that I could hit back, when they commenced tearing me to pieces, and I have since found the critics very courteous."

" They certainly could find little to sharpen their l-lancets upon in the ' P-pleasures of Memory,' " said Lamb. " For m-more elegant English and m-m-more beautiful thoughts seldom m-m-meet us in these days."

" I thank you, friend Lamb, for your kind opinion. The appreciation of a man of letters is not to be despised. I can fully return the compliment upon certain articles in the ' Morning Post ' and the magazines which I am pleased to learn are yours," said Rogers. " We were speaking of them at Lady Holland's the other day, and you will find yourself famous some time.

Though it is seldom one in an unknown set becomes an oracle in London," he added.

Charles Lamb's face was a study during this somewhat modified praise. His fine eyes beamed, and a flush rose upon his olive cheek, at the unexpected commendation. But at the snobbish turn to the compliment, he said, with one of his winning smiles: " Far be it from me to c-c-claim kinship with the L-L-London aristocracy. I leave that to those whose s-s-silver spoon was b-born with them. But for g-genius, such as our L-L-Lake poets p-p-possess, not London or its p-p-palaces can elevate it. It sh-sh-shines, and all the world will see, after these earth d-d-damps are cleared away. The L-L-London critics and *l-l-literati* cannot quench or make the r-r-radiance of true g-g-genius."

" Bravo ! " cried Rogers, turning to Wordsworth and Coleridge, with a smile rare to his cynical face. " I believe the champion is right. I have found genuine delight in ' The Ancient Mariner,' and am most anxious to hear ' Christabel,' which Talfourd and Wm. Hazlitt, who sometimes breakfast with me, think quite remarkable."

" Could you not recite it ? " said Lamb, looking pleadingly at Coleridge ; Rogers and the others added their requests, and Coleridge, with heightened flash in the luminous gray eyes, commenced :

> " The night is chill, the cloud is gray,
> 'Tis a month before the month of May ;
> And the spring comes slowly up this way."

The weird story and exquisite descriptions held the listeners spellbound, as with radiant eye and flushed cheek Coleridge recited it in his rich tones, and the hints of Geraldine's strange origin and influence seemed doubly mystical when told in Coleridge's dramatic way. The spell upon Sir Leoline was growing exciting; Rogers' face showed its effect on him. But when the climax was reached, and the loving father and child were being parted by the deadly spell—so weird, yet so resembling mere magnetic influence—Rogers cried: " Admirable! splendid ! "

Then, as Coleridge stopped, he said: " Well, finish it ! finish it ! Did she succeed—the snake-woman, so like her sisters of to-day ? "

" That is all I have completed," said Coleridge, looking somewhat confused.

" What ! have you left that glorious poem incomplete ? " asked Rogers, in amazement. " Sit down this night. and finish it. It will make your fortune."

" My fortune ! " thundered Coleridge scornfully. " Do you find a muse can be won by gold or power? Nay ! when I court the dainty sprite, I feel 'tis holy ground, and I would fain put off my shoes, and kneel as to a goddess."

" Pish ! a goddess ! A fine quill, and a quiet ingleside, with an ounce of calm determination, will better conquer your goddess," sneered Rogers. " But whether you clip her wings, or woo her, you must finish this inscription—before others steal the fancy," he added, with a sardonic smile.

" Walter Scott has already poached upon my premises and bagged my metre," said Coleridge. " But when I feel the inner voice calling me, I shall complete ' Christabel,'—and not before," he added, glaring at Lamb, who had so often urged the same thing.

" You are right, Coleridge; do not force your muse,

only listen to her when she speaks, " said Wordsworth.

Rogers uttered a scornful " Umph !" and the talk
drifted into other channels. Tom Moore and the young
Byron had not ventured into the discussion of the older
men ; but they had listened attentively. Byron's dark
eyes flashed sympathetically at Coleridge's reply ; and
Tom Moore knew better than to say aught contrary to
the opinion of his rather difficult patron, Rogers.

In the safe chronicles of his note-book he wrote that
evening : " Dined with Rogers—old cock unusually
gracious to a set of poetasters. Some heated discussion
about the muse, in which Rogers was rather quenched by
a long, lank, spectacled poet, named Wordsworth, who
has written some prosy stuff on clouds, mountains, etc.
Note.—Must look up his writings—the critics have killed
them. His friend, Coleridge, is a queer chap, who
lectured at R. S. and seemed likely to capture society,
but failed afterwards for some reason. He is one of
those idealists who takes poetry and life hard. Queer
little chap with droll stammer, named Lamb, actually
struck spurs with the game-cock, and came off—second
best. Had a dig and struck back. One meets strange
people at Rogers'. *Mem.*—Must describe scene to
Lady Holland."

CHAPTER XXIX.

THE HISSED DRAMA.—HOPES AND FEARS.

The tenets which distinguished our society (of damned authors), and which every man among us is bound to hold for gospel, are : " That the public or mob in all ages have been a set of blind, deaf, obstinate, senseless, illiterate savages. That no man of genius in his senses would be ambitious of pleasing such a capricious, ungrateful rabble. That the only legitimate end of writing for them is to pick their pockets; and that failing, we are at full liberty to vilify them and abuse them as much as ever we think fit. . . . . That the terms ' courteous reader' and ' candid critic, ' having given rise to false notions . . . should be forever abolished, etc., etc."

CHARLES LAMB.—Essay on Hissing.

LAMB had no such scruples as Coleridge about courting his muse. He had been scribbling poems, essays, sketches, scraps, yes, even poems, for the London magazines, and the " Daily Courier," and any paper that would pay him. He dotted down his fun and fancies upon bill-heads and letter-backs, and even upon bits of wrapping paper saved from parcels; for Charles and Mary were frugal people, and wasted nothing. He was too glad to add a few shillings to their empty coffers to be fastidious about his subject. But whatever he wrote was in a style so entirely unique, that his scribblings found a ready market where his friend's deeper and more serious articles were rejected or forgotten.

He had written a farce which he called " Mr. H.,"
and had given it to Charles Kemble, hoping he would
play it at Drury Lane. But the Kembles were in a
world of trouble over the debts and expenses of the
theater, and the farce was thrust aside and forgotten.

Meantime Mary Lamb's many illnesses and flights to
the asylum had so drained their scanty income, that
the India-House clerk determined to jog Kemble's
memory about " Mr. H."

Mr. Kemble received this quaint little message :

" Dear Kemble,

" ' Mr. H.' has been in a trance these twelve months, in
the custody of one Charles Kemble, of Newman Street.
His friends and relatives being uneasy at his long
absence, desire information as to his condition. We
hope he is improving, and have reason to think that
the long continuance may augur a favorable result.

" Yours very sincerely,

" Charles Lamb & Co."

Kemble, feeling rather ashamed of his delinquency
regarding his friend's play, decided to have it brought
out. It was carefully studied and well placed upon the
boards, the *clacqueurs* were in readiness, and tickets
were sent to the Lambs and a certain number of their
friends.

Charles and Mary had confidently counted upon its
success, and Lamb had written very hopefully to Thomas
Manning and others of the many uses he would find
for the hundred pounds he expected to receive from it.

With all an author's pride in his work, and nervous-
ness over its first appearance, Lamb with Mary pro-

ceeded early to the theater and proudly took the conspicuous places reserved for them in the pit. Mary looked as gentle and placid as ever, yet she could not conceal her admiration for her gifted brother; and Charles's brown eyes beamed upon the audience—*his* audience. True, it was but the afterpiece. But they scarcely knew what the main play was, so excited were they over their first appearance in public. The prologue was widely applauded, as it deserved. Lamb's friends turned to him, and the applause lasted until he was forced to bow his recognition of the honor. Cheers filled the building. From pit to gallery, all was excitement. But as the play progressed, from the pit, where the link-boys and coachmen assembled in those days, certain ominous growls fell upon the ears. Shouts of " Stop it ! " " Smother that out ! " " Where's the fun ? " sent cold chills down our friends' backs. The *clacqueurs* clapped vigorously at every possible point; but audible yawns and hisses fell like hot bullets upon actors and audience.

It was useless for the friends of the play to applaud " Mr. H.'s " rather heavy fun. The louder they clapped, the louder grew the groans. Lamb glanced at Mary, fearing for her nerves, and, smiling cheerily, as a fresh burst of hisses arose, he joined in the horrid din, and then said, " Well, Bridget, ' Mr. H.' is a lumbering f-fool, and I'll have the s-s-satisfaction of being the f-f-first author who has d-d-damned his own play. And b-by Heavens! it d-d-deserves it ! "

Poor Mary's tears were slowly rolling down her cheeks, and without waiting for further demonstrations, the doomed author and his sister slipped out of the theater.

" Oh, brother, how awful those hisses were," sobbed Mary; " I could only think of a den of snakes."

" Pooh, P-Polly ! don't take it so to heart," said Lamb, smiling grimly at his defeat. " It is b-b-better to be a d-d-damned author than a d-d-damned fool. An author can t-t-try again, but a f-f-fool has no chance at all."

Nevertheless his letter to Manning, describing the impression of those hisses, and his essay on " Hissing at Theaters," written years afterwards, showed how deep was the sting.

To Thomas Manning he wrote :

" DEAR MANNING,—I suppose you know my farce was damned. The noise still rings in my ears ! Were you ever in the pillory—being damned is something like that. . . . . In general . . . . my spirits are pretty good ; but I have my depressions, black as a smith's beard—Vulcan—Stygian. At such times I have recourse to my pipe, which is like not being home to a dun. He comes again with tenfold bitterness next day. . . . So I go creeping on since I was lamed with that cursed fall from the top of Drury Lane Theater into the pit, something more than a year ago ! " *

This was written about a week afterwards, yet his quaint way of expressing the weariness of the disappointment was understood by his friend. He also wrote : " That hiss was like mad geese with noisy unction, like bears, mows, mops, like apes, sometimes snakes, that hissed me into madness. 'Twas like Anthony's Temptations. Mercy on us, that God should give His favorite children, men, mouths to speak with,

* " Letters of Charles Lamb."—AINGER.

to discourse rationally, to promise smoothly, to flatter agreeably, to encourage warmly, to sing with, to drink with, to kiss with, and that they should turn them into mouths of adders, bears, wolves, hyenas, to hiss like tempests and emit breath.... like distillation of aspic poison ; to asperse and vilify the innocent labors of their fellow-creatures, who are desirous to please them. Heaven be pleased to make their breath stink and the teeth rot out of them all!   Make them a reproach to all that pass by them, to loll out their tongues at them ! ' Blind moths !' as Milton somewhere calls them . . . .

"Brahm's singing bewitched me! I follow him as the boys followed Tom the piper. He cures me of melancholy as David cured Saul ; but I don't throw stones at him as Saul did at David in payment.

"I was insensible to music until he gave me a new sense. . . .

Brahm's singing, when impassioned, is finer than Mrs. Siddons' or Mr. Kemble's acting. . . . Coleridge delivered two lectures, but was sick, and omitted the other two.   He sits up two pairs of stairs, at the ' Courier ' Office, and receives visitors."

Thus did he ease his heart, by pouring out the pent-up wrath and disgust to his sympathizing friend.   And he let the whip of his sarcasm fly, in the essay that pictures the various serpent-hisses of critics and audience. "The common English snakes of the auditory, who, having no critical venom in themselves, stay till they hear others hiss, and then join in for company. . . The Rattlesnake—your obstreperous talking critics— the hiss always originates with these. . . . The Whip-snake—he that lashes the poor author the next day in

"* Letters of Charles Lamb."—AINGER.

the newspapers. . . . The Deaf-Adder—that portion of the spectators who, not finding the first act of a piece answer to their preconceived notions, positively thrust their fingers in their ears, etc. As the degree of malignancy in people vary according as they have more or less of the Old Serpent (the father of hisses) in their composition."*

As "Mr. H." failed, and that hope perished, Charles and Mary tried to think of some new scheme for adding to their slender means.

Mary looked up from her writing one evening, as Charles came in from India House. "Brother! I have an idea."

"Well, write it d-d-down, Polly; you may never f-f-find another," he said, lovingly pinching her ear.

"I am going to write some stories," she said, flushing, and looking anxiously into his eyes.

"Whew! And after they are written, who will p-p-publish them?" he asked.

"I have attended to that part first," she answered, proudly. "Mr. Godwin wants some children's stories from Shakespeare, and I have promised to do it, and I have already written 'The Merchant of Venice,'" she said, holding a rather scratchy-looking manuscript up to his astonished gaze.

"W-well done, little w-w-woman, let me be s-silent partner."

And together the two wrote the charming "Shakespearean Tales" that have been the classic treasures of little ones ever since the year that "Mr. H." was damned.

Mary also wrote "Mrs. Leicester's School," a pretty

* "Essays of Elia."—On Hissing in Theaters.

fancy which still holds its place in the world. This unpretentious work of Mary Lamb, assisted by her brother, brought them £200. But her satisfaction in thus being able to add her share to their income was dashed to the ground by her old enemy, that crept in upon her at all times and seasons.

Among the many friends who frequented the Lambs' hospitable rooms was William Hazlitt, the critic and satirist. Hazlitt always found, in the Lambs, the restful friendship his perturbed spirit craved. There he could lash the politicians of the day, or extol the despised Napoleon with unchecked freedom, only rousing a smile or witticism from the impartial Lamb.

Another friend was Sarah Stoddart, a bright, wayward girl, sister of John Stoddart, Queen's Advocate at Malta, who had lately been knighted. Sarah was always in some love-scrape. She used her bright eyes with too effective power, and, like many another coquette, complained that her friends always turned lovers, and so deprived her of their society by getting themselves rejected. To her surprise, the bright-eyed, witty brother of her friend Mary Lamb never succumbed to her charms. Despite her long visits and quick repartee to his incessant puns, he showed but a brotherly interest in Miss Sarah, which made his friendship the more piquant.

But among the many visitors at Mitre Court, on those pleasant Wednesday evenings, the moody, brilliant Hazlitt made the deepest impression upon her susceptible heart. Lamb watched the increasing friendliness between the two with much amusement and some alarm, not knowing whether this flirtation was mere coquetry or something more serious.

Mary also watched the course of affairs with keen interest. She had long been in Sarah's confidence, and had sympathized deeply in several tangled love troubles. Although Mary knew that lovers and marriage could never be factors in her own life, she had a woman's relish for the romantic, and a warm sympathy for the hopes and fears that accompanied the love episodes in the lives of her friends. They knew just where to go for advice and help in their troubles, and the demure, soft-eyed woman, who dared never think of appropriating man's love for herself, in her blighted life kept her heart warm and young by sharing her friends' hopes and desires.

Charles determined to save Hazlitt an irrevocable mistake, if his evident admiration were not returned. So one day, after an unusually pleasant evening, he said to their guest :

" Well, Sarah, the constant errands of Mr. Hazlitt after b-books, etc., etc., etc., are a new ph-ph-phase of his character. He is always espousing lost causes and g-g-getting himself into d-d-difficulties—has a mania for being on the wrong s-s-side of everything, and trying to wrench it r-r-right-side-out. I hope he is not becoming interested in another f-f-fatality ? " he asked, looking seriously at the blushing girl.

" How do I know what Mr. Hazlitt is doing ? " she asked, looking guiltily at Mary. " Has he time to spare from his lost illusions for any other subject ? "

" He s-s-seems to find ample t-t-time ; I hope he is not p-p-pursuing another *ignis fatuus*," he replied.

" I hope not, if he is not able to take better care of himself than you seem to fear," said Sarah, laughing.

Since her friends thought the matter so serious with

Hazlitt, the warning made her look more carefully into her own heart. She really did not know how to answer her self-questioning. She had seen enough of his cynicism and impetuosity to fear a life-union with so violent a man. Yet she admired him more than any one she knew. She disliked his moody spells, yet she found that she held the magic key to unlock the closed doors of his heart. She wavered, and we all know when a woman wavers she is lost.

CHAPTER XXX.

And now, beloved Stowey! I behold
Thy church-tower, and, methinks, the four huge elms
Clustering, which mark the mansion of my friend,
And close behind them, hidden from my view,
Is my own lowly cottage. . . .
My spirit shall revisit thee, dear cot—
Thy jasmine and thy window-peeping rose,
And myrtles fearless of the mild sea-air.
And I shall sigh fond wishes, sweet abode!
Ah,—had none greater! And that all had such
It might be so,—but the time is not yet.
Speed it, O Father! let Thy kingdom come!

COLERIDGE.

AFTER his Shakespeare and Milton lectures, Coleridge had fled from London to Grasmere, where Wordsworth and Dorothy warmly welcomed him. Sarah, hearing that her husband was at Wordsworth's, came also, and spent some days there, hoping to woo her wanderer back to his deserted home.

But Coleridge was not ready to settle down at Keswick, under Southey's reproachful eye. He shrank from the implied reproof in Southey's incessant literary toil amid his heavy family cares.

Their old Stowey friends, the Pooles, had written the Coleridges often, begging a visit. So together, with little Derwent and the tiny Sara, they took the coach for Stowey. Thomas Poole welcomed them eagerly to the well-remembered home, and the little pique he had felt at Coleridge's long silence melted away at sight of his wan face and broken, spiritless manner.

After a week amid the pleasant old scenes, Coleridge's depression yielded to the sunshine of Poole's society. His rheumatism was so much better that he seldom used the fatal drug. Sarah watched him tenderly, and suppressed every word or look that might suggest anything unpleasant.

The little children, so like him, were a sweet comfort, and it was a pretty picture to see the tiny maiden in her mob cap and quaint long gown, toddling everywhere after " Papa," who shuffled along, timing his heavy step to her tiny footsteps.

Sarah watched them with breathless interest, hoping against hope that at last, through his little daughter, the restless husband and father would be lured back to the comfort of home life.

Poole's hopes of reforming the " Poor Laws," and so benefiting the masses upon a large scale, had been so nearly checkmated by the unsettled state of the country after the deaths of Pitt and Fox, that he returned to his quiet cottage at Stowey, and turned his attention more than ever to the poor at home. Always ready to help all in distress, he had planned a " Friendly Society " for working women, to give them shelter during childbirth, widowhood, and old age, without driving them to the plane of pauperism. The whole community subscribed, the poor adding their mites to the large donations of the rich.

Coleridge and Sarah took great interest in this scheme, and as the opening ceremonies occurred whilst they were visiting Poole,* Coleridge wrote the motto for this first " Female Aid Society " :

> " Foresight and Union,
>   Linked by Christian Love,
>   Helped by the good below
>   And Heaven above."

They had a long procession, with banners, headed by all the ladies of Stowey. After the meeting, the gentlemen drank tea with them. The family of John Poole, the Wedgwoods, and the Cottles from Bristol were over; and amid all these dear friends of their early-married life the Coleridges entered joyously into the pleasant celebration of the new charity.

From this beginning, many " Women's Aids " and " Exchanges " have emanated. To-day, England and America are teeming with " Friendly Inns," Homes, and Retreats for helpless, sick, or aged women, and they should remember that one kind, generous, old bachelor in quiet little Stowey started the ball rolling, and Coleridge wrote their first motto.

Until this visit, Thomas Poole had never understood the cause of the change which had crept over Coleridge. He now saw with dismay the shattered nerves and weak body, with the once great mind literally chained to it by the unnatural craving for opium. He felt deeper pity and more tender love than ever, and determined to make a great effort to save Coleridge from the fatal habit. He watched him, entertained him, and so guarded him from *ennui* and despondency, that his health improved greatly, and the drug was almost

* " Thomas Poole and his Friends."

abandoned. The fortnight's visit was prolonged to several months.

After the happy summer among her old friends under the pleasant shelter of Poole's hospitable roof, Sarah felt it was quite time to return to Keswick. Coleridge had again been written to about delivering another course of lectures in London, during the fall. He felt so much better and so much more hopeful that he willingly consented, and they bade farewell to their kind host.

They made a short stay in Bristol, where De Quincy joined them; and for months Poole heard nothing of the guests who had spent a pleasant summer with him.

After Christmas, a letter came from Sarah, which rather surprised him : *

" Keswick, Dec. 28, 1807.

" MY DEAR SIR,—

" If Coleridge has not written to you lately, I guess, from the interest you have always taken in our affairs, you will not think a few lines, even from my feeble pen, an unpardonable intrusion. But where shall I begin ?   I cannot endure presupposing you have never heard anything of us since Coleridge left your most hospitable dwelling; yet what is more likely?   When he joined us at Bristol in such excellent health and improved looks, I thought of days of 'Auld Lang Syne,' and hoped and prayed it might continue.   Alas ! in three or four days it was all over.   He said he must go to town *immediately* about the lectures, yet he staid three weeks without another word about removing, and I durst not speak, lest it might *disarrange* him.   Mr.

* " Thomas Poole and his Friends."

De Quincy, who was a frequent visitor to Coleridge in College Street, proposed to accompany us and the children into Cumberland, as he wished to pay Wordsworth and Southey a visit. This was a pleasant scheme for me, only I was obliged to give up my visits to Birmingham and Liverpool. Towards the end of October I packed up everything—C.'s things, as I thought, for London—and we all left Bristol. We reached Chester the third night, and the next we reached Eastham. I crossed to Liverpool.

" On the second night we all arrived at Grasmere, at Wordsworth's, and they wishing us to stay overnight, we sent back the chaise to Ambleside, and ordered it for the next afternoon. At Keswick they were all in expectation of us, and although it was quite dark, they were out with lanthorns.

"Coleridge, I left (as I thought) ready to jump into the mail for London. Lo! three weeks after, I received a letter from him dated ' White Horse Stairs, Piccadilly.' He was just arrived in town; had been ill owing to wet clothes, and had passed three weeks in Mr. Morgan's house, and been nursed by his wife and sister in the kindest manner.

"Yours sincerely,

" SARAH COLERIDGE."

But the lectures : what of them ? They had been promised for the early course. As the time approached, and no word came from Coleridge, Sir Humphry Davy, learning he was at Bristol, wrote him that he was expected to lecture the next week. He started from Bristol, as we know. But meeting friends upon the coach, he gladly accepted their invitation to stop at Calne and pay them a short visit. He was wet from riding upon the outside in a pouring rain. He could escape the discomfort of further travel in the rain, and still be in time for those tiresome lectures, that ever pursued him with relentless persistence. But alas! the wet clothes brought a return of the old rheumatism and gout, and, as Sarah wrote, he was utterly helpless for weeks.

The lecture day came and no Coleridge. But Mr. Morgan wrote of his condition to Sir Humphry Davy, whose own lectures were substituted at the last moment. Coleridge was placed upon the list for the later course.

He returned to London by Christmas, shattered, feeble, with swelled and aching limbs, and more than ever under the spell of opium. Only that relieved his terrible pain. He could not even fight against it, for fate seemed to drive him right into his enemy's clutches. His friends saw he was in no condition to lecture; but he was anxious to try. At the appointed time he appeared, and lectured upon Dryden. He rambled aimlessly over the ground, and quoted and commented; but the old charm of his eloquence was gone. Each lecture was less consecutive than the last. His parched tongue almost refused to move, and his thick utterance won only pity, and finally but scant toleration. Pity is but one step beyond contempt, and soon descends to disgust and resentment. So the once popular lecturer lost his place through the misfortune of his ill-health and its consequences.

The society released Coleridge from a part of the lectures, giving him £100 for the few he did deliver. He fled once more to the comfort and shelter of Wordsworth's home.

CHAPTER XXXI.

> Flowers are lovely; love is flower-like;
> Friendship is a sheltering tree ;
> O the joys, that came down shower-like,
> Of friendship, love, and liberty !
> > Ere I was old!
> *Ere* I was *old !* ah, woful ere !
> Which tells me youth's no longer here.
> > COLERIDGE.

WILLIAM HAZLITT'S courtship had progressed so favorably that the wedding arrangements were being planned and discussed by Sarah Stoddart and Mary Lamb.

Sir John Stoddart had yielded a reluctant consent, but stipulated that the marriage was to take place from Sarah's home, rather than from the Lambs', as Sarah preferred. Sarah had long ago gone home to prepare for her wedding, and she insisted upon Mary being her bridesmaid.

"What shall I wear?" wrote Mary; "Manning has sent me from China the most delicate and lovely silk, just tinted, or shall I wear the pretty muslin you sprigged for me last year? I have always kept it for a great occasion." * The important decision was finally given to the China silk.

Mary looked very pretty in the unaccustomed stylish

* "Letters of Charles and Mary Lamb."—W. C. HAZLITT.

gown and pelerine of creamy pongee. And Sarah was so handsome in her wedding-gown of delicately embroidered muslin and lace as to completely overwhelm the shy bridegroom.

They were married at old St. Andrew's Church, High Holborn, where Lamb and his friends of the "Round Table," and the Stoddarts' more aristocratic acquaintances, assembled to witness the ceremony.

The absurdity of the solemn and reserved Hazlitt taking a wife, and being the prominent feature at a fashionable wedding, so upset Lamb, that his endeavors to preserve a proper bearing were fruitless. He nearly disgraced himself and Mary with his half-suppressed merriment, which was but too contagious to all in his vicinity. The more Rickman and William Godwin scowled at him for his levity, the more difficult it became for him to quiet down. He afterwards wrote to Manning, who was still in China :

"When, man of the many faces, will you return from contemplating the mandarins and riding in palanquins? Methinks your eyes will forever have that upward squint at the aft-side, and you will never bring them down to the focus of ordinary London acquaintances.

"Can you bring your imagination to bear upon William Hazlitt as a Benedict? He has captured the skittish Sarah Stoddart, and the wedding was quite a grand affair at Holborn Church, with wedding fixings, and Mary as bridesmaid, in the China silk you sent her. Hazlitt was terrified enough to suit a hanging on Tyburn Hill, with himself the victim. George Dyer was arrayed in those antique nankeen trousers, which he fancies clean and the height of style; but, by the bells of Edmonton, they are encased in the dust of ages, and hang like ancient battle-flags around their poles. Dear old Dyer twitched in, like a crab shedding its last month's coat, murmuring his approbation during the service, like an imprisoned bumble-bee. (He has been browsing amid the book-stalls, and buying antiquated treasures until his rooms are knee-deep in books, and his larder is bare as Mother Hubbard's cupboard.)

"I was edified as usual upon solemn occasions, and came so near disgracing myself, with laughing at the incongruities, that I feared the verger would usher me out.—Yours, C. LAMB."*

When the friends gathered around the whist-table on the following Wednesday, there was a new topic for discussion. The new gas corporation had introduced gas-lamps upon Pall Mall in place of the usual smoking oil-lamps.

Of course Lamb resented such an innovation.

"G-g-gas!" he exclaimed. "What is the world coming to? These experiments with the b-b-bottled-up st-st-stench will drive us out of London."

"Yes! it was not enough to take out tinder boxes, and have every servant-wench crying for lucifer matches, but they must blow us up with their new-fangled gas," growled Godwin.

"L-lucifer matches are an invention of the d-d-devil," cried Lamb, "and I'll none of them!"

"But you will! Sir Knight of the Olden Time," said Francis Jeffrey. "Mark my words; you will live to

* "Life and Letters of Charles Lamb."—AINGER.

use sulphur matches, and we will yet have our 'rub-bers' under a twenty-candle power gas-light. The world is progressing, man, and we must go with it."

" It m-m-might be as well to blow up some of those old B-B-Bond Street dandies," retorted Lamb.—" It will meantime give them a new excuse for their p-p-per-fumed handkerchiefs, for the st-st-stench of those lamps is unbearable."

" Perhaps the manufacturers will learn some better process of making gas without odor," said Jeffrey.

" G-g-gas without odor would be like f-f-fire without f-f-flame," said the conservative Lamb. Any innovation in his beloved London must be frowned down. " It is bad enough to have a m-m-mad King and a d-d-dandy Regent without b-b-blowing us up with g-g-gas."

" Come, Brother Lamb, don't don your wolf-skin, or we shall all run. Besides, you have banished politics," said Rickman.

" Here's to Light, Liberty, and L-Legitimacy, then," cried Lamb, holding up his smoking punch. They fol-lowed his example and enjoyed their whist by the sputtering candles as much as if they had had a festive illumination.

During this winter, Mary Lamb wrote many verses for children, some wholesomely didactic, and some merely to amuse. Her little volume, with some poems in the same vein by Charles, was very popular and brought them quite a nice little income. The whole edition was sold and enjoyed by the children of that day. And now, ninety years later, when the little volumes have been scattered to the four winds, and lost to sight, an interest has sprung up to collect all the writ-ings of that unpretending sister and brother, and for long this little book seemed out of existence ; when behold ! a bachelor in Australia had all his old books and treasures sent him from his early English home, and in recalling childish memories and delights, over the old souvenirs, he found a copy of the now precious book.

So, in the whirligig of time, some who have been lowly come to the top ; and many who have shone brilliantly in their day go into the depths of the unknown and are extinguished. And who can tell what his future destiny may be, if he live and work his best ? Charles Lamb scarcely foresaw that his odd fancies and antiquarian reminiscences, written as much for necessary money as for amusement, would, in half a century, become classical English essays. But he did prophesy that his friends, Wordsworth and Coleridge, would live when their detractors should be forgotten.

Lamb was deeply grieved at the failure of Coleridge's lecture on the English Poets. He watched him tenderly and encouraged him faithfully. But when he saw the brilliant talker stumble and maunder along, with most unusual platitudes, and found his ideas drag as painfully as his words, he realized the hopelessness of the struggle.

Thomas Poole, hearing of Coleridge's wretched condition, wrote, reminding him of duty and opportunity, and begging him to bear his sufferings rather than fly to such a remedy as opium.

He answered Poole in the following sad lines :

"Let the eagle bid the tortoise sunward soar.
As vainly strength speaks to a broken mind."

He wrote further : " In truth, I have been for years almost a paralytic in mind, from self-dissatisfaction—

brooding in secret anguish over what, from so many baffled agonies of effort, I had thought and felt to be irremediable; but which yet, from moral cowardice, and a strong tyrannous reluctance to make any painful concern of my own the subject of discourse—a reluctance, strong in exact proportion to my esteem and affection for the persons with whom I am communing, I have, after great reluctance, submitted my case to a physician. . . .

"I have never struggled all I can with myself, without instantly wishing for a nearer communion with you. For as you were my first friend, in the highest sense of the word, so you must forever be among my dearest.

"S. T. COLERIDGE." *

The struggle did indeed seem almost hopeless. At this time he constantly took a pint of laudanum a day, and sometimes even more—enough to kill a dozen men unaccustomed to the poison. Having saturated his system with it, he simply could not live without it.

* "Life of Coleridge."—BRANDL.

CHAPTER XXXII

WORDSWORTH AND THE LAKE COUNTRY.

And when—O friend, my comforter and guide,
Strong in thyself and powerful to give strength.
COLERIDGE.

On man, on nature, and on human life,
Musing in solitude, I oft perceive
Fair trains of imagery before me rise—
And I am conscious of affecting thoughts,
And dear remembrances whose presence soothes
Or elevates the mind, intent to weigh
The good and evil of our mortal state.
To these emotions, whencesoe'er they come,
Whether from breath of outward circumstance,
Or from the soul—an impulse in itself—
I would give utterance in numerous verse.
Of truth, of Providence, Beauty, Love, and Hope,
And melancholy fear subdued by faith,
Of blessed consolations in distress—
I sing.
WORDSWORTH.

COLERIDGE was now living with Wordsworth at Allan Bank. This pleasant cottage upon the sloping hillside, overlooking Grasmere, was their home for several years, until Mr. Wordsworth bought "Rydal Mount," a couple of miles below. Here, with luxurious foliage, and beautiful views of the encircling mountains and the lakes nestled at their feet, the two friends wrote and read and discussed their favorite theories.

Coleridge improved in health and spirits during this summer. The tall poet, with his shepherd's plaid to protect him from the evening damps of the chilly Lake country, and his owlish green spectacles, might be seen at all times and seasons, with his shambling companion, whose blowsy hair, now fast turning gray, responded to every passing breeze. They paced back and forth along the bracken and sedge-grass of the lake-sides, and clambered through the heather, over all the fells and peaks of the mountains, always arguing, talking, reciting, like great buzzing bees. The farmers and yeomen of all the country round became accustomed to the daily sight of the two friends, and shook their heads over the busy idleness that seemed mysterious to them. " Ees do climb oop and on loike the verra de'il war after 'em ; and back ees coom again, belike, wi' moss or stanes to hand. Nawbut a speerit o' onrest do seem to guide ees," said these worthies over their pipes in the village ale-house when their day's ploughing or haymaking was over. Little did they know of Wordsworth's interest in their homely lives and toil. That he should find poetry in their daily prose, or make them immortal through his art, was an honor unsuspected.

The humble church on Kirkstane Pass, and its equally unpretending vicar, who—

> " Turned to this secluded chapelry
> That had been offered to his doubtful choice
> By our unthought-of patron, *

are better known than many a bishop of large diocese and stately cathedral.

> " Bleak and bare, they found the cottage, their allotted home,
> And far removed, ...

* " The Excursion."—WORDSWORTH.

> The chapel stood, divided from that house
> By an unpeopled tract of mountains, waste . . . .
> Yet cause was none, whate'er regret might hang
> On his own mind, to quarrel with the choice,
> Or the necessity that fixed him here." *

The shepherd Michael,† on " the forest side in Gras-mere Vale," "near the tumultuous brook of Green Head Ghyll," never knew that he was living a poem for the wandering poet to write. He never suspected his steady, patient toil to be either praiseworthy or pathetic, and when he impoverished himself of his life-long earnings, for the only son, who turned rascal and broke his parents' hearts, he had but done his best, and received fate's cruel reward.

But the poet saw the poetry beneath life's bitterest prose, and the world will never forget that cottage—

> "High into Easedale, up to Dunmail Raise . . . ·
> And from this constant light, so regular,
> And so far seen, the house itself, by all
> Who dwelt within the limits of the Vale,
> Both old and young, was named the *Evening Star*."

Here, at Allan Bank, Wordsworth planned and wrote " The Excursion " and many of his finest poems. Mrs. Wordsworth and Dorothy were always his ready helpers, writing out the lines he hummed to them after a long ramble, or when lying in the sunshine on a mossy bank. And Coleridge was also his ardent worshiper. The sick, discouraged poet felt his energies revive in this sweet, wholesome atmosphere of love and labor, but not for poetry ; that seemed left be-

* " The Excursion."—WORDSWORTH.

† " Michael."—Pastoral Poem by Wordsworth.

hind with his youthful hope and aspirations. But he wrote political, metaphysical, and philosophical essays far into the night. And feeling the possibilities still awaiting him, he urged Wordsworth to help him start a new periodical, which he called " The Friend." As usual with his plans, Coleridge had great schemes of work and usefulness laid out, to be accomplished by " The Friend." Wordsworth became as enthusiastic, and placed all the money he could spare at Coleridge's disposal. Thomas Poole assisted him with subscriptions and articles, as did many old friends, glad to know that he had again shaken off his lethargy. His letter to Thomas Poole would have moved a less generous and loving man than Poole : " Do what you can for me, old friend, by yourself and your influence, or the influence of your friends ; for this is to make or mar me. . . . You must write me a number for ' The Friend ' upon that infamous lace-beslavered set of lazzaroni, these rascally male servants in and out of livery, in these stinking Gold and Silver Fish-ponds, the Squares and Places and Grandee Streets of London. Likewise an essay on the means by which a man may make his wealth conducive to, productive and augmentative of, his happiness. You may call it ' Ariadne's Clue Improved,' or ' Jason (Theseus) with a Golden Fleece.'

" Joking apart, some evening, throw yourself into a day-dream. Suppose yourself, with your present notions unchanged, at the age of 21, with £20,000 a year. Live through fifteen years—(21 to 36). Your biography of this should be written. Then from 36 to 55 the second, and from 58 to 70 or 80, on, as you like. People it with friends—only be married (and take precious care to *whom*), and have sons and daughters." *

Poole understood Coleridge's sarcasm, and while not approving of the fling at his own marital relations, he pitied the unfortunate friend who found even his marriage a failure. He helped him with subscriptions and articles for " The Friend," and with Wordsworth's and Dorothy's ready assistance, it prospered for awhile. Both Poole and Southey begged the impetuous fellow to pay more regard to public feeling.

Southey said: " Do not give offense by too plain speaking, and by sneering at the ways of the world. Those very people you hold in such contempt are the ones who can make or mar your magazine."

For once Coleridge listened to advice. He tried to be cautious and tolerant; but the effort was evident in the work. He wrote faithfully night after night; but the articles were too serious, too metaphysical, for a weekly magazine. The tone was not light enough for the popular taste. His plan was too grand, and he rambled over too wide a field. Subscriptions failed, and week after week the numbers accumulated, as the demand decreased.

Wordsworth added money to the increasing expenses, but neither he nor Coleridge knew anything about the practical poet publishing a magazine. Coleridge saw a hopeless muddle of debts, expenses, and necessities increasing continually. In despair he wrote to Lamb : †
" Send more of your sparkling nonsense : the paper is sinking like lead, and carrying me with it. Stamps, duties, paper, expenses, are swamping it. I have made a faithful effort, and have again found my Nemesis.

* " Thomas Poole and his Friends."
† " Life of Coleridge." BRANDL.

Poole, Wordsworth, Cottle, all write for it; do what you can for me."

The Lambs had read the magazine with delight, and were surprised and pained to hear of Coleridge's discouragement. Charles wrote: "I think the account of Luther at the Wartburg is as fine as anything I ever read. God forbid that a man who has such things to say should be silenced for want of £100. This Custom and Duty age would have made the Preacher on the Mount take out a license; and St. Paul's epistles would not have been missible without a stamp. But alas! where is Sir G. Beaumont?

"What is become of the rich auditors in Albemarle Street? Your letter has saddened me." *

And so it was: no support from the crowds who had thronged to hear him lecture, and who had been ready to lionize the popular favorite. 'Tis the old story of the multitude the world over. One day they cry, "Hosannah! hosannah!" and the next, "Away with him!"

Far into the night, Coleridge's light sent its rays out upon the hill slope above Grasmere Lake. It might be another beacon, like old Martin's upon Nab Scar, for struggling wanderers.

But no homeless tramp could feel more forsaken than did the writer in the sheltering home of his dearly loved friends. Failure was stamped upon his work, and his friends must lose their money and confidence through him! He was struggling against his fate, and against his tempter too, and day by day his strength for resistance grew less. He sent out twenty-seven numbers of "The Friend." They contained fine essays upon the times, and upon great epochs of the world's

* "Letters of Charles Lamb."—AINGER.

history, but—the world did not want them, and when there was nothing left but debts they stopped.

From Greta Hall, Sarah Coleridge was eagerly watching the progress of "The Friend," seeing in it the hope for Coleridge and promise of her future, and the hope that a life of activity might recall the old desire for wife and home. She and Southey knew nothing of the discouragements of the undertaking; and Southey fed her hopes by his praises of the work. She felt a wild longing for her husband, until it became unbearable, and she took little Sara and went to visit the Wordsworths.

How her heart throbbed as she passed the frowning old Helvellyn, and beyond Thirlmere Lake saw Grasmere lying along the silver thread of the Rothay. The stage seemed to crawl, the horses to creep, as they neared the Rothay House. There, at Allan Bank, was her husband with his old friend, Wordsworth. Timidly she approached, sending little Sara before to announce their visit. Coleridge saw the little fairy and clasped her to his breast, giving Sarah an awkward greeting, from the unexpected pleasure of the meeting.

Wordsworth went to the house to announce them, and for a short time the husband and wife were left together. Sarah noticed the gray hair and pallid face, and taking his hand said: "You are not well, dear; I hoped to see you looking better. We read your papers with such pleasure, that I fancied you must be better and happier than when we were last together."

Coleridge looked nervously away, and clasping little Sara closer, said: "I am better at times; but the old pains are getting the mastery again. And you, Sarah, are you not contented with your home? Are you not more happy among your friends, than in the old, anxious days, when my vagaries were always bothering you ?"

"Oh, no, Coleridge, come back to your home, to your children ; they are growing away from you.   I, your wife, need you sorely."

He looked restlessly at the house, hoping for a break in their trying meeting.

And Sarah, seeing his troubled, unresponsive face, felt her heart sink, and knew only too well that he was still a wanderer.   She made a terrible effort to master her disappointment, and as Mrs. Wordsworth and little Dora came hurrying to greet them, she gained composure.

It was awkward to be a mere visitor to her husband's home ; and although Mary Wordsworth was tender and sisterly, and Dorothy's cheeriness made the visit pass pleasantly, Sarah remained only a few days, but was prevailed upon to leave the little girl with her father.

The blue-eyed little woman in her quaint cap, where the little golden rings would curl over the border, and the brown-eyed witch of Allan Bank were great friends. They were a pretty pair, and Coleridge and Wordsworth loved to watch their innocent games and prattle. Dora's big brothers somewhat alarmed the "little fairy," as they called Sara.   But her quick wit and responsive sweetness soon won the rough fellows as champions. They were a merry, happy party ; and Coleridge's pride and delight in his child were touching.   She must sleep with him, and he was only happy when she was trotting over the hills by his side.   He had an endless store of fairy tales and "wonder-dreams" to tell her, and she followed him like his shadow—a midday shadow was this tiny maiden.

"Little daughter," said Coleridge, one day, taking her into his arms and holding her close, " if you could choose, would you live all the time with mother or with father ? "

"I must *live* with my mamma ; but I will *stay* with you," she answered quickly. " But I would like to have both of you at once, like Edith and Dora. Why will you not come home with me to my mamma ? " she asked, looking wistfully into his loving eyes.

It was a touching appeal, and Coleridge sighed heavily as he left the little girl with her companions, and climbed wearily up Green Head Ghyll to the mountain top.

When, at last, Sarah came for her little one, and Coleridge saw her cling to her mother, glad to leave friends, father, and everything, to return with her, he realized that he must return to his children, or lose their love.

CHAPTER XXXIII.

> Hence viper thoughts that coil around my mind,
>   Reality's dark dream !
> I turn from you and listen to the wind
>   Which long has raved unnoticed.   What a scream
>   Of agony, by torture lengthened out !
>
> COLERIDGE.

DURING the fall Wordsworth persuaded Coleridge to accompany him to Keswick. He thought there would be more hope of a reunion between husband and wife if Coleridge found himself a welcome guest at Greta Hall. Sarah had pleaded earnestly with Wordsworth to use his influence to this end.

On a crisp, sunny Monday of September, the tall poet with green goggles, shrouded in the folds of his gray plaid, and the shorter man in rusty black, with heavy step and luminous eyes, set out to scale Dunmail Raise and reach Keswick before dinner hour.

The thirteen miles of mountain and valley were but a pleasant morning walk to the friends who spent their lives in studying Nature and prying into her secrets. Even in the warm sunshine Helvellyn rose cold and grim, its great rugged boulders hanging threateningly over Thirlmere Lake. At its base, moss and purple heather hid its scars; and ferns and bracken, and innumerable blue-bells and broom, fringed the lake. But Thirlmere cannot smile in the sunshine as do the other lakes : it lies sullen and black under the frowning shadow of Helvellyn, its watchful giant.

" I like this mountain least of all the great brotherhood," said Coleridge, shuddering in the breezes from its stony crown. " It is so dark and gloomy ; it seems always turned away from the sun. And it is so full of mysteries, and great purple chasms."

" How differently the same point appears to different minds or temperaments," said Wordsworth. "To me, Helvellyn is the finest of our hills. It bears the scars of centuries, and seems to have the ruggedness of age and strength, whilst the others are yet in their youthful freshness and bloom. They have their trees and mosses to shield them from the storms ; but, save for the grass that veils all nature, Helvellyn stands up, brave and uncovered, to the pitiless elements here."

Southey and his household greeted the poets warmly, showing by every attention their pleasure at the visit. Hartley and Derwent Coleridge had much to tell their father of their school-life and studies ; and little Sara clung to him as at Allan Bank. Yet, on Wednesday, when Wordsworth proposed to leave, Coleridge returned with him. He felt more at home beneath his friend's roof than with his own family.

He remained during the winter and spring, suffering terribly with rheumatism, neuralgia, and gout. He was seldom free from pain, and again his remedy held him in bondage. De Quincy had taken the little cottage by the roadside, all screened in ivy ; and he was a daily visitor. The Clarksons and Professor Wilson, who lived near, were also constant visitors and most sympathizing friends. The Scotch giant, Wilson, with his splendid figure and tawny hair, was a striking contrast to the shuffling, stooping man he was proud to call his friend. Being a young poet, he appreciated and worshiped the genius of Wordsworth and Coleridge, and he was indefatigable in his efforts to reclaim Coleridge from his fatal habit. Perhaps Dorothy Wordsworth's laughing brown eyes had some power to attract the handsome young Hercules. William Wordsworth always said she had bewitched him. But whatever the cause, he was a most constant visitor, and added much to the charm of the group of poets that congregated at Allan Bank.

After the failure of "The Friend," Coleridge felt no incentive to work, and as idleness is always the highway to ruin, he grew worse in health and became more unsettled and restless. It was torture to him to have Wordsworth and his family see his helpless weakness. He therefore decided to return to his home, if he might still so consider his deserted fireside and family.

Sarah was only too happy to welcome him, and faithfully nursed him back to health and strength. The summer was beneficial to his rheumatism, and her tender care soothed his spirit. The children and Southey were a wholesome stimulus to his ambition, and he was again enabled to throw off his chains, and become almost free from opium torments. He taught his boys Latin and mathematics, and found such pleasure in their development that Sarah hoped against hope that home would satisfy him.

But he grew impatient of her anxious watchfulness. He felt the ignominy of his shattered powers and broken hopes; and their contrast with Southey's hard, patient labor and growing success galled him into restlessness. He must be doing something, and only London could offer him a field of action.

Sarah's anxious eyes had already divined his purpose. She saw his increasing irritability, and all her womanhood rose within her against his injustice and weakness. If he left her again, it should be forever. She would steel her heart against the husband who could so easily throw off all claims of wife and children. And she succeeded in this her last struggle. When Coleridge departed for London this time, both felt it was a final severing of the sacred tie.

Sarah's indignation at being so unjustly treated, cured her of the pangs of such a separation. Coleridge's repugnance to his home-life was almost incomprehensible to himself. He could scarcely find an excuse, even to himself, save that he was unfit for the friction and jarring of domestic life. Yet he was an honorable, Christian man, with a most sensitive conscience. But his fiend had perverted his vision and weakened his resistance. Sarah's quick temper and ready reproaches always galled him. He considered himself unable to be happy in his home, and unfit to make his wife happy. They misunderstood one another continually; and as he felt rather a cipher in his home, and fancied reproach before he even saw it, he departed, this time, forever.

He went to London with his friend Basil Montagu, and accepted an invitation to stay at his house. The Montagus lived among a more fashionable set than our poet relished. The stately dinners and brilliant assemblages at their house soon grew irksome to Coleridge. He welcomed his old friends, Lamb and Hazlitt and Procter and Samuel Rogers, when they came to Mrs. Montagu's *salon* evenings, but he grew morose when Jeffrey or Lord John Russell, or any of the Holland House coterie appeared. He answered their courtesies so brusquely that his hostess resented his rudeness. Mrs. Montagu was a charming hostess, brilliant, witty, genial, with her own especial charm, as she flitted from guest to guest, always a pretty picture of a medieval dame, in silver-gray flowing robe, with ruff and laces. She could forgive Coleridge's rusty black small-clothes, so unfashionable in cut and careless in adjustment; but she could not overlook the dusty shoes and unkempt head, and the sullen air he assumed in the presence of her especial friends.

At a dinner, he sat beside young Monckton Milnes, and commented rather savagely upon his politics and his popularity among the aristocrats.

"Why, sir," said Coleridge, "you cannot expect to understand the Reform Question if you spend your days driving around with snobs, and your nights dining and wining in this fashion. No man can lead an artificial life, and keep a clear brain for the important questions of the day."

Monckton Milnes flushed and looked surprised at the uncalled-for attack, but before he could reply, Sydney Smith said in his quick way:

"No, Mr. Coleridge, reform should always begin at home, and only those can appreciate that who have succeeded in their own lives. It is a pretty question, but a better answer when applied practically."

Coleridge felt the rebuke, and turning his great eyes upon Sydney Smith, said: "You remind me then of the old saying: 'Let him who is without sin among you cast the first stone?'"

"Nay, I never preach out of the pulpit," laughed Sydney Smith; "'tis work enough to fit text and sermon when I'm paid to do it; I cannot spare it, gratis," and the ever-ready wit turned the edge of the sarcasm and brought back the smiles and good-humor that always followed that clerical wag.

But Coleridge's antagonism to the set accustomed to flattery, and his criticisms upon fashionable life, soon made a breach between him and the Montagus, and he removed to the more humble home of his friends the Morgans, at Hammersmith, where he remained a year, until the increasing debts and poverty of the Morgans compelled him to seek new lodgings. He feared he was some tax upon their straitened means, although he always paid his board, when he could squeeze anything out of "The Courier" for his writings.

He finally made an arrangement with Street, the proprietor of "The Courier," by which he was to write regularly for that paper, and also to condense the police and political reports, for which he received four or five pounds a week. He worked faithfully and wrote constantly and regularly; his friend, Mrs. Morgan, watching him and guarding him from opium as at Calne. He rose at six and took the early coach to the Strand each day; but he walked the whole distance back at night to save the fare.

As Coleridge was accustomed to walking whilst in the Lake Country, the daily exercise was beneficial rather than otherwise. His engagement upon "The Courier" became most irksome and trying. His articles were used or thrown aside at the mere whim of Street, who never appreciated their charm, and who had but the low standard of popular favor. In his long walks to Hammersmith, Coleridge had ample time to churn up his wrongs, and the result was a serious quarrel between him and Street. He told Street that "The

Courier " was degenerating into a mere gossip grind, and he insinuated that that gentleman knew about as much of literature and the standard of taste as an Italian organ-grinder.

So, naturally, his connection with the paper ceased, and the poor poet, who was so willing to be a mere journalistic drudge for his daily bread, had even that certainty fade into shadow.

The Morgans could no longer live amid their debts at Hammersmith, and they returned to Calne, where Mr. Morgan gathered a few pupils, and so eked out a scant living. Coleridge removed to a garret in South-ampton Building, near Charles Lamb.

Once more a streak of luck came at an opportune time. He was engaged to deliver a course of seventeen lectures before the " London Philosophical Society." He gathered all his forces and made the most vigorous effort of his life, and resolutely walked off his wild cravings for opium. Fortunately he was less tormented than of late by neuralgia and gout, and with rigorous care and constant encouragement from Charles and Mary Lamb, who were always his good angels, he delivered the best lectures of his life.

There were usually a couple of hundred people present, and the lectures upon Shakspeare and Milton were admirable. The cynical Rogers found more to praise than to criticise, which alone was great encouragement to the drowning man who was clutching his last straws. Byron was charmed, and was ready to assist in any way within his power. Crabbe Robinson and Landor and Basil Montagu and Leigh Hunt, and many more of the literary men of London, were delighted at the reawakening of the eloquence of this born orator.

During this winter of 1812 the hall was crowded, and the lectures were most brilliant and satisfactory, if somewhat discursive ; for Coleridge followed no rules, and traveled on, in his own brilliant fashion, rambling over wide fields and pouring floods of unpremeditated eloquence upon all the ramifications of his subject.

None but a genius could dare confront such an audience with so unprepared a lecture. But Coleridge's mind was a reservoir of valuable information upon all subjects, and he had but to let the torrent loose, to charm all listeners. Though a risky style, it was none the less charming for its digressions.

He greatly needed the substantial sum he received for these lectures, and was glad to send a large share of it to his family.

Another piece of good fortune came to him through Lord Byron, who was at the height of his popularity in London. His old, forgotten play, " Osorio," which had been lying unheeded for a dozen years among the waste paper of Drury Lane Theater, was hunted up by Byron, who was one of the managers of the theater. He saw possibilities in the play, and was eager to help his brother-poet, upon whom fate had so long frowned. He induced Coleridge to rewrite and remodel the piece, and give it another name. It was brought out under the title of " Remorse," and had a run of a month or so, bringing Coleridge popularity and a nice sum of money.

CHAPTER XXXIV.

O framed for calmer times and nobler hearts,
O studious poet, eloquent for truth !
Philosopher ! contemning wealth and death,
Yet docile, childlike, full of life and love.
. . . 'Tis true that, passionate for ancient truths,
And honoring with religious love the great
Of elder times, he hated to excess,
With an unquiet and intolerant scorn,
The hollow puppets of a hollow age,
Ever idolatrous, and changing ever
Its worthless idols.

COLERIDGE.

It seemed as if brighter days were dawning for Coleridge. Within a year he had had two successes which had netted him several hundred pounds. He felt so encouraged that he wrote another play, "Zapolya," but the critics tore this to bits, and, having been written more for its ideas and literary points than for the stage, it fell dead. Coleridge's health also failed : the old rheumatism attacked him, and again the remedy was worse than the disease.

He visited Joseph Cottle, who was shocked to see the ravages disease and opium had made upon him. He now gave himself up to his enemy more than at any other time, being in a constant state of exaltation or stupor from the poison, and the victim of terrible suffering from neuralgia. If not allowed the drug, he walked the floor whole nights. Yet Cottle was so determined to save him, that he employed a man to follow him about Bristol and prevent him from buying the poison. But with the cunning of a madman he would elude the very man whom he besought to prevent him from buying opium. He resorted to every device to get it, and in spite of himself, and despite Mr. Cottle's utmost care, he obtained it. He had sunk to a state of mere animal existence, with a burning craving for the drug that dragged him still lower—leaving neither will nor strength for the conflict of soul against body.

He fled to Calne, where the Morgans were again living, and begged Mrs. Morgan to save him from the devil that had possession of his faculties. She, better than any one else, could exorcise the evil spirit, and, with her kind woman's heart and keen woman's wit, could soothe his sufferings of body and mind.

After some months with them, where he was paying two pounds a week for his board and lodging (thus helping along their straitened finances), he gradually became somewhat better.

He wrote whenever his tempter left him with mind enough for work. Here, in the quiet of the little country town, he wrote many philosophical articles, and those broken and disconnected memorials of his life and philosophies—the " Biographia Literaria."

In these rambling memoirs he gave his finest tribute to his friend Wordsworth ; and he discussed, in his discursive way, his own wanderings through German metaphysics, and his return to the safe shelter of the Church of England. Whilst bearing traces of his enfeebled physical condition in its style, the book is a fascinating sample of his deep and earnest thought, and deserved a better fate than the sneers that met it upon the threshold of its career. The critics tore it limb from limb and scattered it as worthless trash, not reading the heart-story beneath its lines, and not appreciating its summing up of the eager gropings of a lifetime.

True, he rambled, and went off upon innumerable side issues; but he pictured his hungry grasping for soul-food as a warning to other seekers after truth amid the husks of metaphysics. He pieced together the fragments of his deeply studied theories, and showed the fallacies of the different systems of philosophy, that had driven him, little by little, back to the Church of England, as nearest to the Bible teaching. He hoped to lead other doubting souls back to the saving faith in Jesus Christ, the only belief that satisfies both heart and intellect. What mischief his early wanderings and doubting may have done, he prayerfully hoped his later convictions might undo. It was his atonement. How was it received? The magazines sneered at it as a piece of hypocrisy. They called it "wandering, maudlin trash of the past, dragged into view."

Even Southey, co-editor of the "Quarterly Review," gave it no help; he took no notice whatever of it, and said to a friend, "Coleridge had better reform his habits before he preaches to the public." Thus easy is it to condemn and throw mud at a fallen friend!

Lamb wrote to Coleridge, praising the book in highest terms.

"Come to me, old friend," he wrote. "I want a good old-fashioned talk with my philosopher. We have the little garret snuggery waiting for you. Come up to London and see what we can do to stop those hissing serpent-mouths, that spit their venom at what is far beyond their comprehension."

Coleridge went for a visit to his comforters. Charles and Mary could always soothe his troubles ; and the quiet fireside and pleasant evenings with the Lambs alone, or the whist evenings with their friends, seemed an elysium of home comfort.

One evening, soon after he had gone to London, Coleridge sauntered slowly up Cheapside to meet Lamb on his return from the India House. The throngs of pedestrians and vehicles, passing along the crowded thoroughfare, did not rouse him from the heavy reverie in which he walked rather blindly. A new attack upon his writings and character had just appeared in " Blackwood," and he was stung as with nettles ; too stupefied with his pain to notice the enticing book-stalls and shop-windows along his favorite Paternoster Row, until he descried a small, black-clad figure, all head and luminous brown eyes, tripping briskly along.

" Hello ! Ph-ph-philosopher, what problems are you s-s-solving now ? " called Lamb, as he approached and linked his arm in his friend's.

" Ah, Charley ! they're at it again, flaying me alive ! ' Blackwood ' has just come in with a vicious stab at the ' Biographia.' They call me ' hypocrite,' ' dreamer,' and say I have no right to foist my trash upon the public," he spoke with tears of mortification and grief in the eyes turned so piteously upon Lamb. " And William Hazlitt, your friend Hazlitt, is trying his scalpel upon me," he groaned. " I did my best ; I am but a broken man, Charley, ruined in mind and body ; yet I gave earnest, patient labor to that book, and I need its success for my daily bread."

"Sh-sh-shameful! c-c-cruel!" stammered Lamb, stamping his little foot, until a passing baker's boy stared in round-eyed wonder, and held his steaming roast closer for fear of some sudden collision. "I'll write to Hazlitt this n-n-night, confound his imp-imp-impertinence," added Lamb.

"Ah, Charley! you and I cannot stop them. Even Southey refuses the help he might give. I tell you, I am discouraged. Life has nothing left for me. It has neither hope nor the right to work for my bread. I have failed at every point. What I have done has found small sale and brought no money. What I have meant to do has been frozen back by the world's cruelty and pitiless scorn at what I have written. The critics have murdered me."

"So they have abused S-S-Southey and W-W-Wordsworth," said Lamb. "The 'Edinburgh Review' and 'B-Blackwood' have s-s-s-sneered for years; but they have gone steadily on writing and paying no heed, until the t-t-tide has turned, and Southey can now have his t-t-turn at them. Your ebb t-t-tide must be nearly run out, old f-f-fellow. It is d-d-deuced hard; but t-t-trim your sails, and come in at the f-f-flood."

"I will not, I cannot write to be torn piecemeal, and spit out of those Scotchmen's mouths, while Tom Moore's little jigs, and Byron's sulphur fumes are called 'poetry.' Poetry! such mewling, puking, drawing-room dilettante nonsense, spun by the yard, and twanged to harps and viols! This, poetry! Look at Lady Blessington, with her hundred pounds for album sweeties. And Mrs. Hemans, with some common-sense, and a pretty knack at rhyming, is supporting her family with her *poems !* Campbell and Rogers, having friends and money, have found favor with the public censors who build up or destroy a man's reputation, according to their prejudices."

" Do not feel it so b-b-bitterly, Esteecee. Do not let them b-b-bridle your mouth. W-w-write for the world and for Truth's s-s-sake, and Truth shall some day own you."

" And starve in the mean time ! like Chatterton and all the rest of the poets ! I tell you, I have dropped poetry forever. They don't know it when they see it. I am writing sermons for stupid and lazy divines at sixpence a page. I am doing the ' Courier's ' dirty work at five shillings a column. I am a poor devil of a literary hack, since I must find my daily subsistence somewhere. But let a man curse the day that made him a poet and a seeker after truth. There is no place for poetry, and I am done with it ! "

Lamb winced visibly when he read the article, calling Coleridge a " fantastic braggadocio, full of self-admiration, with little feeling and no judgment." The " Biographia Literaria " was pronounced " execrable trash, treating the most ordinary commonplaces like mysteries."*

He and Mary comforted Coleridge for his abominable treatment by their warm sympathy. They watched him tenderly and suggested many pleasant diversions. The political events and war news were great sources of interest to the "Round Table" as well as to all England. Bonaparte's hesitations and defeats, and the gradual pursuit by the Allies, until, after their great

* " Life of Coleridge."—BRANDL.

victory at Leipsic, they followed him to Paris, stirred the world. So under the protection of England, and the other allied powers, Louis XVIII. returned from his residence in England, and became King of the French, promising to administer the laws according to the new constitution.

He signed, with Great Britain, Austria, Russia and Prussia, a treaty of peace, restoring French boundaries to their old limits. Thus was the troublous chasm of twenty-two years, bridged over. And the torrents of blood that had flooded those years had at last swept away the French republic and the usurper's throne, and carried the Bourbons back. London was in a continual state of enthusiasm, parades, and illuminations. The coffee-houses and clubs teemed with life and excitement. Whigs and Tories united in the common rejoicing. There were a few more anxious days after Napoleon's return from Elba and his advance upon the Allies on the Belgian frontier during the Hundred Days.

Waterloo and the surrender of Bonaparte was a magnificent climax, and the enthusiasm and pride of the English knew no bounds. "Waterloo and Wellington," "Victory and Peace" were upon all arches, banners, and lanterns, and the newly-introduced gas added greatly to the splendor of the illumination. London was ablaze with light and as full of mad revelry and street processions as Rome during the Carnival. Coleridge and Lamb of course shared the general excitement. At one of the Wednesday evenings, Talfourd and Procter came hastening in with a hurried: "Have you heard the news?" "Is it another W-W-Waterloo; is the k-k-king dead?" asked Lamb.

"Better than that: you'll never guess. Southey is

made poet laureate," said Procter, glancing quickly at Coleridge, who flushed a deep red, and then paled again.

"Good for him!" said Lamb, "you, s-s-see, Coleridge, you p-p-poets are g-g-gaining the foot of the throne; you will f-f-find your pedestal one of these d-d-days."

"Not by cringing to royalty or bending my knee to ask favors of aristocrats," said Coleridge hotly. " Southey has been clipping his wings these many days to avoid flying in the face of royal providence. Well! he has his reward; but I do not envy him his honors."

" Nay, Coleridge, Southey never sought the position," said Rickman, who had entered during the discussion. " His work has well deserved this public expression of approval. He works like a giant, and this is the only literary distinction within the power of the Crown."

" We shall see Southey's muse chained to the christening car and the triumphal chariot," sneered Coleridge.

"Well, even that is better than to be d-d-drowned in the depths of the s-s-sea," stammered the peace-loving Lamb. " I'd write odes to his m-m-majesty's pint-pots myself, if I might sign myself ' P-P-Poet to the Crown,'" laughed Lamb.

" No, ' Elia,' that thou wouldst not," said Rickman. " Our quaint philosopher would not wear cap and bells for any prince."

"Let not that prince, then, tempt me with too shining gold, else might I f-fain forswear my p-principles."

" Gad! does he too hanker after Egypt's flesh-pots ? " asked Hazlitt.

" Small aid he'd ever get from you, knight of the

scalpel," said Coleridge, who was still stinging from that critic's thrusts.

" Perhaps no aid to climb to royal favors," said Hazlitt; "but if ever 'Elia' needs my help, he knows my opinion of him."

" The world knows your opinions of most people," said Coleridge. " You certainly do not hide your light under a bushel; the smoke and stench announce its presence, and the flames soon burn through, and leave charred reputations in your wake."

Hazlitt's eagle face looked dangerous at this retort; but the general laugh warned him that Coleridge had the majority upon his side. Moreover, a twinge of conscience told him poor Coleridge had a right to retaliate, after certain pretty keen attacks from his pen.

CHAPTER XXXV.

"THE COURSE OF TRUE LOVE NEVER DID RUN SMOOTH."

> The cataracts blow their trumpets from the steep,
> No more shall grief of mine the season wrong.
> I hear the echoes through the mountain throng,
> The winds come to me from the fields of sleep,
> And all the earth is gay.
>
> WORDSWORTH.

> But we sailed onward over tranquil seas,
> Wafted by airs so exquisitely mild
> That e'en to breathe became an act of will, and sense of
> pleasure.
>
> SHELLEY.

AT Lamb's Wednesday evenings in the old Temple precincts, the well-known group of writers and philosophers strolled in from Fleet Street under the arches on the Strand, and paced the fine old gardens lying around the Temple buildings, until they reached the dingy red-brick quadrangles, and climbed the creaking stairs to his apartments. There, in these upper rooms, where the long twilight and the sunset-glow showed them the silver glimmer of the Thames, with its many sails, gathered these men who were carving their names upon the records of the busy, driving London. Of the throngs that crossed these gardens and Inns of Court, in the early days of this nineteenth century, these visitors of the India House clerk stand out in full relief.

Hazlitt, the merciless satirist and critic, who spared few
men of his times the thrusts of his probing criticisms;
Procter, the " Barry Cornwall " whose name is still a
power in the world of letters; Talfourd, the shrewd
lawyer, destined to be prominent among the barristers
of his day; Rickman, the politician of liberal views and
deeds; the Burneys; Godwin, the philosopher and
socialist; our Lake Poets and their friends; Rogers,
the rich poet and banker; Walter Savage Landor, and
Leigh Hunt, whose places in *belles lettres* are undis-
puted :—all still gathered here, year after year, held by
the magnet of Lamb's genial wit, and the attractions of
genius and congenial spirits.

It was an understood thing among Lamb's coterie
that Godwin found the whist club a most peaceful
refuge from the uncertain tongue and temper of that
" Elisha-bear," as Lamb still called the second Mrs.
Godwin. She had angered Lamb by misrepresenting a
remark of his to Godwin; and Lamb could not forgive
the spirit that prompted her to slander him. So Charles
and Mary had seen little of Mary Wollstonecraft's
little girl during all these years because of this step-
mother. " She's s-s-swallowed by the ' Elisha-bear,' "
he would say, when Mary wondered about the girl.
Godwin was not very communicative, and Mary learned
little from him. The impecunious philosopher seemed
to care more for his quiet naps over the punch-bowl
than for the cards or friendly chatter of the " Round
Table," although he was always sufficiently awake to
do full justice to the cold roast or the veal pie.

Mary said the Amazon kept him upon short allow-
ance at home, and herself always managed to give him
the lion's share of the simple collations that were

served after their noisy rubbers of whist. Of late Godwin had seemed more silent and troubled than usual, and had confided to Mary that family cares were pressing rather heavily. As he was in a chronic state of borrowing from Lamb or any of the coterie who seemed ready to lend, they supposed debts were pressing, as usual.

Godwin had spoken to Lamb and Coleridge of a young scamp of a poet who had been expelled from Oxford for revolutionary sentiments, and for holding atheistic and Platonic theories, and challenging the professors to reply. It was at a time when the ferment of free-thought was causing the college authorities some trouble, and they pounced upon the erratic young Shelley as a scapegoat, and banished him.

Whilst stinging under the disappointment of a spoiled career, under the ban of Church and State, and thrust out from home for his vagaries, Shelley had rushed into a foolish marriage with a girl of humble origin. The poet found himself with no future, and no money, tied to a wife with whom he could find nothing in common. True, he had himself to thank for this early shipwreck of his life; but being a poet, with a poet's keen sensibilities, this did not make his trouble lighter to bear. His wife flirted and coqueted with other men, so he left her, and plunged into foreign travel; but he could not adjust his life to its lot. The apostle of the Necessarian creed gave the young poet much comfort. And being frequently at Godwin's house, he was thrown with the two pretty young daughters, Fanny Imlay and Mary Godwin, Mary Wollstonecraft's children. Of course their sympathies quickly followed the handsome young poet who had already tasted so much of the injustice and bitterness of life. Shelley soon recognized the ardent and gifted nature of Mary Godwin. The oftener he visited his friend Godwin for philosophic comfort, the more solace he found in the bright eyes and tender glances of Mary Godwin. They were both poetic, enthusiastic, and ardent, and life had used both badly; for Mary felt her motherlessness the more, as her sensibilities developed, only to be checked and curbed by the hard and practical stepmother.

So, upon her mother's grave, in the old churchyard in Holborn, Shelley and Mary Godwin plighted their troth—such a troth as a disappointed married man and Mary Wollstonecraft's motherless daughter could promise. The Necessarian, who held erratic views upon marriage, had not impressed very clear ideas of duty upon the young minds under his care. With her own mother's sad history before her, the young girl could scarcely have formed correct ideas upon matrimony under Godwin's tuition. So, in her loneliness and infatuation, she agreed to elope with Shelley, and become his wife and his comforter. His high-flown fancies seemed a beautiful religion to the girl of sixteen. To make the elopement more proper, Claire Clairmont, the second Mrs. Godwin's daughter by a former marriage, insisted upon accompanying the fleeing lovers, whose plans she had discovered.

They crossed to France, and started upon a pedestrian tour of the Continent with the small capital of a few pounds, great poetic enthusiasm, and unbounded affection and sentiment. This strange elopement, including a second young madcap as a chaperon, could scarcely realize the ideal of these young dreamers.

" M-Mary, who do you suppose has d-d-decamped ? " asked Lamb, hurrying back from the India House, the next day.

Mary looked blank for a moment, as if running over the list of possibles and impossibles, and said, in quicker time than I can tell it, " Mary Godwin and that little fool-poet ? "

" How did you g-g-guess it, old girl ? " said Lamb. " Trust you for smelling out a m-m-matrimonial alliance ! "

" I feared it," said Mary. " William Godwin has talked so much about that scapegrace Shelley; and that child is so beautiful, and so enthusiastic and unguided ! The Amazon has kept her too close, and the rebound was sure to come."

" Humph ! I should s-s-say she was not kept close enough. B-b-but that is not the worst of it, the Amazon's g-girl has gone with them ; and this morning the Elisha-bear herself f-followed."

" To bring them back ? " gasped Mary.

" Well, he could h-h-hardly marry the th-three of them," stammered Charles. " Poor old G-G-Godwin ! No wonder he has looked s-s-solemn lately; I suppose he f-f-feared some entanglement."

Mrs. Godwin returned in a few days, without her daughter. Shelley and the two girls had left Calais, and she could find no clew to their whereabouts.

Poor Fanny Imlay was left to bear the full brunt of her baffled wrath, as Godwin haunted the " Three Feathers " and the " White Cat " more than ever; and Charles and Mary Lamb encouraged him to take many a quiet nap at their cosy chimney-corner.

As for the lovers, they soon learned that even love

cannot escape the thorns and brambles of life's vicissitudes. They had to walk many weary miles in their wanderings. A little donkey which Shelley had bought gave the girls intervals of rest, as they took turns in riding him. But the meager fare and poor accommodations their scanty means could give them were hard upon the two delicate English girls. The beautiful scenes of Switzerland scarcely compensated for the terrible fatigue. Mary and Shelley, in their perfect congeniality of tastes, could have forgotten fatigue and privations in the enjoyment of the glorious mountains and exquisite lakes; but the sympathetic *tête-à-têtes* were always shared by the much complaining Claire. She had cast in her lot with theirs, and must now share the privations without their compensating love. She had soon become the skeleton at the feast, and since they had been unwise enough to take her from her home, the skeleton must share their weal or their woe hereafter. They were all three drifting along, rudderless, with mistakes and wrong-doing in their wake, and no safe harbor ahead. Perhaps the drifting was often pleasant, over sunset-tinted lakes, but there were many rocks waiting to wreck so ill-guided a bark.

They had thrown duty and reputation to the winds, and they could scarcely expect to reap aught but the whirlwind of condemnation, poverty, and the pricks of conscience. Despite their imperfect religious training and their vagaries of belief and imagination, they could not break God's recognized laws, and hold up their heads as though they were upright and pure in heart. Whilst feeling around, in the pride of his intellect, for a formula and plane of belief to suit his imagination and love of independence, the young poet had made shipwreck of his college career. For revenge and the gratification of a passing fancy, he had married a woman utterly unsuited to his station and nature. Becoming disgusted with her and with his own folly, he had deserted her and turned to the sympathy of the charming, gifted child, whom he had easily induced to try to make amends to him for his spoiled life. And now they were enjoying their stolen sweets under the fairest skies, and amid the loveliest scenes of God's beautiful world. But such roses have their thorns.

Shelley's poet-soul found stories of all the great castles clinging to the rocks. He learned or invented legends for every one. He made the girls shudder over the sad story of the rival brothers of Sterrenburg and Leibenstein. He pictured the army of rats and mice that besieged Bishop Hatto and devoured him in the square tower at Bingen, opposite the old castle of Ehrenfels. He pictured the myriads of little heads and claws emerging from the slimy stones, and forcing their way through windows and under doors, until the girls fairly shrieked with fright. He sang of the Lorelei and the mystic maidens, with their luring voices, who beckoned and called to the passing boatmen, until they clung to the side of their little boat, and implored him to hurry by, lest they too should fall under the witching spell.

And so they sailed along, week after week, stopping when and where they pleased, exploring the quaint old towns, and climbing over many a grand old ruin of fallen castle and dismantled tower. Never would any of that trio forget the wanderings of those idyllic days, charming in spite of the lowering cloud of conscious wrong-doing that ever followed them. The wronged wife, though left behind, was an unforgotten presence in their midst, and the anger of the outraged father, who had been so kind to the girls despite his poverty, haunted the sensitive Mary Godwin.

CHAPTER XXXVI.

" HONOR TO WHOM HONOR IS DUE."

Say, what is honor? Tis the finest sense
Of *justice* which the human mind can frame—
. . . . Honor is hopeful elevation—whence,
Glory and triumph.

WORDSWORTH.

IF the tidings of Southey's appointment to the Laureateship were criticised by Coleridge and some other old friends who did not like to think of Southey as a recipient of Court favors, the news was received far differently at the busy home at Keswick. To the simple women who adored him as their god, Southey was only receiving the just tribute to his genius.

Edith Southey, careful mother and housewife, clung with gratified pride to him, and Aunt Lovell and Sarah Coleridge warmly congratulated him upon being appreciated at last. The boys were vociferous, and the two sweet young girls, Edith Southey and Sara Coleridge, danced like fairies around their charmed Prince.

"Oh, now you will take us to London, won't you, papa?" "Won't you, dear uncle?" they cried, hanging around his neck, and jumping around him to snatch kisses, like doves pecking at an eagle.

"To London indeed!" he cried, laughing, whilst dodging and trying to ward off their well-aimed kisses.

" I suppose you think I shall have a chariot, and ride in the Queen's processions, with nodding plumes in my helmet," he said, laughing.

" No, uncle, poets wear a mantle and a laurel wreath, like Dante, don't they ? " asked Sara.

" So you young humbugs would like to see me look like a player in a Twelfth Night play ? " laughed Southey.

" And you would be the image of Dante, with your long nose and dark eyes," said Edith.

" Well, don't anticipate any such schemes ; I fear you will not see any access of grandeur. I have even bargained that I need not attend the Court fêtes— being such a modest man."

" Oh, papa !" " Oh, uncle !" said the girls in one breath, " we had even planned what we would wear."

" *Vanitas vanitatum !*" he exclaimed. " Well! I suppose peacocks will be peacocks ! "

" Even though they be males ! " added Edith wickedly.

It was a pretty sight to see the many inmates of that pleasant home grouped about the tall, handsome man. He was never too busy for a pleasant word or a joke, and he was ever ready to help the mother in her tasks, or the boys with their Latin or mathematics, or the girls in some frolic or mischief. Dora Wordsworth, the poet's only daughter, was very intimate with the two cousins, and a lovely trio they made. Sara Coleridge was fair as a lily, with soft blonde curls and luminous gray-blue eyes ; sensitive, dainty, full of the poetic sentiments that her delicate face portrayed, and with a well-cultured mind, that had developed finely under her Uncle Southey's fostering care. She was even now spending much of her leisure in translating Dobrizhoffer's "Account of the Abipones, an Equestrian People of Paraguay," which she published anonymously in 1822, for the purpose of helping Derwent at college. Coleridge's pride in this difficult work of his modest daughter was touching. He often spoke to his friends of her wonderful patience and perseverance in translating this three-volume-octavo Latin book. He said, "It is, in my judgment, unsurpassed for pure mother English by anything I have read for a long time." Charles Lamb also wrote to Southey of his wonder at the quiet girl's patience in "digging through this rugged Paraguay mine."

"How she *Dobrizhoffered* it all out puzzles my slender Latinity to conjecture," he wrote.[*]

The imagination, inherited from her father, found vent, later, in the dainty romance, "Phantasmion," which peopled her own Lake country with the nymphs and wind-sprites which the girls used to picture in their childhood.

The daughters of the three poets lived in a charming dreamland of their own evolved from their environment and the influence of the exalted literary and poetic atmosphere of their fathers and their friends. Southey's ever-increasing library and literary work was a wide field; Wordsworth's poetic dreams invested their rustic life with high ideals; and Coleridge's philosophies and eloquence made these children of the Lakes at home amid the elevations of genius. There was no dead level of commonplace in their world. Childhood and youth, sprung from such surroundings, develop into finer essence than those from common clay—although the children of geniuses seldom create or perpetuate similar

[*] "Lamb's Letters."

effusions. In Wordsworth's charming tribute to the three girls in "The Triad," he pictures Sara in such terms, that friends of Coleridge's supposed the sketch a personification of Faith.   He wrote :

> " Her brow hath opened on me—see it there
> Brightening the umbrage of her hair.
> So gleams the crescent moon that loves
> To be descried through shady groves. . . .
> Nor dread the depth of meditative eye,
> But let thy love upon that azure field
> Of thoughtfulness and beauty yield
> Its homage, offered up to purity.
> . . . . In sunny glade,
> Or under leaves of thickest shade,
> Was such a stillness e'er diffused
> Since earth grew calm, while angels mused ?
> Softly she treads, as if her foot were loth
> To crush the mountain dew-drops, soon to melt
> On the flower's breast. As if she felt
> That flowers themselves, whate'er their hue,
> With all their fragrance and their glistening,
> Call to the heart for inward listening.''

Of Edith Southey, gravest, most sedate of the three, the kind, helpful daughter, he wrote :

> " O lady, worthy of Earth's proudest throne,
> No less by excellence of Nature fit
> Beside an unambitious hearth to sit—
> Domestic Queen, where grandeur is unknown."

And of Dora Wordsworth, the youngest of the three ; wild as a gypsy, yet timid and gentle as a doe, he wrote :

> " How vivid, yet how delicate her glee.
> Flower of the Wind. . . .
> For she, to all but those who love her shy,
> Would gladly vanish from a stranger's sight. . . .

> Her happy spirit, as a bird, is free. . . .
> A face o'er which a thousand shadows go. . . .
> Like the lowly reed, her love
> Can drink its nurture from the scantiest rill."

The poetic appreciation of her bright, lovable qualities, added to the father-love, makes the tribute especially pleasing.   In his praise, one sees the restraint he puts upon his pen, lest his own child should have more than her share of the eulogy given to the three friends.

Was ever sweeter praise from worthier source ?

The daughters and sons of these three families formed a charming, social group in the quiet Lake country. They formed warm friendships among their neighbors; but the home circle was ever the dearest spot to all, save to Hartley Coleridge, who had something of Coleridge's love of genial company and wayside oratory.

Sara and Hartley inherited much of their father's talent.   They both wrote charming verses, and had that delicate susceptibility to the beautiful in Nature and Art that marks the truly poetic temperament.   Robert Southey watched them and the sturdy Derwent with as warm an interest as his own children.   He dreaded the tendency that Hartley showed towards self-indulgence and idle dreaming.   He feared the indications of these inherited traits, and, with Sarah, did all in his power to combat this weakness of will.   The only severity that Southey ever showed was when Hartley shirked some task or lesson, or slipped off for an evening at the Inn, where his wit and talents made him a most welcome visitor.

He had been sent to Oxford by his uncle and by some friends of Coleridge, who felt they would like in this way to help the unfortunate poet.   But while

Hartley was always a great favorite, certain eccentricities made his family anxious about him. His college record was not as good as it should be. Still, he was his sister's darling. And one of the little group of friends was especially interested in everything belonging to Hartley. Dora Wordsworth had clung to him from babyhood, and now she vied with his sister and cousin in fashioning mittens and comforters and Christmas surprises for Hartley. And when the examinations came, and Hartley failed to bring home the honors that they expected, Dora had the tenderest excuses and the warmest comfort for poor Hartley. At last, in the midst of eager Christmas preparations and loving Christmas secrets, when Hartley should come home with honors and crown them with the radiance of his glory, he came back sullen and disgraced. He and some companions had fallen into careless, desultory ways, and had been reprimanded several times, and finally, after some escapade, he, with several others, had been expelled!

Oh, the misery of it to the poor, anxious, disappointed mother! She had so watched him, and agonized over his careless, easy-going ways. She had prayed over him and warned him, and now her boy had come back disgraced! The knowledge of his son's lost career nearly broke Coleridge's heart. He remembered his own wasted opportunities, and grieved the more that his son should lose the chance of fitting himself for the life-battle. And Hartley, himself, was never again the same light-hearted, high-spirited fellow.

He came home more eccentric than ever, and would disappear for days together, and return, morose and silent, allowing no word of remonstrance.

Through his friend's influence he secured the position, at Ambleside, of teacher of the village school, which unpretending office he retained for many years. Here he was nearer Wordsworth, his father's dear friend, and he could easily seek Dora for comfort and encouragement. But William Wordsworth and his wife and the vigilant Aunt Dorothy could not let their darling waste her young heart upon as uncertain and unsteady a fellow as Hartley Coleridge.

Aunt Dorothy herself had a warm spot for Coleridge's son ; but she kept close guard upon Dora, lest Hartley Coleridge should come a-courting.

Only when they feared danger to their pet did they fully realize what it would be for her to be allied to a man as erratic and uncertain as was Coleridge. Hartley should never have the chance to treat their Dora as his father had treated Sarah Coleridge. It was only through their fears of the son that they understood where the great fault of the father lay, and realized that Hartley had inherited Coleridge's tendency to a weak will and erratic life. Even now, Hartley's good stories and bright wit made him so popular at the Inn and by the roadside, that he never knew when to go home.

CHAPTER XXXVII.

"THE WAGES OF SIN IS DEATH."

O world ! O life ! O time !
On whose last steps I climb,
Trembling at that where I had stood before,—
When will return the glory of your prime?
No more—oh nevermore !

Out of the day and night
A joy has taken flight;
Fresh Spring and Summer, and Winter hoar
Move my faint heart with grief,—but with delight
No more—oh nevermore !

SHELLEY.

THE Shelleys had returned to London, poor and friendless. Godwin refused to see the girls, and Shelley's father would have nothing to do with him. So the two girls had a mean little lodging, and Shelley slept wherever he could, coming to see his wife every day, and bringing whatever pittance he could earn by writing, and all the tenderness and comfort that a sincere love could offer. Mary Shelley was sick and wretched, and the only comfort she could have—her husband's ministrations—was denied her in these days of extreme poverty. She remembered her good friend Miss Lamb, and sent a message begging her to visit her. Mary Lamb hastened to the poor young thing, and found her lacking the very necessaries of life, with Claire fretful and fault-finding—a wretched burden to the young couple. Often the poet and his wife would not have a penny to pay for a dinner, but would dine upon a few cakes or buns that Shelley would bring in. Yet they were cheerful and even hopeful, and only Claire complained. When Mary's baby was born, and the little thing died, she grieved sorely, although it was well there was not another mouth to feed.

Mary Lamb was as tender and kind to the poor outcast as she was to everything that needed her help. She carried the sick girl clothing and food from her own little store, and she made Godwin do what he could for his daughter.

One morning, before the breakfast dishes had been cleared away, the sloppy little drudge announced " Miss Lamb " to the astonished couple.

Godwin looked alarmed and somewhat foolish, and Mrs. Godwin straightened up defiantly, as she stiffly greeted the mild-looking guest.

"It is a long while since you have honored us, Miss Lamb," she said, tartly.

"I am but a poor visitor," said Mary, flushing. "You know my poor health prevents me from doing much visiting ; but this morning I wanted particularly to see you—both," she added, as she saw Godwin preparing to escape. "I have spent several days with your daughters, who are most anxious to see you both. Mary's baby died yesterday, and she has not even the means to bury it, or food enough to build up her wasted strength," said Mary, with tears in her kind gray eyes.

Godwin twisted uncomfortably in his chair, and Mrs. Godwin said, with a snort, " You have no right to come here upon such a matter; you know these wretched girls have disgraced us."

" I think, Mrs. Godwin, they have suffered enough to atone for their foolishness.   Shelley and Mary have simply nothing to live upon, and yet they must share their crusts with your daughter, who should at least be under her own mother's roof and protection."

" And whose fault is it, pray, that she is not?" asked Mrs. Godwin wrathfully.

" Ah! Mrs. Godwin, it is too late now to talk of whose fault it may be.   Who of us lives up to our whole duty?   I say, again, your daughter's place is at home with her family, before worse comes to her."

" Then let her crawl back and ask pardon, if she is penitent," said the angry mother.

" May I tell her so?" asked Mary gently.   " She is afraid to come here when she has so deeply offended you.   May I tell her you will forgive her if she asks your pardon?"

" It seems odd for a stranger to be interfering with our affairs," said Mrs. Godwin angrily.

" Not a stranger, but a real friend of those foolish girls," said Mary, timidly holding her ground and looking full at William Godwin.

" Yes, yes, Mary Lamb, thou hast ever been kind to the little hussy," said Godwin.   " We will see those poor foolish children.   I have but little help I can give them ; my own debts press heavily; but Claire shall come home, and I will see Mary and that young fool." So Claire came home, and Godwin and the Lambs did what they could to help the Shelleys.

A month or two later, Charles Lamb hurried home one evening, with such alacrity in his step, and such especial good-humor beaming from his eyes, that Mary knew he had good news for her.

"Well, brother, is Coleridge or Manning coming up to town that you seem so gay?"

"No, B-B-Bridget, but s-s-somebody's dead."

"Dead!" said Mary, aghast; "what do you mean?"

"An old s-s-scion of the aristocracy has 'sh-sh-shuffled off this mortal coil,' and some b-b-beggars will ride to his funeral. Not knowing the d-d-defunct, I can but rejoice with the b-b-beneficiaries. Shelley's grandfather has k-k-kindly departed in the n-n-nick of time, and couldn't c-c-carry his estates and p-p-possessions to old Nick with him," said Lamb, with a wicked twinkle, "and they are entailed upon Shelley."

"Does not that seem like the hand of Providence,— just when those poor Shelleys are at their wits' ends for a living?" asked Mary.

"Umph! you know they say the d-d-devil takes care of his own," said Lamb; "but, God or devil, it is a blessed windfall for them."

"You know 'God tempers the wind to the shorn lamb,' Charles."

"Now, Polly, have we not waited these t-t-twenty years, and the only t-t-temper I have found has been thy tongue, when I have tried to find c-c-comfort in my c-c-cups."

Mary laughed at his adroit allusion to their little battles over Charles's propensities. She had to watch this genial brother carefully, especially upon their whist evenings; for he was becoming more and more addicted to drowning cares and disappointments in the steaming punch-bowl.

After the Shelleys received their inheritance, or rather the pension allowed the young poet by his father, in place of the direct inheritance, they lost no time in settling in a comfortable place, where Shelley could write, and Mary could learn the happiness of having a home of her own.

And happiness might have dwelt with these two who seemed so well adapted to enjoy each other, if the shadow of their wrong-doing had not pursued them. Harriet, Shelley's legal wife, followed the poet with angry complaints, and compelled him to divide his pension with her. Even this did not satisfy her, and she insisted upon seeing Mary and tormenting her with the wrong and suffering they were causing her. Verily "the way of the transgressor is hard," as Mary Godwin learned every day. She knew his former wife was using all her wiles and claims to lure her husband back; and between her fears and her conscience she did not know whether indignation at, or pity for, this deserted wife was the stronger in her heart. She knew that Shelley loved her now; but would he, who had once forsaken duty and love, be true to her who had only the claims of love upon him? So the young girl grieved and feared, and they decided to leave England, where both had found so much of disappointment and sorrow. Shelley made generous provision for the father-in-law who had so grudgingly forgiven him, and for his wife; and again Claire accompanied them, having become entangled in a love affair with Lord Byron, who had but lately married the cold and haughty Miss Milbanke. Byron's great popularity, as poet and social favorite, was waning. Many ugly rumors were afloat about the handsome young *roué*, whose burning glances and passionate poems made him so fascinating and dangerous a companion to the London *débutantes*. Mammas were beginning to look anxious when he bent over their pretty daughters, and society was gradually turning a cold shoulder towards this last year's favorite.

His stately wife watched him nervously, and was not able to conceal a certain disdain or unhappiness which had settled upon her rather plain face.

The gossips had wondered at the match, as she seemed scarcely the woman they would have expected a pleasure-loving poet to choose.

And equally did her friends wonder at her choice; for she was considered rather a prude, and Byron was a recognized libertine. But when, a few months later, Lady Byron left her husband's home, and refused to return or make any explanation, the storm broke and fell gradually upon his head.

The gossips had known him to be a wicked rake. They did not know how he had treated poor Lady Byron; but they did know he was a monster. Their doors were closed upon him. There was no pity, no sympathy. His pious wife would not, or could not, live with him. There was something wrong, something so terrible, that only silence could express it. No explanations were given; no explanations were needed. He was an outcast from that day, with no chance to defend himself. They forgot " Childe Harold." Doubtless the man who could write " Don Juan " was a heartless libertine; but he had not written it then. That emanated from his later life, when he was an outcast and an exile from home and country, wife and child. Doubtless his life was full of imperfections, in a day when men lived high and gave free rein to passions and vices that a later civilization holds in check —at least, outwardly. But whatever his deserts, his fate was hard, as society used him as the scape goat for a loose state of morals that needed reforming in England. Every now and then the morals and manners of "Society" need purification and a wholesome lesson, and the culprit who is caught at that time bears his own and his neighbors' punishment. Lord Byron was that culprit in his decade, and was pursued with a scorn and hatred for his many known and unknown sins, that made him a wanderer on the face of the earth, and ended his young life in an ignominy where there was no room left him for repentance or reformation.

It is not strange that Shelley and Byron should have become intimate. Poetry is a strong magnet to attract its votaries, and these two poets were similarly scorned by their countrymen, and ruthlessly banished from society by the rigors and narrowness of newly-awakened public opinion. Each was the scape-goat of his day, and bore the punishment due to the whole race of similar offenders : Shelley, as skeptic and free-thinker ; Byron, as libertine.

In his gloomy days, when society was fast closing its doors to him, Byron was thrown much with the Shelleys, and was comforted by Claire's unstinted sympathy and adoration. In his banishment from wife, home, and country, the tie grew closer between Byron and the Shelleys. In Italy they could enjoy God's beautiful world, screened from the venom of critical and gossiping tongues, and enjoy a happiness denied them in their own country.

The Godwins kept this new trial as quiet as possible. Some few old friends heard rumors of Byron's intimacy with Mrs. Godwin's daughter, but nothing was known positively, and the flight to the Continent might be but a continuation of the first folly. But poor Godwin had grown very taciturn. Married life and the very unusual cares it brought him, with his increasing poverty and debts, wrought a sad change in the old philosopher.

At home, Mrs. Godwin's temper was not sweetened by this fresh blow to her pride, and poor Fanny Imlay had the whole brunt of the domestic woes and cares thrust upon her. She saw her kind step-father overwhelmed with debt and disappointment. She suffered keenly from the obloquy that had fallen upon the family ever since Mary and Claire had first left home. And now, with this new complication, and the comments and questions about Claire that she could not endure to hear, her patience and endurance were gone. There was nothing in life but sorrow and dis-grace. She tried to support herself by teaching or as a companion, but the scandals about her family closed all doors upon her. She brooded in uncomplaining bitterness of spirit, day by day and week after week. Mary Lamb was a kind friend and comforter; but the shy girl could not speak of the worst of her troubles to any human ear, and the Heavenly Father seemed so far away, so pitiless! Daily she grew sadder and more pathetic in her lonely sorrow. The angry step-mother visited her own misery upon the patient young thing who was in her power. Fanny sat in her bed-chamber through many long nights, softly moaning and weeping. There was no escape, no future for her, no hope, even no work, to help keep her foster-father from the debtor's prison. All the grief in Mary Wollstonecraft's heart, when deserted by the faithless

Imlay, seemed poured out in her daughter's nature. Poor Fanny was overwhelmed, bewildered, by the cruelty of her fate. " Why should she live ? There was no place for her," was repeated over and over in her tired heart, until there was but the one thought—Death. Death seemed such a blessed relief from the daily repetition of worry, anxiety, and despair.

One morning, filled with the thought of life's endless dreariness and death's kind reprieve, she dressed herself carefully in plain clothes, leaving behind all articles that might give a clew to her identity.

She left home, pretending she would seek a situation of some sort until she found one. She took a boat to Swansea and paid her last shilling for a room at the inn. She wrote a letter that compromised no one, saying, " she was but a lonely woman of unfortunate birth and no connections, who was weary of life. . . . She would pass unknown from a life that held no place for her, and she prayed Christian burial for the body that she hoped and believed had wronged no one, praying a merciful Father to save her soul,—if she had a soul." *

The London papers, two days afterwards, were filled with accounts of a suicide at Swansea of a beautiful girl of about twenty, describing the delicate features and dark eyes and hair, and publishing the letter found by her bed.

The Godwins had become alarmed at Fanny's long absence, and finding she was not at the Lambs', some one suggested the possibility that her evident depression had affected her mind. The notices of the unknown suicide at Swansea seemed ominously like Fanny Imlay ; and William Godwin and Charles Lamb

* " Life of Mary Godwin Shelley."—ROSETTI.

went to the inn at Swansea, and at once recognized poor Fanny, still and cold in death. They wept bitterly at the sad sight, and buried the poor child with as little publicity as possible.

They were able to hush up the affair, and very few persons ever knew that the young suicide at Swansea was Godwin's step-daughter, the quiet little Fanny Imlay. The poor little life had gone out like a snuffed candle, and she had, as she said, so small a place in the world that it never missed her.

The life, shadowed by her mother's sin and her sister's wrong-doing, had never shone out into notice, and the feeble light had gone out into the thick darkness of the great unknown.

The Shelleys had wandered hither and thither in Switzerland and Italy. When the news of Fanny's death reached them, they were with Byron at Lake Leman, sailing and rowing over the lovely blue waters. They had visited Chillon Castle, and watched the sun playing upon the fine towers and over the gray walls, and sending its one shaft at sunset into the black, pillared dungeon where Bonnivard and his sons had watched that same evening ray pierce the narrow slit in the wall, at sunset, all those weary years. Here, and in the beautiful garden adjoining the castle, with its oranges and roses and wisteria, Byron wrote the poem that has given him his widest fame.

And here, in this same lovely spot, where they leaned over the marble balustrades, all ivy-grown, and watched the moon silvering the turrets and towers of Chillon, did the Shelleys and Claire hear of the death of their half-sister.

They had been rioting in the beautiful scenes about

them—these poets full of passion and the love of the beautiful.

They had watched the rosy and blue tints of the many hills and mountains encircling Lake Geneva, and changing their opal hues with each turn of the boat, or passing cloud. They had watched the violet and blue mountains stretch off to the glowing silver lines of the *Dents du Midi* where they peep over the shoulders of the rosy peaks that enclose them. And they had floated idly for days upon the blue, blue-waters, under the clear blue skies. They had dreamed of love and poetry; of the olden days and the stately castle, in the rose-covered cottage which was now their home. They had written songs and poems, and had sung them in the evening glow, upon the lake. Now, again their golden idyl was shattered. Death had awakened them from their poets' dreams. They all felt that in some way, they had helped poison that poor patient life. The shadow hung over them, in castle, lake, or cottage. Their stories grew weird and wild, and their overwrought nerves fancied death and mourning in every sigh of the breeze. To shake off remorse and grief, they challenged each other to write stories and poems to amuse and crowd out sad memories during the evenings.

Shelley and Byron, Mary and Claire, with an occasional visit from Trelawny, who was also staying near, spent their days writing stories for those haunted evenings. Byron's " Dream of Darkness " was one of his contributions to their evenings' entertainments. And Shelley's wild stories, and Claire's more commonplace ones, were all eclipsed by the fascinating horrors of Mary Shelley's horrid inspiration—" Frankenstein." This girl of eighteen created a monster of strength, cunning, and wickedness—a great distorted body, without a soul. The psychological questions, the mocking of evil without the balance-wheel of principle and conscience, are so well understood, and so carefully depicted, that we realize that her talent was well mated with Shelley's inspired genius.

Mary Shelley's companions were as astonished at her story as the world has been ever since its publication. It shows, however, the nervous and unsettled condition of the writer's mind at this time. Fortunately, the arrival of a little son turned the channels of her thoughts, and perhaps saved her mind from becoming utterly unbalanced. The little baby claimed her time and attention, and filled her heart with sweet new thoughts and love.

Another shock was awaiting them. Harriet, Shelley's wife, becoming a prey to remorse, jealousy, and despair, drowned herself in the Serpentine, in Hyde Park. Here was another blow and mortification. Shelley's sensitive nature was stung to the quick.

He felt the full force of his part in this tragedy. Harriet had been vain and foolish, and had driven him to leave her by her conduct with other men, yet he knew she always loved him, and had taken her life in her despair at losing him. He was haunted with misery and self-reproach. The one consolation remained, that he and Mary could now marry, which they did at once.

Beautiful Geneva Lake became hateful to the Shelleys, and as soon as possible they gave up their charming little cottage and settled here and there in Italy, as the spirit moved them, or their restlessness permitted. They visited Milan, Florence, Pisa, Leghorn, the baths of Lucca, Venice, and settled in Rome for the winter. They lived in Byron's castle at Este, but Claire lost her little girl (Byron's child), and they again craved change and spent the following winter at Naples. Here, in this land of art, Shelley absorbed the spirit of art and love of the pictures and sculpture that abound in Italy. Here, at the Doria and Colonna palaces, he saw the exquisite pictures of Beatrice Cenci which inspired him to write the beautiful drama of the Cenci. But at Rome they lost their eldest boy, and again fled from their gloom and sorrow to Florence, and finally settled at Lerici, on the Bay of Spezzia.

CHAPTER XXXVIII.

CHANCE AND CHANGE.

The man must have a rare recipe for melancholy who can be dull in Fleet Street.—Often when I have felt dull at home, have I rushed into the crowded Strand and fed my humor till the tears have wetted my cheek for unutterable sympathies with the multitudinous, moving picture. . . . I love the very smoke of London, because it has been the medicine most familiar to my vision. Thus an act of extracting morality from the commonest incidents of a town life is attained by the same well-natured alchemy by which the foresters of Arden " find tongues in trees."

CHARLES LAMB.

WHILST the Shelleys were roaming through Italy, the Lambs and Coleridge had both changed their homes.

The Lambs moved from the Temple building to No. 20 Little Russell Street, over a brazier's shop—a strange situation for two nervous people to select.

They were temptingly near two theaters, Drury Lane Theater being just in front of their house, and Covent Garden Theater directly in the rear. And the Lambs were both fond of attending the theater, although this could scarcely have been their reason for selecting a home in a neighborhood so full of noise and discomfort. " I can s-s-step around the corner and f-f-find the first vegetables and greens in market," said Lamb.

" Cresses and beans with the morning dew upon them, and f-f-fruits in their early bloom. And Mary likes nothing better than w-w-watching the carriages and c-c-cabs rushing by in the evenings, and listening to the halloos and wrangles of the link-boys, as they s-s-swing their torches."

" I cannot say that I p-p-particularly enjoy the h-h-hammering in the shop below ; but they stop work at night, and M-M-Mary says it is c-company for her during the day," he said to Procter.

Poor Mary liked almost anything that drew her thoughts from herself. She dared not let her mind dwell upon the symptoms that seemed forever threatening her with those dreaded spells of insanity. They were always returning, always creeping upon her, like some hidden enemy. Her attacks were more frequent than formerly, and they made fearful gaps in the quiet home-life of the devoted sister and brother. Just when Charles needed her most, she was sure to be overtaken by her tormentor. It was an ever-present terror to the unfortunate pair, and it was wearing Charles's nerves thread-bare.

During all the merriment of the noisy evenings over whist, Charles was always furtively watching his sister. And whether he was flinging his witticisms among the many friends who loved to gather in his cheerful rooms, or quietly reading some beloved old folio to Mary, he was ever watchful and thoughtful of her. No lover could be more tender or anxious. The bright-eyed little man and his sweet-faced sister became known around the flower-market, and the vegetable women and fish-wives learned to look for their pleasant morning greeting.   When he wandered there alone, looking so pensive, they would ask after the pretty lady, and win his heart by their comments and praises of his sister.

Often the constant chatter of his many friends wearied him.   He was the oracle of his friends, and they sought him continually.   But as she grew more popular, he complained that his friends left him no time for quiet thought.   They met him as he strolled through the Temple Gardens and up Fleet Street and Cheapside, on his morning walk to India House. They joined him upon his return in the afternoon. They looked in during the evening to consult him about this book and that essay ; and they talked and smoked and played cards with him until midnight.   This constant excitement wearied both his and Mary's sensitive nerves until he decided upon some escape.   Lamb wrote to Wordsworth, " I am never alone. . . . .   I can never walk home from office, but some officious friend offers his unwelcome courtesies, to accompany me.   All the morning I am pestered.   Evening company I should like, had I my mornings, but I am saturated with human faces (*divine*, forsooth), and miss all the golden mornings."

" I am never Charles Lamb, but C. L. & Co.   He who thought it not good for man to be alone, preserve me from the more prodigious monstrosity of never being by myself." *

This letter was partly the result of a frustrated effort to write out the thoughts that were becoming so acceptable to the public, and partly the whimsical exaggeration that made his letters so welcome to his friends.

Lamb loved his friends, and was the last man on

* " Letters of Charles Lamb."--AINGER.

earth to show the least impatience at their endless claims, but he always liked the relief of emptying his moods into the bosom of his letters.

"Wh-who of us c-can endure to be robbed of our leisure and privacy? N-n-nothing so upsets a writer as interruptions when he f-feels his inspiration upon him," said Lamb to Mary, after an evening's interruption by guests.

Most writers claim and insist upon a certain amount of seclusion ; in fact, who can think and write without it? It is the besetting sin and daily temptation of people gifted with individuality, to shrink into themselves, and retreat into the sheltered haven of home.

Tennyson was at last almost a hermit, and even the social Dickens fled from his friends and the world when he was evolving his own world. Writers must live among their creations. But Charles Lamb's mornings were filled with his accounts and India House work, and his scanty leisure from public service was borrowed and stolen by the endless demands of an ever-increasing circle of friends. It was indeed a time to say : " Good Lord ! deliver us from our friends ! " And not one of these friends ever guessed that the gentle " Elia " was chafing for quiet and freedom. With the courtesy of the true gentleman, he had a smile and joke for all, only relieving his ennui by such an occasional letter as the one just quoted.

He often said : " The neighborhood of such a man as Coleridge is as exciting as the presence of fifty ordinary persons, and if I lived with him or the author of ' The Excursion ' I should, in a very little time, lose my own identity." * Yet he loved both tenderly, as few men

* " Letters of Charles Lamb."—AINGER.

love those of their own sex. He gave the sympathy of a woman to poor Godwin in all his trials and tribulations, and often shared his slender purse with " the philosopher " when creditors became too clamorous.

He and Mary watched over the impractical Dyer, and gave him many a good dinner when the book-stall treasures had left him no margin to buy the, to him, unimportant necessaries of life. They suffered with the Hazlitts, at the illness and death of their child. They soothed the disappointments of disgusted politicians, and shared the griefs of ill-used authors. They rejoiced with Rickman over a successful Reform Bill, and they shared Sergeant Talfourd's pride in a legal triumph. In fact, Charles and Mary Lamb had the gift of ready sympathy and thorough appreciation for every human being that cared to claim such munificence. The gentle, soft-eyed sister was as great a favorite as Charles Lamb. But even this wealth, when poured out so generously drains the donor's coffers. They both needed a change of scene to replenish the overtaxed nerve forces. The Wordsworths, the Hazlitts, Manning, all their friends besought them to pay them visits. But this would still require the effort of social intercourse, from which they both craved a rest. The Shelleys' descriptions of Switzerland and the Rhine had made Charles Lamb feel that there was grandeur and beauty in the world, even beyond Skiddaw and Helvellyn, and the Westmoreland lakes.

Mary had lately recovered from a long spell of her malady, and the time seemed favorable for a visit to the Continent. The task-masters at India House were gracious enough to accord a holiday, and with great glee they started for Paris. The horrors of a packet-boat upon the English Channel were graphically described by Lamb, when he could look back upon its misery. He and Mary were keenly alive to the charm and novelty of the old French towns and cities along the route to Paris. They were charmed with the quaint old streets of Amiens, its fountains and statues, its gray old palaces and splendid cathedrals, and exquisite Gothic pinnacles of St. Ouen and the fine bridges over the meandering river.

Charles's quaint taste was satisfied by the solidity and age of the buildings in the towns through which their coach-route lay. And Mary's with the bright-eyed children, the babies in their caps, and the profusion of flowers everywhere.

They stopped at old St. Denis, to see the abbey and its stately monuments and tombs, and walked with keenest interest through the crypts and chapels, where the insane mobs of the Reign of Terror had torn open the tombs and desecrated the bodies of the many kings and bishops and royalties who had been, for ages, buried here.

They followed the course of those infuriated mobs, who had marched out from Paris on their tour of destruction and vengeance. But ere they reached Paris, Mary was attacked by her old malady, and in the stage-coach Charles put the strait-jacket upon her; and his first business in Paris was to find some asylum for his raving and delirious sister. He placed her in the care of some nuns at an insane asylum. But the charm of his holiday had vanished. Poor Mary was among strangers, and he must visit these longed-for scenes alone. Paris, in that year of 1822, was not the Paris of to-day. Long, over-crowded streets, packed with swarming humanity, and darkened from the height of the great rambling tenements that almost met across the streets, stretched and intertwined for miles ; almost concealing in their close embrace the palaces which rose in stately grandeur behind their walls, and the noble churches encroached upon by these close-pressing streets. The Palais Royal and its gardens, the Tuileries and its beautiful park, the splendid Louvre and Luxembourg palaces were screened by their gardens and enclosures behind the narrow streets. But the wide, straight avenues of to-day, with their fair, roomy hotels, stretching for miles in all directions, are souvenirs of the Napoleons.

The Republic of this latter end of the nineteenth century must thank the Bonapartes for the stately avenues that follow and cross the Seine in all directions, and make Paris the fairest city on earth, if not the most interesting. To gain this beauty she has sacrificed much that was interesting and historic.

The sight-seeing of the next few days amid the ruins of the Bastille and the Reign of Terror scenes ; the noble façade of Notre Dame, and pillared Madeleine, and the delicate gorgeousness of the Sainte Chapelle, scarcely diverted Lamb's thoughts from his trouble.

The charm of the new scenes and historic streets and palaces had departed. Charles wandered for weeks around Paris and its suburbs, visiting the art galleries and palaces, with but half a heart for the interesting sights. He visited the salons of the Tuileries open to strangers, and meditated upon the changes which it had lately witnessed. Here Napoleon had lived in splendor with Josephine, and, after the cruel divorce, he had brought the young *Austrienne* to this same palace. And now they were all gone, and Louis XVIII. the Bourbon, had returned. The mighty Napoleon Bonaparte had risen to the pinnacle of his fortune and success, and was now dying at St. Helena. As Charles Lamb visited the splendid palaces of Versailles and Fontainebleau where Napoleon had lived in those elegant apartments, adorned and frescoed for the magnificent Louis XIV. and representing his grandeur and pride in every hall and corridor, he could but wonder afresh at Napoleon's audacity, and pity the downfall of such splendid ambition. At Versailles he sought the chambers whence Marie Antoinette had fled from that horrible mob; and he marveled that the gentle Josephine could have occupied those apartments, so filled with the very recent memories of that sad downfall. And after her came Marie Louise into the same beautiful suites of rooms, with only the exquisite white silk draperies and hangings changed to cover the traces of those happy yet anxious years, ere Josephine, too, had been driven away from home, husband, and throne.

"I am living over the history of this strange people in my glimpses of their palaces and art galleries. It is appalling to think of the great revolutions and changes within the past twenty years—the overthrow of the Bourbons; the Reign of Terror; the advent of the mighty Napoleon; his rise and setting like a gorgeous comet; and now, his utter humiliation and the return of the Bourbons, with the modification caused by that revolution. These people are so fiery and volatile, that each new change seems the supreme blessing to be desired—until a newer sensation takes their fancy. Then, phiz! bang! chop off their heads! and try another revolution."

Thus wrote Lamb, while taking his lonely views of Paris. Mary, who would so have enjoyed these scenes and memories, was in a lunatic asylum, personating a grand dame—perhaps one of those very personages whose history was brought before them. The simple-hearted nuns in attendance could not understand the English jargon of the " court-lady " who made such fine speeches, and gave such stately orders ; but they did understand the gentle kindliness underlying the veneer of her stately illusions, and the poor stranger was treated kindly, and even made friends among her attendants.

After her recovery, they could do but little sight-seeing together, and could go no further, as Charles's leave-of-absence was over.

" I am always interfering with your plans, brother," said Mary sadly, the day they left Paris for home.

" No, Bridget ! that you are n-n-not ! I have no p-p-plans apart from you, and the b-b-best thing in life is to see your ch-ch-cheering smile again. It d-d-drives out all the cobwebs that g-g-gather in my brain."

As they were journeying towards home, Charles filled in the time and relieved the tedium of the long stage rides, by making the acquaintance of such of their fellow-travelers as seemed disposed to be sociable.

One young Scotchman just returning from Germany attracted his notice by his unusual attention to small personal comforts.

" Ah ! driver ! have we any hot breeks ? " he asked, after a change of horses at an inn.

" Eh, Monsieur ? Breeks ? h-h-hot ? *Qu'est-ce que c'est ?* "

" *Quelque chose chaud, pour les pieds,*" answered the impatient Scotchman, drawing his traveling shawl close round his shoulders.

" C-c-cold ? " asked Lamb sympathetically.

" Umph ! " snarled the Scotchman, giving his long mane a shake.

" Perhaps you would l-l-l-like a good d-d-dram to warm you," said Lamb, offering his pocket-flask.

" No, sir ! no, sir ! Nothing of the kind ! Rank poison, sir ! " said the Scotchman.

But Lamb was not to be bluffed off in this unfriendly manner, and after a half hour's silence, he again addressed his surly companion.

" What do you th-th-think of Paris, sir ? "

" It is as infernally dirty a hole as ever was built, and those confounded Frenchmen chatter like a set of monkeys. I spent a month there collecting material for a history of the Revolution, and that month nearly killed me."

" Ah ! you are a writer ? " said Lamb, with an accent of reverence in his tone. " I do something in that l-l-line myself. Possibly you have st-st-stumbled upon some bits in the ' N-N-New Monthly ' signed Elia ? "

" Ah ! ' Imperfect Sympathies,' ' Oxford in Vacation ! ' Indeed I have read them with pleasure ; I am pleased to meet a fellow-worker. Perhaps you have read my translation of ' Wilhelm Meister ' ? "

" Aye, that I have," said Lamb, with a sunny smile, " and I am proud to know Mr. Thomas C-C-Carlyle. It is strange we have not m-m-met before. We have so many mutual friends in L-L-London. I have often heard S-S-Samuel Rogers and L-L-Leigh Hunt speak of you. And that young marplot, Shelley. You would not be l-l-likely to have heard them mention Ch-Ch-Charles Lamb, we little f-f-fish are s-swallowed up in the great London whirlpool."

"I am so seldom in London that I meet but few people. The atmosphere and horrible din of that place tear my nerves to pieces," said young Carlyle.

"How d-d-different we are! London is the finest tonic I can take. I p-p-pine for it, wherever I may be, and only breathe freely in its b-busy streets."

"Then you must have enjoyed the turmoil of Paris?" asked Carlyle.

"N-no. I abhorred it, even as y-you did. P-P-Paris can no more be c-c-compared with London than Old Bow with S-S-St. Paul's."

"And neither can be mentioned in the same breath with Edinburgh, or even with the fens and moors, for a dwelling place," said Carlyle, in a tone which admitted no contradiction.

So Lamb slid off into more general topics, and the restless young Scotchman drummed upon the window-glass and shuffled around in his seat, and finally settled down for a nap, which was an impossibility, with the stage-coach plunging and tilting and rattling like thunder.

In after years, when Thomas Carlyle had become one of the lions of his day, and Charles Lamb had won his place among the first of the British essayists, each recalled this stage-coach meeting with the other.

"The Scotch philosopher reminded me of a b-b-bear with a sore head and a very alarming g-g-growl," said Lamb, in describing that meeting.

"Charles Lamb is a pitiful little fellow, with the sort of a bleat you would expect from the aimless wanderings of his sketches.   He is always stammering into a bog and fishing himself out, and calling upon every one to come and see how limp he is," said Carlyle.

Before Carlyle tore himself from his adored Scotland, and settled in London, " Elia " had ceased to find his stage, his philosophy, his comfort, and his world, in its busy streets.

CHAPTER XXXIX.

> But he is weak; both man and boy
>   Hath been an idler in the land,
> Contented if he might enjoy
>   The things which others understand.
> Come hither in thy day of strength,
>   Come weak as is a breaking wave!
> Here stretch thy body at full length,
>   Or build thy house upon this grave.
>
> WORDSWORTH.—*Poets' Epitaph.*

As I have already said, both Lamb and Coleridge
had changed their homes.   Coleridge becoming utterly
discouraged at the fresh hold taken upon him by opium,
and at the continued scorn of the critics, which caused
his best efforts to fall dead, placed himself under the
care of Dr. Gillman at Highgate.   He confessed his
weakness to Dr. Gillman, and begged him to give him
such care as should help him fight off his besetting
temptation.   Dr. Gillman, becoming greatly interested in
the gifted man, who seemed so in earnest in desiring to
reform, invited him to his own home.   There he was
received as one of the family, and Mrs. Gillman became as much attached to their strange inmate as her
husband.   They watched him incessantly.   They had
an attendant accompany or follow him in his long

walks from Highgate to Hampstead Heath, to prevent him from buying opium. They warned all chemists and shop-keepers not to sell it to him.

Yet, such is the cunning that these tyrannical habits implant, he often found opportunities to get the poison. He wanted to be prevented from buying opium, yet he was impelled by the secret craving to elude every vigilance and procure it.

From months, his stay lingered on into years. He became known throughout the neighborhood, and many of his and Lamb's friends took the London coaches and visited Coleridge at the Gillmans'. Leigh Hunt, Tom Hood, De Quincey, Edward Irving, the eccentric young divine who was making such a stir in London, all sought him out, and spent many pleasant evenings with him. Charles and Mary Lamb spent many evenings, and an occasional Sunday, at Dr. Gillman's. Here in this peaceful, pleasant home,—a wide stone house set in a shady garden, amid fine old trees—Samuel Coleridge grew calmer and happier than he had been for many years. He wrote incessantly, and many excellent books resulted from these quiet, peaceful years. His "Aids to Reflection," written at this time, although ignored, or only sneered at by the prejudiced critics, became a regular text-book in America, where, in those days, Coleridge found more appreciation than at home. Long before he found recognition as a thinker and philosopher in England, America regarded him as one of the leading spirits of the day. The "Biographia Literaria" and "Aids to Reflection," which had no chance whatever for sale at home, were widely sought by his brothers across the water. Longfellow, Emerson, Holmes, Hawthorne, and a host of young writers who were just beginning to try their powers, looked upon Coleridge's poetic and prose writings as models of thought, recognizing the divine genius of his poetry and the depth of his philosophy.

A congenial coterie formed around him at Highgate, and listened with delight to his wonderful flow of eloquence. Friends followed him here, and settled around him, and he held a sort of literary court to which an ever-increasing set of satellites flocked. A nephew, Henry Coleridge, settled near, and spent his leisure with this revered uncle, and his daughter Sara paid him long visits, charming him with her sweetness and ready appreciation. A strong bond steadily increased between father and daughter. Sara flitted around him in this pleasant home, where he was more like a brother than a mere boarder. His family and friends were ever welcome, and for the first time in many years, Coleridge felt the comfort and satisfaction of having a home. He was tenderly watched and cared for, with no complaining or reproaches at his occasional relapses into the trammels and subsequent melancholy of his infirmity. He grew stronger and better, as the years went by, and a genial, benevolent smile replaced the old eager, restless look. Little children always crowded around the tottering, silver-haired man, who gathered them to him with winning smiles and fascinating stories, as he slowly paced the shady lanes and breezy uplands of Highgate and Hampstead Heath.

"They say you are a poet, Mr. Coleridge," said a little fellow, slipping his hand into his friend's. "What is a poet?"

Coleridge looked at the earnest eyes and eager face, and, shaking his head, said:

" Ah, Willie, a poet is a queer fellow that tries to fly instead of walking. He tries to live with his head in the clouds, and only stumbles along, having a body too heavy to follow his thoughts."

" Can you fly, sir? " asked the child, astonished.

" I used to try, my boy ; but a hard set of fellows always held me back and plucked all my growing wings ; " and he smiled so sadly that Willie nestled closer, and held tighter to the kind hand, and, with a cloud in his sympathizing eyes, asked : " And did the feathers never grow again, sir ? "

" No, Willie, they never grew again ; they only turned into quills, and I pluck them myself, and write a lot of things, very different, and dry, which sometimes turn into silver and help me to live."

" Father says your talk is like diamonds and pearls. I have often watched you, but I never saw any fall."

Coleridge laughed heartily at the boy's comments, and told him a wonderful tale of the East : of gorgeous palaces and jeweled attendants, and brilliant birds and charmed princesses, until the boy beamed with pleasure, and understood better about the pearls and diamonds.

Coleridge earned enough in these years to pay his board and send Derwent to college. Life seemed floating into smoother currents, and a gentle peace stole into the weary man's heart. He had drifted through life almost penniless, helped here and there by kind friends when in danger of ruin. In his premature old age he was as penniless, but friends and almost constant work still kept the wolf from the door, and left him a trifle for the dear ones who had enjoyed so little of his fatherhood. Hartley and Derwent came to visit him and worship him as often as possible ; but traveling was expensive, and stage-coaching was very wearying, and many miles lay between them. So they could not very often have the benefit of his gentle admonitions.

Sara was with him most frequently, and he showed tenderest pride in the excellent work she was doing—careful translations of Spanish and Italian works, full of a certain charm of style which she had caught from constant study with her Uncle Southey. Her lovely, delicate face won her friends and sympathy wherever she went, and by her writings she was earning a nice support for herself and a little nest-egg "for a dowry," said her careful mother. Sara would blush and smile at the suggestions and hints of her mother and aunts, when the great Wordsworth boys would tramp weekly, and oftener, from Rydal to Keswick. There was always some errand to bring the two noisy young fellows to Greta Hall. And Sara Coleridge and Edith Southey would often walk miles over the mountain roads to accompany "the boys" part way home. And the picnics and boating and fishing excursions of the holidays, when the Wordsworth and Coleridge boys were home from college, kept life fresh and merry for this pleasant group of young friends.

But, somehow, the love-making was such a cousinly, brother-and-sister affair, that the years flew by, and there was no especial mating of the girls and boys who had become men and women in each other's society.

Aunt Dorothy Wordsworth need not have so feared trusting her lovely Dora with Hartley Coleridge. Dora grieved over his shiftless ways and lax habits as over an erring brother, and Hartley never knew which of his three sisters was the dearest. And the

Wordsworth boys brought all their college scrapes and love-tales to the sympathetic trio. Every one knows that this friendly state of affairs seldom wakens the tender passion. A little opposition and difficulty of access are much surer to kindle the flame of pursuit and waken dormant fancy. What we have always had, and can always enjoy, has no charm of novelty or surprise, which seems an important element in love-making.

If Sara's heart quickened at the approach of John Wordsworth, with his fine eyes and chestnut curls, she kept the flutter carefully concealed. Her tender blue eyes smiled just as gayly upon William. If half-formed dreams flitted before her fancy, she chased them back with a hot blush, and would not let an arrow stick that had not been aimed at her. She was always shy; so when she and Edith were discussing "the boys," Edith never guessed that John was dearer than the rest. But mothers see deeper than words; they know the fluttering of pulses, no matter how carefully the young hypocrite may feign calmness.

Sarah Coleridge guessed Sara's secret, and planned many a trip for her into new scenes where the overwrought nerves could find a new stimulus and again grow quiet. Hence the frequent visits of Sara to her father, in the Gillmans' pleasant home. Here, in the society of her father and cousin, Henry Coleridge, Sara's nerves quieted, and peace and happiness filled her heart and life again.

CHAPTER XL.

Oh weep for Adonais—he is dead!
  Wake, melancholy Mother, wake and weep!—
Yet, wherefore? Quench within their burning bed
  Thy fiery tears, and let thy loud heart keep,
  Like his, a mute and uncomplaining sleep;
For he is gone where all things wise and fair
  Descend. Oh dream not that the amorous deep
Will yet restore him to the vital air;
Death feeds on his mute voice, and laughs at our despair.

SHELLEY.

ABOUT this time Leigh Hunt had found debts accumulating around him, and, his wife's health failing, he decided to close their home at Chelsea and join Byron and Shelley upon the Continent. The Shelleys and Byron were in Italy. Byron, living a very gay life near Florence with the Guicciolis, had his name coupled with that of the Countess Guiccioli, and many rumors had come back concerning his *liaison* with Claire Clairmont, who had just lost her little daughter, Allegra, and was as heart-broken as the Shelleys, whose eldest son had died near Florence. The Shelleys, unsettled again by this new sorrow, had been spending the summer at San Arenzo, near the Bay of Spezzia. Byron and the Shelleys had made all arrangements for Leigh Hunt to join them. Hunt had reached Byron's home, and had written, asking Shelley to visit him at once. He had sent Shelley a copy of Keats's new volume of poems, " Lamia," which he had just brought from England.

Shelley read many of the poems to his wife that evening, and they discussed the new poet with the Williamses who shared the villa of Casa Magni with them. Shelley and Captain Williams decided to take their yacht and meet Leigh Hunt the next day at Pisa. There was a heavy storm raging without; the wind was moaning, and the waves boomed drearily against the shore. The windows rattled and groaned against the casements; and the olive trees and vines encircling the house whispered and hissed in the storm, as green things do when tossed and twisted by the wind. Hot gusts of wind broke through the house, bearing heavy odors of orange-flower and wisteria, and the thunder crashed and lightning glared, as the inmates tried to read and talk. But conversation flagged, and the storm held full sway. Mary Shelley had never recovered from the shock of her little one's death. She clung nervously to Shelley at each crash of thunder and wail of the moaning wind.

" Don't leave me, Percy," she cried. " Do not go to Leghorn to-morrow; Lord Byron will look after Leigh Hunt. Do not go; I am afraid to be left alone, even for a day. Something black hangs over us; I see it, I feel it; do not leave me."

" You are only nervous, little wife," said Shelley tenderly. " We will wait until the storm is spent. You will feel all right to-morrow, when the sun is shining and the waves are rippling like diamonds. It would not do to disappoint Hunt. You will bid us

God-speed to-morrow. Dear old Hunt! he will have such budgets of news for us from old England." And Shelley sighed, as he always did whenever he spoke or thought of home.

The next morning was beautiful and clear. The waves were dancing and curveting, with myriads of diamonds sparkling on the blue waters. The trees and vines sparkled and glistened, and the orange-blossoms filled the whole atmosphere with their rich, heavy fragrance. Captain Williams and Shelley laughed at Mary's foolish fears, and set off merrily in the dancing yacht—their pretty Ariel.

> "' I'll bring you, my lassie, a bunch of blue ribbons,
>   To tie up your bonny brown hair,'"

sang Shelley, as they skimmed and dipped over the bounding blue sea. But Mary turned pale with unaccountable terror, and shut herself in her room to ease her foolish fancies by shedding floods of tears. She was a fanciful little body, and her dreams and visions always held her in complete possession until her sky cleared.

They met the Hunts and passed a pleasant day with them at Pisa, and in spite of a threatened storm Shelley and Captain Williams sailed from Leghorn the next morning. Leigh Hunt and Trelawny urged them not to start in the teeth of a storm, but they were determined.

The squall broke with such fury, that Hunt and Trelawny watched the little yacht from the light-house tower, until the rain and clouds hid the fluttering speck from view.

Meantime the anxious wives waited and watched for

the return of the Ariel. From Monday to Thursday they waited in terror and suspense: Mary knowing the worst, by her fatal gift of prescience, that foresaw evil at the very start ; Jane Williams hoping and praying for their return. On Friday, when a letter came for Shelley from Leigh Hunt, expressing his fears for their safety after the squall of Monday, Mary knew her fears were reality, and they started in haste for Pisa, to inform Hunt and Trelawny of their terrible fears, and to hunt for some traces of their lost husbands. Leigh Hunt's letter to Charles Lamb will tell the result better than words of mine.

"DEAR LAMB,—I hardly know how to write of the terrible event of which you have doubtless heard by this time—the drowning of poor Shelley. It was so sudden and terrible that I can scarcely write of it ; but his friends will want particulars. He and Captain Williams had visited us at Pisa, and established us in Byron's villa at Este, and started to return in the face of a storm ; but their light yacht must have capsized in sight of land, as the storm caught them before they had been out a half-hour. Finding they had not reached home by Friday, Trelawny and I spent days searching the whole coast for their bodies, after discovering the Ariel drifting, bottom up, upon the bay. When found, poor Shelley had Keats's 'Lamia' open in his pocket. Those poems had been his last thought. We could not remove him, after all those days in the water (the bodies were only recognizable by their clothes when found), so we built funeral pyres and burned the two bodies. which were found miles apart. Byron, Trelawny and I gathered fagots and bits of old wreckage from the beach to build the funeral pyres. We added cedar and olive wood to Shelley's, and tenderly placing all that remained of poor Shelley upon it, we applied torches and waited until all had burned to ashes. It was the most weird and horrible scene, with the flames licking greedily that splendid ruin of a fallen temple, and the waves booming and moaning under the cold, clear moon! Yet it was a fitting funeral for a poet, and for one so unlike other mortals as poor Shelley.

" And, stranger still, after all else had turned to 'dust and ashes,' his heart was left untouched—that manly heart that had so loved and suffered. We placed it in a small casket for his wife. Of course we hastened to the lonely spot where the poor wives were waiting in terror and suspense, fearing, almost knowing, the worst, after those dreadful days of watching. Their little home is a lovely bower of flowers and vines and fragrance, but so isolated that we cannot leave these grief-stricken women alone here, and shall wait until they can pack and leave with us.

" Byron and I are living together at Este, and, for the present, Mrs. Shelley and her little one will live with us.

" Mrs. Hunt insists upon this, and it seems the best thing at present. This calamity has left us no thought or recollection of our trip, or the scenes we have enjoyed. I will write again.

" Yours,

" LEIGH HUNT."

In those days of slow transit, when the mail-coach was the most rapid communication between friends and countries, the news of Shelley's death had not reached

London until Leigh Hunt's letter carried it. At the gathering about the " Round Table " Lamb read the letter to the friends. Many of them had seen or known the erratic young poet and had commented upon his foolish, unworldly freaks, and criticised or admired the poems he had published from time to time.

Now the sentence of death had been passed upon him and his mistakes and his efforts. Charles Lamb had held his poetic powers in high esteem, and even Hazlitt had found his poems " bits of rainbow color, dainty and most sweet." Death came now to silence criticism and recall what was pleasant and winning, and they mourned another young poet, so soon following poor Keats.

" The romances and changes one sees in a lifetime are startling," said Talfourd ; " they follow like the transformation scenes upon the stage. Look around upon our very friends and associates. Look at Byron's great popularity and success, and see him now, an outcast and wanderer. Look at Coleridge's great promise and scanty results, at Bonaparte's rise and fall, and now at the sudden snuffing out of this undoubted genius."

" Startling changes and unexpected results we must and ever shall find ; " said Hazlitt, " but a close observer can foretell much that will happen. It is no blind chance that makes or mars men's lives. The germs of all that overtakes them lie within themselves. Even Bonaparte's downfall could be predicted, when all Europe combined against him ; his indomitable will challenged the world, and he dared his own fate."

" C-c-could you have foretold p-p-poor Shelley's death ? " asked Lamb.

" I did prophecy his end many a time. His blind

recklessness in all things, and his passionate love of boating needed no seer to foretell his doom," replied Hazlitt.

" Perchance you would t-t-tell my h-h-horoscope, since you are so s-s-sure of your powers ?" said Lamb.

Hazlitt's eagle eye rested searchingly upon Lamb's " Titian head " and diminutive figure, and with a smile unusual to his severe face, he said, laying his hand on Lamb's shoulder :

" I would I could prophesy for you all the blessings you deserve, dear Charles Lamb. I do see brighter years in store for you than those of the past."

" Ah, Hazlitt ! you are l-like the Delphian Oracles, w-w-wise about the past, and r-r-rather general about the f-f-future. But, for your good wishes, m-m-many thanks ! "

And the years did flow more smoothly than of old, to the loving brother and sister. They lived on quietly for six years, in the house over the brazier's shop. Lamb wrote, during these years, many of those exquisite bits of humor and satire which have raised him to a level with the best of England's Essayists. His sketches, those " Essays of Elia " were sought by the first magazines of the day, and were noticed favorably by the critics, and greatly enjoyed by the public.

He was well paid for his writings ; and he stole many an hour from the tiresome desk-work at India House, to pen the quaint fancies that appeal so strongly to one's humor and sympathies. He loved to fill up quiet evenings at home with his writing; but his many friends left him little leisure. He and Mary could never settle down for a cosy home-evening with books and writing, but some friend or friends would drop in and stay

until bed-time, and headache from smoking and drinking, would prevent further work for that night.

As Lamb became more popular and better known,
the whist-club grew to larger proportions. It became
a rival to the brilliant *salons* at Holland House and
Gore House; and many of the *habitués* of these more
fashionable centers found the freedom, wit, and intellect
at Charles Lamb's " Round Table," the most attractive
rendezvous. Here they met writers and thinkers. They
could freely discuss their hobbies and their opinions,
untrammeled by party lines or fashion's decrees.

Amid the pomp and pride at Holland House speech
was more fettered. Poets and writers met there the
heads of the great Whig party, and the rich patrons of
art and letters. Free speech was modified by the
thousand little barriers of polite society. This lord
was too powerful to be offended, and that lady had
great influence at court. Tom Moore understood all
the unwritten code of decorum and intolerance, and
became a great favorite in this brilliant circle. He was
intimate with Lord Lansdowne and Lord John Russell, and was a devoted slave to all the whims of Lady
Holland. Walter Scott and Rogers and Campbell,
Landor and Procter, were equally welcome; but the
barrier between this coterie and the Lamb party and
Lake Poets was never thrown down.

After Southey and Wordsworth became stanch
Tories, the breach was wider than before. Southey, as
Poet Laureate, was often in London, and frequently the
guest of Samuel Rogers, who seemed to stand between
these different literary factions. But they never entered the charmed circle at Holland House.

In these days Wordsworth was gradually becoming

recognized as a poet. His "Excursion" was finding its way into drawing-rooms, and his name was becoming known. The grave, quiet man from the hills sometimes met many of the Holland House set at Lamb's Wednesdays. He also visited the stately home of Rogers, and at his celebrated breakfasts met the poets and authors who gathered there. During one of these visits to Rogers, a "Drawing-room" was held, and Rogers insisted upon presenting Wordsworth at Court. He would take no denial. Even the plea of want of Court dress could not release him from the importunities of his host, who insisted upon lending Wordsworth the requisite suit. The country poet crowded his long limbs into Rogers' velvet breeches, and squeezed his tall form into the elegant ruffled shirt and stylish coat.

"Picture the bard in poor little Rogers' small-clothes!" said Rickman. "He kneeled so long at the Queen's feet that we thought him stricken with sudden deep reverence for royalty; but he confessed afterwards that he absolutely feared to move for fear of splitting his breeches."

The vision of the serious and spectacled bard of the Lakes doffing his long plaid cloak for Court dress and small-clothes was too much for Charles Lamb.

"Fancy Wordsworth masquerading in cap and bells," he wrote to Manning. "Can you see him bowed in reverence before royalty, and bowed so low that the lion's skin was stretched too tight for him to get up again? I had rather not think of the great Wordsworth bent so low. Yet we are all actors in this drama called Life, and who knows at what entrance or exit we shall find ourselves."

CHAPTER XLI.

A WELCOME CHANGE.

I was fifty years of age, and no prospect of emancipation presented itself. I had grown to my desk, as it were, and the wood had entered into my soul.—LAMB.

For the first day or two I felt stunned, overwhelmed. I could only apprehend my felicity; I was too confused to taste it sincerely. I wandered about, thinking I was happy, and knowing that I was not. I was in the condition of a prisoner of the old Bastile; suddenly let loose after a forty years' confinement. I could scarce trust myself with myself. It was like passing out of Time into Eternity, for it is a sort of eternity for a man to have his time all to himself.—CHARLES LAMB.—*Superannuated Man.*

SIX years of uneventful life passed over the Lambs in their Russell Street home. Charles's writings for the "New Magazine" and other periodicals brought him ever-increasing fame and money. During these years the "Essays of Elia" were collected and published in book form, and the modest India House clerk found himself growing famous. With the increasing demand for his essays and character-sketches, and the diminishing of his leisure time, as their purse grew less scanty, Lamb was growing yearly more weary of the drudgery of his desk-work. He would fain stay at home and write the thoughts that were crowding upon him for utterance. But the tread-mill never stopped, save on the Bank holidays and upon the Jewish Church festival days recognized by his task masters. A weariness of work, of life, even of friends, grew upon him. Mary's illnesses continued, and left long gaps of melancholy in their frequent wake ; and Coleridge's life at the Gillmans' even shut apart their old close intimacy. They longed for a change, as sick spirits do long for new scenes, and homesick souls for the quiet haven of home.

Mary suggested the country. They often took long strolls into Islington, and it seemed sweet and restful to her amid green fields and quiet country roads. Charles shuddered at the thought of the country—at the idea of leaving London. But at least it would be nearer the hospital where he so often had to leave his sister.

They hunted up at Islington a pretty little white cottage with six rooms, with fine trees and a pretty garden, and the New River gurgling past their garden wall. They moved once more, and Charles graphically described the packing and flitting in one of his letters. It was a genuine move this time—from city to country, from the scenes of a life-time to new environments. He often walked to the city, following the broad road along the little stream, past fields and cottages, until the straggling buildings merged into the London streets, and turned into Holborn and stretched out to Cheapside and the India House.

He always walked one way, and often both, reaching Colebrook cottage in better health and spirits for the long exercise after work. But the country did not appeal to Lamb as to most poets ; and he wearied of his Islington home, so far from Coleridge and from his dear shops and book-stalls, and the busy London crowds that were such familiar studies to him. He describes this home to Bernard Barton as, " A white house with six good rooms ; the New River (rather elderly by this time) runs (if a moderate walking-pace may be so termed) close to the foot of the house. Behind is a spacious garden with vines (I assure you), pears, straw-berries, parsnips, leeks, carrots, cabbages to delight the heart of old Alcinous. You enter without passage, into a cheerful dining-room, all studded over and rough with old books ; and above is a lightsome drawing-room, three windows, full of choice prints. I feel like a great lord, never having had a house before." *

Here Charles and Mary settled down to enjoy a rural peace and quiet ; for before their door was a broad country road bordered with fine old sheltering trees. The little garden was a wonder and delight to these cockneys, who had seldom stepped beyond the confines of London. Mary had her cosy tea-table in the little garden, in the shelter of their "own vine and fig-tree." Charles would read their favorite books, while Mary served and poured tea. Here Leigh Hunt and Bernard Barton, the Quaker poet, the Procters, and Martin Burney would often join them, and enjoy the quiet serenity of sunset and evening. For, although Lamb often growled about his want of leisure, no one ever welcomed friends more cordially.

Charles wrote to Mrs. Hazlitt an amusing account of George Dyer's visit : " Yesterday week, George Dyer called upon us, at one o'clock (bright noonday), on his way to dine with Mrs. Barbauld at Newington. He sat with Mary about half an hour, and took leave.

* "Letters of Charles Lamb."—AINGER.

The maid saw him go out, from her kitchen window, but, suddenly losing sight of him, ran up in a fright to Mary. G. D., instead of keeping the slip that leads to the gate, had deliberately, staff in hand, in broad, open day, marched into the New River. He had not his spectacles on, and you know his absence. Who helped him out, they can hardly tell; but between 'em they got him out, drenched thro' and thro'. A mob collected by that time, and accompanied him in. . . . . The patient was put between blankets; and when I came home at four to dinner, I found G. D. a-bed, and raving, light-headed, with the brandy and water which the doctor had administered. He sang, laughed, whimpered, screamed, babbled of guardian angels, would get up and go home; but we kept him there by force; and by next morning he departed sober." *

Charles enjoyed this episode hugely, picturing most graphically the drenched and maudlin philosopher to their friends, and, ever after, teasing him about it.

" T-t-to think that at last these n-n-nankeen trousers should have f-f-found their way to water," he said. " I always t-t-told you you reminded me of a c-c-crab, old fellow. It was instinct, p-p-pure instinct, that l-l-led you h-home."

Not only did friends seek Lamb at Colebrook cottage; but he was invited to the Mansion House, to a dinner given to authors. " The dinner was costly and served on massive plate; champagne, wines, etc., forty-seven present, among whom the chairman and two other directors of the India Company. Here's for you ! and I got away pretty sober. Quite saved my credit," * he

<hr>

* " Letters of Charles Lamb." AINGER.

wrote. Of course this public notice was immensely gratifying to Charles and Mary. " The Essays of Elia " were most favorably noticed by the reviews and papers. Little by little the India House clerk was growing in popularity. And now to dine with other notables, and even with the august India House directors, was a great event. Mary swelled with pride, but apart from a little joking, Charles bore his new honors as meekly as he had always borne his troubles.

He regarded a dinner with the Lake poets as a far greater honor and pleasure. He wrote to Barton: " I dined in Parnassus, with Wordsworth, Coleridge, Rogers, and Tom Moore—half the poetry of England, constellated and clustered in Gloucester Place. It was a delightful evening. Coleridge was in his finest vein of talk—had all the talk ; and let 'em talk as evilly as they do of the envy of poets, I am sure not one there but was content to be nothing but a listener. The Muses were dumb, while Apollo lectured on his and their fine art." *

This was one of the occasions when Coleridge shone with his old splendor, and Lamb basked in his effulgence. Coleridge, with his son and daughter, visiting him at Highgate, and himself the center of the ever-widening circle of brilliant men who came to Highgate to visit him, was better and happier than he had been for years. He was proud of his children : both Hartley and Sara wrote good poetry and were brilliant. The careful nursing and watching of Dr. Gillman and his wife had helped him gradually to throw off the fetters of opium. And, although the critics gave him no place in the world as a writer, still he wrote and worked

* " Letters of Charles Lamb."—AINGER.

regularly for duty's sake, and to pay his board. And it was a pleasure and benefit to him.

His treatment by the papers and magazines, while it cut him to the quick, was greatly compensated by the sympathy of friends.

Even the celebrated Edward Irving, the great Scotch divine who was making such a stir in London, came to Coleridge, as to a master, for advice and instruction. He confessed many of his difficulties to the " silver-tongued orator," and found Coleridge's experience of the comforts of Christianity, after his wide wanderings into mysticism and philosophy, a wholesome and bless-ed lesson.

Coleridge, whilst appreciating Irving's brilliancy and earnestness, frequently warned him against the dangers of his emotional nature and ascetic tendencies. The philosopher of Highgate and the humorist—the anti-quarian and seer of Colebrook cottage met sometimes in London, and sometimes at the Gillmans', and there was ever the same tender interest when they met, and the same regrets that their paths now lay so far apart. Each was rapidly ageing and needing more the rest and retirement of home. Coleridge, at sixty years, was now an old man in appearance and feelings; and Charles Lamb was also greatly aged, from the constant, wearing desk-work, and the more nervous strain of his anxiety about Mary. He fretted like a nervous woman over every symptom which threatened a spell of insanity. He was always watching for them and dreading them. And by his very fears he often worried her into an attack that might have been warded off had she been in a less exciting environment. Mary's own melancholy before and after her illnesses, was most terrible to them both. It is small wonder that they tried different resorts in the few vacations Charles could beg; and imagined that a change of home and location could lift their cloud.

The ceaseless desk-work in the gloomy den, by candle-light, so wore upon Lamb that he determined to send in his resignation to the India House directors, hoping that after his thirty-three years of faithful service he might receive a small pension. He heard nothing from them, as the weeks went by, and feared a mere acceptance of his resignation, without the accompanying enrollment upon their pension list. He dared not tell Mary what he had done, fearing to excite her; but his over-wrought nerves were almost as bad for Mary's peace of mind as a share of his uncertainty would have been.

After nearly two months, he came hurrying in one mid-day, with a face so beaming with joy that his appearance at that unusual hour failed to startle her.

"Guess, Polly, what g-g-good news I have b-brought thee," he shouted. "P-p-put on thy thinking-cap and w-w-wish for the best!"

"Is anybody married?" asked Mary.

"N-n-no, Polly, but somebody's divorced, with alimony, from the most tiresome mistress on earth. I've quit India House, with a pension of £441 a year for life, and the half of it for you if I d-d-die first!"

"Charles!" said Mary, with a flush of pleasure lighting her pale cheek, "I cannot believe it!"

"Nor I, Polly. I've hoped for it these two months, and now that it has c-come, I don't know how to b-b-bear it. All holiday you know—time to r-r-read, t-time to write, t-t-time to th-th-think! and money enough to l-l-live on! What nabobs we'll be!"

But with the contrariness of human nature, no sooner had this hoped-for release come than he was like a child with too much cake.

When morning came, there was no duty awaiting him. The habit of years was suddenly snapped, and the relief caused a revulsion of feeling. He commenced to look back tenderly upon the old busy days that had the coveted evening at their close, and upon the eagerly counted and expected holidays. He wrote to Wordsworth: "Holydays, even the annual month, were always uneasy joys; their conscious fugitiveness, the craving after making the most of them. Now, when all is holyday, there are no holydays. I can sit at home, in rain or shine, without a restless impulse for walkings. I am daily steadying, and shall soon find it as natural to me to be my own master as it has been irksome to have had a master. . . . Leigh Hunt and Montgomery, after their releasements (from prison), describe the shock of their emancipation much as I feel mine. . . .

"Tuthill and Gillman gave me my certificates. I laughed at the friendly lie implied in them; but my sister shook her head and said it was all true. Indeed, this last winter I was jaded out. Winters were always worse than other parts of the year, because the spirits are worse, and I had no daylight. In summer, I had daylight evenings. The relief was hinted to me by a Superior Power, when I, poor slave, had not a hope but that I must wait another seven years with Jacob: and lo! the Rachel which I coveted is brought to me!"*

The Lambs had invited a little daughter of Mr. Isola,

---

*" Letters of Charles Lamb."—AINGER.

a teacher of French ar.d Italian at Cambridge, to visit them, and the visitor had staid with them until such an attachment grew that they decided they could not part with her. So the " pretty, nut-brown maid " became one of the family—the adopted daughter of this bachelor and spinster, who were too full of the milk of human kindness to be forever childless. She accompanied them upon their long walks, and her young life added a zest to their quiet home.

Charles found an interesting occupation in teaching her Latin, and Mary helped her keep up her French, and both gave her of their best stores of knowledge, to fit her for the position of governess, as she grew older. She was a charming girl, and their kindness to her was well repaid by her tender affection for her foster-parents. Emma Isola took a daughter's place in the household duties, and lightened the home cares by her youthful spirits and interests.

As Charles grew accustomed to his liberty, he enjoyed visiting and receiving his friends more than for years past. He and Mary made frequent trips to Highgate, and enjoyed the charms of Coleridge's society more than ever.

CHAPTER XLII.

EVENING SHADOWS.

> The clouds that gather round the setting sun
> Do take a sober coloring from an eye
> That hath kept watch o'er man's mortality;
> Another race hath been, and other palms are won,
> Thanks to the human heart by which we live,
> Thanks to its tenderness, its joys, and fears,
> To me the meanest flower that blows can give
> Thoughts that do often lie too deep for tears."
>
> WORDSWORTH.—*Ode to Immortality.*

COLERIDGE had just written the most earnest and conscientious work of his life, his " Aids to Reflection." His improved health and spirits had enabled him to give more careful thought and work to this effort than was usual with him. Readers and thinkers eagerly sought the book, and prized its wholesome lessons. It is the epitome of a philosopher's theories and experiences. He wrote from his heart, in the sincere hope of helping men struggling to the Light and Truth, as he had done. The whole summing up of his experience and philosophy was, that Christianity is to be found in Christian living rather than in beliefs or doctrines ; practical Christianity being of so much higher importance than this or that formula. Faith in the Bible, in all its teachings and miracles, being wiser than all the wisdom of all the schools.

Thus, in his weakness and age, Coleridge reached out a helping hand to humanity. He had solved the riddle "What is Truth?" for himself, that riddle that had so puzzled his youth, and upset his manhood. And the other question, the "Why, why?" that had also so disturbed all his early life, was answered by the sweet childlike faith and trust that sheltered his age. He had learned that, "when I am weak, then am I strong," and after all the discords and the unrest of the weary seeking, had come this blessed finding of the Heavenly Father's infinite love and pity. He had at last learned peace, the "peace that passeth all understanding." It shone from the kind, gray eyes; it brooded over the venerable silvery head, and with its own wondrous luminousness, it shed its light upon others. Coleridge, the chastened, childlike Christian, was happier, better, greater, than Coleridge the poet, or Coleridge the philosopher. And, because of his humility, because he now only wished to help and not to teach, his influence was far greater than in his days of pride—the greater for the years of deep humiliation he had undergone. Men of all denominations felt the power of his earnestness, and came to learn of him.

It was a time when the question "What is Truth?" was stirring the colleges and the churches. The Oxford movement was growing; and the spirit was driving formalism and perfunctory ceremonials out from the temple. The young Newman was striving against the bonds of dogma, and preaching new doctrines at old St. Mary's, within the very walls of Oxford. He sought out Coleridge, and had long, earnest talks with him, whilst trying to adjust duty and conscience. He found the "Aids to Reflection" a great help, as did Julius

Hare and Edward Irving, and all that set of thinkers who were trying to follow the leading of God's Spirit, and to discern between duty, conscience, faith and feeling.

Carlyle, he whose leaven was of another yeast, also sought Coleridge and tried to sound his depth. But Coleridge's world was of another order, and these two great thinkers were on planes too different to furnish common meeting ground. Each despised the conventional and false; each loved to hear his own flood of eloquence, and each sought Truth above all else on earth.

But Coleridge's law was tolerance and love, and Carlyle's law intolerance and scorn. The fiery young Scotchman found little in the broken veteran beyond a certain musical eloquence spoiled by the nasal, stumbling utterance of his physical infirmities.

Charles Lamb marveled at the calm and peace that had descended upon his best-loved friend. His own sweet, trustful nature had worn somewhat fretful through these long years of strain and anxiety. And now he found the restless Coleridge grown calm and almost happy; and he wondered, while he rejoiced.

In these days of leisure, the friends were often together, yet less often than they wished, because of Mary's many illnesses and long interruptions, which, for the time being, shriveled Charles's heart into a suffering void—paralyzed with misery, and dead to friendship. His letters of this period were either invitations to old friends to dine or sup with them, or warnings of a dismantled household, and its suffering need of absolute repose.

During these years, and for the rest of his life, Lamb

haunted the British Museum, studying his favorite old dramatists and the musty treasures of the library and records. Almost any day, in the least gloomy corner of the great library, could be seen the attenuated figure with the fine silvered head and sparkling brown eyes, bent over piles of folios, browsing here and there among them. He always loved to dip and skim through his favorite authors, like a bird in an orchard. His own writings give one pleasure in the same way—a delicious bit here, a fine thought there, a quaint picture or humorous touch, to whet the fancy for new discoveries.

At the library, and amid the collection of engravings and curios of the Museum, where his fine taste and excellent judgment made him quite an oracle, he widened his circle of friends.

Men of similar tastes in letters and art flocked around Lamb wherever he was. At the Royal Academy he was in his own element. Who so well understood the Hogarths, the Turners, the Reynolds, the Titians of the art gallery as the quaint little fellow who spent hours studying, criticising, weighing, and comparing them? He knew every turn and line of the Hogarths —every point and insinuation of their satire was delicious to this artist of the quill, and he had as true an instinct for color as for form. Hayden, Hazlitt, and other artists prized his criticisms beyond that of professionals. He had spent weeks of his scanty leisure decorating his garret in the Temple with the prints and engravings of his favorite Hogarth. And he knew each one as intimately as a good Christian does his Bible. He had always visited all the picture sales and the galleries within reach, and now no collection escaped his attention.

He was sent for as a connoisseur, to verify the genuineness of certain disputed "old masters," and he became familiar with the gems in the many fine private galleries of London. At Bridgewater House and Dudley House, and in many of the superb private galleries, Charles Lamb knew the Titians, and Da Vincis, and Guido Renis, Murillos, and Poussins better than did their owners. " What need to have the c-c-care of t-t-treasures, when you can have your f-f-fill of them at other men's expense?" asked this fastidious connoisseur who did not own a painting. But with books it was different. He never could pass the fascinating old bookstalls and junk-shops, where musty treasures, as mellow and odorous as old cheese, could be picked up for a few pence, without stopping to buy. It was his hobby; he knew all these disreputable old corners in London, and indulgence in this very inexpensive taste was his one extravagance. The great old book-case, that had followed them from one home to another, was crammed with these rare skimmings, and overflowed into shelves and corners, in a way that would have distracted any other housekeeper than Mary. But as she shared all her brother's tastes and indulged all his whims, she adored these same old folios, as contributing to his happiness and welfare. She did try to keep them from the chair-seats and mantel-shelves, but if "brother" had required them to adorn the center of the breakfast-table, it would have been all right. She had the same tender way of looking after the comfort of their intimate friends. She mothered Coleridge and George Dyer, and all the impractical dreamers that had no other woman to mend their linen and collect their scattered belongings.

Years ago, she and Sarah Hazlitt had undertaken to tidy up poor George Dyer's untidy den. They had mended and hung up the innumerable articles of wearing apparel that were piled up around the floor. They had cleared a path among the books that lay scattered in all directions, and had piled in a corner those kept in the seat of the only easy-chair in the room. They brought order from the chaos, and beamed upon their afternoon's work. But George's look of consternation, and his blank expression when he found the havoc they had wrought in his familiar surroundings, kept them from ever again trying to reduce him to order. Now, there was no need of such tidying up by pitying friends, for George Dyer had blundered into matrimony. He, the eccentric, the book-worm, had somehow found himself blessed with a caretaker; and history will not lift the veil that mercifully covers the adjustment of such life-long vagaries to the more wholesome jog-trot of married life.

CHAPTER XLIII.

Art thou a statesman in the van
  Of public business trained and bred?
First learn to love one living man
  Then mayst thou think upon the dead.

Plain living and high thinking are no more,
  The homely beauty of the good old cause
Is gone.   Our peace, our fearful innocence,
  And pure religion, breathing household laws.

WORDSWORTH.

WHILST our friends, Lamb and Coleridge, had been
steadily drifting down the tide, towards the great sea
that swallows all, the world, too, had been drifting on.
The poor old king, George the Third, had been
"gathered to his fathers," and the Regent had become
George the Fourth, with little change in ministry or
events, as he had for a dozen years held the reins.
Strange compound as he was of dandy and brute, he had
always taken some interest in the literary development
of his country.   He prided himself upon his literary
tastes, and gave pensions and aid to a number of writers,
among them, in an indirect way, to Coleridge.   He had
established a Royal Literary Society for the advance-
ment of *belles lettres* and general literature, and this

Coleridge had joined, and besides the F. R. S. attached to his name as mark of especial honor in the world of letters, he was invited to deliver the annual lecture, and receive one hundred guineas for his services.

This addition to his earnings assisted Coleridge in sending Derwent to college, and helped him to feel less cramped for money than in his earlier life.

Sydney Smith's long cherished scheme of Catholic Emancipation, in spite of all obstacles, was growing in favor. The Liberals had gained ground, and the "No Popery" cry was dying out, after long struggles, frequent riots, and troubles. The great clerical wag who had steadily fought for the removal of Catholic disabilities had bravely stood in the way of his own promotion to preferment; but his wit and wisdom steadily bore down barriers and helped redress the wrong. Public meetings all over the country endorsed the reform. In one of Sydney Smith's speeches upon the subject, his description of the old woman sweeping, sweeping back the tide that swelled to her door, to her house, and her fruitless effort to keep back the sea with her vigorous broom, carried all before him. Such a powerful and picturesque argument helped the cause more than all the pleading and logic of Daniel O'Connell. Even Mr. Peel, one of its strongest enemies, became an advocate for the "Catholic Emancipation Bill," and as the years sped on the chances of its success increased yearly.

During the canvass for the "Catholic Bill," in 1824, came tidings of Lord Byron's death at Missolonghi, Greece. The shock of Shelley's tragic death had made Byron more cynical and morose than ever; and after a quarrel with the Countess Guiccioli, and a severance of that *liaison*, his restlessness led him to fling himself into the Grecian struggle for liberty. Outcast as he was from home and country, his resentment against social, religious, and political tyranny grew into a passion. He offered his money and personal services to the people of Greece who were rising against their oppressors. He had become utterly reckless, and, longing for death, feverishly hoped to find his deliverer upon the field of battle and of glory. His welcome visitor came, not upon the battle-field, however, but from cold and exposure and malarial poison ; and the troubled spirit was at rest—at least in this world. His last wishes were disregarded, his last command disobeyed. He forbade them ever to send his body to England. He wished to lie where he fell, that the country which had expelled him from its pity and society during life, should never again hold his body. Even this last request was denied the brilliant poet who had lived through all life's phases, and burned out its fires at the age of thirty-six. His body was sent to England, and was met by a handful of friends who followed him to the grave. On a gray, rainy day, the few coaches, in which were Samuel Rogers, snarling at a long ride in such weather, Leigh Hunt, Tom Moore, and a dozen others, wound slowly to the vault near Newstead Abbey. There was laid the wanderer who had shot like a meteor across England's cold skies.

Another poet was fallen, but the world wagged on. Kings and poets, lords and commoners but drift to the same ocean, and its waves close over them, and rise and fall as musically, waiting for the next victims. To some, who are weary of the drifting, and are listening for the boom of the waves on the shore, the voyage seems endless.   But to many who are bravely, eagerly steering against the tide, it seems to sweep them on all too soon for their ambitions and their pleasures.

But whether we wait wearily for our summons to cross the dread Styx, or shrink from the inevitable doom awaiting us, it comes to all—this summons to lay down life's burdens and struggles.

CHAPTER XLIV.

BLIND MAN'S HOLIDAY.

I have been laughing, I have been carousing,
Drinking late, sitting late, with my bosom cronies;
All, all are gone, the old familiar faces!

Ghost-like I paced round the haunts of my childhood,
Earth seemed a desert I was bound to traverse,
Seeking to find the old familiar faces.

How some they have died, and some they have left me,
And some are taken from me : all are departed;
All, all are gone, the old familiar faces.

CHARLES LAMB.

CHARLES LAMB found his long holiday dragging on rather wearily. Heavy colds and nervous affections frequently unfitted him for writing, and Mary's more frequent absences from home left him unsettled and uneasy.

Emma Isola had taken the governess's position and was away in Hertfordshire, and the cottage seemed to grow solitary and gloomy. True, the old friends hunted him up and new friends sought him. Dr. Carey, librarian of the British Museum, a most genial man, as well as finished writer, became one of Lamb's most intimate friends at this epoch of his life. The two were of congenial tastes, and liked nothing better than the oft-repeated sparring over the old dramatists or some new writers who were claiming attention. Thomas Wainwright, who was the brilliant "Janns Weathercock" of the "London Magazine," was another crony, until he turned villain and was disgraced.

Lamb's essays in the "London Magazine" had won for him a permanent place in the literary world. Invitations to dinners and gatherings of the London *literati* poured in upon him.

"If I had as many st-st-stomachs as a c-c-camel, I could fill them all in these days," he said to Dr. Carey. "I could s-s-sample the *patés* and p-peacock's tongues of the very aristocracy, as often as Tom Moore, from the numbers of *billets doux* that p-p-pour into Colebrook Cottage; but my nerves won't stand that sort of thing," he said, rather regretfully. "I have to confine my d-d-diet to newspapers and m-m-magazines," he laughed, as he promised to attend the annual dinner of the "London Magazine," at which he had become high-priest. These Fleet Street dinners were a great function. Here were gathered John Scott, the editor of the "London Magazine," the publishers, the directors, and many of the most important contributors.

De Quincey, brilliant and satirical, yearly growing more shriveled and weird, "Barry Cornwall," Leigh Hunt, the fanciful John Reynolds, Dr. Carey, dignified and solid, and many other well-known knights of the quill, were regular guests. How they did fling satire and criticism over the efforts of those "young goslings," who were just struggling to the front!—the young Tennysons who had presumed to publish a sleek little volume of poems—"poems, forsooth! those pretty little cacklings and quackings of the young pullets who thought to hatch a brood." "New Byronics!" said

Lamb, somewhat contemptuously, as a few of the verses from "Poems by Two Brothers" were read or quoted over the punch-bowl.

Thus coolly and indifferently was the future author of "In Memoriam" and "Idyls of the King" passed on to oblivion by those who had been so dealt with by the critics at their own start. The young dandies, Bulwer and D'Israeli, who had just published their first novels, were handled unmercifully.

"It seems to me that such froth as 'Pelham' and 'The Disowned' are not worth notices in a respectable magazine," said Dr. Carey. "The very condemnation of such falsities and perverted views of life calls attention to them. I think we should give no place or notice in the literary world to such books."

"How could two such f-f-fops as Bulwer and that l-l-little curled Jew D-D-D'Israeli write anything b-b-better?" asked Lamb. "I s-s-saw Bulwer strutting be-curled and be-jeweled along Piccadilly the other day, and I c-c-could only recall poor B-B-Beau Brummel; the mincing g-g-gait and b-b-bored stare were identical. And Rogers tells me the author of 'Vivian Grey' is w-w-worse yet."

"You ask, how could such young puppies write better? Why need they write at all?" asked Leigh Hunt.

"Your friend Coleridge says it is only such light stuffing that the reading world cares for in these days."

"Dear old Coleridge has f-f-found too little favor for his own g-g-gold to endure having b-b-brass take the place of true c-c-coin," said Lamb.

"Ah, well, you are all too hard on those boys. Give the lads a chance; show 'em their faults; they're young and will improve," said Procter. "I remember how awfully I felt when the 'London' chopped up my maiden efforts ; but it did me good."

"You did not start in as a coxcomb," said Dr. Carey.

" Even a coxcomb may have something to say ; you cannot always judge the kernel by the husk," said " Barry Cornwall."

" Snuff them out ! snuff them out !" piped in De Quincey. " Lamb and Coleridge and Carey are right : unless men have something to say, and know how to say it, they'd better keep quiet. Perfume, pomatum, and powder are not good brain fertilizers."

In the general laugh that followed this sally of the confirmed opium-eater, Lamb whispered to his neighbor : " Ask him what g-g-guano he uses."

These dinners and an occasional poets' breakfast at Rogers', where the old friends were invited to meet "the young pretenders," as Rogers called them, with visits to Coleridge and occasional evenings at home with the old whist-club set, were the only dissipations Lamb's failing health would allow. His nerves and digestion were thoroughly impaired, and he and Mary tried another change. They went to Enfield to visit some old friends, and finally decided to take rooms in a pleasant little house there, where Mary could be nursed during her spells of insanity.

Of the new house, he wrote to Thomas Hood : " We have got our books into our new house. I am a dray-horse, if I was not ashamed of the undigested lumber, as I toppled 'em out of the cart, and blest Becky that came with them for having an unstuffed brain with such rubbish. We shall get in by Michaelmas. 'Twas with some pain we were evulsed from

Colebrook. You may find some of our flesh sticking to the door-posts. To change habitations is to die to them ; and in my time I have died seven deaths. . . . My house deaths have generally been periodical, recurring after seven years ; but this last is premature by half that time. Cut off in the flower of Colebrook !"*

The cottage at Enfield was a pretty, low cottage with ivy growing over the front, and in the back garden were yew trees and old apple trees and pretty garden flowers—the pinks and larkspurs and sweet-williams that Mary loved. Of course the packing and moving excited poor Mary, and brought on another spell, but after she recovered and they got their old books and furniture into place, it was very homelike.

"I think, Polly, we must just spend the rest of our d-d-days here. This m-m-moving around is such a t-t-tearing up of roots. Mine are b-b-bleeding yet from the wrench. If our dear old New River had not f-f-followed us down, I f-f-fear I could not strike root again."

"Yes, brother, God willing, we will stay here until He calls us away," she answered, laying her hand lovingly upon his shoulder.

"You must go first, you know, Mary," he said, smiling up into her face with that exquisite, tender smile, that so bound his friends to him.

"Yes! I must go first, Charles. What should I do in this world without the kind care that has watched me these thirty years?"

And Dash, the great rollicking dog of Hood's, that summered with the Lambs, looked beseechingly into their faces, as they talked thus earnestly.

*"Letters of Charles Lamb."—AINGER.

He thumped his fringed tail on the floor, and sighed so heavily, that Charles and Mary laughed. "What, Dash, are you afraid you'll have to st-st-stay in London when we're g-g-gone?" And Dash's howl of delight and slobbering caresses led to a change of topic.

At pretty Enfield, with its shady trees and fine meadows, Charles Lamb and Mary and the frisking Dash became well-known features, during their long daily walks.

Often Emma Isola was with them, at the holiday seasons, and during vacation. She had grown very handsome, this brown-eyed lassie, and some of the Lambs' visitors and friends became much attached to her.

Among them was the young publisher, Edward Moxon, who had published Lamb's Essays, in the collection called "Essays of Elia."

He came very often on business, especially when Emma was at home. And after a long spell of brain fever, from which she was slow in recovering, he asked Charles and Mary to give him their child.

"Is this the way you w-w-want to keep your p-p-promise, miss?" asked Charles, pinching the hot cheeks. "Is this the way you are g-g-going to cheer an old age, flying off with the f-f-first young r-rooster that c-crows?"

"Humph! that's all you know about it, if you suppose this is my first offer," said Emma, saucily.

"Shade of my g-g-grandmother! Who else could there be? Why you were only hatched the other day!"

"My children down at Farnham thought me quite an old person," said Emma, laughing, "and if you cannot guess who was the disappointed swain, I'm sure

I'll not tell you," she added, tossing her pretty brown curls. So Emma Isola became engaged to Edward Moxon, and again Mary had the pleasure of aiding and abetting a happy pair of lovers, and brooding, like a motherly hen, over the courtship.

The other wedding over which the Lambs had presided had not turned out as happily as they had hoped. Sarah Stoddart was too high-spirited a woman to tamely submit to Hazlitt's many whims and eccentricities. She had come to Mary, and even to Charles Lamb with complaints and tales of unhappiness, as the years went by. The keen sarcasm that Hazlitt used so unsparingly upon the writers and artists of his day was too often turned upon his wife. That dangerous weapon is certain death to peace and happiness, if used too freely at home.

The Lambs urged forbearance, and patched up many a quarrel between these two; but lately they had not even lived together.

The Lambs, pitying and condemning both, stood between the parted husband and wife as the friend of both, hoping that time would soften the asperities that held them apart, and would draw them together again.

" We old maid and old bachelor pair s-s-seem better m-m-mated than our m-m-married friends," said Lamb. " Look at Coleridge and Hazlitt, at Godwin and D-D-Dyer, and all the rest of the married c-c-couples."

" Perhaps our tie is the closer for being less binding. But I cannot imagine your being disagreeable enough to lose the love of a wife, in spite of sundry little failings," said Mary, smiling.

" Eh, Polly, you have had to b-b-bear many a year with my old m-m-mistresses, Tobacco and Punch, and you think even a w-w-wife could learn to st-st-stand them?"

"Maybe she could have supplanted them, brother," said Mary, with her usual gentle caress.

" Aye, there's the rub ; w-w-wives try to f-f-force their lords to leave old h-h-habits, instead of t-t-trying to win them and w-w-wean them. I do hope for great happiness in this union; Emma and M-M-Moxon are better suited to each other than m-m-most people who marry."

As the months passed, Mary's illnesses became so frequent that both she and Charles found home cares weighed too heavily upon them. After many discussions they decided to sell off all their household goods but the beloved book-case and books, and their bedroom furniture, and board with their neighbors, the Westwoods.

Charles sighed for London, and wearied of the dreadful monotony of the little village of Enfield. " I know every bit of old g-g-gingerbread in these accursed little shops," he said.

And after settling Mary comfortably at the Westwoods, he took a room in London, and comforted his soul with long walks around his beloved streets, and prowls around the well-known book-stalls and haunts.

But much of the old charm was lost. He had no home now to hold the treasures he coveted.

So many of the old friends were gone. Godwin was dead, and Hazlitt had died lately, and many were scattered in different directions, and much of the old relish for the bustle and hurry of London streets was gone, for Charles Lamb was growing old and feeble. His overtaxed nerves had reacted, leaving him full of pains and aches, with a restlessness and feebleness far greater than should naturally belong to a man of fifty-six years of age. Many men, most men of fifty to sixty, are still in their prime, with scarcely a foreshadowing of the end. But Coleridge and Lamb were prematurely old. Life had gone hard with both. Anxieties and endless strain had worn out Charles Lamb's vitality, and disappointment and opium had sapped Coleridge's strength.

Within a few miles of each other the two friends were rapidly drifting down life's stream, farther apart, in their ill-health and weakness, than in the wider separations of early life.

Coleridge seldom came to London, and very rarely did he visit the Lambs, although the tie of love and friendship was as close as ever. Sometimes Charles and Mary Lamb visited Coleridge at Highgate, stopping over night at the Inn near by, and spending a happy day and evening together. But often long intervals elapsed without a meeting or a letter.

This same year that gave Charles and Mary a happy wedding, also brought new life and love to Coleridge. His daughter Sara was married to the Cousin Henry who had been as a son to Coleridge during his residence at Highgate. The young couple settled at Highgate, near their beloved and revered father, and were often with him.

Emma and Mr. Moxon were married at St. George's Church, in July, 1830, having quite a fashionable wedding, with many distinguished writers among the guests. Holcroft and Talfourd, Procter, Martin Burney, Tom Hood, the Cowden Clarkes, Rickman, and Rogers who was a sincere friend of Moxon, with many others, attended the wedding. A trip to Paris and Northern

France followed, and the happy couple sent to the Lambs a number of pretty sonnets extolling their happiness amid the new scenes. The wedding preparations, in which Mary had so keen an interest, were too much for her nerves, and at the very time she was struggling with a violent spell of insanity, from which she recovered suddenly when the attendant spoke to her of Mr. and Mrs. Moxon. The horrid blank of wandering wits was broken suddenly, as when the sun bursts through a heavy cloud, and she returned to full interest and comprehension of all the details, and tender sympathy with the happiness of her friends.

CHAPTER XLV.

'Tis the sunset of life gives me mystical lore,
And coming events cast their shadows before.

                        CAMPBELL.

     How wonderful is Death,
     Death and his brother Sleep.
     One pale as yonder waning moon,
     With lips of lurid blue;
     The other rosy as the morn,
     When throned on ocean's wave,
     It blushes o'er the world.

Unfathomable Sea, whose waves are years !
   Ocean of Time, whose waters of deep woe
Are brackish with the salt of human tears !
   Thou shoreless flood, which in thy ebb and flow
   Claspest the limits of mortality !

                        SHELLEY.

AT Dr. Gillman's, on the hillside at Highgate, the white-haired poet was daily growing more feeble. As his bodily strength wasted, his noble soul expanded, until he seemed to his many devoted friends more angel than man. He suffered terribly from intense restlessness, and spent many hours of the day and night in pacing slowly back and forth along the sunny garret-room, which had been raised and enlarged for him. He was happy with the Gillmans, and they warmly welcomed the many friends who still flocked around him to enjoy the beautiful eloquence that never deserted him. He rambled on, pouring the same musical flow of talk into the ears of all who listened. A gentle peace soothed these last years. He had fought a terrible battle against the most insidious foe that can attack man. He had suffered many a defeat, and had gained many a victory, but at last the soul rose triumphant over the weakened body. In the days of his humiliation he had written books that are sought and studied by scholars, for their clear philosophy and their Christian teaching. The mists of doubt and questioning had long since cleared away, and his faith grasped the Bible and all its teachings as the only sure guide. He had wandered in darkness whilst seeking the Truth; but had found the rottenness of mere human reasoning, and was glad to accept the Church of England's teachings, as a tired child clings to its mother, penitent for its wanderings, and safe in the happy shelter of her love. He had written the confession of his wanderings in the "Biographia Literaria," and was now patiently waiting delivery from his pains and weakness, confident in God's mercy, through Jesus Christ.

At this time, during the long days and nights, when the Past with all its phases and mistakes rose before him, he could feel that at least he had always believed and written honestly, and that the principles of his youth were the principles of his age, only modified by the clearer vision gained by life's varied experiences. His early friends were still the friends of his last years, and he had never stooped to truckle for favor or influence.

The world's history had shattered many of his ideals,

and forced him to change his political party to accord with his principles, which were modified, though not changed. Liberty, human rights, individual freedom, were still his ideals, and, over all, a faith in His loving care. Charles Lamb, his boyhood's friend, and manhood's companion, was still the dearest friend of his age, although the growing infirmities of both had kept them so much apart of late.

Charles and Mary had made one more change of residence during these years. They had removed to a pleasant cottage at Edmonton, near the pretty church with the square tower with battlemented top. Here, in the low, cosy cottage of Mr. Walden, where they had choice rooms, the sister and brother played piquet, read, and even studied together, during the intervals between Mary's spells of insanity. Charles wrote to Wordsworth :* " Her illnesses encroach yearly. The last was three months, followed by two of depression most dreadful. I look back upon her earlier attacks with longing—nice little durations of six weeks or so, followed by complete restoration—shocking as they were to me then. In short, half her life she is dead to me, and the other half is made anxious with fears and lookings forward to the next shock. With such prospects, it seemed to me necessary that she should no longer live with me, and be fluttered by continual removals ; so I am come to live with her at a Mr. Walden's and his wife, who take in patients, and have arranged to lodge and board us only. They have had the care of her before. I see little of her. Alas ! I too often hear her. *Sunt lachrymæ rerum !* and you and I must bear it. . . . . I am three or four miles nearer

* " Letters of Charles Lamb."—AINGER.

the great city. Coaches, half-price less, and going always, of which I will avail myself. I have few friends left there—one or two, though, most beloved. But London streets and faces cheer me inexpressibly."

So he still loves and longs for London. To Bernard Barton he writes : " I dread the prospect of Summer with his all-day-long days. No need of his assistance to make country places dull. With fire and candle-light I can drown myself in Holborn. With lightsome skies shining in to bed-time I cannot. . . . Give me old London at fire and plague times, rather than these tepid gales, healthy country airs, and purposeless exercises."*

Thus, through all the long weary years of his anxious life, he remained the same London-loving, gentle-hearted cockney. Starting a true, though unorthodox, Christian, Charles Lamb never wavered, never wandered into mazes of unbelief, but held steadily to his God and his Bible, seeing with his wise philosopher's eyes through all the petty shams, right into the heart of men and life. And seeing the shams and masks, he never grew bitter, but humored the delusions, and found the disguised princes beneath their masquerades, smiling always at the paint and powder and the make-believes, honoring them, sometimes, as the mere cloak of self-respect, worn to hide the tatters of poverty. Such is his picture of Captain Jackson, who represents a whole class of men and women that make the world better for their cheerful, uncomplaining gayety.

He unconsciously painted himself in this sketch ; for

* " Letters of Charles Lamb."—AINGER.

was not Charles Lamb's whole life one endless struggle concealed by the pleasant jests and wit that endeared him so to all ?

Because of their frequent illnesses, Charles and Mary had not seen much of Coleridge during the past year. They had corresponded and sent books to one another, but had seldom met. Lamb, suffering with colds, rheumatism, dyspepsia, and the many ills of increasing age, did not know how rapidly Coleridge was failing. And Coleridge, during the restless days and wakeful nights, longed for those dear friends of his heart. Hunting among his books for a rare old copy of "Beaumont and Fletcher," with his marginal notes like his own personal chats all through, he wrote on the fly-leaf :

"Midnight. God bless you, dear Charles Lamb. I am dying. I feel I have not many weeks left, in Gillman's, Highgate.—Yours, S. T. C."

Another hand had added : "Died July 25, 1834."

Coleridge hoped to see his friend once more, but knowing he had been ill with nervous and rheumatic disorders, feared this would be his last farewell.

And it was.

The wonderful hazel eyes, that Carlyle said "were full of sorrow as of inspiration," gazed out into the future and back into the past, and again he wrote :

> "Dew-drops are the gems of morning,
> But the tears of mournful eve !
> Where no hope is, life's a warning
> That only serves to make us grieve,
> When we are old ;

> That only serves to make us grieve,
> With oft and tedious taking-leave,
> Like some poor nigh-related guest,
> That may not rudely be dismist.
> Yet hath out-stay'd his welcome while,
> And tells the jest without the smile."

He sighed at the truth of these last pathetic words, thinking how true they were of his own life—a guest—where wife, children, family, all, were gone from his side.

His daughter and her husband were, indeed, often with him, bringing their little babe ; but Sara's delicate health and her baby prevented her from remaining constantly at his side. "Barry Cornwall" and Leigh Hunt lived near, and frequently cheered him with loving words.

But at the end only Sara and Henry Coleridge were near to give him earth's last farewell, and to close those beautiful eyes that mirrored his poet's soul.

Under his pillow was found, written with feeble hand :

> "Stop, Christian passer-by—stop, child of God,
> And read with gentle breast. Beneath this sod
> A poet lies, or that which once seemed he—
> O lift one thought in prayer for S. T. C. !
> That he who many a year with toil of breath,
> Found death in life, may here find *life in death*,
> Mercy for praise—to be forgiven for fame,
> He asked and hoped, through Christ. Do thou the same.
>   "S. T. C."

To one loving heart the news of Coleridge's death came as a knell that kept repeating its monotone in his ears : "Coleridge is dead ! Coleridge is dead !"

Charles Lamb was shocked, not knowing that the end was near, and for weeks and months kept repeating : "Coleridge is dead ! Coleridge is dead ! "

He had received a message from the Gillmans about Coleridge's illness, upon his own recovery from a spell of sickness, and took the coach to London, and thence to Highgate, hoping for a last farewell, a last look. But he was too late, his friend was dead, and as he hastened up the steps of the closed house, dreading, fearing to see that loved face, perhaps in its last agony, perhaps rigid in death, he found they had that morning laid his dear brother in the churchyard beneath the cloister.

"We sent you word of the death and funeral, which you must have missed, although we thought you were too ill to attend," said Dr. Gillman. "He died as peacefully as a little child falling asleep in its mother's arms."

" Ah, my friend, my friend ! " was all Charles Lamb could say.

They gave him the book with Coleridge's last message written for him, and he spent the rest of the day pacing around the new-made grave of him who for more than fifty years had been his dearest friend, his more than brother. He found the nurse who had soothed his friend's last hours, and pouring the contents of his purse into her hand, he moaned : " 'Tis all I can do, my friend, my friend ! "

Like a wounded creature, he crept back to Edmonton, where Mary was singing and raving and rambling on, in ceaseless flow of disjointed eloquence and fragmentary memories. Her ravings reached him through the closed doors, reminding him that, with Hazlitt and

Godwin gone, and now with Coleridge—his Coleridge—dead, there were still duties left for him.

She would become herself again and need him. So, taking his pipe and book, he schooled himself into a calm ; but ever through heart and brain were surging the words : " Coleridge is dead !   Coleridge is dead ! " The mourning ring which Coleridge had ordered for him was also a ceaseless reminder.

The papers and magazines began also to take up the theme that was haunting him. They seemed suddenly to awake to the fact that the poet whom they had slighted and scorned for so many years was a man upon a higher plane than one meets every day. They eulogized his poems ; they praised his prose ; they remembered his " fine lectures and wonderful eloquence." He was dead, so they lavished the applause upon his memory that would have saved his living heart many a bitter pang. He was deaf to all praise now that they remembered the rare beauty of his verse and song. As so often happens in this contrary world, they now began to build a pedestal for him. " He was one of England's Bards "—he whom they had scorned and discouraged, without stint and measure. * " Blackwood's Magazine," that had sneered at his " Christabel " as " impudent lunacy," now remembered that " Coleridge, alone, of all men that ever lived, was *always* a poet, in all moods." And the " Edinburgh Review " and the " Quarterly," that had given him naught but criticism, and refused him a place in literature where he might earn his bread, now became generous—nay, even fulsome—in their praises of the dead poet. Too late, too late, to help him in the weary

<hr>

* " Life of Coleridge."—HALL CAINE,

struggle, or to encourage the genius they had succeeded in stamping out, they gave him his deserts. Ah, the pity of it all! The pity! the shame! that men who might build up and help should spend their energies and powers in stinging a poet's genius to death, and then atone by praising him—too late!

Lamb wept bitter tears over these late tributes to his dead friend, that kept appearing in the magazines and papers.

"Too late to comfort or encourage his t-t-tired heart!" cried Lamb over the "Edinburgh Review." "Oh, why did they not s-s-say all this before? He l-l-longed for it, he waited for it, until he was w-w-worn out, and n-n-now his ears are d-d-deaf to it. He c-c-cannot know that justice has c-c-come at last."

"He was a crushed and broken man," said Talfourd. "The failure of every effort cut him to the very soul. He knew his weakness, but he felt his poet's powers, and the cruel attacks upon each book he offered were stabs he could not bear."

"Yes; they killed the poet in him," said Leigh Hunt; "his beautiful peace and sweetness in those last years was the absolute yielding to resignation; he had ceased to struggle for his place in the world."

"And yet such yielding is not mere c-c-cowardice; it is but accepting one's f-f-fate," said Charles Lamb. "There always c-c-comes a time when effort must succumb, and one must ac-ac-acquiesce in one's l-l-lot."

CHAPTER XLVI.

BREAKING THE KNOT.

Mr. Lamb has the very soul of an antiquarian. The film of the Past hovers forever before him. He is shy, sensitive, the reverse of everything coarse, vulgar, obtrusive, and commonplace.

There is a fine tone of *chiaro oscuro*—a moral perspective in his writings. He delights to dwell on that which is fresh to the eye of memory. He *blurts* out the finest wit and sense in the world.

WM. HAZLITT.—*Spirit of the Age.*

THE summer faded into autumn, bringing the cold November rains, and fresh pains and weakness to Charles Lamb. Mary was well again, and was once more the watchful care-taker, tenderly guarding and comforting her invalid. He could no longer bear the noise and jolting of the rumbling coach, so his only exercise and change were his short walks to the " Bell " at Edmonton for his glass of ale or whisky. In returning, one sleety day, he slipped upon the icy stones and fell, bruising his face. Erysipelas set in, and after a few days of fever and suffering, softened by the merciful unconsciousness that dulls the pangs of death and partings, it was all over. The gentle " Elia " passed away, leaving Mary alone in her helpless affliction.

The Blue-coat boy had already become known and famous far beyond his modest ambition. Little by little his quaint fancies had taken hold of the popular heart and being so unpretending, the critics gave him help rather than hindrance. When he died, his heroic life of self-sacrifice and self-surrender was known to few besides his intimate friends. He never claimed the least merit for surrendering life's ambitions at the very start, and taking up its burdens in the path of duty. His quiet generosity to friends in need was known only to himself and the recipients of his charities; but the fragrance of his sweet, blameless life clung around his memory, and expanded as the years passed, until his life, as well as his works, gave him his place among the best beloved of the English essayists.

Dear, quaint Charles Lamb! who does not know and love his pictures of English life, and London scenes and characters—his gathered and crystallized memories, given in his matchless style!

They buried him quietly, in the little churchyard at Edmonton, and placed a plain stone over him, and a tablet to his memory in the church.

For thirteen years after his death did Mary survive him. She, the helpless invalid, who for nearly forty years had been his first care, was left alone and unprotected to bear her burden of illness and helplessness.

True, the Moxons were left to see that she was comfortably cared for, and their many friends never forgot the gentle woman who had always so warmly welcomed them to the cosy fireside. And the half of the India House pension was continued to Mary during her life. Besides this pension, Charles had saved nearly two thousand pounds of his hard-earned money from his salary and his writings, to keep the loved sister from want or anxiety.

But what need to picture the loneliness of these years

of alternating illness and recovery. She was too brave and sweet a woman to spend them in hopeless repining. The calm strength that had sustained her through all those years of trial was hers still. The faith that was able to reconcile her to life, after the horrible deed committed during her insanity, sustained her through this loss and the lifelong loneliness that followed. Her bodily health even improved as years went by, and the spells of insanity were less frequent. She grieved over the long illness and the shattered faculties of her friend Dorothy Wordsworth. And when the poet's loved daughter married and died so soon afterwards, Mary Lamb sent tenderest messages to the Wordsworths.

It is strange how many of this once closely allied circle were doomed to suffer the same misery that had pursued Mary Lamb throughout her life.

For several years Edith Southey, the poet's wife, had shown signs of mental trouble. She was extremely variable, at times wildly excited over mere trifles, and suddenly depressed and melancholy. Southey had watched her, silently and anxiously, for a long time before her state became noticeable to others. But the latent insanity was unmistakable before the time of Coleridge's and Charles Lamb's deaths; and now Southey's own health suffered severely from the constant tax upon his nerves.

The life-long strain upon her, of family cares and the constant effort to keep increasing expenses within the limited income, had worn out the mind and body of Edith Southey. She was a brave woman, who ever had the tenderest co-operation and sympathy from her husband; but his increasing prosperity came too late to mend the overtaxed nerves. They yielded to the pressure, and she became entirely insane, and finally Southey was forced to place her under medical care and restraint. Fortunately, the poor woman did not live long in her pitiable condition. But when Southey himself, a few years later, just after his marriage with Caroline Bowles, sank into the strange confusion and the settled torpor of softening of the brain, it did seem as if some cruel Nemesis were pursuing the different branches of our party of poet-friends.

For a fine, well-balanced mind like Southey's to sink into ruin seems most strange and terrible. Perhaps the constant, unremitting labor of fifty years was a heavier drain than human nature could endure. But the great number of his books and writings are evidence of his ceaseless mental activity, and the fiat, " Well done, good and faithful servant," is the reward for such lives as his and the venerable Wordsworth's, who afterwards wore the Laureate's mantle, fallen from the shoulders of his departed friend, Robert Southey.

He, the eldest, the calmest, the greatest, of this galaxy of poets, was the last to pass away.

They, whose lives met and flowed so pleasantly together, often intermingling on their way to the great sea of eternity, lie scattered in their last earthly resting-places. Coleridge lies beneath the cloisters of the new school at Highgate, which has supplanted the old church. The memorial shaft is as hidden away as was his life, though the site of building and monument lies upon the beautiful heights of Highgate, which look down upon Hampstead Heath, and have the distant towns and spires of London as a mirage upon the horizon, glistening in the sun, or fading out in the soft veils of mist that often drown the lovely view.

Charles and Mary Lamb sleep well, " after life's fitful fever," in the quiet churchyard at Edmonton, in the shadow of the low, square tower. There, quite close to the shady village street, amid many plain old tombs and slabs, stands the simple headstone that marks the grave of the sister and brother whose lives were as simple and unpretentious. Methinks a corner in Christ's Hospital churchyard, where a few old graves lie clustered in the shadow of the Blue-coat walls, would have been a more suitable resting-place for him who loved those scenes so well, or a secluded corner in his beloved Temple precincts. But the gentle spirit is as happy in the reunion with his loved ones upon the shores of the great sea, as though his cast-off body of the flesh had received this tribute.

Robert Southey sleeps in Crossthwaite churchyard, near Keswick, with great Skiddaw and its " giant brotherhood " keeping watch above him, with the Greta still murmuring the song he knew and loved, near enough to sing his requiem. His recumbent statue, in the church close by, and the medallion in the wall will ever keep his memory fresh in the spot he loved and honored.

Wordsworth, too, lies amid the scenes he so revered during his long life. At the foot of his own yews in Grasmere churchyard, where his ·loved Rothay ever whispers its sweet secrets close to his last bed, he lies surrounded by his loved ones : Mary (his wife), Dora, Dorothy, Hartley Coleridge, and all his little circle.

Truly he is at home here, at the foot of Nab Scar, in the beautiful Grasmere Vale where he spent so many happy years as Nature's own interpreter. No need of the medallion and tablet graven upon the wall of yonder pretty stone church that was his sanctuary for so many years. The rocks, mountains, and vales of all that beautiful Lake Country are his ineffaceable monuments. He haunts them still. No crag or hidden corner, no group of yews, or tender heather-bed, or rippling waterfall, but belonged to him, and was consecrated by his verse to all humanity. And when we climb those grassy slopes, and see those crowns and shoulders still standing sentinel over the lakes and nestling tarns, we know the Lake Poets are not dead, but sleeping, and each loving visitor has power to bid them " Arise ! "

THE END.